KILL 'EM WITH CAYENNE

This Large Print Book carries the
Seal of Approval of N.A.V.H.

A SPICE SHOP MYSTERY

KILL 'EM WITH CAYENNE

GAIL OUST

THORNDIKE PRESS
A part of Gale, Cengage Learning

GALE
CENGAGE Learning·

Farmington Hills, Mich • San Francisco • New York • Waterville, Maine
Meriden, Conn • Mason, Ohio • Chicago

GALE
CENGAGE Learning·

LIBRARY OF CONGRESS CATALOGING-IN-PUBLICATION DATA

Oust, Gail, 1943–
    Kill 'em with cayenne / by Gail Oust. — Large print edition.
        pages cm. — (Thorndike Press large print mystery) (A spice shop mystery)
    ISBN 978-1-4104-7878-8 (hardcover) — ISBN 1-4104-7878-5 (hardcover)
    1. Women detectives—Fiction. 2. Cooks—Crimes against—Fiction. 3. Murder—Investigation—Fiction. 4. Large type books. I. Title. II. Title: Kill them with cayenne.
    PS3620.U7645S68 2015b
    813'.6—dc23   2015012486

Published in 2015 by arrangement with St. Martin's Press, LLC

Printed in Mexico
1 2 3 4 5 6 7 19 18 17 16 15

Lightning can strike twice.
Jessica Faust and Anne Brewer,
you're the best!

ACKNOWLEDGMENTS

It takes a village, or in this case a publishing house, to turn a manuscript into the finished product. To all the talented people who work behind the scenes — editor, copy editor, production editor, publicist, compositor, and sales team — my sincere thanks for all you do on my behalf. Lea Shaw, thank you for speaking brisket to me when *Kill 'Em with Cayenne* was still a mustard seed of an idea. To the hosts of the Savannah Point Pig Roast, thanks for introducing me to Southern cuisine and the notion of a butt rubbin' party. Most of all my humble gratitude to my readers, old and new, who have taken the time from their busy lives to tell me they enjoy my stories. I appreciate each and every one of you. Last, but not least, thanks to my husband, Bob, who enriches my life in so many ways.

CHAPTER 1

"Change is a good thing, right?"

I wasn't quite sure how to respond to my BFF's question. Sometimes change wasn't either good or bad, it was just change. And I ought to know. Ask anyone in Brandywine Creek, Georgia, and they'll tell you Piper Prescott was the Queen of Change. Not only had I divorced the low-down lying skunk I'd been married to for over twenty years, but I traded being a country club wife for proprietress of a fledging business, Spice It Up!, in a building older than Methuselah. Since a certain cute veterinarian arrived on the scene, I'd also abandoned all thoughts of entering a convent in order to avoid further contact with the opposite sex. When it came to change, I could write a book.

"Well, girl, don't just stand there; say somethin'?" Reba Mae pirouetted in front of me. "Do you like my new do or don't you?"

I set aside the yogurt I'd been eating before Reba Mae burst through the door. Reba Mae owned and operated the Klassy Kut. "The best little ol' beauty shop in the South," as she liked to tell folks. One of her favorite pastimes was changing hair color. "It's s-so . . . so . . . black," I stammered.

She smoothed her fringe of bangs. "The box called it Bewitched."

Canting my head, I studied the transformation more closely. Yesterday she'd sported magenta locks. Today her hair was dark as a raven's wing. Regardless of her adventures in Crayola-land, Reba Mae Johnson is a striking woman. At five foot seven, she towered over my petite five foot two even without the high heels she favors. Platforms, wedges, stilettos, bring 'em on.

"Bewitched, eh? If I meet up with Dracula, I'll tell him where to find you."

"Seriously, hon, is it too much?" she asked.

"No, no," I said. "It's edgy . . . striking." The style with its shaggy bangs, cheek-hugging wisps, and mold to the nape was sort of punk-meets-pixie.

"I was aimin' for sophisticated."

Sophisticated? You could cut my tongue out before I'd tell her she'd missed her target by a country mile. Reba Mae, bless her heart, was about as "sophisticated" as Minnie Pearl. She'd once confessed over margaritas that the only time she'd ever left Georgia was to attend a stylist convention in Myrtle Beach, South Carolina. Call me a snob, but family vacations on pristine beaches aside, I have trouble equating a place that hosts a biannual Bike Week with cosmopolitan. Harley-Davidson gear is hardly my notion of haute couture.

"It's just going to take some getting used to, is all."

"Reba Mae? That you?" We turned to see Maybelle Humphries, manager of the Brandywine Creek Chamber of Commerce, push through the door. "Why, I didn't recognize you," Maybelle gushed. "That new look of yours puts me in mind of a gypsy."

"Gypsy . . . ?" Reba Mae looked crestfallen. "I thought it made me look chic."

" 'Chic,' that's the word I wanted," Maybelle hurriedly corrected herself as I tried to hide a smile. "I always admire your sense of style, Reba Mae. You're never afraid to experiment. Take me for instance. I've worn my hair this way since high school."

In Maybelle's case, change might be just the ticket. Her salt-and-pepper bob looked like a do-it yourself scissor job over a

11

bathroom sink. Maybelle was sweet as they come but outwardly as plain as vanilla pudding.

"Fess up, Piper," Reba Mae said. "Aren't you even a teensy bit tempted to try a new look? With your fair skin and green eyes, you'd make a fabulous blonde."

"Thanks, but no thanks." I tucked a wayward red curl behind one ear and changed the subject. "What brings you here, Maybelle?"

"These are hot off the press." She plunked a pile of brochures on the counter next to my antique cash register. "It's that time of year again — the Annual Brandywine Creek Barbecue Festival. Mayor Hemmings wants all you merchants to pass out flyers to customers."

Picking one up, I read it out loud, " 'Blues concert, street dance, fireworks, shag contest.' "

Reba Mae's eyes lit up. "Shag contest?"

Maybelle nodded. "The mayor persuaded the town council to approve funds for a shag club in Myrtle Beach to come and show us how it's done."

"Sign me up," I said. "I've always wanted to learn how to dance the shag."

Reba Mae perched on the counter and swung one long leg over the other. "The shag's considered the official dance of South Carolina. I learned the basic steps years ago, but could stand a refresher course."

"According to the brochure the group sent, it's a cross between swing dancing and the jitterbug," Maybelle said.

Reaching for the half-finished yogurt, I scooped up a spoonful. I felt proud of myself for adding crystallized ginger to the granola topping I concocted. It added a sweet, citrusy note. "Are you entering the cook-off this year?" I asked Maybelle.

"The Chamber's kept me so busy, I haven't had time to perfect a decent Cajun-style rub."

"As long you're here, Maybelle, take a look around. I got a new shipment of chili powders that might inspire you. Feel free to browse."

"I'll do just that." She took one of the little wicker baskets I kept on the counter for customers' use and wandered off.

Reba Mae glanced at the regulator clock on the wall. "Wish I had time to browse, but I got highlights waitin' on me."

She'd no sooner left when two gentlemen I'd never seen before strolled into Spice It Up! The pair paused just inside the door. They stood there, unsmiling, for such a protracted moment that I began to feel jittery. Who were they? The board of health? Had someone reported me for keeping a dog on the premises? I darted a look over my shoulder and sighed with relief. Casey, the little mutt I'd rescued, snoozed peacefully behind the baby gate erected across the storeroom. Casey's bladder was worse than his bite. His most serious offense thus far was peeing on a customer's very expensive Ferragamo sandal. In my humble opinion, it couldn't have happened to a more deserving person.

At last, the taller of the men strode forward and stuck out his hand. "Tex Mahoney."

I set my now empty yogurt carton on the counter. Before returning the handshake, I swiped my hands down the sides of my sunny yellow apron with "Spice It Up!" embroidered over a red chili pepper. "Piper Prescott."

"Nice place you have, ma'am." The man's deep voice had a definite twang that suited his rough-and-tumble appearance. He was tall, rawboned, with a weather-beaten face and mop of brown hair gone mostly gray. The elaborate silver belt buckle he wore was befitting a rodeo champ. Only things missing to complete his Western ensemble were spurs and a six-shooter.

"Thank you, Mr. Mahoney," I said. "Are you in town for the barbecue festival?"

"Yes, ma'am, I am. And, please, everyone calls me Tex."

"Are you looking for anything in particular, Tex? You'll see that I carry a wide range of spices. Everything from *A* to *Z*."

The second man stepped closer. "Z . . . ?"

"*Z* for zedoary, also called white turmeric," I said to Mr. Fancy Dresser. "In its powdered form, zedoary is a common addition to curries."

"I'm impressed," he said with a thin-lipped smile. "The lady knows her spices." The complete opposite of his companion, this man was a natty dresser in a striped short-sleeved button-down dress shirt with a horsey logo and dark pants with a razor-sharp crease. He had a sturdy, compact build, eyes the color of mud, and a gleaming bald head.

"My livelihood depends on it, Mr. . . ." He reminded me of an actor, but I couldn't recall a name to go with the face. Maybe Yul Brynner, the star of one of my favorite musicals, *The King and I*? No, I decided with a shake of the head, not Yul. The name would come to me . . . eventually.

"Porter." He extended his hand. "Wally Porter, certified master barbecue judge."

We shook hands. I noticed his were smooth, callus-free, the nails buffed. "Nice to meet you," I said.

"Did I hear someone say 'barbecue judge'?" Maybelle asked, coming out from behind a row of freestanding shelves. Shame on me, I'd forgotten Maybelle was in the shop browsing. Not to be be mean, but the woman had that kind of effect on people.

"Yes, you did," Wally said, turning to Maybelle.

Tex gave her a warm smile and, taking her basket, peeked at the contents. "I reckon you must be a mighty fine cook judging by your choice of spices."

Maybelle looked flustered in the machismo-charged atmosphere, so I proceeded with the introductions. "Maybelle not only runs the Chamber of Commerce with the precision of a Swiss clock, but she's one of the finest cooks in the county."

Embarrassment turned Maybelle's usually sallow complexion into a becoming shade of pink. "Piper's too kind," she said, dismissing the compliment with a wave of her hand. "I take it you two gentlemen are well acquainted?"

"Our paths cross from time to time on the circuit," Wally explained.

"Are you one of the judges, too?" Maybelle asked Tex.

"No, ma'am. I'd druther be on the cookin' end than the judgin'. I'm always experimentin' with various rubs and sauces. Tryin' to find the perfect combination of spices."

"Tex happens to be a champion pitmaster," Wally told her. "Quite by chance, we both happened to arrive in town early for a little relaxation before the festivities begin in earnest."

I removed the items from Maybelle's basket — juniper berries, star anise, and Szechuan peppercorns. "Have you found a place to stay yet?" I asked the men. "If not, I can recommend a nice bed-and-breakfast."

"The Turner-Driscoll House?" Wally unfastened the lid on a jar of Grenadian nutmeg, sniffed, then nodded his approval. "Tex and I just checked in. Mrs. Driscoll — Felicity — said she was expecting her final guest to arrive shortly."

Maybelle handed me her credit card. As I started to run it through my machine, I noticed she was staring at a figure in the doorway. Maybelle's features contorted with dismay. I followed the direction of her gaze. A woman dressed head-to-toe in pink had her hand on the knob about to enter Spice It Up!

Uh-oh, I groaned silently. *Here comes trouble.*

CHAPTER 2

Becca Dapkins, pretty in pink, breezed through the door. "Hey, Piper."

"Hey there, Becca," I said, pinning on a smile.

Wally's and Tex's heads swiveled to view the new arrival. Both men drew themselves taller and did the gut-sucking thing males often do when around an attractive female. And though it grieved me to admit, Becca was attractive. That is, if one harbored a soft spot for barracudas. As usual, every dark hair on Becca's head was in place, her makeup artfully applied. While Maybelle's shape resembled that of an ironing board, Becca's was soft and curvy beneath the frilly blouse and flowing skirt.

Maybelle remained silent, choosing to glare at the woman she'd known since high school. Can't say I blamed Maybelle, considering their history. Becca Dapkins had stolen Maybelle's man. That would be enough to rile any red-blooded woman.

Becca turned the full wattage of her smile on the two men watching her with interest. "You gentlemen must be new in town. I'd remember you if you'd dropped by my office at the water department. I never forget a face. A God-given talent, according to my grannie."

"Wally Porter, senior barbecue judge." Wally inclined his bald head. "I'm looking forward to spending some time in your quaint little town."

Not to be outdone in the gallantry department, Tex stepped up to the plate. He tipped an imaginary Stetson. "Tex Mahoney at your service, ma'am. Like Wally, I'm here for a little R and R before it's time to fire up the grill."

"Better be prepared for some stiff competition, Tex." Becca wagged a finger with a nail lacquered Pucker Up Pink. I recognized the shade instantly 'cause my toes were painted with the same bright color.

"What category are you enterin', Miss Becca?" Tex asked.

"Taster's Choice," she replied without hesitation. "It's the one where pro or amateur, all contestants are equal. The public gets to decide the best of the best."

Wally rocked back on the heels of his polished loafers. "That's quite an ambitious plan. The winner of Taster's Choice walks away with not only a trophy but a sizeable check."

"Oh, come off it, Becca," Maybelle snapped. "That's the most ridiculous thing ever to come out of your mouth. Unless a recipe calls for cream of mushroom soup, you can't cook well enough to keep a sparrow alive."

"Cream of mushroom soup . . . ?" Tex looked horrified at the notion.

Becca whirled to confront Maybelle. "No, not soup. I happen to have a secret weapon that will put my brisket head and shoulders above the rest. Just you wait and see."

I didn't like where this conversation was heading. Attempting to divert open warfare, I slid a charge slip across the counter. "Um, sign at the bottom."

Ignoring the hint, Maybelle planted her hands on her narrow hips. "Mr. Porter," she said, her tone clipped. "I advise you to keep an eye on this woman. She's got a whole bag of tricks up her sleeve. No telling what she might do. She's entirely without scruples."

"What . . . !" Becca slammed a knockoff designer bag on the counter with enough force to make her charm bracelet jangle. Her red face clashed with her frilly pink blouse. "Maybelle Humphries, what the devil are you implying?"

"Here's a pen." I offered Maybelle a ballpoint, trying to hurry her out of the shop and avert bloodshed.

My suggestion went unheeded. Maybelle was too incensed to back down. "I'm not *implying* anything," she said. "I'm simply telling it like it is. You're a sneaky, conniving bitch."

Wally and Tex followed the confrontation between the women like spectators at Wimbledon. Venus and Serena — change that to Becca and Maybelle — continued to lob insults with ease and precision.

"Admit it, Maybelle." Becca moved into Maybelle's space. "You're jealous Buzz picked me, not you."

Maybelle blanched as the barb hit home. "We'd still be engaged if you hadn't set your sights on him. He'll come around once he's wise to your ways."

"Over my dead body," Becca sneered.

"Ladies, please . . . ," I tried again. Soon I'd be dialing 911 to report an assault and battery.

"You deliberately lured Buzz away from me," Maybelle charged.

"So what if I did?" Becca fired back. "If you can't get a man to marry you after twelve years, then you don't deserve him."

"Thirteen," I corrected.

"Thirteen?" Tex and Wally chorused.

I nodded confirmation. "Maybelle and Buzz dated eight years and were engaged for another five before he broke it off."

"I'd like to meet this Buzz," Tex commented to no one in particular. "He must be quite a guy."

"We were making wedding plans when this homewrecker showed her true colors." Maybelle made a supplicating gesture and addressed first Wally, then Tex, as though they were the judges in her personal court of appeals. "Day and night, this brazen hussy started calling the pest control business where Buzz works. Always asking the boss to send Buzz. First, it was to check for termites. Then, she wanted him to spray for spiders. After that, she claimed she found a wasp's nest. Before I knew what was happening, she was feeding him pork chops cooked in cream of mushroom soup and Tater Tot casserole."

"Hmph!" Becca snorted. "Buzz is a grown man. He needs a real woman in his life — not a mother."

Maybelle's scrawny hands bunched into

23

fists. "So help me, Becca Dapkins, I've half a mind to slap you upside the head."

"Lay one finger on me, Maybelle Humphries, and I'll have you arrested so fast it'll make your head spin."

Rounding the counter, I wedged myself between the two women. *Sheesh!* I felt I'd blundered into a taping of *The Real Housewives of Brandywine Creek,* albeit neither Becca nor Maybelle was a housewife. I handed Maybelle her purchases. "Here," I said. "Go deliver those flyers you brought along."

Maybelle snatched the sack from my hand, then grabbed the brochures from the counter. "I meant every word I said," she flung at Becca as she stormed out.

An excruciating loud silence followed her departure. At last, Tex cleared his throat. "I'll see if I can find Miss Maybelle and calm her down," he said, and headed out the door after her.

Unperturbed, Becca glanced at her watch with its pink leather wristband. "My break's nearly over. Unless I hurry, I'll be late getting back to work. I'll come another time, Piper, to pick up the things I need."

"Sure thing," I said. Next time she came, I'd take great pains to make sure Maybelle was occupied elsewhere.

Becca shot Wally a coy smile and pivoted on her pink high heel — and stopped dead in her tracks.

Curious, Wally and I glanced over to see a late-model white Cadillac Escalade cruise to a stop in front of Spice It Up! A drop-dead gorgeous woman with platinum-blond hair emerged. As the three of us gawked, the woman shoved a pair of movie star–size sunglasses to the top of her head.

Becca exhaled a long sigh. "As I live and breathe. My day just keeps getting better and better."

"Who is she?" I inched forward straining for a better look.

"Barbara Bunker," Becca said, never taking her eyes off the blonde. "I never thought I'd live to see the day she'd show her face again."

Giving her long hair a careless toss, the blonde hoisted a designer tote over her shoulder and strode across the sidewalk toward us. With the self-assurance of a diva, Barbara Bunker sailed into Spice It Up!

CHAPTER 3

Was the curtain going up on Act Two of *The Real Housewives*? I wondered. Next to me, I sensed Wally Porter's avid interest in the statuesque blonde. I could practically see the man's antennae twitch. Once again I witnessed the gut sucking and posture straightening. If Wally had hair, he'd have run a comb through it.

Becca deliberately stepped into the woman's path. "What brings you here?"

The bombshell's shoulders rose and fell in a nonchalant shrug. "Let's just say I felt nostalgic for the old hometown and leave it at that."

Becca's eyes, dark as burnt toast, glittered with malice. "What have you been doing all these years? Working as a stripper?"

"Becca," I gasped. "I've about had it with you. I'm going to have to ask you to leave."

No one budged. No one even blinked. I might as well have been invisible.

"Some folks never change," Barbara said coolly, addressing her comments to Becca. "You're still the same vicious person I remember. And Becca — I think I'm entitled to call you that since we're both adults — I'm Barbara Quinlan now. Most people refer to me as Barbie Q."

I watched, puzzled, as Wally smacked himself in the forehead with the heel of his hand. "Duh!" he exclaimed. "So you're Barbie Q!"

Totally out of the loop, I glanced from Barbie to Wally, then back at Barbie. "Will one of you kindly fill me in?"

"Barbara Bunker Quinlan." Wally gave me a look as if to ask what planet I was from. "Barb-B-Q. She's the gal set to host *Some Like It Hot,* the new show on the Cooking Network."

Barbie graciously inclined her head, pleased there was one less moron in the group. She held out a manicured hand to Wally, and the two shook. I couldn't help but notice the rock on the third finger of her right hand. The stone was so large I questioned whether it was real or cubic zirconium.

Wally seemed oddly reluctant to release her hand. "I'm Wally Porter, master barbecue judge, here in Brandywine Creek for the festival."

"And I'm here to film it," Barbie drawled. A trace of pure Georgia lingered in her low, sultry voice.

"So, you have a TV show. Big deal," Becca sneered. "You've certainly come a long way since your trailer trash days."

Becca Dapkins was a vindictive woman. Mean as a wild hog. "Becca," I said, my voice sharper than usual, "don't you have to get back to the water department?"

Becca darted a look at her watch and frowned. "Now I'm really late," she said as she hurried off, leaving a trail of overly sweet perfume in her wake.

"I'm sorry Becca was so rude," I said to Barbie. "I hope that won't prevent you from visiting my shop in the future."

Barbie turned and studied me for flaws. All her inspection lacked was a jeweler's loupe. As long as she was taking my measure, I felt free to take hers. The blonde was Reba Mae's height, maybe an inch taller, and equally well endowed. While Reba Mae's cleavage was part of the original package, I had the sneaky suspicion Barbie's was an after-market addition. Eyes a clear blue-green aquamarine were the most outstanding feature in a face just shy of being beautiful. Her ivory slacks and lightweight ivory cardigan worn over an aquamarine silk blouse were obviously expensive. She'd come a long way, baby, from a "trailer trash" background.

"Allow me to introduce myself," I said, breaking the stalemate. "I'm Piper Prescott."

"Prescott . . . ?" Barbie's penciled brows drew together. "I recall a CJ Prescott from high school. I heard he's a hotshot lawyer now. I've seen his face plastered on billboards up and down the interstate. He your husband?"

I'm not in the habit of discussing my marital status with strangers. In a town the size of Brandywine Creek, however, all anyone had to do was ask the butcher, baker, or undertaker and they'd tell you. "CJ's my ex," I said on a sigh.

"Hmm."

Hmm? Maybe I'm persnickety, but I prefer words with vowels. "Hmm" can be hard to interpret. It can run the gamut from "that's mighty interesting" to "that's the most boring drivel I've ever heard."

Wally took the pause in our conversation as his cue to exit. "I'll leave you ladies to get better acquainted."

After he'd gone, I reverted to shopkeeper mode. "Are you looking for anything special?"

"I just want to take a look around. If I like what I see, I might decide to shoot a segment here. Use it as a focal point, since the name of your shop segues nicely with the title of my show."

The prospect of free publicity made me want to flip cartwheels. Instead, I tried to act as though an offer like this came my way every day. "Go right ahead," I said. "If you have any questions just ask."

I busied myself behind the counter but watched Barbie out of the corner of my eye. She seemed to wander aimlessly among the shelves, pausing here or there to pick up a jar of this or that. I saw her open a jar of ancho chili powder, sniff, then set it back on the shelf. Moving on, she repeated the smell test with coarsely ground chipotle peppers. When she disappeared behind a row of shelves, I forced myself to concentrate on placing an order with a supplier in the Southwest.

My finger hovered over the send icon when the front door opened. I glanced up and all thoughts of chili peppers vanished. When it came to heat, Police Chief Wyatt McBride topped the chart of Scoville units. "Hot, hotter, and hottest," in his case, translated into "tall, dark, and handsome."

Brandywine Creek's native son McBride had recently returned home after a stint as a Miami-Dade homicide detective.

"Hey, McBride. If you're looking for handouts in the form of cookies or muffins, you're out of luck."

"Hey yourself." He flashed a smile that showed off the cute dimple in his cheek, which always made me weak in the knees. "Cookies and muffins might constitute bribing an officer of the law. There might be consequences."

"Hmm . . ." Now it was my turn to resort to a vowel-less vocabulary. I opened my mouth to make a snappy comeback but was interrupted by a loud shriek.

"Wyatt!"

I watched in amazement as Barb-B-Q, no longer cool, calm, and collected, hurled herself into the arms of Wyatt McBride. My mouth hung open as he laughingly lifted her off her feet and swung her around.

Finally, McBride set Barbie down. "You look fabulous."

"So do you," the bombshell purred.

Giving myself a sound scolding, I went back to ordering chili peppers. I happened to be dating a pretty terrific man by the name of Doug Winters. I had no call to feel

31

the least bit irritated at watching old friends reunite.

Unable to sleep, I woke around 3:00 A.M. Except for an occasional gentle snore from my pup, the apartment over Spice It Up! — where I'd lived since my divorce — was quiet. Now that summer school was behind her, my sixteen-year-old daughter, Lindsey, was spending the week at a friend's lake house. My son, Chad, a pre-med student at University of North Carolina at Chapel Hill, had opted to spend his summer working as a lifeguard. I missed the noise and chaos of family life. What I didn't miss was trying to please a man impossible to please. I'd tried hard to make our marriage work, I really did, but in the end I'd been upgraded for a twenty-four-year-old former beauty queen in a miniskirt.

I shook off my nostalgia. No sense dwelling on the past.

Yawning, I got out of bed and padded into the living room to stare out the window at the square across the street. A statue of a Confederate soldier, rifle at the ready, stood sentry atop a stone pedestal. The square's grassy expanse was the heart and soul of Brandywine Creek's downtown. A tidy row of shops and businesses lined both sides.

Like stately bookends, a pillared courthouse presided over one end, the renovated opera house the other. Willow oaks provided shade; flowering shrubs added color. The scene was peaceful, serene. Small-town America at its finest.

Stifling another yawn, I trudged back to bed and promptly fell asleep.

When the alarm sounded later, my first impulse was to slap it silly. I'd planned to take my snazzy new sneakers out for a spin. Jogging was a recently acquired habit of mine. It's something I'm trying on for size to balance my pizza addiction. So far the verdict is still out. Before I could talk myself out of crawling back under the covers, I climbed out of bed.

Ten minutes later, garbed in a faded UNC T-shirt, old gym shorts, and a ridiculously expensive pair of neon-green running shoes, I was good to go. I snapped on Casey's leash and designated him my jogging partner.

After a few simple warm-ups, I started down Main Street with Casey trotting obediently at my heels. It was a glorious morning. Billowy clouds drifted across a bright blue sky. Birds chirped in the willow oaks. I jogged past the opera house, then turned onto a residential street. I passed my ex-mother-in-law's house and kept going.

The soles of my shoes rhythmically slapped concrete, and I hit my stride. I felt I could run forever.

No sooner had the thought crossed my mind when a throbbing, burning pain shot down my shins. Shin splints. I'd apparently overestimated my athletic prowess. Slowing from a jog to a walk, I decided on a shortcut through the town square.

Casey seemed happier with the slower pace, too. Tugging on his leash, he pulled me toward a clump of azaleas. I gave him more leeway, thinking he wanted to do his business. Instead, Casey began to bark and strain on the leash.

"What is it, boy?"

Casey answered with another series of barks, punctuated by growls.

I edged closer. When I saw what Casey saw, bile rose in my throat. I thought for a moment I was going to be sick. Beneath the greenery and what at first glance appeared to be a bundle of rags lay a body.

Becca Dapkins, no longer pretty in pink, was deader 'n' roadkill.

CHAPTER 4

"I found a dead body," I blurted the instant my 911 call was answered.

"Piper, hon, that you?"

"Precious . . . ?" Relief flooded over me at hearing Precious Blessing's familiar drawl. Precious manned the front desk at the police department with the aplomb of a concierge at a five-star hotel. "I thought you worked afternoons."

I inwardly berated myself for the inane comment. How stupid was that? Guess it goes to show the state I was in.

"Dorinda's daughter went into labor. I'm fillin' in. What's this about a body?"

I clutched my cell so tight my knuckles ached. "It's . . . she's . . . under an azalea bush in the square."

"Sugar" — Precious clucked her tongue — "I'd sure hate to see you in a heap of trouble. Makin' a false nine-one-one call is a serious offense. If you want to talk to the chief, dial his cell. I'd be more'n happy to give you the number."

I huffed out a breath. "Precious, this isn't a joke. Call McBride and tell him to get his butt over here on the double."

"Ain't findin' one dead body enough for you, girl?" she asked, referring to my recent track record. "Sit tight. Cavalry's comin'."

No sooner had I disconnected when the wail of sirens split the air. Glancing over my shoulder, I saw the flash of red and blue lights. The rapid response didn't come as a surprise, since the police department was located on Lincoln Street two blocks away. Seconds later, two squad cars screeched to a halt at the curb.

Wyatt McBride leaped out of the lead car. His long strides ate up the space that separated us. "What's this about a body?"

Even under ordinary circumstances, McBride at six foot one and probably two hundred pounds tends to be intimidating, but when in full cop mode he's a force to be reckoned with. I resisted the urge to take a step backward. I pointed. "Over there."

I watched as McBride shoved branches aside and glimpsed the crumpled form of Becca Dapkins. Bending down, he felt for a pulse. I could've told him it was useless, seeing how Becca's skin was the color of day-old mashed potatoes, but kept my own counsel.

"Recognize the vic?"

The vic? I shivered at the clinical term. "Becca Dapkins. She works at the water department. Better make that 'worked,' " I amended.

Running an impatient hand through his military-short black hair, he scowled at me. "How is it that in the brief time I've known you, you've managed to find more bodies than most cadaver dogs?"

"For your information, *I* didn't find the body. Casey did."

At hearing his name, the pup's ears perked up and he gave McBride his best doggy smile.

"Casey might not be a cadaver dog, but he's every bit as smart," I said.

"Please tell me neither you nor your four-legged friend touched anything?"

"I know the drill, McBride," I replied heatedly. "I'm not exactly a newbie in the dead body department." I thought I heard teeth grind, but I could've been mistaken.

"Did you happen to see or hear anything suspicious?"

"I didn't notice anyone hanging around if that's what you mean. There aren't many people out and about this early in the morning."

McBride turned to the officers who hovered nearby, awaiting orders. "Tucker, cordon off the area," he barked. "Moyer, get the camera. Start taking photos."

The light sweat I'd worked up while jogging was beginning to evaporate on my skin, leaving me chilled. I rubbed my arms. "Am I free to leave?"

"Not so fast." McBride swung his attention back to me and zapped me into obedience with his laser-blue eyes. "In concise terms, tell me how you — of all people — happened upon the vic?"

My teeth started to chatter as a delayed reaction at finding Becca finally set in. While Becca and I were more acquaintances than friends, I felt terrible about what happened to her.

"Piper . . ."

I realized McBride was still waiting for an answer to his question. "Sh-shin splints," I managed to stammer.

His gaze narrowed. "You okay? You're white as a ghost."

"I'm f-fine," I muttered. "Or at least I will be once I warm up."

I thought he muttered something that sounded like "danged skimpy clothes," but

I wouldn't swear to it on a stack of Bibles.

"Have a seat in the patrol car and wait for me. I still need to ask you a few questions."

"B-but —"

He held up a hand to forestall a protest he saw forming. "No argument. Right now, I have to make sure the crime scene is secure."

"Crime scene . . . ?" I echoed, but I doubt that he heard me. He was already hurrying away.

Shoulders hunched and Casey trotting alongside me, I slowly made my way to the cop car and slid into the driver's seat. No way was I going to sit behind a mesh screen in a spot reserved for miscreants and felons. I wrapped Casey's leash around the door handle, and the little dog settled down to regard the goings-on with watchful eyes.

The interior of the car felt warm. I detected a faint, lingering citrusy scent. *McBride's aftershave?* I wondered. *Or air freshener?* Eager to take my mind off Becca — and McBride — I concentrated on my surroundings. With its myriad of dials and gadgets, I likened it to a landlubber's version of an airplane cockpit. A police radio crackled and hummed. A radar gun rested in a special holster on the dash. The stainless-steel arm of a hand-operated spotlight jutted out left of the windshield. The console boasted a state-of-the-art computer. McBride had Facebook, Twitter, and YouTube at his fingertips.

I was about to look away when I noticed an item of even greater interest — a stainless-steel coffee mug — sitting in a cup holder. I plucked it out and held it to my nose. The smell of fresh-brewed coffee tantalized my taste buds. I couldn't help myself. I took a sip, then another. Hot and strong, it warmed my innards. Surely McBride wouldn't notice if the mug wasn't quite as full as he'd left it.

As my insides began to thaw, my brain clicked into gear. *Crime scene?* Who'd want to kill Becca? I distinctly recalled McBride saying "crime scene." Surely he was mistaken. I closed my eyes and envisioned Becca lying on her side, her right hand outstretched as if to break a fall. The hair at the back of her head had appeared sticky, matted. Certainly there must be a reasonable explanation for her death. Maybe she'd tripped over a root or slipped on a hickory nut. Maybe she'd suffered a heart attack. Or had a seizure. Whatever the case, she'd fallen and struck her head. A simple accident. Not foul play.

Then doubt pricked a teensy hole in my

theory, letting the air out of my bubble of self-deception. If Becca had fallen — and landed in her present position — she'd have struck her forehead, not the back of her skull.

I mulled this over as I drank coffee. Yellow tape now decorated shrubs and bushes like a child's clumsy attempt at putting garland on a Christmas tree. I watched McBride, notebook in hand, prowl the scene in ever-widening circles. The paramedics arrived, armed and ready to administer CPR to a corpse. The fire department followed minutes later in their hook and ladder in a show of solidarity for their crime-fighting buddies. The men climbed out of their respective vehicles and congregated in a tight knot outside the roped-off area. Last, but by no means least, John Strickland, local mortician and county coroner, pulled up in a van, then toted a medical case over to where Becca lay under the azaleas.

"Hey, girlfriend." Reba Mae sidled up to where I sat. "What's this about you findin' a body? Wasn't one enough?"

Sheesh! I hissed out a breath between clenched teeth. One would think I made a habit of seeing dead people. And all because several months ago I'd happened upon a local chef who'd been murdered in his own kitchen.

"I swear, Reba Mae, if one more person asks me that, I'm going to scream bloody murder." I clapped my hand over my mouth. "Please," I groaned. "Poor choice of words. Forget I just said that."

"No problem, honeybun," she said. "News is spreadin' like a brush fire. Good thing you're sittin' up front or else folks would really have somethin' to talk about."

At hearing this, I glanced around. Folks were fighting a losing battle not to stare my way. I'm not clairvoyant, but I could read their minds. They were asking themselves and one another what Piper Prescott was doing in a police car. Was I a suspect in an assault and battery? Or a murder? Was I about to be arrested? And how was it a person could find more than one dead body in an entire lifetime? Tired of being a sitting duck, I popped out of the police car and leaned against the rear bumper.

Reba Mae leaned next to me. "So fill me in."

"Blame it on shin splints," I grumbled, taking another sip of McBride's coffee.

"What did I tell you when you bought those fancy runnin' shoes?" She shot a glance at my psychedelic-green footwear. "I tried to warn you that exercise isn't all it's cracked up to be. Look where it's gotcha."

"I overdid too much of a good thing," I confessed. "If it hadn't been for those darn shin splints, I'd be standing *behind* the crime scene tape instead of being stared at by my friends and neighbors."

"So, tell me" — Reba Mae lowered her voice — "did you recognize who the body belongs to? Promise, I won't tell a soul."

I debated the pros and cons of revealing too much information. Pro being that in a town the size of Brandywine Creek the cat would be out of the bag soon enough. The con being possibly eliciting McBride's wrath. I opted for life on the edge. I'd take my chances with McBride's temper. I leaned closer and whispered, "Becca Dapkins."

"Becca?" Reba Mae's eyes rounded. "You're kiddin', right?"

"Wish I was."

"You sure?"

I nodded. "Looked like she was still wearing the same pink blouse and skirt she had on yesterday."

Reba Mae let out a low whistle. "Whooee, think it might've been an accident? That all this fuss is for nothin'?"

"McBride's being pretty closemouthed, so I can't say for sure." Frowning, I bent down and gave Casey's head a pat. "Funny, but something tells me this isn't going to turn out to be a death from natural causes."

CHAPTER 5

"Hiya, Scooter." My ex-husband separated himself from a knot of onlookers and sauntered toward me.

"Hey, CJ."

I had cringed at hearing the hated nickname. What had once been endearing now was an irritant. Once upon a time the love of my life, Chandler Jameson Prescott IV, had deserted me in the pursuit of hefty lawsuits and a toothy brunette.

Arms folded across his chest, my ex lounged beside me on the rear bumper of the squad car. "You in trouble again? Sources tell me you're up to your behind in alligators. Thought I'd wander over. See if you're in need of my legal expertise."

"What's the matter, CJ?" Reba Mae drawled. "Can't find any ambulances to chase?"

"That you, Reba Mae?"

CJ's head had swiveled so fast I heard the

bones in his neck creak. I almost giggled at the double take — almost.

"In the flesh." Reba Mae grinned. "Must be my new do."

"Yeah, well, it's a durn sight better than that purple color I'm used to seein'." He dismissed her with a frown and turned his attention back on me. "What's this I hear about you murderin' a customer?"

"I *didn't* murder anyone," I all but snarled. "I found a body in the bushes."

"Easy, darlin'." He held up a hand. "Don't go all PMSing on me. I'm just tryin' to help the mother of my children."

"Your sources need to do some fact-checking. And, for your information, I am not PMSing."

"Sorry, Scooter. Guess at your age it's more likely menopause that's makin' you cranky."

"Do you want to sock him or want me to do it for you?" Reba Mae asked.

Menopause is no laughing matter to women of a certain age. There's nothing funny whatsoever about hot flashes and biological clocks low on battery life. "Don't bother, Reba Mae. Knowing CJ, he'd probably have us hauled in on assault charges."

"We'd get off if we had a woman judge."

"Or an all-female jury."

46

Affronted, CJ stepped back and straightened his tie. "Well, since my services aren't required, I'd best be on my way. You've got my number, Scooter. Call if you need a good lawyer, you heah?"

Oh, I had his number all right, but it was no longer on speed dial. I watched him wander off to exchange pleasantries with his cronies who were clustered under one of the willow oaks drinking coffee from Styrofoam cups and engaging in idle gossip.

"Out of my way! Get out of my way!"

Reba Mae and I turned toward the shouting. Harvey Hemmings, esteemed mayor of Brandywine Creek, shoved through the swarm. Harvey's round as a dinner plate face was flushed crimson. A gray fringe of hair encircled a head shaped like a bowling ball. A furry caterpillar of a mustache crawled across his upper lip. Sad to say, but our mayor looked more like a cartoon character than many cartoon characters.

"McBride, hold up a sec! What's this about a dead body?" Hizzoner ducked under the crime scene tape, obviously under the impression DO NOT CROSS didn't apply to him. "Why wasn't I notified of the goings-on?"

"G'mornin', Mayor," McBride returned. " 'Fraid I'll have to ask you to step to the other side of the tape. This is an official crime scene, sir. Need to preserve evidence."

Hemmings's face went from bright crimson to dull red. "You're forgettin' who you're talkin' to, son. I head up the city council who hired your ass."

From my vantage point, I saw a muscle work in McBride's jaw. "You hired me to do a job," he said with remarkable calm. "Kindly step aside and let me do it."

Reba Mae and I exchanged glances. A standoff. Neither man seemed willing to back down. Harvey Hemmings liked to throw his weight around — which was considerable — and most folks didn't challenge him. His jovial demeanor belied his tendency to carry a grudge. "Don't get mad, get even" was the motto he lived by.

"Better watch your tone, boy, if you know what's good for you," Harvey blustered.

"Until we know otherwise, we're treating this as a possible homicide."

"Homicide . . . ?" Hemmings repeated, sounding more angry than shocked.

Homicide . . . I tried to wrap my mind around the possibility that Becca had been murdered. Times like these, denial can be a blessing. Numbs the mind. Possibly McBride's stint at Miami-Dade had him seeing homicides behind every tree in the woods. Or in Becca's case under every azalea bush.

"What the Sam Hill you talkin' about?" Harvey shouted. "Should've known your big-city ways would've rubbed off. Prove more hindrance than help. I thought havin' a hometown boy head up the force was a smart move. Now I'm not so sure."

If McBride was affected by Hemmings's tirade, he didn't let his irritation show. "Mayor, can we discuss this in your office later? Right now, I have a job to do."

"Hrmph!" Hemmings ducked under the tape and stomped off. Instead of making a beeline for his office, though, he held court on the sidelines with CJ and his good ol' boy cronies.

"Poor Harvey. He doesn't look none too pleased right now," Reba Mae observed.

"You can say that again," I replied. "He's used to being the only rooster in the henhouse. When it comes to orders, he doesn't like to be on the receiving end."

People continued to gather as word spread. These days even octogenarians were adept with cell phones, texting, and e-mail. I personally knew some who had Facebook and Twitter accounts or were LinkedIn. The whole town was turning out for the show.

"Mind if I record you standing by the

49

police car?"

I turned at Barbie Quinlan's seductive drawl. The blond bombshell dressed all in black for the occasion in slim-leg jeans and low-cut ribbed tee. But it wasn't her ensemble that drew my attention. It was the iPhone she held, its camera aimed directly at me. "Why would you want a recording?" I asked.

"It'll make a good promo for my new show," she said with a shrug. Not bothering to wait for my response, she continued to film. "Are you considered a suspect at this point or merely a person of interest?"

"Neither," I snapped. "And turn that dang thing off this instant!"

"Feisty little thing, aren't you?"

Reba Mae whipped Barbie around to confront her. "And you're about to get a personal demonstration of just how feisty my friend really is if you don't stop filmin' her."

Barbie shook off Reba Mae's hand. "And who might you be?"

"Reba Mae Johnson. Piper's BFF and owner of the Klassy Kut, should your roots need a touch-up."

"Sorry, I won't be in town long enough to worry about touch-ups." Barbie smoothed a hand over her hair, which she'd pulled back and secured with a clip. "I let my stylist worry about such things."

Well, whoop-de-do. I drained the remainder of McBride's coffee. "Must be nice to have a stylist of your very own."

Barbie ignored my sarcasm, her attention on Reba Mae. "Being a Johnson means you're kin to half the folk in the county. I thought I knew most of them, but you don't look familiar. You from Brandywine Creek?"

"Next county over. Butch and I met at a football game when his team played ours."

"Butch Johnson? That name rings a bell. I remember him from high school, but we didn't run with the same crowd. Be sure and tell him Barbara Bunker's back in town and says hey."

"Be happy to," Reba Mae told her, "except Butch died some years back."

Barbie had the grace to flush. "Sorry to hear that. He seemed like a nice enough guy."

"The best."

Barbie turned her back on us and panned the parade of emergency vehicles lined up and down Main Street. "My videographer isn't due to arrive until tomorrow, so I'll have to make do."

"What do you intend to do with all that video?" I asked.

51

"The promos alone will bring in a host of viewers. I might even be able to sell the rights to CNN or one of those investigative journalism shows like ABC's *20/20* or NBC's *Dateline.* A fond reunion in my old hometown turns into a full-blown murder investigation. I can't believe my luck. It'll make for a great debut."

Her smug attitude annoyed me. "What makes you so sure it's murder and not an accident?"

"The look on Wyatt's face says it all."

Reba Mae's brow shot up at the disclosure. "Just how well do you know McBride?"

"Since we were kids. It's his intensity. I've seen it before. If you knew him as well as I do, you'd recognize it, too."

As if sensing he was the subject of conversation, McBride strolled toward us. "Ladies, I hate to break up this tea party, but I've got a few questions for Piper."

The two women didn't argue but headed off in opposite directions without another word.

He slipped his notebook into his shirt pocket. "When I asked you to wait, I didn't mean hold a press conference."

"You asked me to wait, not to remain silent."

"I stand corrected." He eyed the coffee mug I still held. "Don't s'pose there's any left?"

"Nope." I tipped the mug upside down. "Nary a drop."

He scrubbed a hand over his jaw. "Damn shame. I sure could use some about now."

"Sorry," I mumbled, contrite. "I owe you."

"Big-time," he agreed. "Now," he sighed, "let's get down to business. Tell me again how you happened upon the body of Becca Dapkins."

"How many times do I have to tell you?" I asked plaintively. "Shin splints."

He gave me a once-over. "Funny, I didn't take you for a runner, but your shoes are a dead giveaway."

"I just started jogging. Figured I needed the exercise and shoes were cheaper than a health club membership."

"Do you have peas in your freezer? If not, rice will work just as well."

I stared at him, dumbfounded. "What am I supposed to do with peas and rice? Make a pot of soup?"

"Icing your shins for twenty minutes will help with the pain. It won't hurt to down a couple ibuprofens either." He removed his notebook and got down to business. "You can come to the department later to sign your statement."

I stared over at the coroner and crew clustered around Becca's body. "I took a shortcut across the square. Casey started poking around the azaleas. At first it looked like a bundle of rags laying there. When I took a closer look, I realized it was Becca Dapkins."

He made a note of this. "How did you know who the body belonged to?"

"Becca always wears pink even though it's not her best color. She had on pink when she came into my shop yesterday. A blouse with ruffles and a flowered skirt — just like she's wearing now."

"Don't suppose you know Ms. Dapkins's next of kin? Does she have family in the area? Is she married? Divorced?"

I frowned, trying to recall the little I knew about Becca's personal life. "She's divorced, but dating Buzz Oliver. I believe she has a son and a daughter. One lives in New York. The other's out west somewhere — Phoenix or Tucson."

McBride jotted this down. "Call if you recall any further details. If not, I'll expect you to drop by my office to sign a formal statement."

"McBride, wait up." He'd turned to leave, but I caught his arm. "Can you tell me what happened? Do you think Becca was murdered? How? Why?"

"We'll know more after the autopsy."

I swallowed. "Autopsy?"

"It's required in cases like this. The coroner is getting ready to transport the body. The autopsy itself will be done at GBI's — the Georgia Bureau of Investigation's — headquarters by one of their medical examiners. I should have the preliminary results soon after its completion."

I would have liked to ask more questions, but just then Buzz Oliver ran up. Puffing and out of breath, he looked pale beneath his summer tan. I noticed the shirt of his pest control uniform was buttoned haphazardly, the tail sticking out of his pants. "Is it true?" Buzz asked McBride. "I heard talk about a body being found. I've been trying to reach Becca all morning, but she doesn't answer her phone."

McBride regarded the man calmly. "Why is it so urgent you reach Ms. Dapkins?"

Buzz ran a hand over his gray crew cut and looked down at the ground. "We had a terrible fight the other night. I wanted to apologize."

"I see," McBride said, his tone noncommittal. "And what is your relationship to

Ms. Dapkins?"

Buzz hesitated a moment before answering. "I'm . . . a friend."

I couldn't say what made me glance away just then, but I chanced to see Maybelle Humphries standing apart from the rest of the crowd. She stood with her arms hugging her thin body, her expression unreadable.

CHAPTER 6

Customers lined the sidewalk waiting for me to open. To borrow one of my dad's favorite Yogi Berra quips, it was déjà vu all over again. A repeat of my grand opening of Spice It Up! Then, as now, my grand opening was made even grander by the fact I'd stumbled upon a dead body. That was definitely something I didn't wish to make a habit.

After McBride had finally allowed me to leave the crime scene, I'd raced home, shin splints forgotten. I'd barely had time to shower, blow my hair dry, and dump Kibbles 'n Bits into Casey's bowl before hurrying downstairs. I left Casey in the apartment curled on his favorite rug, apparently having had enough excitement for one day.

I was relieved my daughter, Lindsey, was visiting friends and not caught up in all the turmoil. My son, Chad, was too hell-bent on entering medical school to pay attention to any local news. Not even his mother finding a corpse could upset his focus

The blood in my veins practically fizzed with an odd mix of adrenaline and dread. Questions buzzed through my brain like bees at a picnic. *Who'd want to harm Becca Dapkins?* topped my list. *Why was she killed?* I was still mulling these over when I switched the sign on my front door to OPEN.

"Piper, dear!" My ex-mother-in-law, Melly Prescott, rushed in. "What a terrible ordeal it must have been, finding poor Becca in the azaleas."

I mustered a smile. "I'm fine, Melly."

"Of course you're not fine," she chastised me. "That's why I dropped everything and hurried over to help. Where's my apron?"

Not waiting for a response, Melly made straightaway for the counter, knowing I kept a stack of cheery yellow aprons with chili pepper logos on a shelf below. Melly Prescott was Southern to the core. Prim and proper on the outside in her signature twin set and pearls, she was a steel magnolia on the inside. Woe to anyone — or anything — that threatened to harm those she held close to her heart. To my surprise, since my divorce from CJ she'd often sided with me, and not her son when it came to disciplining Lindsey and often volunteered to help in the shop.

A trio of women streamed into my shop with gossip on their minds. Dottie Hemmings led the charge, trailed by Diane Cloune, a tall, athletic brunette in golfing togs, and Gerilee Barker, wife of Pete the butcher.

Dottie, plump and blond, her hair teased sky-high in a sixties look, zeroed in on me and enveloped me in a motherly hug. Hugs were dispensed more freely than handshakes in this part of the country. It was a habit I'd grown accustomed to after being raised in the more conservative Midwest. "Piper, you poor thing," Dottie cooed. "Discovering Becca planted among the azaleas must have been a dreadful shock. Shouldn't you be upstairs resting?"

I disengaged myself from Dottie's embrace, knowing her flowery scent would cling to my clothes for the rest of the day. "I'm fine, Dottie."

She clucked her tongue. "You're such a brave little girl."

"Good thing the azaleas weren't in bloom. No telling how long Becca might have laid there unnoticed," Diane commented.

Gerilee quickly agreed. "With all the pink Becca liked to wear, she would have blended right in with the flowers."

"Gee," I murmured. "Lucky for Becca some psychopath didn't get to kill her in April."

The women regarded me worriedly. No doubt trying to differentiate whether I was verging on hysteria or merely being sarcastic.

"Why don't I put the kettle on for a pot of tea?" Melly chirped. "Chamomile, I think. Nothing like a nice cup of chamomile tea to soothe the nerves, I always say."

Needing to keep myself occupied, I picked up a feather duster and ran it over a shelf of exotic salt and peppercorns from the far corners of the globe. Melly bustled to the rear of the shop, where I heard her running water into a kettle.

"I heard someone remark it might have been an aneurysm," Gerilee, an attractive sixty-something woman with short wavy brown hair, volunteered.

Diane nodded vigorously. "My uncle Ray died of an aneurysm. He was sitting in his recliner watching golf one minute and dead the next. Doctor told my aunt the thing in his belly was probably big as a baseball before it burst."

"Might've been all the chemicals Becca was exposed to in her job with the water department," Dottie suggested.

Gerilee rolled her eyes. "You're forgetting, Dottie, that Becca worked in an office — not a sewage treatment plant."

"Oh, right," Dottie muttered, then turned her attention back to me. "Could you tell anything just by looking at Becca, what happened to the poor thing?"

I concentrated on a speck of dust hiding behind a jar of pink Himalayan peppercorns. "I really can't say. I expect McBride will let people know once he hears from the medical examiner."

"Well, my husband the mayor is worried sick about the whole incident." Dottie smoothed a helmet of blond curls that could have withstood a hurricane. "Harvey predicts this will stir up all sorts of negative publicity. Definitely bad for barbecue, he said."

"It might be bad for barbecue, but it's even worse for Becca," I snapped.

Diane and Gerilee traded nervous glances. Dottie, however, remained undaunted by my outburst. "Please don't think I'm not heartbroken about the terrible fate befallen our dear Becca. In fact, I'm planning to bring an extra-nice dish to her memorial service."

"Do you know when that might be?" Diane twirled her ponytail around a finger. "I'm playing in the member-guest tournament at the club, and I've already paid the entrance fee. I'd hate to have to chose between them."

Melly rejoined the group carrying a tray with five Styrofoam cups and a plate of cookies. "I thought we could all use a calming influence. I brought some gingersnaps I made yesterday. They're Lindsey's favorite."

Leave it to Melly to turn a solemn occasion into a tea party. Though often irritated with my former mother-in-law, I was rarely angry. She tended to be outspoken, but her intentions were good.

No sooner had these thoughts passed through my mind when Melly berated me, "Really, dear, Styrofoam is *so* tacky. You need to have some pretty china teacups on hand for when you entertain guests. As a matter of fact, I think I might have some at home that you can have."

Gerilee helped herself to tea and cookies. "Becca was in my bunco group. I met her son and daughter during their last visit. They weren't a close-knit family, but her children were shocked at the news of her passing nevertheless. When I offered to plan a nice memorial service for their mother, they were pleased to accept. All they asked is to let them know the details so they can book flights."

"I've just had a marvelous idea," Dottie beamed happily. "Wouldn't it be lovely if everyone honored Becca's memory by bringing a cream of mushroom soup dish to the reception? Everyone knows how fond Becca was of soup recipes."

"Excellent idea, Dottie," Melly said, quick to jump on the cream of mushroom soup bandwagon. "I have the perfect recipe in mind."

Diane sipped her tea. "Who do you suppose will be Becca's successor with green bean casserole? She brought it to every single covered-dish supper since she moved back to Brandywine Creek."

The thought of a successor boggled my mind. I sank down on a stool behind the counter to contemplate the conundrum. It was better than wondering why Becca died and how. I sipped my tea and, remembering I didn't have breakfast, helped myself to one of Melly's gingersnaps.

"Speaking of cream of mushroom soup," Gerilee said, "do you think Buzz might've been bearing a grudge? Pete swears the man blamed Becca's cooking on his recent gallbladder attack."

"Buzz needed emergency surgery," Melly

recalled.

Dottie brushed cookie crumbs from her flowered polyester blouse. "And no surgery is risk-free. Buzz could've died — and all because of a can of soup."

Diane smiled a sly smile. "Last time I saw Buzz and Becca they were arguing. It wouldn't surprise me if Buzz had tired of Becca and regretted breaking up with Maybelle. Let's face it, Becca could be demanding. Next to her, Maybelle's a saint."

Interesting. "Do you think Maybelle would take Buzz back if he asked?"

"Yes, of course," Melly insisted.

"No way," Gerilee contradicted.

Gerilee's answer surprised me. "What makes you say that?" I asked.

"I've known Maybelle for years. She's not the sharing type."

Further speculation on Buzz Oliver and Maybelle Humphries's love life halted when the door opened and a stylish woman in her midfifties with short dove-gray hair and an infectious grin entered.

"Hey, y'all," Felicity Driscoll sang out, waving a sheet of paper in one hand.

"Hey, Felicity," we chorused in return.

Felicity was the owner of the Turner-Driscoll House, a newly opened bed-and-breakfast in the historical district. The house had been in Felicity's husband's family for generations but had fallen into disrepair during the last decade or two. When Felicity's husband, a successful neurologist in Birmingham, Alabama, passed away suddenly, she packed up her antiques and moved to Brandywine Creek. As someone who loved people, loved to entertain, and loved to play hostess, Felicity found running a B and B a perfect fit.

✓ She handed me the list she held. "Piper, one of my guests needs some special spices for a dish he's preparing. I hope you have them in stock."

I scanned the sheet. Cayenne pepper, Hungarian-style sweet paprika, black Tellicherry and white Sarawak peppercorns, cumin, and Turkish — not Mexican — oregano. "Your guest seems to know his way around a kitchen. His requests are quite specific."

"Yes." Felicity smiled. "He wasn't satisfied with the spices in my pantry. He lectured me on the importance of fresh spice and the folly of buying in bulk."

I picked up one of the small baskets I kept handy and began to circulate among the shelves. "This shouldn't take long."

"You and Piper both took a pretty big risk starting businesses in this economy," Dottie commented. "How're things going, Felicity? Are you managing to break even?"

"Dottie, really!" Melly interjected. "That's not polite. Stop being such a busybody."

Dottie dismissed the criticism with a flick of her wrist. "Inquiring minds want to know such things. How do you know if you don't ask?"

"No offense taken, Dottie," Felicity said. "Thanks to the upcoming barbecue festival, I'm pleased to report business is booming."

"So who do you have staying at your place?" Diane asked. "Anyone important?"

"All my guests are important," Felicity said, her tone prim. "Every single one."

"That didn't come out the way I intended," Diane said, trying to backpedal. "What I meant was, are any of your guests playing a . . . pivotal . . . role in the contest?"

"Well, there's Wally Porter, a charming and cultured man, who's a certified master judge." Felicity ticked them off on her fingers as she spoke. "Then, there's Tex Mahoney, a champion pitmaster, winner of various barbecue festivals all over the Southeast. And last, but by no means least, Ms. Barbie Quinlan, better known as Barbie Q, the host of a new cooking show. You might recognize her, ladies. She said that she grew up here in Brandywine Creek."

Melly frowned. "Funny, I don't remember any families by the name of Quinlan."

I stuck my head out from around a display of chili peppers. "She was Barbara Bunker back then."

"Barbara Bunker . . . ? My word." Melly toyed with her ever-present pearls. "Never thought she'd return to Brandywine Creek."

"Well, she's back — and with a vengeance." I located the last item on Felicity's list and dropped it into the basket.

"My husband the mayor mentioned she was filming all the goings-on this morning. He's afraid once word gets out about Becca, it'll keep folks away. Brandywine Creek will get a reputation for murder like New York City or Chicago."

"Or Detroit," I said as I started to tally the order. "By the way, Felicity, what dish is your guest making?"

"Brisket," she said with a laugh. "Tex called it his Braggin' Rights Brisket."

CHAPTER 7

The workday was finally over. It was now after six o'clock. Time to pay McBride a visit. Guilt had niggled at me throughout the day for drinking all his morning coffee. The poor guy sure had looked as though he needed a strong jolt of caffeine. Probably hadn't had a chance to grab a bite to eat all day. I decided to bring him a peace offering of sorts. Before I could reconsider, I reached for the phone and placed a take-out order. Twenty minutes later, I arrived at the Pizza Palace.

"Hey there, Miz Prescott," Danny Boyd, a slight young man with pale-blue eyes behind John Lennon–style glasses, a wispy goatee, and a wannabe mustache, greeted me with a friendly smile. "Just took your pie out of the oven."

"It smells wonderful," I said. "Suppose you could add a Greek salad to my order?"

He shoved his glasses higher on the bridge

of his nose. "Sure thing."

"And don't be stingy on the feta." I watched Danny heap lettuce into a plastic carryout container, then add tomatoes, black olives, and slivers of red onion. "How's business at the Palace since Gina and Tony opened their new place?"

Danny glanced up from his salad making. "Couldn't be better. The Pizza Palace is strictly carryout. Pizza, subs, calzones. If people are in the mood for sit-down Italian, they go to Antonio's. Tony's got a great menu. His lasagna's the best."

"I'll keep that in mind." One of these days, I knew I'd have to bite the bullet and give the new restaurant a try. Tony Deltorro and I haven't exactly been on the best of terms since I gave his name to McBride as a possible suspect in a homicide. Funny how little things like that damage a relationship.

Danny slid the salad into a bag and rang up my order. "Tony's attracting a lot of new customers with the home-style Italian cooking. His momma makes all the pasta. Gina does the tiramisu and cannolis. What's not to like?"

"Thanks, Danny. Have a good one," I said as I left.

I inhaled the spicy scent of Tony's superb

marinara sauce. My stomach rumbled in appreciation. I hoped McBride was in a sharing frame of mind when I arrived at his office bearing gifts. The Brandywine Creek Police Department was only a couple short blocks away, so I opted to walk. All I needed was a nice bottle of red wine to complete my menu, but knowing McBride as I did, he wasn't the type to drink on duty. I shoved open the double glass doors and stepped into the inner sanctum.

Precious Blessing, her hair in elaborate braids and her ample figure stuffed into a uniform a size too small, manned the front desk. "Well, lookee here," she drawled in a voice sweet as sorghum. "Today must've been declared National Feed-a-Cop-Pizza Day."

I frowned. "What do you mean?"

Precious eyed the box I carried. "Just my way of sayin' that if you brought that for the chief, you're a mite late. He already done had supper."

"Ohh," I said, feeling my spirits deflate. Although loathe to admit, even to myself, I looked forward to our . . . encounters, I always found them . . . energizing . . . for lack of a better word.

"Sorry, sugar." Precious's round, brown face mirrored her sympathy. "Miss Barbie-doll beat you to the punch. She brought the chief a pepperoni mushroom pizza not more 'n a half hour ago. Heard the chief say he was hungry enough to eat the box."

"Swell." I set the pizza and salad on one of the battered wooden benches rimming the front of the room. "She still in there with him?"

"She ought to be off mindin' her own business. I'll buzz the chief and let him know you're waitin' on him."

I plunked myself down next to the pizza box and picked up a dog-eared copy of *Field & Stream.* I flipped through the pages while Precious announced my presence, but couldn't seem to concentrate. My eyes roamed around the shabby surroundings. A large wall calendar from a local lumberyard adorned one wall; a bulletin board with Maybelle's flyer along with the FBI's Most Wanted posters occupied the other. Except for the addition of the wall calendar, nothing else had changed since McBride had taken over the role of police chief from Reba Mae's uncle through marriage, Joe Johnson.

"Doesn't look like McBride's hired an interior decorator since he accepted the job," I commented.

"No, but he's makin' progress. Just last week, he got the city council to cough up funds for a couple cans of paint. Place ain't seen a paintbrush since Clinton was president."

I idly leafed through ads for fishing rods and hunting rifles. "So how's Dorinda's daughter? She have her baby yet?"

"Not yet." Precious's face crinkled with worry. "If she don't have it soon, doc's doin' a C-section. Dorinda always said Lorrinda's hips were wide enough to push out a linebacker, but I guess she overestimated."

I winced. "Wide hips or not, that's a lot of baby."

Precious cocked her head to the side and listened. Then, I heard it, too, the *click-clack* of high heels against tile. Glancing up, I watched Barbie Quinlan sashay down the hall. Upon seeing me in the waiting area, she smiled. Her shrewd gaze took in the pizza box next to me on the bench.

"What's that old saying?" she mused. "Something about great minds thinking alike?"

Feeling at a disadvantage, I rose to my feet. That didn't help one iota. The blonde, dressed for the occasion in mushroom-and-pepperoni chic — formfitting black capris and leopard knit top — towered over me. I wished I'd taken time to change out of my work clothes. Maybe spritz on some perfume. No doubt I smelled of cinnamon, cloves, and nutmeg. A scent more suitable for a gingersnap than a femme fatale.

"I didn't expect to see you here," I said in a poor excuse for clever repartee.

"I hoped to persuade Wyatt to give me an interview about what transpired today."

"And did you?"

The woman smiled, the cat with a canary kind of smile. "Not yet."

"Why would he allow you to interview him?"

Barbie shrugged. "Wyatt and I go back a long way. I thought he might be willing to do a favor for old times' sake."

I clenched my jaw to keep from asking her how well she and McBride knew each other. And if they were planning to pick up where they'd left off. But I didn't. That would make it look as though I were jealous. And I wasn't. McBride's love life was none of my business. After all, he was single — a widower actually — and free to date whomever he wished.

I shifted my weight from one foot to the other. "I thought you were in town to film the barbecue festival. Only thing McBride has to do with the festival is keep the peace."

"You've gotta be joking," Barbie snorted. "This whole thing is turning into a journalistic sideshow. It's a developing story, and I intend to stay on top of things."

"Dottie Hemmings, the mayor's wife, said her husband's worried you'll show your hometown in an unfavorable light. Hinted you had an agenda. Any truth to her theory?"

"Dottie Hemmings?" Barbie scoffed. "That old biddy? All she cares about is keeping her hubby's reputation squeaky clean. She's afraid a dead body in the town square will reflect poorly on him and his fair city." Dismissing the subject, she pointed a red-nailed fingertip at the rapidly cooling pizza. "Interesting," she purred. "I didn't know you and Wyatt had that kind of a relationship."

I could feel my face heat. "What kind of relationship is that?"

"The let's-chat-over-pizza variety — especially considering you're CJ's ex."

"What does that have to do with anything?"

"Those two have been at each other's throats since they were boys. Just because CJ dumped you doesn't mean the guy wants to watch you cozy up to his old nemesis. Don't be fooled, honey." She lowered her voice. "Wyatt's just using you to rattle CJ's cage."

My jaw dropped. Words deserted me. I'd known from the get-go there was no love lost between the two men. But it never once occurred to me that Wyatt McBride and CJ might be playing a game of one-upmanship with me as the pawn. I didn't believe it for a New York minute; still the thought rankled.

Barbie seemed pleased at my reaction. Tossing her long hair over her shoulder, she sauntered toward the exit. "Bye-bye."

"Don't pay that bimbo no nevermind," Precious counseled. "She's the type who likes to cause trouble. I've seen her kind in action before."

"Thanks." I sounded as dispirited as I felt.

"Chief just signaled for you to report to his office," Precious said moments later. "You need anythin', just speak up, you heah?"

"Yes, ma'am." Precious's offer coaxed a smile from me. I placed the pizza box on the countertop in front of her. "Help yourself."

"Don't tempt me." She shook her head until the colorful beads on her braids rattled "I'm on a diet. Got my eye on a new man — friend of my brother Bubba. Had me a Lean Cuisine and a diet soda when I had my break. Just leave the pizza. I'll guard it for you."

I knew the way to McBride's office from previous visits. *Time to put on your big-girl panties and not let Barbie's words affect you,* I lectured myself as I walked down the hall. Drawing a deep breath, I knocked on his door, then entered without waiting for an invitation. McBride glanced up from behind a mountain of paperwork on his desk. "Hey," he said.

"You told me to come by later to sign my statement."

"Right, right." He shuffled through a stack of papers until he found the one he was looking for and handed it to me. "Read it over carefully," he instructed. "Make sure it corresponds to what you told me earlier. Then sign it."

"All righty." He sounded a bit testy, so I didn't want to try his patience further. Clearly, he was feeling the pressure of a long day. Sinking down in the chair opposite him, I read the typed report and slid it back to him unsigned.

"What's wrong?" he asked, skewering me with a look from his frosty blues.

"I can't sign this."

"And why can't you?"

Some folks might've squirmed at his tone, but I held my ground. "Because the statement is incorrect. It should read that Piper Prescott's dog, Casey, found the body and *not* Piper Prescott found the body."

McBride appeared as though he wanted to argue, then changed his mind. "Fine," he agreed. "I'll have Precious correct your statement to read: 'Mrs. Prescott states her dog, Casey, discovered the body.' Is it accurate to include that Mrs. Prescott proceeded to make the nine-one-one call since her pet was otherwise occupied being a cadaver dog?"

"No call to get sarcastic," I retorted.

"I'm not being sarcastic. I'm merely aiming for accuracy, since you always seem to think I'm in need of correcting."

"Only when it's necessary."

He huffed out a breath. "You're doing it again — correcting me."

When I refused to engage in a verbal sparring match, he issued orders to Precious via an intercom to make the requested changes. I studied him covertly. Even though his navy-blue uniform was as crisp as it had been that morning, his face looked tired. I felt an unbidden flood of sympathy for the man and his job. My eyes chanced to fall on a handful of paint chips in various colors at the edge of his desk. "Getting ready to give this place a face-lift?" I asked to lighten the mood.

He appeared puzzled at first, but his expression cleared when he realized what I was referring to. "Yeah, it's long overdue. Getting money for a couple gallons of paint was tougher than asking to pay for a root canal out of petty cash. I even offered to do the painting myself."

"So," I said, examining the samples, "what color did you decide on."

"It's a toss-up between Belgian Waffle and Banana Cream Pie."

"Mmm." I studied first one swatch, then the other. "I'd pick the Belgian Waffle. Maybe use Whipped Cream for the trim."

"I take it Whipped Cream is a paint color."

"Right up there with Banana Cream Pie. I used the color to paint the woodwork in my apartment, if you'd like to see what it looks like."

A ghost of a smile flickered across his mouth. "I'll have to check it out one of these days."

Once again, I felt my face flush. I'd brazenly just gone and invited the man to my apartment. With Becca dead was I going to be the next "hussy"? Thankfully, I heard Precious's footsteps in the hall and was spared further self-flagellation.

"Here you go, Chief," she said, handing

him the edited version of my statement. "Seein' as how you have a long night ahead of you, I put on a fresh pot of coffee. I'll bring some soon's it's done. What about you, Piper? You want a cup?"

"Thanks, Precious, but I can't stay."

She left and I scanned the changes she'd made, scrawled my name at the bottom, and shoved it over to him. "There you go. Signed, sealed, and delivered."

McBride added it to a folder, then leaned back in his chair and pinched the bridge of his nose. "Hard to believe there's been two murders in the short time I've been in office. A regular crime spree. Mayor's demanding to know if someone tampered with the drinking water."

Murder? A *Titanic*-size iceberg seemed lodged in my chest. "You're absolutely certain Becca was murdered?"

"No doubt about it," he sighed. "The medical examiner just faxed over preliminary findings. Becca Dapkins's death appears to have been a robbery gone south. Jewelry gone. Handbag missing."

"Becca wasn't rich. She worked at a low-paying job. Who'd want to rob her?"

"We're in the process of checking things out. In some cases, the killer often turns out to be the husband or significant other."

I stared at McBride in disbelief. "Surely you don't think Buzz Oliver had anything to do with Becca's death? He wouldn't hurt a fly. Well, actually that's not true," I admitted in the spirit of full disclosure. "The man *is* in the pest control business. Termites and scorpions are normally his targets, not the woman he's dating."

"You'd be shocked at the inhumanity people inflict on one another — even those they profess to love."

Silence permeated the room for a long moment. It was obvious McBride had seen more than his share of death at the hands of loved ones. Finally, I cleared my throat. "Did the medical examiner give the cause of death?"

McBride nodded grimly. "Becca Dapkins was bludgeoned."

"Bludgeoned . . . ?" I gasped. "Did you find the murder weapon?"

"No, not yet. Murder weapon might not be so easy to find in this case."

"Why is that?"

McBride drummed his fingers on the desk. "The ME found traces of fat and connective tissue in the head wound."

"What kind of weapon would leave fat and connective tissue behind?" I wondered aloud.

"The ME's running more tests, but he's convinced it was a beef brisket."

"Unbelievable," I murmured. "Becca Dapkins killed with a cheap cut of meat."

Chapter 8

"Pizza delivery," I sang out.

"Someone's got their wires crossed. I didn't order —" Reba Mae ended her tirade mid-sentence at finding me on her doorstep. "Piper, what on earth?"

"Hungry?" I asked when she stepped aside

"Well, yeah, kinda sort of," she admitted, eyeing the box in my hand. "I was just about to fix myself a peanut butter sandwich. The boys are playin' in a softball tournament tonight. Said not to bother fixin' 'em supper. They'd grab a burger after the game."

I headed for her kitchen. "Well, since that's the case, can I interest you in a pepperoni-and-mushroom pie with a side Greek salad?"

"Heck yeah. How about a nice glass of merlot to help wash it down?"

"You don't have to twist my arm. A glass of wine is just what the doctor ordered after the day I had." I turned the dial on Reba

Mae's oven and set the temperature to low. "I need to pop this baby into the oven to reheat. It's been setting for nearly an hour in McBride's waiting room while I reviewed the statement I gave this morning."

Reba Mae got out a baking sheet and watched me slide the pizza onto it. "I take it my favorite lawman wasn't in the mood for pizza."

"Actually, I arrived too late."

"How's that?" Reba asked over her shoulder as she took plates from a cupboard.

"Seems like the Cooking Network's shining star, aka Barbie Q, had already brought him a piping-hot pizza." I found silverware and napkins and proceeded to set the table. I knew Reba Mae's kitchen like the back of my hand. And she knew mine. That was part of being BFFs.

"What the . . . ? Barbie brought him pizza? How well do the two know each other?"

"Quite well, judging from my front-row seat at their reunion tour," I replied.

Reba Mae worked the cork out of a bottle of merlot and poured us each a glass. "I'd bet my last bottle of peroxide that woman's up to somethin'."

"She said she dropped by to ask McBride for an interview."

"And you believed her?"

I shrugged. "Yes and no. On one hand, Barbie's ambitious and thinks a dead body in the town square might be a big break careerwise. Yet on the other side of the coin, she and McBride share a history, so her interest in him might be strictly personal."

While Reba Mae divvied up the salad, my eyes wandered around her cozy kitchen. Like Reba Mae herself, the room was unpretentious and straightforward. Formica countertops, aging appliances, and a no-wax vinyl floor. In spite of her weakness for flashy clothes and even flashier shoes, Reba Mae pinched pennies.

I took a sip of wine and reminisced. Once upon a time, we'd been next-door neighbors. We'd bonded over teething, potty training, and *General Hospital*. Then CJ's struggling law practice took off and, in keeping with his image, we'd moved to a bigger house in a newer development. The one thing that hadn't changed though was mine and Reba Mae's friendship. That had remained constant. Not even a country club membership, fancy car, or gold Visa changed that. Reba Mae's twins, Clay and Caleb, were best friends too with my Chad and treated Lindsey like the baby sister they never had.

When Butch died in a tragic accident

while bass fishing, Reba Mae discovered they were deep in credit card debt. Butch was a great guy but not one to worry about tomorrow. He thought he'd live to a ripe old age. After things settled down, I'd loaned Reba Mae money for beauty school. Later, I helped her finance the Klassy Kut and let CJ think I'd used the money for a tummy tuck. She'd paid back every dime — with interest.

"Might as well start while the pizza warms up." Reba Mae set a plate piled high with salad in front of me. "Dig in."

I speared a cherry tomato. "Mmm. I'm famished."

"Any chance McBride mention what killed Becca?"

"More like a 'who' than a 'what.' "

"Who . . . as in a person?" Reba Mae missed the cherry tomato she aimed at and it skittered across the table.

I picked it up and popped it into my mouth. "That would be correct. The medical examiner said she was bludgeoned."

Reba Mae stared at me, her fork poised halfway to her mouth. "No kiddin'."

"Even more to the point, the ME's almost certain the murder weapon — get ready for this — was a beef brisket."

Her salad forgotten, Reba Mae set down

her fork down and reached for her wine. "Wow," she said after taking a gulp. "I wasn't expectin' that."

"I would've been less surprised if she'd been beaned with a can of soup." I got up and removed the pizza from the oven. "All this publicity will be bad for the barbecue festival."

"Or it might work just the opposite." Reba Mae helped herself to a slice. "Nothin' like morbid curiosity to draw a crowd."

"Well, if Barbie Quinlan has a say this town will turn into a three-ring circus. She fancies herself Lois Lane, girl reporter." I bit into pizza smothered in gooey mozzarella. "Then fade to gray as she and Wyatt McBride ride off into the sunset."

"Think you're makin' too much out of two old friends seein' each other again?"

"You don't have to know Morse code to interpret the signals she was sending out. I don't know why I'm obsessing over it. I already have a terrific man in my life," I said, referring to Doug Winters, the very nice vet who not only had saved Casey's life but also bought expensive saffron from my shop.

"There you go," Reba Mae said. "Doug's not only a great guy, but he likes to cook.

What more could a girl put on her wish list?"

"You're absolutely right. Doug is . . . special. It was my lucky day when he happened to waltz into Spice It Up! Not only that, he's been a positive influence on Lindsey since she started working part-time at his animal clinic. Because of him, she talks about becoming a veterinarian one day. Speaking of Doug and cooking," I said, reaching for my wineglass, "he called to tell me he entered the backyard division of the competition. Said he's been experimenting with mopping sauces. Wanted to know if I'd object if he asked Lindsey to be part of his team."

"Sounds like a good idea if you want my opinion. It'll help keep Lindsey's mind off breaking up with that no-'count boyfriend of hers." Reba Mae took another slice, then pushed the pan in my direction. "Does McBride have any suspects?"

"It's still early yet. He mentioned it might've been a botched robbery. Becca's jewelry was missing and so was her purse. He also said something to the effect that husbands and significant others were often the guilty parties. I gathered he was going to question Buzz."

"Buzz?" Reba Mae topped off our wine.

"McBride surely can't think Buzz would harm Becca?"

I shrugged. "I'm no mind reader, but he might have heard talk that Buzz blamed Becca for his gallbladder attack. After all, she was the reason he had to have emergency surgery. The quiet ones like Buzz are the types you have to watch. They keep things bottled up and then . . . pow! They explode."

Reba Mae rolled her eyes. "Where did you hear that? Dr. Phil?"

I kept silent, too embarrassed to admit that might well have been my source.

Reba Mae leaned back, wineglass in hand. "Gossip goin' around the Klassy Kut has it that Becca was spittin' mad 'cause Buzz paid more attention to Maybelle at the Baptist church ice-cream social than to her."

"Blame all his attention on the fact that Maybelle baked her to-die-for Hummingbird Cake. Not a soul alive can resist her Hummingbird Cake. She's been asked for the recipe dozens of times, but refuses to share."

"When it comes to cooking, Becca can't compete with a five-year-old, much less Maybelle. Without a can opener, she's as helpless as a fish out of water."

"Change that to past tense," I reminded

Reba Mae.

"Duly noted," Reba Mae agreed somberly.

"At any rate, McBride intends to call Buzz down as part of the official murder investigation."

Reba Mae was about to comment further when the back door swung open.

"Hey, Mama," Clay said, then turned to me. "Hey, Miz Piper,"

"Hey yourself," I said, giving him the once-over. Reba Mae's boys were big, strapping lads with her dark hair and good looks and their daddy's pretty hazel eyes. The easiest way to tell them apart was by their hair. Clay favored his cut short while Caleb's, much to his mother's chagrin, reached almost to his shoulders.

"Your mama's going to have to use her bag of tricks to get that softball uniform clean," I told him, taking in the sweat stains under his arms and the Georgia red clay ground into the knees.

"Naw, Mama's a mean one." He grinned. "She makes me and my brother do our own laundry. Said she's trainin' us to be good husbands."

"Darn right," Reba Mae retorted. "You're home early, Son."

Clay fixated on the half-eaten pizza on the table. "I'd sure hate to see that fine-lookin' pizza go to waste when there's starvin' children in the world."

"Charity begins at home," I said, shoving it toward him.

"You might want to save some for your brother," Reba Mae commented as she watched her boy wolf down a slice.

"Caleb hooked up with a cute little blonde in a red halter top," Clay said around a mouthful. "She offered to buy him a burger."

Reba Mae laughed and shook her head. "That boy is so easily bribed, it's pitiful."

Clay reached for another slice. "Could have told the girl to save her money. It was a done deal with just the halter top. Take me for instance; I'm just the opposite when it comes to the ladies."

"How's that?" I asked, forever curious to learn the workings of a man's mind.

Pizza finished, Clay headed for the fridge and pulled out a gallon of milk.

"No drinkin' straight from the jug," Reba Mae was quick to admonish. "Use a glass."

"Didn't I tell you Mama was a meanie?" He winked at me but took a glass from the cupboard. "Now, as to my technique with women, I'm more subtle than Caleb. I'm taking cues from Chief McBride and play-ing hard to get."

"McBride?"

"Yep." He downed the milk, then refilled his glass. "I've seen how women look at him all smiley-like. He could have his pick, but he pretends not to notice. Drives the gals crazy."

Hmm, I thought to myself. I hope I didn't fall in the same category all "smiley-like" and calf-eyed. If Barbie Q wanted him, she could have him. I intended to play it safe and stick with Doug. He might not be tall, dark, and hunky, but he was a gold medalist when it came to kissing. His kisses made me weak in the knees. Besides that, he was sweet, thoughtful. And he listened, really listened, whenever I talked. What could be sexier than a man who hung on to your every word?

Reba Mae got up and cleared the dishes. "Clay, you still haven't mentioned who won tonight's game."

"We did. Cloune Motor Cougars beat the Bugs-B-Gone Braves four to two." He placed his glass in the dishwasher. "Say," he said as a new thought occurred to him, "either of you know why the Chamber of Commerce was closed today? Is it some sort of holiday?"

"That's odd." I looked to Reba Mae for confirmation, but she shrugged. "The

Chamber's usually open nine to five Monday through Friday and till noon on Saturdays."

"I stopped by to pick up some flyers like my boss asked, but the place was locked up tighter 'n a drum."

Reba Mae began loading the dishwasher. "Perhaps Maybelle came down with the flu, though I've never known her to be sickly."

Frowning, I tapped my nails on the tabletop. "I'm pretty sure I saw her this morning on the sidewalk near the square."

"Did she look like she was ailin'?"

I closed my eyes briefly, trying to picture Maybelle the last time I'd seen her. "Now that you mention it, her complexion seemed even more pasty than usual. And she seemed distant . . . distracted. I don't think she even noticed me."

"Probably upset about Becca."

"I'll try the Chamber again tomorrow," Clay said. "Right now, I'm headin' for the shower."

Grabbing a dishrag, Reba Mae wiped down the counters. "It's not like Maybelle to close up shop."

I stared into the dregs at the bottom of my wineglass. "Someone — I think it might've been Dottie Hemmings — made a comment that Maybelle wasn't the type who liked to share what was hers."

Reba Mae stopped wiping. "Such as Buzz . . . ?"

"You don't suppose . . . ?"

Reba Mae instantly read my mind. "No, of course not," she replied. "Maybelle wouldn't step on a spider."

"Good point," I said. I felt guilty as sin that such a thought even crossed my mind. "If Buzz has a solid alibi for the time of the murder, suspicion will shift to Maybelle in a heartbeat. Mark my words, she'll be the next one lined up in McBride's sights — and in the court of public opinion. Maybelle's a friend. I'd hate like heck to see that happen. I know what it's like to be wrongly accused."

"I'm worried about her," Reba Mae admitted. "You said she didn't look well when you saw her earlier."

I jumped up and grabbed my purse. "Let's go."

Reba Mae tossed the dishrag into the sink. "Where we goin'?"

"We're off to visit a sick friend."

CHAPTER 9

Maybelle Humphries lived in a brick ranch-style home with black shutters and neatly trimmed shrubs. Her wide front porch held two white wicker rockers — rockers are a requisite for Southern homes — and several clay pots filled with bright red geraniums.

I rang the bell while Reba Mae opted for the less subtle approach, which consisted of pounding on the door. Between the two of us, the din was loud enough to wake the dead.

No response.

Disappointed, we stared at each other in the gathering darkness, trying to decide on a course of action. "Maybe she's not home," Reba Mae suggested.

I pointed toward the side of the house. "Then how do you account for her Honda in the carport?"

"Oh, yeah, right. S'pose she's sleepin'?"

"Not with the racket we've been making."

I jabbed the doorbell again.

"Could be she went for a little exercise," Reba Mae offered. "It's a nice night for a walk."

I stood on tiptoe and peered through the small diamond-shaped pane of glass set into the wood door. "Looks like the TV's still on."

"Might be Maybelle's in the little girl's room."

I stepped off the porch and wedged myself between the boxwoods under the picture window. Cupping my hands around my eyes, I tried to peek through a narrow slit in the drawn blinds. "What if Maybelle's fallen and can't get up? Like in those television commercials."

Reba Mae edged closer. "You mean the one with the lady layin' on the floor all old and helpless? Then she's all happy again after buyin' herself one of those gadgets to wear around her neck?"

"That's the one." I straightened and stood, hands on hips, staring at a nearby crepe myrtle ready to burst into bloom. "You stay here while I go around back."

"You don't think Maybelle is avoidin' us on purpose?"

"Nonsense," I replied, although privately that's exactly what I thought. Still . . .

"What if Maybelle *is* hurt and needs help? What kind of persons would we be if we turned our backs on a friend? We need to make sure she's safe. We owe it to her."

"You're right," Reba Mae agreed. "Maybelle could've sprained an ankle. Or broken her hip. Do you think we should call nine-one-one? Ask McBride to send one of his men over to check on things?"

"Umm . . . Let's wait," I said as she started to reach into her pocket for her cell phone. I knew Maybelle to be a private person — a very private person. She'd never speak to us again if we called the police to break down her door. "Why don't we check this out more thoroughly before calling for reinforcements?"

"Piper . . . ?" Reba Mae raced over to me and clutched my arm, her eyes wide. "I just thought of something. What if the same psycho who killed Becca came after Maybelle? After all, the two of them are single women, livin' alone, and approximately the same age."

"Are you nuts?" I hissed. "Surely you're not suggesting there's a serial killer on the prowl in Brandywine Creek? A killer who bludgeons his victims with a brisket?"

"Stranger things have happened," she retorted, her tone defensive. "You read about serial killers all the time in the news-papers. Or see stories about them on TV. I even saw a show once about vampire serial killers."

I fought the urge to roll my eyes. "Next you'll try to convince me Buzz Oliver flipped out and is systematically knocking off all the women in his life."

"That's exactly what I'm talkin' about. Just think of it as a possible movie of the week on the Lifetime channel."

"Stay here," I instructed. "Keep ringing the bell and pounding on the door while I check around the back." I didn't know what I expected to find but thought it worth a shot. Maybe the kitchen curtains would be open and give me a better hint of what was going on inside. Could be Maybelle was playing possum. Could be she really was injured or ill and needed help.

I'd no sooner gone a half-dozen steps when the front porch light flicked on, bath-ing us in its jaundiced glare. A lock snicked and a door opened, revealing a haggard-appearing Maybelle Humphries clutching a fleecy robe tightly around her throat.

"What in heaven's name!" she exclaimed at seeing us. "You two are making enough noise to disturb the neighbors."

"Hey, Maybelle," I said, taking in the

woman's drawn face, the dark circles under her eyes. "Reba Mae and I were worried about you. Thought we'd stop by and make sure you're all right."

Reba Mae stepped forward, motioning for me to return to the porch. "My boy Clay said he came by the Chamber this afternoon to pick up some flyers, but the office was closed. In all the years I lived in this town, I've never known the Chamber to be closed in the middle of the week."

"Do you mind if we come in for a minute?" I asked. "I promise we won't overstay our welcome."

Much too genteel to slam the door in our faces, Maybelle stood aside grudgingly and allowed us to enter. Her neat-as-a-pin living room with its green-and-gold plaid sofa, matching love seat, and walnut end tables was as plain and simple as the woman herself. I recognized the smiling faces of Rachael Ray and Bobby Flay on the covers of cooking magazines fanned across the polished surface of a coffee table.

Reba Mae and I plunked ourselves down on the sofa, leaving the love seat to Maybelle. She lowered herself primly, lapping the robe more securely around her thin frame. Picking up the remote, she clicked off the television. "It's nice of you girls to worry about me, but as you can see, I'm fit as a fiddle."

Maybelle didn't meet my criteria of looking "fit as a fiddle." Her complexion was the color of bread dough, her eyes bloodshot. "You sure you're okay? You're awfully pale."

"Is there anything we can get you?" Reba Mae asked. "Chicken soup, ginger ale, aspirin, cold pills?"

Maybelle managed a wan smile. "That's sweet of you, Reba Mae, but as you can see, I'm fine. No need to fret. Probably just allergies kicking up. You can tell your son it'll be business as usual tomorrow at the Chamber."

"That's not why we're here. We're your friends and thought you might be sick."

"Or hurt," I added for good measure.

"Well, it was a wasted trip," Maybelle snapped. "I'm neither."

Reba Mae and I gaped at hearing the sharp rebuke. It wasn't like Maybelle to be irritable and out of sorts. And it certainly was out of character for her to bite our heads off. I couldn't help but wonder if Becca's death had a more profound impact on Maybelle than she cared to admit.

"Sorry for how that must've sounded," Maybelle apologized, her hands tightly clasped in her lap. "It's been a . . . difficult . . . day."

"No apology necessary, hon." Reba Mae popped off the sofa. "I gotta pee. Pushin' out two future football players three minutes apart wrecked my bladder somethin' fierce. Mind if I use your bathroom?"

"Go right ahead. Down the hall, first room on the left."

As we had exhausted the subject of Maybelle's health, it was time to tackle a different subject. "I caught a glimpse of you at the square this morning," I ventured. "Learning Becca had been killed must have come as a quite a shock."

Maybelle wrapped her arms around her waist and shivered. "Yes, quite a shock."

Following her admission, she lapsed into silence. I could hear the *tick-tock* of a clock from another room of the house. I was relieved when Reba Mae finally returned. She smiled and, when she was certain Maybelle wasn't watching, gave me a thumbs-up.

Puzzled, I returned my attention to Maybelle. "Who do you suppose killed Becca?" I asked, trying to keep my tone conversational rather than confrontational.

"How should I know?" Maybelle moistened dry lips with the tip of her tongue. "A lot of folks disliked Becca."

"Do you know anyone who 'disliked' her enough to want her dead?"

Maybelle stood abruptly and began pacing back and forth. "Don't think I don't know what people are going to be thinking? Everyone will be looking at me sideways and wondering if I'd finally had enough of Becca's thieving ways."

"You know how folks are, Maybelle," I said, soothingly. "Once you prove you have an alibi, they'll turn their attention elsewhere. You do have an alibi for last night don't you?" At least I assumed that's when the murder occurred. Aren't most crimes committed under cover of darkness?

"Of course I do," she said a shade too quickly. "I volunteer at the food bank down in Augusta the second Tuesday of every month with Gerilee Barker."

"That's great," I told her. "Then you have nothing to fear if McBride questions you."

Maybelle ceased pacing, her eyes wide with alarm. If possible, her pale face became even paler. She looked as if I'd just given voice to her worst nightmare.

Reba Mae, seemingly oblivious to Maybelle's distress, abruptly changed the subject. "Speakin' of food and such, my boys rave about your Hummingbird Cake no end. I was wonderin' if you'd be kind enough to share your recipe."

Maybelle's lips pursed. "Forgive me, Reba Mae. I'm truly sorry, but I never divulge recipes that have been in the family for generations. I hope you understand."

Reba Mae reached over and patted Maybelle's arm. "Don't think twice about it, sugar. I guard Meemaw's recipe for Hungarian goulash with my life."

"Now if you ladies don't mind, I've had a rather trying day and would like to get some rest."

I rose and signaled Reba Mae to follow suit. Maybelle escorted us to the door and shut it firmly behind us. The *snick* of a dead bolt sounded overly loud in the sudden stillness.

A huge golden moon hung from a star-spangled sky. Cicadas buzzed and tree frogs chirped in a discordant symphony. After the heat and humidity of a summer day in Georgia, the evenings were often bliss. "Well, that was odd," I commented as Reba Mae and I headed toward our respective homes.

"I thought the entire visit was weird," Reba Mae agreed. "Did you happen to notice that when Maybelle's robe separated she was still wearin' her street clothes?"

I nodded. "The same ones she wore this morning at the crime scene."

"That's what gave me my first brainstorm."

"Girlfriend, the notion of you having brainstorms gives me the heebie-jeebies."

"I'm more than just a pretty face," Reba Mae reminded me with a jab to the ribs. "Anyhow, as I was about to tell you, seein' her fully dressed made me want to take a gander at her bedroom. See if her bed looked slept in or if the spread was wrinkled. That's why I made up the story about needin' a bathroom."

"Was her bed mussed?"

"Nope," Reba Mae said smugly. "Smooth as a baby's bottom. I got the impression she threw on her robe and pretended she'd been sleepin' when we refused to go away. Probably afraid we'd break her door down — or call the cops — if she didn't answer."

"What was all that stuff about Hummingbird Cake?" I asked as we continued on our way.

"Hummingbird Cake is Maybelle's specialty. She insists it's a family recipe, but I overheard my customers talkin'. According to them, Maybelle found the original version in an out-of-print cookbook she picked up at Second Hand Prose. It makes

103

me wonder, is all."

"Wonder what?"

"Makes me wonder if it's true what folks say about Maybelle not sharin'."

We paused under the glow of a streetlamp where our paths diverged. "Take pity on me, girl. I've had a long day, too. *What* are you getting at?"

"If Maybelle doesn't like sharin' recipes, I'm thinkin' about the lengths she might go to not share a fiancé with Becca Dapkins?"

"Reba Mae Johnson!" I scolded. "Shame on you! Maybelle wouldn't swat a mosquito."

"Maybe, maybe not," Reba Mae said with a shrug. "It's no secret there were hard feelin's between the two. I'm just sayin' . . ."

"I remember all too well what it's like to be number one on McBride's hit parade of suspects. To be honest, Reba Mae, I'd rest easier knowing Maybelle was truthful about her alibi."

Reba Mae and I said our good nights and started off in the direction of our respective homes. The entire time, I couldn't rid myself of the thought that Maybelle's actions had been evasive. The woman was clearly hiding something.

But what . . . ?

"Be prepared" might be the Scout motto,

but it was also good advice when it came to dealing with a wily police chief who happened to be a stickler for such things as alibis. Maybelle might not be ready to admit it, but she needed our help.

CHAPTER 10

I was on the floor restocking spices the following afternoon when Casey's frenzied barking startled me so much I bumped my head on one of the shelves. "Dang!" I said, getting to my feet.

"Want me to kiss and make it better?" a familiar voice asked.

I turned to find Doug Winters, veterinarian extraordinaire, behind me. The brown eyes behind rimless glasses twinkled with good humor. A youthful face belied the premature gray hair that I found quite attractive. Instead of his usual golf shirt and chinos, he wore a lightweight linen sport coat in a muted gray-and-cream glen plaid, white dress shirt open at the throat, and gray slacks. Before I could scold him for making light of my injury, he moved in for a kiss that made my toes tingle.

"Hey," I said, slightly breathless when we broke apart. "I thought it was the bump on my head that needed attention."

He grinned boyishly. "Head, lips, I always get the two confused."

"Fine doctor you are," I teased. "You better pray word doesn't get around town that you flunked Anatomy."

"I'll take my chances. Miss me?"

I opened my mouth to reply, but Casey, tired of being ignored by his favorite vet, hurled his small body against the baby gate I'd fastened across the stairs leading to my apartment. "Enough, Casey," I admonished. "Settle down."

"Sure wish I had that kind of effect on everyone." Doug laughed.

Since I knew Doug wouldn't mind, I unlatched the gate. Casey scampered over to enthusiastically greet our guest. "Everyone doesn't spoil him rotten with doggy treats."

"Hey there, fella." Doug bent down and rubbed the little dog behind the ears, sending him into a fit of puppy ecstasy. Casey demonstrated his affection by lathering the vet's hand with his raspy pink tongue.

"You're Casey's knight in shining armor," I said, smiling. I'd first discovered the little mutt at death's door after he'd been stabbed and rushed him to the vet at breakneck speed. Doug saved his life.

"Casey loves anyone who brings him treats." Doug modestly shrugged off his role of savior. Reaching into the pocket of his sport coat, he tossed Casey a handful of nuggets resembling Tootsie Rolls.

Humans forgotten, Casey scrambled after them.

"How was your seminar in Atlanta?" I asked. "Learn any new tricks?"

"One or two." He folded his arms across his chest, all traces of humor vanishing. "What's all this talk I hear about you finding a dead body? I learned about it from the clerk at the Gas and Go on my way into town."

I sighed. "Technically, Casey is the one who discovered a body, not me." I then proceeded to relate the details of finding Becca Dapkins, pretty in pink and deader 'n a doornail, under the azaleas.

He let out a low whistle when I finished my story. "That's quite a feat for a pup his age. The little mutt's got a good nose. You might want to consider enrolling him in cadaver-dog training. I can give you some information if you're interested."

I held up both hands in protest and stepped away from the vet. "Thanks, but no thanks. I don't intend to make a career out of finding bodies — and neither does Casey. I've already found more than the recommended quota."

"It must have been a terrible experience," Doug sympathized. Reaching out, he trailed his fingers down my cheek. "You all right?"

" 'Terrible' doesn't begin to describe what it was like." I resisted the urge to rest my head on his shoulder and assume the role of damsel in distress, but I was made of sterner stuff. Instead, I smiled gamely. "I'm thinking of swearing off jogging and listing my gecko-green running shoes on eBay."

"Did you know the woman well?"

I picked up a jar of crystallized ginger, then returned it to the shelf. "I knew her, but I wouldn't say we were friends. Becca left Brandywine Creek years ago, but after her divorce she came back to a house her grandmother had bequeathed her. She worked for the water department, but I don't think she was happy."

"The clerk at the gas station mentioned she was seeing someone."

"Buzz Oliver."

"Buzz Oliver the exterminator?"

"That's him." I wandered over to the counter where I'd left a stack of mail. "Before Becca came back to Brandywine Creek, Buzz was engaged to Maybelle Humphries. You might know Maybelle. She manages the Chamber of Commerce."

Hands in his pockets, Doug strolled over to join me. "Yeah, I know Maybelle. We met when I was establishing my business. Efficient, friendly, helpful. She's a nice lady. I like her. I happened to know of a cute little calico looking for a good home and tried to convince her it would make the perfect pet. Alas." He chuckled ruefully. "Maybelle seemed interested, but her allergy to cats stood in the way."

"Poor Maybelle." I idly sorted through mail comprised mainly of charities' asking for donations. "Her allergies were giving her grief yesterday. So much, in fact, that she closed up shop for the day, went home, and said she climbed into bed."

"Hmm, that's strange," Doug said, rubbing his jaw. "Allergies usually flare up in the spring and fall."

Interesting, I thought. *Good-bye, Maybelle's excuse for going home early. But if not allergies, what explained her drawn face, the reddened eyes?*

"So bring me up to speed on local gossip," Doug continued. "Maybelle and Buzz were an item before Becca arrived on the scene?"

"Theirs had to be one of the longest engagements in history. Maybelle was devastated when Buzz broke it off and started seeing Becca."

Doug's brow furrowed. "You don't suppose . . . ?"

You don't suppose . . . ? Those words could be put to music.

"Can we change the subject please?" All this worrying and wondering was starting to give me a headache. "What brings you here in the middle of the afternoon? You in the market for more of my pricey saffron?"

He chuckled. "Every time you mention 'saffron,' I swear I can see dollar signs light up those green eyes of yours."

"Well," I drawled, "a girl's gotta make a living. Need I remind you, saffron *is* the world's most expensive spice? Not much call for saffron in a town where mac and cheese is a staple."

"Don't forget collard greens and cornbread."

"Not to mention fried green tomatoes."

"Guess I haven't been south of the Mason-Dixon Line long enough to acquire a taste for grits or greens. Once the barbecue festival is over, I intend to appoint you as my guinea pig. I stumbled across a recipe for shrimp remoulade that I'd like to try. Are you game?"

"Count me in." Doug was an excellent

cook. Absolutely fearless in the kitchen. Exotic dishes calling for rare spices made him one of my best customers. And also my favorite.

"In the meantime, I'm perfecting pulled pork. I have my eye on winning the trophy for backyard division in the pulled-pork category. The winner is often invited to compete with the professionals next year. Which brings me to why I'm here. Is Lindsey around?"

"Hmph," I sniffed. "And all this time, I thought *I* was the reason you stopped in."

"You know I look for any excuse I can to see you," he said, his expression earnest. "My pantry is filled to overflowing with spices. Some, like nigella, mahlab, and kokam, I'd never heard of before, much less used."

"Nigella and mahlab have a nutty flavor," I told him, showing off the knowledge I'd accrued. "Kokam is more acidic and fruity."

"Thank you, teacher," he said in mock seriousness. "Is that going to be on the final exam?"

I gave his arm a playful swat. "Don't be a smart aleck," I said. "And as for Lindsey's whereabouts, she's spending the week at a friend's lake house. What did you want to see my daughter about?"

"She volunteered to be part of my pit crew for the festival. I wanted to ask if she had any friends who might be interested in joining the team."

"I expect her home, tanned and tired, on Sunday."

"She's scheduled to work at Pets 'R People the next day, so I'll ask her then." He stole another kiss, then strolled out, leaving me wanting another. I stared after him with a bemused expression.

After Doug left to tend to his practice, I filled the hours until closing restocking shelves and planning an eye-catching display designed to draw customers into my shop during the barbecue festival. A glance at the clock told me it was quitting time.

I started around the counter when in walked Wyatt McBride. I automatically ran a hand over my rebellious curls and smoothed my apron — the female equivalent of gut sucking and spine straightening. McBride has that kind of effect on the ladies. I'm ashamed to admit I'm no exception.

"McBride," I said all businesslike.

"Piper," he replied, aping my tone.

I folded my arms across my chest. "Since you don't cook, I know you're not here to buy spice. Unless you've taken my advice and purchased a copy of *How to Boil Water.*"

"Too drastic. I'd rather load up on doughnuts and other edible donations."

Donations such as pepperoni pizza delivered by a certain platinum blonde?

"Not my idea of a well-balanced diet."

Six foot one, broad shoulders, trim waist. It was hard to believe someone who looked like a living, breathing ad for fit-and-trim was a junk food addict. Speaking for women the world over, it just wasn't fair! I knew for a fact McBride was in his mid- to late forties, yet he looked like he could bench-press with youngsters half his age. Maybe he secretly existed on a diet consisting of tofu and soy. When my defenses were low, I caught myself fantasizing what he'd look like without a shirt.

It took willpower, but I managed to pull my errant thoughts back to the present. "If you're not a customer, what brings you here?"

"I thought you might've remembered some detail from yesterday that might prove helpful."

McBride subscribed to the theory that memory was a funny thing. That details that at the time seemed insignificant lodged in the hinterlands of the brain and might resurface at a later date. In his experience as a hotshot detective, he claimed these details often cracked a case wide open.

"I tried, but can't think of anything I might've missed. I don't recall seeing anyone or hearing anything unusual. Just me and Casey."

Hearing his name mentioned, the pup awakened from his nap, raised his head, opened one eye, then promptly went back to snoozing peacefully next to the counter.

"Any clues who might have killed Becca?"

"For now, we're treating her death as a random act of violence. A crime of opportunity. Becca Dapkins happened to be in the wrong place at the wrong time."

Tugging on my apron strings, I pulled it over my head. "Was the coroner able to establish the time of death?"

"Estimating time of death isn't an exact science," McBride cautioned. "Judging from body temp and rigor, however, Strickland puts it somewhere between ten o'clock and midnight."

Mechanically, I folded the apron into a neat square. "What was Becca doing in the square at that hour? Why wasn't she home watching reruns on TV? Or getting ready for bed?"

"We're theorizing she might have been

taking a brisket over to Buzz Oliver. A peace offering of sorts."

"That's ridiculous! Who ever heard of beef brisket as a peace offering? Chocolate-chip cookies or brownies, but a chunk of meat?" I shook my head in disbelief. "By the way, did you ever find the brisket?"

"No sign of it." He hooked his thumbs in his belt. "I figure the mugger panicked and skipped off with it. One of my men raised the theory that an animal might've carted it off. A large dog maybe. Or turkey buzzards."

Turkey buzzards were incredibly ugly birds that ate anything that wasn't moving. The notion of them feasting on Becca made me queasy. I swallowed hard and asked another question that had been plaguing me. "What about Buzz? Did you talk to him? Rumor has it he and Becca had argued."

"Buzz's alibi is rock solid."

"Are you sure? Isn't the husband or boyfriend supposed to be the guilty party? That's the way it always works on TV." I tossed my apron at the counter, but it missed by a mile and slid to the floor. "So what was Buzz doing the night Becca was bludgeoned? Playing poker with the guys? Watching a Braves game?"

The corner of McBride's mouth lifted.

"He had an emergency."

I threw up my hands. "For crying out loud, the man's an exterminator, not a brain surgeon."

"Don't rush to judgment." McBride's smile widened ever so slightly. "Seems a bedbug infestation was reported at the Beaver Dam Motel on the edge of town. Guests were freaking out, screaming bloody murder. Threatening to call the board of health. The manager called Buzz's company and offered to pay double if he'd send someone ASAP. Buzz was there until the wee hours. The manager backed up his claim still grumbling about the bill."

"Isn't the Beaver Dam Motel also known as the No-Tell Motel?"

Turning, McBride sauntered toward the door. "One and the same."

"Did Buzz find any bedbugs?" I called after him.

"Nope." He flashed a devilish grin over his shoulder, showing off the cute dimple in his cheek. "Cockroaches. Lots of 'em."

CHAPTER 11

"You're pullin' my leg, right?" Reba Mae asked. "McBride can't really believe Becca's the victim of a muggin'? No way, José."

"Way."

I dunked a tortilla chip into the spicy salsa. We were seated at a booth in one of our favorite eateries, North of the Border. Mariachi music blared over a loudspeaker. Though Brandywine Creek isn't a mecca for fast-food joints, we citizens fancied ourselves a cosmopolitan bunch. Mexican, Chinese, and Italian restaurants all did a thriving business. And if you're more in mind for burgers and beer, there was High Cotton Bar and Grill out on the highway.

"Where does Wyatt think this is, New York City?"

"Don't shoot the messenger. I'm just repeating what McBride told me."

"We've never had a muggin'." Reba Mae idly stirred her slushy margarita with a straw.

"That's not to say it can't happen," I pointed out. I helped myself to another chip and critiqued the salsa. It seemed spicier, hotter, than usual. *A tad too much poblano pepper?* I wondered. Good thing I'd stocked up on antacids.

"It wasn't a simple muggin'," Reba Mae reminded me. "It was a murder. Do you s'pose it might've been done by a kid high on drugs?"

"I wasn't aware Brandywine Creek had a drug problem."

"Honeybun, don't kid yourself," Reba Mae chided. "You'd have to be livin' on the moon to get away from drug problems. They're everywhere."

As though the tequila could dull the fact we didn't live in a perfect world, I took a big swallow of icy-cold margarita. I was relieved when Nacho, one of the owners, delivered our food.

An ever-present smile wreathed his round face. "Is there anything else I can get for you, señoras?"

"No thank you, Nacho," I said, returning his smile.

When he left to wait on a table of newcomers, Reba Mae and I dug into our dinners. Chicken chimichanga for me, beef enchiladas for her.

"Did McBride and his men give Becca's house a look-see?" Reba Mae asked as she cut off a bite-sized piece of enchilada.

"They probably did, though McBride didn't mention it. To be honest, I wouldn't mind taking a look myself."

Reba Mae stared at me as if I'd lost my marbles. "Why'd you want to do a fool thing like that?"

I concentrated on my chimi and avoided eye contact. "Just because."

"Because why?" she persisted. "What do you expect to find that the cops didn't?"

I shrugged. "I don't *expect* to find anything. I just thought it might be, well . . . you know . . . interesting."

Leaning forward, Reba Mae waggled her fork at me. " 'Interestin" covers a boatload of meanin's, sugar."

"A quick peek was all I had in mind. We might spot something others missed. Be a fresh set of eyes. Just think, Reba Mae. What if the police overlooked a tiny detail that could lead them to Becca's killer?" I went for the jugular. The kill shot. "You know how unobservant men can be," I added.

"Ain't that the truth." Reba Mae nodded knowingly. "Once Butch was so busy tellin' me about a fifteen-pound crappie he caught, he failed to notice I'd gone from blond to brunette while he was reelin' it in."

"Butch was a good guy." I added a dollop of sour cream to my chimi, spread it around. "He adored you."

Reba Mae returned her attention to her food. "Butch was never a smooth talker. I think I started to fall in love with the big lug when he told me I was prettier than a speckled trout."

"Aww . . ."

"Times I feel myself wishin' I had a man in my life," she confessed. "I miss the little things. Stuff like gettin' all dolled up, then catchin' that certain gleam in your man's eye and knowin' how — and where — the evenin's goin' to end. I miss havin' someone ask about my day. Someone who after listenin' to me whine gives me a hug and tells me everythin's gonna work out."

A lump the size of a baseball seemed lodged in my throat at hearing this. Reba Mae wasn't one to host a pity party or go squishy sentimental. She was the no-nonsense practical sort who faced problems head-on. But she was lonelier than I imagined. Not knowing what to say, I simply reached over and squeezed her hand.

Reba Mae blinked several times, then shrugged off her somber mood. "I'm thinkin' of givin' Internet datin' a whirl. Brandywine Creek's not exactly overrun with eligible bachelors."

I finished my chimi and pushed my plate aside. "I hear Buzz Oliver is available," I teased. "On the plus side, with Buzz around you'd never be bothered with termites."

"Mark my words, Maybelle will snap him up in a heartbeat. She's probably already whippin' up a Hummingbird Cake to lure him back."

"True."

"While we're on the subject of eligible gentlemen, you, hon, have already staked a claim on the two hottest guys in the Peach State. Doug Winters is cute as a bug's ear. And I've seen you and McBride together. With a little effort on your part, you could fan those sparks into a ragin' forest fire."

"McBride's out of my league." I crumpled up my napkin, tossed it aside, and drained the last of my margarita. "He's reported to have escorted starlets to premieres in South Beach, and now Ms. Bombshell has her sights set on him. Barbie Q went as far as insinuating McBride's only interest in me is to even a score with CJ dating back to when they were boys."

"Blondes are the root of all evil," Reba Mae theorized. "I'd bet good money Jezebel was a blonde."

"Amen, sista!" I clinked my empty margarita glass against hers.

Reba Mae lounged back in the booth and eyed me speculatively. "You still dead set on checkin' out Becca's digs? 'Cause if so, I figured out a way to do it without gettin' busted for breakin' and enterin'."

I watched in amazement as Reba Mae pulled out her cell phone and punched in a number. Minutes later, she'd persuaded Gerilee Barker, who lived three doors down from Becca, to leave Becca's spare key under the mat for us. In exchange, Reba Mae promised we'd take over the tending of Becca's extensive collection of African violets.

"Easy peasy." Reba Mae grinned.

We were standing at the counter waiting to pay our checks when Wally Porter came through the front door. His dress slacks bore a crease sharp enough to slice cheese, and his striped oxford cloth shirt was starched stiff as a sheet of plywood. The guy looked out of place in a town where jeans and shorts were the uniform du jour.

Wally beamed a smile at us. "If I'd known I'd be treated to the sight of two of the town's lovelies, I would have timed my arrival to coincide with yours. Maybe you'd have taken pity on a lonely bachelor in a strange town and invited me to join you. Any chance I can buy you a drink? I heard the margaritas are excellent."

Reba Mae cast me a hopeful glance. "Well . . ."

"Sorry, but we're on our way to an errand," I explained. It occurred to me Reba Mae and Wally hadn't met, so I hastily performed the introductions.

Reba Mae handed her credit card to Nacho, who patiently waited for us to finish our conversation. "We offered to water the plants of a recently deceased friend," she confided. "And we're gonna take a look around while we're at it. See if the police missed anythin'."

"Is this 'deceased friend' the woman who was murdered in the town square?" Wally asked.

"Yes, I'm afraid so." I handed some bills to Nacho and told him to keep the change.

"I'm sorry for your loss," Wally said, his expression grave.

"Can we have a rain check on the drink offer?" Reba Mae gave him an arch smile.

I elbowed her in the rib cage. What was she thinking? She'd just met the man.

Wally turned his charm on Reba Mae, his gaze lingering a fraction too long on the endowments Mother Nature had generously bestowed. "Better yet, perhaps I can persuade you to dine with me one evening."

"No coaxin' necessary." Reba Mae dug a business card out of her purse, then, using the pen she'd signed her credit card with, scribbled her cell phone number on the back. "Here," she said, handing it to Wally. "Call me."

Reba Mae pouted all the way to Becca's. "It's been a long time since a nice-lookin' man invited me for a drink. I don't see why we couldn't have stayed and had another margarita."

"Because, to paraphrase a popular song, tequila makes your clothes fall off. That's why. Besides, those plants of Becca's need watering."

By this time we'd reached Becca's tidy little bungalow. A gable roof, supported by twin columns, covered a charming little front porch. Its entrance was flanked on either side by trailing Boston ferns. Pink petunias filled window boxes. The house itself, however, was showing signs of wear, as evidenced by the peeling paint and crumbling concrete steps.

I picked up several newspapers lying scattered on the porch. "I'd better notify *The Statesman* and tell them to cancel her subscription."

Reba Mae lifted the flap of a mailbox mounted near the door and drew out a handful of mail. "Better remind the post office, too."

We found the key under the mat as promised and let ourselves in. The door opened directly into what was Becca's living room. We stood for a moment in silence, getting the lay of the land so to speak.

"If I'm not mistaken," I said, "this is one of those Sears and Roebuck catalog homes from the nineteen twenties. There was an article about them in the paper a while back."

"No kiddin'? Folks ordered homes from a catalog?"

"They were sold as a kit. Lumber, shingles, floors, ceilings, siding, hardware, and paint. The whole shebang. Only extras were cement, brick, and plaster."

Becca's furniture consisted mostly of outdated pieces that to my unpracticed eye appeared more flea market than antique. A chintz-slipcovered sofa held a half-dozen throw pillows embroidered with Bible verses. A pink-and-blue crocheted afghan more suitable for a nursery than a living room was flung over its back. The décor consisted of blue wall-to-wall carpet, threadbare in spots, a large flat-screen television, and lots of lace doilies.

And dozens of African violets.

Darkness was rapidly settling in, swaddling the interior in shadow. "This place creeps me out," Reba Mae complained, edging closer. "Think Becca's ghost will haunt her grannie's house?"

"Don't be such a fraidy cat. We won't be long."

Reba Mae gestured toward a coffee table and tea cart. "Becca might not be thrivin', but her houseplants sure are."

"I doubt they'll fare as well under my care. My plants have to survive long periods of drought followed by flash floods," I said, and then inspiration struck. "If her kids don't want them, maybe we can give them away. You know, free to good homes. Like puppies or kittens."

"Whatever." Frowning, Reba Mae placed her hands on her hips and looked around. "Where do we start?"

"Why don't you take a peek into the bedrooms? See if you can spot anything out of the ordinary. I'll check the dining room."

After flicking on a table lamp, Reba Mae reluctantly left to do as I asked. Meanwhile, I entered the adjoining dining room. I made quick work of searching through the drawers of a mahogany buffet but didn't find anything more interesting than musty yellow linen tablecloths.

I shoved a swinging door aside and entered the kitchen. Black and white speckled linoleum on the floor, red Formica countertops, and aging appliances. Another flat-screen television, this one smaller, sat on the counter next to a toaster oven. The room itself was immaculate. I sniffed the air, then sniffed again. What did I smell?

Chlorine?

"Becca was a TV addict."

I jumped, startled by Reba Mae's voice directly behind me. "Did you find anything of interest in Becca's room?" I asked once I'd recovered from my fright.

"Jewelry, mostly costume stuff, and a bunch of perfume bottles. Only thing of value is a television set that looks fairly new." She wrinkled her nose in distaste. "What's with the bleach smell? Becca's whites need an extra boost?"

"Your guess is as good as mine," I said absently as I started opening and closing cupboards. I pulled out a drawer next to the cookstove and stared at the contents in surprise. "Reba Mae, what do you make of this?"

Reba Mae peered over my shoulder. "Well,

I'll be darned. Flavor injectors. Every shape and size they make 'em. No wonder Becca was so all-fired sure of winnin' herself a trophy. She planned to cheat."

"According to the festival rules, contestants are disqualified for injecting marinade or tenderizer into their meat."

"Only if they're caught."

Flavor injectors and meat went hand in hand. This in mind, I walked over to the refrigerator and opened the freezer. "Well, well, well," I said. "Look what I found."

There, stacked like cordwood, were five frozen beef briskets. Except for the briskets, a quart of strawberry ice cream, and a bag of frozen peas, the freezer was empty.

"Findin' a brisket in a freezer right before a barbecue festival isn't kin to discoverin' a stash of Confederate gold buried in a rose garden," Reba Mae pointed out. "I bet Meat on Main and Piggly Wiggly can't keep up with orders."

"Don't you think it strange Becca's murder weapon might be something she kept in her very own freezer?"

"Coincidence." Reba Mae drifted over to examine a deep-purple African violet with double blossoms on the kitchen table. "I'm thinkin' we should give Becca's plants a nice drink of water before we go."

I continued to rummage through drawers and cupboards. "I've heard African violets are fussy. Too much water and they contract weird diseases with names you can't pronounce."

"My mama used to have a way with 'em. She always felt the soil before waterin'." Reba Mae poked her finger into the pot, then came away with a small, shiny object. "Look what I found. What do you s'pose it is? A shell of some sort?"

I took it from her hand and placed it in my palm. "Neither," I murmured, nudging it gently. "It's a broken fingernail. A tip torn from a manicure-polished Pucker Up Pink."

"Becca would never venture out in public unless her nails were perfect."

"No," I echoed. "Becca was much too vain. Unless . . ."

Closing my eyes, I tried to imagine Becca as I'd last seen her, sprawled on her side, one arm outstretched as if to break her fall. I willed myself to visualize that arm.

And that hand.

McBride always preached that memory was a funny thing. "Funny" isn't exactly the term I'd use. In this instance, it was downright weird. Becca Dapkins's perennially perfect manicure had been less than perfect. The nail on her middle finger had been broken down to the quick.

"I think Becca was killed right here — in her own kitchen," I told a wide-eyed Reba Mae. "Time to call McBride."

CHAPTER 12

"Let me see if I got this straight." McBride's brows drew together in irritation. "You insisted I drop everything and hurry over — all because you found a broken fingernail?"

I had to admit at hearing it come from McBride's mouth my theory sounded pretty lame. Judging from the fact he was in civvies rather than in uniform, I assumed I'd interrupted his plans for the evening. He didn't look any too pleased at the prospect.

"Becca would never go out in public with a broken fingernail," Reba Mae, bless her heart, rushed to my defense. "It wasn't in the woman's DNA."

I flung my hand out in an expansive gesture. "See for yourself, McBride. The house is spotless. Not a single thing out of place."

"Not even a single water spot on a leaf of an African violet," Reba Mae added helpfully.

"If anything, the place is almost too neat. It doesn't even look lived-in."

He shook his head, obviously not following my logic. "Exactly what does that prove?"

"Do I have to spell it out for you?" I asked in exasperation. "It *proves* that Becca was meticulous. Would a woman that fussy take off to visit her estranged boyfriend with a broken fingernail? No, I don't think so."

Reba Mae nodded vigorous agreement. "She'd at least try to glue it back on until she could get to her nail tech."

McBride scratched his head. "Women do those sorts of things?"

"Yes, but glue is only a temporary fix. Therefore, the break must have been recent. Did your men find a fingernail at the scene of the crime?"

"No, but —"

"Because" — I aimed my index finger at his chest — "if my theory is correct, it was broken during a struggle right here in her very own kitchen."

"Aren't you at least going to check it out?" Reba Mae asked.

"Listen, ladies," he said with exaggerated patience. "I know y'all consider yourselves junior-grade detectives, but you need to leave the investigation to the pros."

I wasn't about to be dismissed this easily — or this condescendingly. "There's more." Marching over to the refrigerator, I flung open the freezer. "Ta-da!"

McBride stuck his head inside to see why the fuss. "Call me dense, but what's so noteworthy about a carton of ice cream and box of peas?"

"Look again," I ordered. "Those are briskets — frozen hard as cement. Five to be exact. If you don't believe me count them."

He took another peek. "So, that's what brisket looks like before it's served up on a plate in a diner along with fries and a side of slaw."

Reba Mae tugged my arm. "Tell 'im about the bleach."

McBride's gaze sharpened. "What about bleach?"

"Can't you smell it?" I asked in disbelief. "The room reeks of chlorine. I've seen enough *CSI*s to know that bleach is used to destroy evidence. What if the killer took time to clean the place up after he did the evil deed?"

McBride didn't answer but instead walked over to the laundry room/pantry. Reba Mae and I trailed on his heels, close enough to be his shadow. A gallon container of Clorox sat on the floor next to the washing machine. When he gave it a nudge with his foot the jug toppled over and rolled across the linoleum.

"Empty," I said, making no attempt to keep the satisfaction from my voice. "Why keep an empty bleach bottle instead of tossing it in the trash?"

McBride turned to study us, his handsome face impassive. "Tell me again what you two are doing here. And make your explanation simple enough for a dumb cop to understand."

"African violets . . . ?" Reba Mae offered.

"We were worried about them," I added.

"I see," he said slowly. "Are y'all members of the garden club? Or maybe some cult that goes around rescuing flowering plants?"

He was doing it again — being condescending. And it made me want to swat him. "For your information, McBride, African violets are extremely temperamental. Knowing they were Becca's favorites, we took it upon ourselves to see to their care."

"We plan to make sure each and every one finds a lovin' home," Reba Mae added self-righteously. "You heard of Adopt-a-Pet? Well, we're gonna have Adopt-a-Plant."

"It's comforting to know Ms. Dapkins has

135

such devoted friends."

I could feel my temper rise higher. "Do I detect sarcasm, Chief?"

"Who, me?" he replied poker-faced.

Reba Mae opted for a preemptive strike. "We didn't do anythin' illegal like breakin' or enterin' if that's what you're thinkin'."

"Gerilee Barker gave us Becca's spare key." I dangled the key in front of him to make my point. "The question is, what are you going to do? On TV, the lead detective on the case usually calls in the crime techs to check for blood."

"Yeah, they use spray bottles and a special light." Reba Mae's gold hoop earrings bobbed up and down as she spoke.

"Times like this, I long for the pre-*CSI* days," he said with a grimace. "Now everyone thinks they know more than the cops."

"So are you, or aren't you, going to check for evidence?" I demanded.

"I'll request experts from the GBI to process the scene. See if they can find any blood traces, fingerprints, or anything of that nature. Satisfied?"

I nodded my head. "What if it turns out we're right? That Becca was killed right here in her kitchen?"

"The investigation will take another direction. In the meantime, I'll continue to ask around, try to find out who might have held a grudge against her. Check out their alibis."

McBride ushered us out the door and locked it. It wouldn't take long for him to find out Maybelle resented Becca stealing her beau. But just because Maybelle didn't like to share didn't make her a murderer. Even so, the woman was hiding something, as evidenced by her odd behavior the night Reba Mae and I paid her a surprise visit. Thank goodness, she had an alibi for the night of Becca's murder.

The following evening, I convinced Reba Mae to join Casey and me for a leisurely stroll. I hadn't jogged since discovering Becca's body. Habits, I'd noted, are much easier to break than they are to acquire.

"Whoo-hoo!" Reba Mae pumped her fist in the air, then pocketed her cell phone. "I've got a date for Saturday night. An honest-to-goodness, bona fide, genuine, gentleman-pays-all date."

"Whoo-hoo," I repeated, but with far less enthusiasm. "Who's the lucky fellow?"

Catching Reba Mae's high spirits, Casey gave an excited *woof* and danced at the end of his leash.

"Wally Porter, esteemed and certified

senior barbecue judge, invited me out for dinner Saturday night. He wants to take me to a seafood place in Augusta. What do you think I should wear?"

Our walk had taken us full circle, ending at the town square where we'd begun. I sank down on a park bench not far from the supposed crime scene. Yellow crime scene tape still festooned the area around the azalea bushes. Casey settled at my feet, his head resting on his front paws, his eyes alert. I could tell from the expression on his cute doggy face that he wasn't keen on the idea of a career as a cadaver dog.

"Wally sure is a snappy dresser. I like all those little horsey logos on his shirts." Reba Mae was too excited to sit still. Instead, she walked back and forth in front of the bench, talking nonstop. "His watch looks expensive. I bet it's a Rolex. And did you see his shoes? They're probably Italian. Italian leather, they say, is the best. I have a hunch the Lincoln Town Car parked outside North of the Border last night belonged to him. It looked like the sort of car he'd drive. I think he's rich."

"Um-hum," I murmured, stifling a yawn. My mind wandered as Reba Mae chattered on. My gaze drifted to Spice It Up! across the square. From my vantage point, I had a clear view of my living room window above the shop. I remembered waking in the wee small hours the night Becca was murdered and staring out that very window.

And all the while, her lifeless body waited for me to discover.

Reba Mae stopped pacing and planted her hands on her hips. "Have you heard a single word I've said?"

"Sure, sort of," I said hastily. "You talked about horses, and Italy, and Lincoln Center."

"Lincoln Center?"

Oops! My bad. Lincoln Center, Lincoln Town Car, close but no cigar. "Sorry, Reba Mae. It's just that memories of this place are still fresh in my mind."

Instantly remorseful, Reba Mae sat next to me and put her arm around my shoulders. "I wasn't thinkin', honeybun. I'm just so thrilled about havin' a dinner date with an attractive man, everythin' else just flew outta my head. Want to talk about Becca?"

I shook my head. "No, maybe another time." I didn't want to prick my BFF's happy bubble. Let her bask in the moment. I couldn't fault Wally Porter's judgment when it came to women. He couldn't have picked a better dinner date than Reba Mae

Johnson.

"Pour yourself a nice glass of wine when you get home, then draw a bubble bath. That always puts me in a better frame of mind. Now," she said, glancing at her watch, "I've gotta thousand and one things to do. Besides decidin' what I'm wearin' tomorrow night, I need to shave my legs, give myself a facial, a manicure, a pedi."

Reba Mae had a bounce in her step as she walked off. But not even the prospect of a glass of wine and a bubble bath was enough to lure me back to an empty apartment just yet. I continued to sit on the bench, Casey content at my feet.

A soft breeze stirred the branches of the willow oaks, fanning my upturned face. The heat of the day was gradually subsiding, though much of the humidity remained. Summers in Georgia are like living in a sauna. I console myself with the theory — totally unfounded — that the excess moisture in the air keeps skin dewy soft and youthful looking. Another theory — also totally unfounded — is that's the reason why so many Southern girls win national beauty pageants.

My peaceful interlude ended when a police cruiser eased to the curb. McBride slid out from behind the wheel and sauntered toward me. "Mind if I join you?" Not waiting for an answer, he lowered himself next to me.

"It's public property," I replied. Why did I always find his closeness unnerving? I immediately switched into denial mode. Surely it had nothing to do with the fact he was almost overwhelmingly masculine. I blamed it instead on the shiny gold badge pinned to his chest and big bad gun strapped to his waist. And then there was the matter of the uniform. I wouldn't be the first girl — or grown woman — to get butterflies for a man in a uniform.

"Nice evening, isn't it?" he said.

"Um-hum."

"Peaceful and quiet." He reached down and scratched Casey behind the ears — the pup's sweet spot. "That's what I remembered most about Brandywine Creek during the time I was away. It's the reason I came back."

"Do you ever regret your decision?" I asked, curious. "Miami has a lot more to offer in the way of excitement than a hick town like Brandywine Creek."

The corners of his mouth curved. "Oh, I wouldn't say that. You seem determined to keep me from being bored."

"What made you leave Miami?"

He stretched an arm along the back of the bench. "Lots of reasons. Guess you could say I OD'd on all the violence. I was ready for a simpler lifestyle. A change of pace. Thought I might find time for a little hunting and fishing. An occasional camping trip in the mountains."

He took a lock of my hair and wound it around a finger. The butterflies in my tummy turned into a swarm of bees. I sneaked a peek at his expression but couldn't tell if the hair twirling was a conscious act or not. "Do you still have family in the area?" I asked, my voice husky sounding.

"Not anymore. My dad died while I was still in the army. I came home long enough to bury him, then headed straight back to my unit. I have a younger sister, Claudia. She lives in California."

"Do you keep in touch?"

"Mostly by e-mail. Phone calls on Christmas and birthdays. We haven't seen each other since Dad's funeral."

"How about you?" He gave my hair a gentle tug. "Any siblings?"

"None. I'm an only child. After my dad retired from an auto plant in Detroit, my parents moved to a mobile home park for 'active' adults in Florida. They're so active, it's hard to find them home."

"Sounds like a good life."

"I've heard rumors that the mayor is making noise about you finding Becca's killer" — I made a slicing gesture across my throat — "or else."

"Hemmings is all hot air and bluster. He pretends to be upset that a murder reflects poorly on the town. On the other hand, he loves the publicity it's bringing the festival."

McBride quit toying with my hair and got to his feet. "As pleasant as this has been, I need to get back to work."

I rose, too, and self-consciously smoothed my curls. "By any chance, did the GBI find anything when they examined Becca's kitchen?"

"A couple blood droplets, but not enough to raise any red flags. For the time being, we're going to continue to treat the case as a homicide committed during an attempted robbery."

"What about the broken fingernail? You don't think it's significant?"

"There's no sure way of determining when or how it happened. Forget about it, Piper. Keep your pretty nose out of police business. I wouldn't want to see you hurt."

My thoughts in turmoil, I watched him walk away.

CHAPTER 13

As it turned out, Reba Mae wasn't the only one with a date for Saturday night. After I'd returned from my unsettling encounter with Wyatt McBride, I saw the red light on the answering machine flashing. To my surprise, I heard Doug's voice asking me to return his call. Amid profuse apologies for the late notice, he'd invited me to join him for dinner at Gina and Tony Deltorro's brand-new restaurant, formerly Trattoria Milano. Tony had rechristened it Antonio's.

A new name. New owners. New menu. Time to give the place a try.

Casey watched me fasten a pair of dangly earrings I'd borrowed from Reba Mae. His tail thumped against the floor in wordless reproach. He'd developed a sixth sense of when he was about to be abandoned and was letting me know he wasn't happy at the prospect.

"Sorry, pal," I told him. "Nothing

personal. This is a fancy place. No dogs allowed."

For my big night out, I'd selected slim-leg white crop pants, a shimmery lime-green top, a cabochon pendant, and strappy high-heeled sandals. Thanks to the humid Georgia weather, my curls were in their usual state of disarray, but little I could do about that. Promptly at six thirty, I heard a knock on the door downstairs. A swipe of lip gloss, a final glance in the mirror, I was good to go.

Doug had dressed for the occasion, too, in khakis and pale-pink dress shirt open at the throat, the cuffs folded back. He let out a wolf whistle when he saw me. "How do you manage to look cool as a cucumber and hot as a firecracker all at the same time?"

I laughed, pleased by the compliment. "Aren't you a silver-tongued devil?"

"That's me all right." He grinned. "I could give Prince Charming a tutorial. Ready?"

I picked up a clutch — also courtesy of Reba Mae — and looped my arm through his. "Let's walk. It isn't far."

"Fine by me." Doug took my hand from the crook of his arm and held it like a teenager on a date.

I recalled how self-conscious I'd been the

first couple of times we were seen together in public. Now I no longer worried what others might think, only that Doug's hand in mine felt right. And made me all warm and melty inside.

"I know this is a last-minute invite, but I couldn't face another beef brisket or pork butt."

"How are preparations going?"

"Good. I'm planning to order T-shirts for the team, but wanted to get your daughter's opinion first."

"Smart move. You don't want to infringe on a teenage girl's sense of fashion. When Lindsey gets home tomorrow, I'll tell her you need advice."

We paused to admire items in the window of Yesteryear Antiques. "Hope the murder of Becca Dapkins won't put too much of a damper on the festivities."

"Maybelle's been slower than usual getting things organized this year, but she always manages to pull it off."

"Any word when Becca Dapkins will be buried?" he asked as we resumed our leisurely stroll.

"Monday."

"Monday . . . ?" he repeated. "Isn't that kind of fast?"

I shrugged. "No reason to drag things out,

I guess. Gerilee Barker told me Ned Feeney, who works at the Eternal Rest, told her the medical examiner released the body yesterday. It's already been cremated. According to Gerilee's hotline, Becca's son and daughter don't want to take any more time off work than necessary. They plan to fly in tomorrow and return home immediately after the reception."

"That seems rather cold and heartless," Doug commented.

"Apparently, Becca hasn't been on the best of terms with her children. With their approval, Gerilee arranged for a simple service for their mother with a reception afterward at the VFW."

Doug pushed open the door of Antonio's, then stood aside for me to enter. A cacophony of clattering dishes, cutlery, and conversation greeted us. I stood for a moment, taking in the transformation that had taken place since the last time I'd visited the restaurant.

Where the former owner had favored the minimalist approach, with lots of black and white, Tony and his wife, Gina, had created a Tuscan-style ambiance. The walls had been faux-painted a warm orangey gold to mimic terra-cotta. Candles glowed on tables covered with cream-colored cloths. The voice of a tenor singing Italian love songs streamed through discreetly mounted speakers.

Gina Deltorro stood at a hostess stand. Upon seeing us, she cast an anxious glance over her shoulder. "Welcome to Antonio's," she said, giving us a nervous smile. "Right this way, please."

We followed her lush figure to a corner table for two at the rear. Doug frowned at the empty tables we passed. "What about one not quite so close to the kitchen?"

"Sorry, sir. The rest are . . . reserved." Gina kept her eyes averted as she handed us menus.

"This is fine, Doug. Really," I told him.

"Guess I only have myself to blame for waiting till the last minute."

"Don't give it another thought. The food will taste the same whether we're sitting here or up front."

"Your server will be over shortly." Gina left us — "escaped" would a more apt description — to contemplate our dinner choices.

"I'm grateful you didn't create a scene," I said. "My ex, on the other hand, would've screamed bloody murder, then stormed out, leaving me to trail behind."

As if on cue, the restaurant door swung

wide and in walked CJ and Miss Amber Leigh Ames, his fiancée and the light of his life. I privately refer to the woman as Miss Peach Pit. Amber is a former Brandywine County's Miss Peach Blossom and later went on to become first runner-up in the Miss Georgia beauty pageant. Flowing brunette locks, mile-long legs, and more curves than Maui's road to Hana, she's the envy of every teenage girl for miles around — my daughter included. If I had to find a flaw — and I felt it my obligation to do so, being Amber was the other woman — she had big teeth. Big, white teeth.

Gina showed the lovebirds to a cozy table for two in a alcove half-hidden behind a ficus. Amber spotted us as she slid into her seat and gave a little finger wave.

I finger-waved back. CJ glanced our way and acknowledged Doug and me with a nod.

Gina hovered solicitously at their table. A waitress in black pants and white dress shirt instantly appeared, order pad in hand. A busboy filled their water glasses. I pretended I wasn't miffed by their preferential treatment.

"I'm in the mood for a glass of white wine," I said, draping a caramel-toned napkin across my lap.

"Excellent idea," Doug agreed. "Pinot grigio?"

I nodded, then stifled a groan when the waitress half-turned and I saw her profile. Marcy Magruder. I'd recognize her baby bump anywhere.

Doug frowned at seeing my expression. "Anythng wrong?"

"Heartburn," I murmured.

Marcy wasn't a member of my fan club any more than Tony Deltorro — and for much the same reason. I'd once pegged Danny Boyd, the father of her future children, as a possible murder suspect. She hasn't spoken to me since. Hey, I'm a newbie when it comes to solving crimes. I wished Marcy would cut me some slack.

Danny, on the other hand, possessed a more forgiving nature. He's friendly and polite whenever I order pizza from the joint he runs. Come to think of it, though, these days I'm getting fewer pepperonis, less sauce. And once he "forgot" the mushrooms.

Marcy left CJ's table and went directly to a party of four seated nearby. I watched her nod and smile, then scurry toward the bar with CJ and Miss Home Wrecker's drink order.

A young man with acne and a starter

mustache sailed out of the kitchen bearing a tray with salads and a bread basket. Doug raised his hand to get the young man's attention, but he must've had blinders on, as he hustled past.

I opened my mouth to protest, but more patrons began arriving. I glanced over, hoping to recognize some friendly faces, but no such luck. The newcomers were none other than Barbara Quinlan and Wyatt McBride. "Tonight just keeps getting better and better," I muttered.

Doug leaned forward, his voice low. "Would you rather we go somewhere else? We could go to my place and I'll rustle up some scrambled eggs."

"I'm no quitter." Doug was a sweetheart to suggest leaving, but I refused to let an audience watch me turn tail. I raised the menu and began studying the list of entrées. The menu also acted as a shield of sorts. I wasn't in any frame of mind to make nice with McBride and Barbie-Q-Perfect.

"They make a striking couple," Doug observed, not sharing my reticence.

"I suppose," I grudgingly admitted, peering at them over the rim of my menu. Barbie looked like a watercolor in pastel shades of pink and rose. In contrast, McBride wore all black, exuding an aura of power and danger. I resolutely turned back to my date. I didn't need "danger" in my life.

Finally, conceding we weren't about to leave anytime soon, an unsmiling Marcy came to our table, took our drink order, then left to get our wine.

"Do you know the blonde's name?" Doug asked. "She looks familiar."

I snapped my menu shut. "Barbara Bunker Quinlan. She's in town to film the barbecue festival for the Cooking Network. Her show's called *Some Like It Hot.*"

"Ahh!" Doug exclaimed. "So that's Barbie Q. I've seen some of the promos for her show. She's even more impressive in person."

Impressive? Couldn't argue with the guy. No man with a drop of testosterone would dispute the fact that Barbie *was* a knockout. Pity she didn't have the same effect on women.

Marcy returned with our wine. She set mine down with enough force to send its contents sloshing over the rim.

Doug and I exchanged glances. I mopped up the spill with a cocktail napkin. "Are there any specials this evening?" Doug asked.

"We have two." Marcy consulted a notepad. "The first is osso buco. Tender veal shanks simmered with root vegetables in their own juices and white wine. It's served over polenta. The second is eggplant parmigiana. Layers of succulent eggplant and cheese baked in a rich tomato sauce." She cracked her first smile of the evening. "Unfortunately, we're out of both."

We stared at her, dumbfounded. Doug was the first to recover from the girl's deliberate rudeness. "What is available?" Doug asked with commendable calm.

Marcy tucked her notepad into her pocket. "I'll have to check with the chef." She turned on her heel and stalked off.

While we waited for her to return, Marcy's counterpart delivered plates of osso buco and eggplant parmigiana to CJ and Amber. Her sympathy as phony as a three-dollar bill, Amber made a moue when she saw Doug and I had only our wineglasses for company.

Just then, a loud crash came from the direction of the kitchen. All heads turned to see the hapless busboy, his face scarlet, scramble to pick up shards of glass. All heads, that is, except those of Barbie and McBride. Out of the corner of my eye, I watched Barbie rise to her feet. McBride tried to stop her, but she shook off his hand. With movements fluid and catlike, she sauntered toward the table where CJ was seated. Wondering what would happen next, I took a sip of wine.

I didn't have to wonder for long.

CJ and Barbie locked eyes with each other while his osso buco turned cool. "It's been a long time, CJ." Barbie spoke in a voice that carried.

CJ, a befuddled expression on his face, put down his knife and fork. "Sorry," he said. "Have we met?"

"Most people know me better as Barbie Q, but I was Barbara Bunker back in high school."

"Y-you're . . . ?"

"So, you do remember me." She laughed, but her laughter had a hollow ring.

Amber, not used to being ignored, interrupted the reunion. "CJ, shame on you," she scolded. "Aren't you going to introduce me to your old school chum?"

CJ's face flushed. "Of course, sweetums. Where are my manners?" Formalities concluded, he returned his attention to Barbie. "You've changed a lot since high school, Barbara. I'm afraid I didn't recognize you."

I eavesdropped shamelessly. I'd repent later.

"I prefer to be called Barbie," she said,

correcting him. "Yes, I have changed. I'm no longer the trailer trash you and your buddies made fun of. Played cruel pranks on. You, on the other hand, don't seem to have changed a bit. Appearances were always important to you, weren't they? You were always on the prowl for something — or someone — to make you look more important than the shit you really are."

"Pooh Bear . . . !" Amber bristled. "Are you goin' to let her speak to you that way? Do somethin'!"

CJ patted Amber's arm reassuringly. "Don't take anythin' she says seriously, sweetums. Obviously, the woman's still nursin' hard feelin's for imagined wrongs datin' back years ago."

"Imagined?" Barbie's voice grew strident.

I drank more of my wine but didn't really taste it. Even without looking at Doug, I sensed that he, along with others, was observing the scenario as avidly as I was.

McBride tossed aside his napkin and approached CJ's table. Sliding his arm around Barbie's waist, he whispered something in her ear, which I couldn't catch. Barbie seemed to mull it over, then nodded. Without so much as a backward glance, she and McBride turned and left the restaurant.

CJ scowled after them, his complexion an

unhealthy shade. Glancing around, he discovered himself the recipient of unwanted attention. "Once trailer trash, always trailer trash, I say," he declared in a loud voice to the room at large. "Same goes for McBride. Good riddance to the two of 'em."

The show over, the patrons went back to their meals. I saw CJ down his Wild Turkey in one gulp and motion for another.

Marcy returned to our table wearing a sour expression. "Chef says to inform you that you have a choice of spaghetti . . . or spaghetti."

I stood and signaled for my date to do likewise. "C'mon, Doug, let's go. I have a sudden craving for scrambled eggs."

CHAPTER 14

I tapped twice on Reba Mae's back door, then let myself in. I found Reba Mae standing at the stove, stirring a large pot. "Mmm. Something smells good."

"I'm makin' Meemaw's Hungarian goulash." She sampled some with a spoon, made a face, and added a pinch of salt.

I placed the earrings and the clutch I'd borrowed for my date last night on the table. When it comes to bling, Reba Mae's my go-to girl. "What's the occasion?"

"I invited Wally for supper," she said. "Travelin' all around the country as much as he does, I thought the man might enjoy a home-cooked meal."

"Well then, he's in for a treat. Your grandmother's goulash is the best." I chose to think it was because Reba Mae used the sweet Hungarian-style paprika I sold at Spice It Up!. The spice imparted a deep, rich color and an extra dash of flavor. The yum factor, as I liked to call it. Reba Mae had a couple other tricks up her sleeve when it came to her favorite recipe. Secrets I couldn't persuade her to part with. Maybelle Humphries wasn't the only cook in town who didn't like to share.

Using the back of her hand, Reba Mae shoved her spiky black bangs aside. "Wanna join us? I made plenty."

"You know what they say about two's company, three's a crowd."

"I just asked to be polite. I was hopin' you'd refuse."

"Well, at least you get an A-plus for honesty," I said. "It's another hot one today. Any Diet Coke?"

"Does a cat have whiskers? While you're at it, I just made a pitcher of sweet tea." She pointed toward the fridge with her spoon. "Pour me some, will you?"

I filled a glass with ice cubes, added tea, and set it on the counter within reach. Now, I have nothing against sweet tea. It's quite delicious but loaded with calories. I heard a story once that as an April Fool's joke some years back the Georgia House introduced a bill making it a "misdemeanor of a high and aggravated nature" to sell iced tea in a restaurant that did not also offer sweet tea.

As far as I know, the bill never went to a vote.

Popping the tab on my Coke, I took a seat at the kitchen table. "I'm expecting Lindsey home soon. I can't wait to hear about her time at the lake."

"The girl will probably come back with a fabulous tan."

"Probably," I agreed. "Take me, for instance. All I ever have to show for time at the beach is more freckles."

"The curse of bein' a redhead. Me, I come back brown as a berry." She turned the dial on the stove to simmer and began gathering the ingredients for her delicious poppyseed dressing. "You fixin' somethin' special to celebrate your baby's homecomin'?"

"Her favorite." I crossed one leg over the other, swung a sandaled foot back and forth. "Shrimp and grits."

Reba Mae grated an onion. "I thought about makin' that, but Wally spends a lot of time in the low country — Savannah, Charleston, Hilton Head. Shrimp and grits are practically on every menu."

"How was your date last night?" I finally asked the sixty-four-thousand-dollar question.

"Fantastic." Reba Mae shot me a grin over her shoulder. "Wally took me to this fancy seafood place. You know the kind. White tablecloths, candlelight, soft music, efficient waitstaff. Lucky for us, Wally had phoned ahead for reservations. Lot of folks had to wait outside on benches."

I took a swallow of Coke. "I didn't know you were fond of seafood — shrimp and grits notwithstanding."

"I'm not, so I let Wally do the ordering. I had Chilean sea bass served with a fruity salsa. Delicious!"

"Sounds delicious."

"It was." She measured sugar, vinegar, salt, and ground dry mustard — from Canada, no less — into a mini-prep food processor and added the onion she'd grated. "How was Antonio's? My clients rave about their specials."

I traced the condensate on my can of soda. "According to Marcy Magruder, who happens to be their waitress, they were out of both the osso buco and eggplant parmigiana. When she finally checked to find out what they did have, the only thing left was spaghetti."

Reba Mae turned on the food processor and gradually added a slow stream of olive oil. "So how was the spaghetti?"

I raised my voice to be heard over the din. "Doug and I decided they didn't want our business, so we left. I glanced back in time to see Tony peek out of the kitchen. You should have seen his smirk."

"I think he's part Sicilian."

"That's not all. . . ." I proceeded to tell her about the confrontation between Barbie and CJ. "That marks the second time I heard someone remark on how much Barbie's changed since high school. The first was Becca Dapkins. Now CJ."

Reba Mae paused to look at me. "Hey, I've got an idea. I still have Butch's high school yearbooks in the attic. He must've been a year or two ahead of Barbie, but it'd be interestin' to see what she looked like compared to now. Sort of before and after shots."

I finished the last of my diet soda. "Why don't you see if you can rustle them up? I don't mean today, when you're expecting to impress a guest with goulash, but soon."

"I'll do just that." Reba Mae stirred pretty blue Dutch poppy seeds — also courtesy of *moi* — into her dressing. "You never did tell me what you had for dinner after leaving Antonio's in a huff."

"Doug came over to my place, and I made omelets."

Reba Mae waggled her eyebrows suggestively. "I'm more interested in what happened *after* the omelets."

"Doug was called away on an emergency. A schnauzer ate his owner's car keys."

"Bummer." Reba Mae gave the goulash another stir.

"What about you?"

Reba Mae gave me a wink. "I'm not one to kiss and tell." As I left her to finish preparations for "date" number two, I gave her a thumbs-up.

Home in my own kitchen, I kept glancing at the clock on the wall. I debated whether or not to take Casey for a romp but decided to let Lindsey have the honors. Becca's funeral was tomorrow, and the reception afterward would be sure to draw a crowd. This in mind, I pulled out my mother's recipe for an old standby — pineapple upside-down cake.

I hauled out cake flour, white and brown sugar, eggs, butter, pineapple rings, maraschino cherries, and the best doggone pure vanilla I stocked. I preferred beans grown in Madagascar rather than darker-flavored ones from Mexico, but to each his own. I wondered if Doug, who always teased me about pricey saffron, knew that vanilla is the second most expensive spice in the world. Like saffron, its production is labor-intensive. Even pollination is done by hand. I made a mental note to inform him of this fact next time we met. Though Doug might be impressed with my knowing this, McBride would deposit my spice trivia into his bank of useless information. All the more reason Doug and I were well suited for each other.

While I went about mixing and measuring, my thoughts strayed to Barbie Bunker Quinlan. It would be interesting to flip through Butch's old yearbooks. See the changes the years had wrought. Neither Becca nor CJ had had recognized Barbie initially. Her eyes, though, should have been a dead giveaway. Their pale aquamarine was a color not usually seen without the advantage of contact lenses.

I suspected the changes that had taken place in the woman were more than superficial. Though I really didn't know much about her, I could tell she was smart, savvy, driven. I was curious about her marital status. And not because of her obvious interest in Wyatt McBride. Barbie flashed a huge diamond — on her right hand, not her left. If she was married, Mr. Quinlan was nowhere in sight. A divorcée? A successful career woman? From the clothes she wore and car she drove, she wasn't hurting for money.

I mentally reviewed what little I did know about her. She'd left town suddenly and under questionable circumstances. And she wasn't averse to showing her hometown in a negative light. The notion that a "prank" CJ had pulled in high school still rankled attested to her tendency to carry a chip on her shoulder. While she and McBride behaved like long-lost pals, she and Becca Dapkins had snapped and snarled at each other like tomcats.

Had Barbie returned to Brandywine Creek with a vendetta? Had she hoped to settle an old score with Becca? How deep did Barbie's animosity run?

A car door slammed just then. Minutes later, I heard Lindsey's footsteps running up the stairs.

"Mom, you home?"

The sound of my daughter's voice erased all thoughts of Barbie Q. "In the kitchen, sweetie!" I called, sliding my cake into the oven.

The instant the door opened, Casey went wild. His shaggy little body quivered with excitement at the return of his favorite playmate. His happy barking even drowned out the *whirr* of the air conditioner.

Lindsey flung her duffel to the floor and

scooped Casey up in her arms. Laughing at his wiggling and squirming, she managed to give me a one-arm hug. "Hey, Mom. Miss me?"

I hugged her back. "You betcha."

Lindsey dropped down on the floor to play Casey's favorite game of tug-of-war with an old gym sock. This gave me an opportunity to study my daughter anew. Sixteen but wavering between twelve and twenty. She favored the Prescott side of the family, with blond hair and blue-gray eyes like those of CJ and Melly.

"Have fun?" I asked, giving Lindsey's sun-streaked ponytail a gentle tug.

"Loads. Taylor's father has a brand-new Jet Ski and let us take it out whenever we wanted. We went tubing and wakeboarding. And . . ." She paused for dramatic effect. "I met this really cute guy. His name is Devon. He's already texted me twice since I left Taylor's."

"Not when driving, I hope."

She rolled her eyes. "Mom, we're not idiots. I know texting while driving is dangerous. We hear that lecture all the time at school. I don't need one from you."

"And I don't *need* that tone of voice from you, young lady," I reprimanded.

"Sorry," she mumbled.

I decided a change of subject might be wise. "I'm making your favorite dinner tonight — shrimp and grits."

She stopped tossing the sock to Casey and looked up at me. "I wish you would've told me sooner. I promised Daddy I'd have dinner with him and Amber when I got home. He's experimenting with a new grill."

I swallowed my disappointment. How could I compete with a brand-new grill? "Well. I wouldn't want you to break your promise to your father. But I'll need you here at Spice It Up! for a couple hours tomorrow while I attend a memorial service and reception."

"Okay," she said, climbing to her feet. "Who died? Anyone I know?"

"Becca Dapkins." I unfastened the beaters from the mixer and dropped them into the sink. "Did you know her?"

Before I could whisk it away, Lindsey grabbed a spatula and licked off the cake batter. "Yeah, she's the lady always dressed in pink. I didn't think she was old enough to die."

"She wasn't." I squirted dish detergent into the mixing bowl and let it soak.

Lindsey pried the lid from a can of doggy treats and tossed one to Casey. "Then what happened?"

166

"Someone struck her over the head hard enough to kill her." I grabbed a dishcloth and wiped flecks of batter from the counter. "Since her purse and jewelry were missing, Chief McBride thinks it might've been a robbery gone awry."

Lindsey leaned against the sink, fiddled with her ponytail. "Wow! Who found her body?"

"Casey did."

Lindsey stared at me wide-eyed. "All by himself . . . ?"

"Not exactly. I happened to be accompanying him at the time." I rubbed harder than necessary at a stubborn stain.

"Jeez, Mom. Wasn't finding one dead body enough? No one finds two! People are going to think you're some sort of a . . . a . . . dead body magnet."

I faced her, dishrag in hand, expression solemn. "I give you my word, Lindsey, it won't happen again. I've joined a twelve-step program."

"That's not funny!"

"Let's look on the bright side," I said. "Doug thinks Casey has the instincts of a great cadaver dog."

Lindsey studied me, lips pursed. Her expression reminded me of Melly's close-lipped disapproval whenever I failed to live up to her expectations — which occurred with regularity. "Where did all this take place?"

"In the square." I waved the dishrag in the general direction. "Under the azaleas."

"You're telling me a woman was killed right across the street?" Lindsey stalked into the living room and peered out the window. She shivered dramatically. "Imagine! A murder practically under your nose."

I joined her. I opened my mouth to offer motherly words of infinite wisdom when a white Cadillac Escalade pulled up in front of the square and parked. Barbie exited the driver's seat. Next, a young man climbed out the passenger side, went around the back, and hauled out a video camera the size of a Confederate cannon. Barbie headed toward a cluster of azaleas and motioned the young man with the camera to follow.

"Who's that?" Lindsey pressed her nose against the glass.

"That's Barbara Bunker Quinlan, known to her admirers as Barbie Q. She's here to film the barbecue festival for her TV show."

"No. Not *her.*" Lindsey shook her head impatiently. "I meant the guy. He's hot!"

Hot? Squinting, I leaned forward, trying to figure out exactly what comprised "hot" in the eyes of a teenage girl. Lean and lanky?

A mop of messy brown hair? Or was it jeans faded and strategically ripped at the knees? The guy didn't do a thing for my libido. Must be a sign of old age. Note to self: get hormone levels checked.

Lindsey turned abruptly and snatched the leash from a hook by the door. "I think Casey needs to go for a walk."

CHAPTER 15

The VFW was wall-to-wall people. Half the town, it seemed, had turned out for Becca Dapkins's send-off. I spotted CJ and Amber chatting with Matt and Mary Beth Wainwright, his law partner and wife. In one corner, Joe Johnson, former police chief, huddled with the mayor and several city council members. In another, Jolene Tucker gossiped with a group of ladies from her bunco group. I recognized Lindsey's language arts teacher along with several others on the faculty at Brandywine High.

Reba Mae gazed in amazement at the array of casseroles that adorned a buffet table. "Who knew there are so many ways to use cream of mushroom soup?"

"Who knew?" I echoed, truly in awe at the spectacle. In contrast, my pineapple upside-down cake and Reba Mae's pecan tassies huddled like castaways on a small table at the far end.

Funerals were always a popular social occasion here in the South, but even more so when murder was involved. Pink balloons floated above tables covered in pink plastic. Bouquets of carnations — pink of course — were scattered here and there. The Thursday night bingo ladies had done themselves proud. If she could've seen the to-do, Becca would've been thrilled.

"Becca's son and daughter," Reba Mae said, pointing to a man and a woman in their late twenties or early thirties, who stood somewhat apart, and lowered her voice. "They didn't seem any too heartbroken about their mother's passin'. I watched the daughter while the minister gave a eulogy. Didn't shed a tear."

"The son kept glancing at his watch the whole time," I whispered back. "Acted like he was late for a kickoff."

"Felicity told me the two are packed and ready to leave the second the reception's over."

"Hey, y'all." Dottie Hemmings bustled over. In keeping with the funeral's theme, she wore a pink flowered polyester dress that strained at the seams. Her blond helmet looked newly sprayed and teased. Reba Mae and I were drab in comparison, a black wrap dress for her, a navy sheath for me. "Did you ever see so many casseroles?" Dottie gushed. "Too bad we didn't think of doing a recipe exchange."

Reba Mae smiled, but I recognized the devilish glint in her eyes. "Maybe it's not too late to ask folks for recipes. Maybe put them in a cookbook. Dedicate it in Becca's honor."

Dottie clapped her chubby hands together. "What a marvelous idea, Reba Mae. I can't think of a more fitting tribute to Becca than a collection of cream of mushroom soup recipes from all her friends and neighbors."

"Perhaps you could sell them at the Chamber of Commerce," I suggested, tongue in cheek.

"Why didn't I think of that?" Dottie beamed, obviously delighted at the notion. "I'll speak with Maybelle and ask her to help."

What had we started? I could envision a no-holds-barred battle between the mayor and Maybelle Humphries if that came to fruition. The thought of Maybelle hawking cookbooks dedicated to her archrival almost made me smile. She'd probably use them for a dart board.

Dottie, oblivious of the irony, rattled on, "For the life of me, I don't understand why folks are so eager to jump on the cremation bandwagon. What about you, Reba Mae, cremation or burial?"

Reba Mae glanced my way, but I gave her my keep-me-out-of-this look in return. "Um, burial?" she said, more question than answer.

"This isn't a pop quiz," I hissed in her ear.

"You had a lovely service at First Baptist when Butch passed. Everyone crying and carrying on. Lots of flowers. Brenda Nash at the organ. Pinky Alexander brought the house down when she sang 'Amazing Grace.' " Dottie dabbed at her eyes with a tissue she extracted from her ample cleavage. "Pinky got a standing ovation."

I didn't have the heart to remind Dottie the congregation was already on their feet at that point.

Dottie smiled fondly in her husband's direction. Harvey Hemmings, busy extolling the virtues of small-town life to anyone within earshot, ignored his wife. I wished Reba Mae and I could do the same. "No carnations or gladiolus for me," Dottie continued. "As for hymns, my favorite is 'Abide with Me.' A good rule of thumb is no hymn composed after 1940. My husband the mayor has clear instructions what to do if I should pass first."

"Pass" was a euphemism for dying — or, in Becca's case, being murdered. I'd never heard the term as a child growing up in Detroit, but it seemed a much gentler phrase than "kicked the bucket," "bought the farm," "cashed in her chips," or just plain "croaked." Since moving to Georgia, I'd adopted the word. "Passed" was now part of my vocabulary right along with "bless her heart."

Melly approached our little conclave. "Pardon the interruption, ladies, but have any of you seen Maybelle?"

I was overcome by a fierce desire to hug my ex-mother-in-law. I don't think I've ever been so grateful for an "interruption" as I was after listening to Dottie prattle on — and on and on.

"Maybelle, the poor dear" — Melly fingered her pearls — "has been feeling under the weather ever since Becca passed."

"Maybelle and Becca weren't exactly on the best of terms —" Reba Mae started to say.

"Best of terms?" Dottie giggled. "My dear girl, Maybelle despised Becca. I wouldn't be the least surprised if she had something to do with poor Becca's untimely demise."

I gaped at Dottie. "Surely you don't believe Maybelle would harm Becca?"

"Shame on you, Dottie Hemmings." Melly shook an arthritic finger at her. "Maybelle is a sweet, good-natured soul. Wouldn't harm a flea."

"Pish-tosh." Dottie dismissed "sweet, good-natured," with a wave of her pudgy hand "Those two were oil and water ever since they were schoolgirls. Becca was the pretty popular one, captain of the cheerleading squad and homecoming queen. Maybelle was the brainy sort, president of the National Honor Society and class valedictorian. She was the perennial wallflower while Becca was queen bee."

I clucked my tongue in sympathy. "It must have been hard on Maybelle when Becca returned after her divorce and set her sights on Buzz."

"Speak of the devil," Reba Mae said, her tone hushed. "There he is now."

In a synchronized move worthy of a water ballet, the four of us turned and locked our gazes on Buzz Oliver. Becca's boyfriend stood alone in the midst of a crowd. His eyes red rimmed, face lined and haggard, the man genuinely appeared grief stricken.

"You darn tootin' Maybelle was mad Becca stole her intended. Madder than a wet hen." Dottie's head moved up and down like one of those bobblehead dolls you see in the rear window of an old Chevy. "I told Chief McBride that very thing when I saw him. Now if you ladies will excuse me, I'd better get in line at the buffet table before the good stuff's all gone."

"Wait up, Dottie," Melly said. "I'll go with you."

"S'pose McBride took Dottie seriously?" Reba Mae asked.

"He's probably hearing the same from people all over town."

"Well, I, for one, will rest easier knowin' Maybelle's alibi is rock solid." Reba Mae looped her arm through mine. "C'mon, sugar, let's have us some dessert before folks realize it's slim pickin's at the sweets table."

The desserts were displayed on a small table more suitable for playing bridge. I helped myself to a small slice of Lottie Smith's Can't-Die-Without-It Coconut Cake that, along with a Texas sheet cake, had joined the meager assortment. Since the cake looked lonely on a plate all by itself, I added one of Reba Mae's tassies, a miniature tart with pecan filling. Reba Mae took cake but left the tassies to the masses. We found ourselves a relatively quiet spot in a corner.

McBride appeared from the direction of the buffet table, holding a Styrofoam plate heaped high with food. "Y'all are to be be commended," he drawled, his Georgia roots evident. "I didn't know y'all were members of the Life's-short-eat-dessert-first Club."

I paused, fork halfway to my mouth, and scowled up at him. He was out of uniform in black blazer and slacks, white shirt. He'd unbuttoned the top button, ostensibly because of the summer heat. If I'd had a top button, I'd unfasten it, too, but not because of the outdoor temperature. It ought to be illegal to look that good.

"Hey, Wyatt." Reba Mae patted the chair next to her. "Sit a spell. Take a load off."

"Don't mind if I do," McBride said with an easy smile. Instead of taking the empty seat next to Reba Mae, however, he plunked himself next to me.

"You here on official business, McBride?" I asked. "Or on the prowl for a free lunch?"

He grinned his dimple-showing-off grin. "Enough can't be said for free lunches for lowly paid public servants."

"Hope you have a weakness for mushroom soup." Reba Mae nodded toward his plate. " 'Cause you're in for a treat."

"Green bean casserole, beef Stroganoff, chicken Stroganoff, cheesy potatoes, mac and cheese." I ticked them off on my fingers.

"And that's only for starters," Reba Mae added.

I'll never know what made me glance toward the dessert table at that particular moment, but as I did I glimpsed Maybelle disappearing out the back entrance. Her signature Hummingbird Cake occupied pride of place on the sweets table. "Well, I'll be," I breathed.

"What's up, honeybun?" Reba Mae asked, seeing my expression change.

"Maybelle brought a cake."

McBride, his back turned from the sweets table, polished off the last of his mac and cheese. "How do you know it's hers?"

"Aside from the fact I just saw her disappear out the door?" I asked innocently.

"Don't be a wiseass," he said.

"No one — and I mean no one — makes Hummingbird Cake like Maybelle. She even lines up those pecan halves perfect along the side. You have any idea how hard it is to make nuts stick without messing up the cream cheese icing?"

"Cream cheese icing is not my area of expertise," McBride commented drily. "I'm better informed on the subject of nuts — and I'm not referring to the pecan or walnut variety."

"That was awful nice of Maybelle to bring

somethin'." Reba Mae sampled her slice of coconut layer cake. "Too bad she didn't stay and visit."

"Ms. Humphries, I'm afraid, spotted me chatting with y'all and decided it prudent to make a hasty departure." He scooped up a forkful of Stroganoff.

"Why is she avoiding you?" I asked.

"I've issued Ms. Humphries a personal invitation to come down to my office later this afternoon and answer a few questions. Too many rumors circulating about her and Becca Dapkins to ignore."

"No wonder Maybelle's makin' herself scarce," Reba Mae said to me after McBride excused himself in response to a summons from Mayor Hemmings. "I don't blame her not wantin' the third degree."

Dessert finished and ready for our second course, we explored the buffet table. I decided to forego dishes in which unidentified objects swam in a gluey gray sea. I played it safe instead with a chicken and rice combo. In Becca's memory, I took a small serving of her specialty — green bean casserole.

"Aren't you afraid of puttin' on extra pounds eatin' all those carbs?" asked a voice sweet as a Georgia peach.

"Hey, Amber," I said, making an effort to

sound equally sweet. "Considerate of you to worry about my figure. Since I took up jogging, however, I can eat most anything I want and not gain an ounce." I had no idea if this was true or not, since I hadn't been jogging long enough to test the theory.

"Joggin's all right for some, I s'pose, but not for me." She smoothed her hair, which didn't need smoothing. Privately, I thought she only did that to flash her two-, maybe three-carat diamond engagement ring. "I don't think," she continued, "that runnin' around all sweaty in public is very ladylike."

But sleeping with another woman's husband is?

I bit my tongue to keep from saying that out loud. Determined to be pleasant even if it killed me, I smiled. "Where's your fiancé? He desert you?"

"CJ wanted to drop by the Chamber of Commerce and give Maybelle one of his business cards. He heard she might be needin' a good lawyer."

Reba Mae sidled closer. "If she needs a *good* lawyer, she won't be callin' CJ."

"That's downright insultin', Reba Mae." Amber turned her back on us and started to stalk off.

"Try the chocolate sheet cake!" I called after her. "It's delicious!"

"I don't eat chocolate," she informed me haughtily. "It makes my skin break out."

"Don't worry, dear." Reba Mae chuckled. "I'm sure you'll outgrow it."

The crowd had begun to thin by the time Reba Mae and I returned to our original seats. "Umm," I said around a mouthful. "The chicken and rice is delish. To quote McBride, 'enough can't be said for free lunches.' "

I was finishing the last bite when Gerilee Barker, an apron over a simple black dress, stopped at our table. "If you two are finished, I'll take your plates."

Reba Mae handed Gerilee hers. "The VFW got you workin' today?"

"The Women's Auxiliary offered to help the bingo ladies since they expected a big turnout. Been back in the kitchen most of the time. Thought I'd get a head start on the cleanup."

I blotted my mouth with a paper napkin. "The women ought to be commended for the fine job they did."

"Thanks, Piper. I'll pass along the compliment."

"Dottie mentioned gathering the cream of mushroom soup recipes into a cookbook. Kind of a tribute to Becca."

Reba Mae reached into her purse and

reapplied lipstick. "She even mentioned sell-ing them at the Chamber. Maybelle will be fit to be tied."

Gerilee added the plasticware to the pile of used Styrofoam plates she carried. Her brow creased into a frown. "I gotta admit, I'm worried about Maybelle. She's been act-ing strange lately."

"I'm sure she's upset, as we all are, over Becca's death." I pushed away from the table and got to my feet. "Considering their history, it's a good thing she has a solid alibi."

Reba Mae stood and hitched her purse onto her shoulder. "Yeah, good thing she was at the food bank with you the night in question."

"With me . . . ?" Gerilee stared at us blankly. "You're mistaken. I went alone that night."

Reba Mae and I exchanged glances. "You sure?" I asked when I found my voice.

"Positive." Gerilee added another plate to the teetering stack she already held. "May-belle called at the last minute and canceled. Said she didn't feel well and didn't want to spread her germs."

We watched Gerilee move off to clear an adjacent table.

"Well, I'll be darned." Reba Mae finally

spoke. "Maybelle lied."

"And what's more," I said, "Maybelle doesn't have an alibi."

CHAPTER 16

"Even though he's going through the motions and questioning suspects, deep down McBride still considers Becca's death a mugging. Call it woman's intuition if you will, but I can't help but think the big-city cop's got it all wrong. I'm convinced the case is much more complicated than the man cares to admit." I climbed into the Beetle and cranked the air to max.

Fanning herself with a program from the memorial service, Reba Mae slid into the passenger seat. "I could see a breakin' and enterin' — a home invasion even — but hittin' a poor defenseless woman on her way to deliver a brisket is, well . . . it just ain't right."

I shifted into reverse, backed out of the parking stall, and pulled out of the lot. "I'd like to take another look around Becca's house. See if we missed anything the first time."

"Fine by me." Reba Mae pulled down the visor and inspected her image in the small mirror. "Her son, Kenny, gave me a key. Told me he and his sister would appreciate havin' someone keep on eye on the place."

I looked at her suspiciously. "When did that conversation take place?"

"While you were visitin' the little girls' room," she said smugly. Satisfied with her appearance, she flipped the visor back up. "I walked over and introduced myself. Told 'em I'd be happy to help any way I could."

"So just like that" — I snapped my fingers — "they gave you a key?"

"More or less," she said. "Becca's kids plan to call a pro to appraise the house for valuables. Kenny gave me a spare house key after makin' me promise not to let the appraiser out of my sight. He and his sister don't want the guy runnin' off with the family treasures."

I made a right at the fork in the road and headed toward town. "From what I could tell, Becca's things didn't seem worth much, but I'm no expert."

"Dividin' up the silver is a big to-do in the South. I'm surprised the kids aren't fightin' over butter knives and seafood forks."

"I got the impression they're the take-the-money-and-run type," I told her. "I'm going to stop by the Chamber for a minute to check on Maybelle. Care to join me?"

"Wish I could, honeybun, but I got a perm waitin' on me."

After agreeing to meet her later, I dropped Reba Mae off at the Klassy Kut and drove to the Chamber of Commerce. Maybelle looked up from her desk behind the counter as I entered. The Chamber could use some sprucing up. A fresh coat of paint over the institutional beige would be a good start. A couple plastic chairs of the stackable variety hugged one wall. The other wall featured blowup photos of Brandywine Creek's "points of interest" — the courthouse, the opera house, the town square.

"Hey, Maybelle," I said cheerily. "Seeing how you didn't stay for lunch, I brought you a plate. Just nuke it in the microwave for a minute or two."

"That's awfully sweet of you, Piper. Maybe later." She took the plate from me and made room for it in a dorm-size fridge next to a file cabinet. "I can't eat a bite these days. Even the thought of food makes me nauseous. I've been a bundle of nerves since Becca . . . died."

"Becca had a real nice turnout. She would've been pleased."

Maybelle tucked a stray salt-and-pepper wisp behind her ear. "Becca always did like being the center of attention."

"Her children didn't seem very distraught at her passing." *Passing.* There it was again, the euphemism of the day. Was there a Euphemism-of-the-Day calendar? If not, maybe there should be. Could be a bestseller during the holidays. Something along the lines of Page-a-Day Sudoku, or 365 Days of Beer.

Maybelle rested her hands on the counter and folded them primly. "Don't think for a minute I don't know what people are thinking. They're saying I had it in for Becca. That I was angry at her for stealing Buzz. Maybe even angry enough to kill her."

"That's just talk, Maybelle. No one who knows you believes that nonsense," I said with more conviction than I felt.

But why lie about her alibi? There had to be a logical explanation for the lie. All I had to do was find out what it was. Easy peasy . . . not.

Maybelle reached into a desk drawer and took out a business card. "Your ex dropped by and gave this to me. Think I should give him a call?"

"I don't think you're in need of a lawyer yet, Maybelle. Besides, CJ's a whizbang at trip and falls, but he hasn't had a lot of experience in criminal cases."

"Criminal" caused Maybelle to wince. *Me and my big mouth,* I berated myself silently. Didn't the woman have enough worries on her plate without me heaping on more?

"Chief McBride's called me in for questioning," Maybelle blurted. "What'll I tell him?"

"McBride doesn't use thumbscrews. Just tell him the truth. He'll have this mess sorted out in no time."

"You really think so?" she asked hopefully.

"Of course I do," I replied, trying to infuse confidence. "Considering the rumors flying around town, talking to you is probably only a formality. Don't forget the man's paid to be suspicious. All you have to do is be honest."

Honest? That brought me to the crux of the matter. I absently picked up a brochure advertising the Brandywine Creek Opera House's fall season. I noticed *Steel Magnolias* was on the schedule. A real tearjerker, that one. "Maybelle," I said, clearing my throat, "there's something I need to talk to you about."

CJ's card clenched tight in her fist, Maybelle nodded for me to continue.

"Gerilee helped clean up after today's

reception, and we got to talking." Did I only imagine it or did panic flicker across Maybelle's face? "According to her, you weren't at the food bank the night Becca was murdered. Gerilee claimed you weren't feeling well and canceled."

Maybelle's clasped her hands so tightly her knuckles shone white. Her face paled, then reddened. "I must've been confused."

"If you weren't at the food bank, where were you?" There, I'd gone and done it. Addressed the elephant in the room.

"I, um, was home . . . alone."

Home Alone was probably a better movie than it was an alibi. From my television viewing I knew "home alone" was a hard one to prove. Or disprove.

"Good," I said. "All you have to do is tell McBride what you told me, and you'll do fine." I placed the brochure back on the pile, careful to align it with the others on the counter. "I'd better get back to my shop and relieve Lindsey."

I gave Maybelle a smile as I left the Chamber, but she didn't smile back.

In the VW once again, I drummed my fingers on the steering wheel. Did finding Becca's body give me a vested interest in the case? Or was I just plain nosey? Nah, impossible. I had an inquiring mind, is all.

But truth be told, the answer wasn't that simple. I worried Maybelle was about to find herself in the same predicament I'd been in not so long ago. I remembered what it felt like to be falsely accused. To have people you'd known for years suddenly regard you as an axe murderer. Or in Maybelle's case a brisket bludgeoner. With Becca's homicide — and Maybelle's uncertain future — uppermost in my mind, I twisted the key in the ignition and headed for Meat on Main.

Pete Barker's ruddy face creased in a grin at the sight of me. A white canvas apron swathed his ample girth. "Hey there, Piper," he said, shoving a tray of ground chuck into the meat case. "How'd the funeral go? Big turnout, I heard."

"Half the town was there. Guess the other half had to work."

Pete stripped the plastic gloves from his hands, bunched them up, and tossed them toward a wastebasket. One glove landed in the intended target; the other hit the floor. "Gerilee expected a crowd. Told me she'd be dead on her feet when she came home. Advised me if I wanted supper, I'd better pick up a pizza after I lock up."

"Never go wrong with pizza."

"Say, can I interest you in today's special?

Boneless, skinless chicken breasts. Want me to wrap up a couple?"

"Sure, why not? I'll make Lindsey and me some nice chicken salad."

Pete donned another pair of gloves, selected a couple plump chicken breasts, and placed them on the scale. "Gerilee raved about the chicken salad you brought for the Friends of the Library luncheon. Said she's never tasted better."

"Tell her I add a touch of curry." I watched him wrap my purchases in heavy butcher paper. "Business must be booming," I said, getting down to the real purpose behind my visit. "With the barbecue festival right around the corner, you must be selling a ton of brisket."

"Brisket, ribs, pork butt, you name it. Can't keep 'em in stock. What about you? Spices flying off the shelves?"

"At the moment, cayenne seems to be leading the pack, with cumin coming in a poor second."

"Folks tend to lose sight of the two essentials for a never-fail barbecue — a low cooking temperature and a cloud of woodsmoke. Some tend to think any old woodsmoke will do, but they're dead wrong. As any barbecuer worth their salt knows, you gotta use hardwood,"

191

"Why?" I asked. "What happens if you don't?"

"Take my wife's nephew for instance." Pete chuckled at the memory. "The fool used scraps of wood he hauled home from a construction site. Worst darn barbecue I ever ate. Might as well have coated them baby backs with varnish, thanks to all the resin in the wood."

"Sounds pretty awful," I commiserated as I followed Pete to the register where he proceeded to ring up my order. "I don't suppose by chance you remember how many briskets Becca Dapkins ordered."

"Let's see now." Pete scratched the bald spot at the top of his head. "Six, she ordered six."

"You're sure about the number?"

"Yeah, 'cause I recall thinking that was strange, since she never cooked anything that didn't call for cream of mushroom soup. But she was a woman on a mission. Bound and determined to win the Taster's Choice award. Wanted to prove to everyone she was every bit as good a cook as Maybelle Humphries."

Six briskets minus one. Reba Mae and I had found five briskets in Becca's freezer. And most likely the missing one was the murder weapon. This information served to confirm my conviction that Becca had been killed at home.

I fished my wallet out of my purse and paid Pete for the chicken. "Thanks, Pete."

He chuckled as he walked me to the door. "I'd be willing to lay odds that most every house in Brandywine Creek has one or more of my briskets in their fridge."

Easy come, easy go. So much for thinking I'd found where the murder weapon originated when, according to Pete, half the people in town had an identical weapon as near as their refrigerator. Perhaps McBride was right when he said I should leave sleuthing to the professionals.

Parking behind my shop, I traipsed through the vacant lot to the rear door of Spice It Up! My constant to-and-fro had worn a path through the weeds and scrub.

"Hey, Lindsey!" I called out. "I'm back!"

Tail wagging furiously, Casey acknowledged my return with more enthusiasm than a Walmart greeter. As I passed through the storage area, I heard people talking, Lindsey's animated voice among them.

"Hey," I said, "care if I join the party?"

"Oh, hi, Mom," Lindsey said, her face flushed becomingly. "This is Carter Kincaid."

Carter turned out to be the same young man I'd seen yesterday stepping out of Barbie's SUV. Up close and personal, he was quite good-looking in a scruffy sort of way. He had nice even features, a stubble-covered jaw, a mop of brown hair, and gray-green eyes. I placed him in his early twenties. "Hello, Carter."

"Nice to meet you, ma'am." He stuck out his hand, which I accepted.

Ma'am? I cringed inwardly. I didn't feel old enough to be called ma'am. I was saving "ma'am" for when I turned eighty. I stowed my purse beneath the counter and slipped on an apron. "What brings you here, Carter? Are you in the market for spice?"

"No, ma'am," he said with an engaging smile that showcased years of orthodontia. "Barbie — Ms. Quinlan — asked me to stop by, check out the natural light. She's considering your place for a segment on *Some Like It Hot.*"

"Carter's a videographer." Lindsey's words tumbled over themselves in her excitement. "He was telling me all about his work."

Carter tucked his hands in his jeans pockets. "Your daughter's extremely photogenic, Mrs. Prescott. She has a keen eye for detail."

Folding my arms over my chest, I cocked my head and studied my daughter, noting her pink cheeks, the sparkle in her blue-gray eyes. "Does she now?"

Lindsey shifted her weight from one foot to the other. "Carter offered to show me how things look from behind the lens. He said he's going to suggest they film me working on Doug's team."

"Naturally, the final call belongs to Barbie," Carter quickly interjected. "And you'll need to sign a waiver."

"Carter says Ms. Quinlan wants to break into investigative journalism," Lindsey offered, all wide-eyed and duly impressed.

"Hmm," I said. "Is that so?"

Carter nodded solemnly. "Barbie thinks murder in a small town on the eve of its annual festival might be the ticket to making the jump to cable news."

"CNN or Fox," Lindsey volunteered. "How cool is that?"

"Cool," I echoed with noticeably less enthusiasm.

A popular drinking song — something about a red Solo cup — suddenly blared from Carter's pocket. He dug out a smart phone and frowned at the display. "Sorry, gotta run. See you around, Lindsey. Nice meeting you, ma'am."

Lindsey and I stood in the front window and watched him climb into the white Escalade and drive off.

"Isn't he something?" Lindsey breathed. "A career in television must be awesome. I think I'd like to have a TV show of my own someday. You heard Carter say I was photogenic."

I stared at her in dismay. "I thought you wanted to be a veterinarian like Dr. Winters."

"Mo-om," she wailed. "That was weeks ago."

"Speaking of Doug, he needs your advice on T-shirts and wants to know if you can recruit a couple friends to help on his team. Unless I'm mistaken, he's expecting you at the animal clinic this afternoon."

"Right. I'm practically on my way." Lindsey ran to the counter and snatched her purse. "I wonder if Ms. Quinlan would let me hang around while she's in town. Give me some pointers."

I sighed wearily. Just what the world needed, another Barbie-Q Bombshell. Oh, happy day — not.

CHAPTER 17

The shop seemed unnaturally quiet after Lindsey left. I took out a pad and studied my notes for a window display aimed at enticing barbecue aficionados into my shop. I reminded myself to ask Reba Mae if I could borrow the compact grill the twins used for camping. Somewhere I had a set of barbecue tools. A sack of charcoal, a red-and-white-checked tablecloth, and one of my yellow Spice It Up! aprons with its chili pepper logo should make a colorful, eye-catching display. As a final touch, I'd add baskets of whole fresh chili peppers in all their glorious shapes, colors, and sizes. My imagination ran rampant. Yellow, orange, and dark-red habaneras. Bright-green jalapeños. Coffee-brown chipotles.

I was so engrossed in planning that I failed to notice the time until the regulator clock bonged the hour. It was then I saw that the roll of paper in my credit card machine needed replacing. *No time like the present,* I thought as I bent down and reached for a refill under the counter.

Letting out a shriek, I leaped back as a spider scuttled out from under the box. I registered the long pinchers, the hook-shaped stinger. This wasn't an ordinary "spider" but a scorpion. Before I could do more than watch, it disappeared under a row of freestanding shelves. Awakened from his doggy snooze by the commotion, Casey raced to my rescue, performing an award-worthy version of a ferocious growl.

"It's all right, puppy. Settle down; it's okay." I gave myself the same advice.

Now I'm not partial to the creatures any more than my daughter is, but I'm less prone to hysterics. Lindsey would've gone ballistic. She's definitely an arachnophobe. Has been ever since she found a big old spider in the restroom at Elijah Clark State Park where CJ and I took the kids camping one summer.

Knowing a scorpion sighting would send Lindsey heading for CJ's scorpion-free home on a golf course, I reached for the phone. The woman who answered at Bugs-B-Gone promised she'd send an exterminator the next day. *Another unanticipated expense,* I thought glumly as I hung up.

There went the ridiculously but oh, so coveted cool pair of running shorts I'd had my heart set on. I locked the front door of Spice It Up! and flipped the sign to CLOSED.

A glance at the clock told me I had plenty of time to prepare chicken salad before meeting up with Reba Mae at Becca's house. I parboiled the chicken while I diced celery, toasted almonds, and halved red grapes. When the chicken was cool enough to handle, I cut it into bite-size pieces. I mixed in mayo, fresh-squeezed lemon juice, and the rest of the ingredients. Last but by no means least, I added a pinch of curry powder that I'd mixed from a combination of turmeric, coriander, and cardamom, to name a few of the spices. When the chicken salad was done, I popped it in the refrigerator for later.

Even at this hour, the July heat and humidity were unrelenting, so I opted to drive the short distance to Becca's rather than arrive dripping wet and out of sorts. Reba Mae's five-year-old Buick was parked at the curb. She waited for me in the shade of the front porch. Apparently, she was also averse to being sweaty and cranky.

"Hope this won't take long," she said as I came up the walk. "Wally's comin' by later and bringin' a bottle of wine."

"You and Judge Wally seem to be hitting it off. Think you ought to slow things down a bit? After all, you just met the guy and don't know much about him."

"It's been years since a man paid me this much attention, so don't go spoilin' it for me." Reba Mae produced a house key and opened the door. "He'll be leavin' soon as the festival's over, and my man drought will start up again."

Inside, Becca's house felt uncomfortably warm, the air stagnant. The air conditioner hummed, but the thermostat had been set to conserve energy. A gray film of dust coated the dark wood of the coffee table and tea cart. Only the collection of African violets livened up an otherwise dismal atmosphere.

Reba Mae planted her hands on her hips and surveyed the scene. "Felicity said Becca's kids stayed at her bed-and-breakfast rather than at their mother's home. They claimed this old place gave them the willies."

"Do you think they'll mind us giving away her houseplants?"

"Heck no. They'd probably say good riddance." Reba Mae walked over to one with ruffled violet and white blooms and stuck her index finger in the soil. "Feels like they can wait another day or two before wa-terin'."

I wandered around the room hoping I might spot something we missed on our previous visit.

"One of my customers, Pinky Alexander, might take a couple plants off our hands."

"Good." I nodded. "Melly has a way with them, too. Maybe she'll take some."

"Pinky said light and proper waterin' were real important. Need to keep the soil moist but never let it get soggy."

I raised a brow. "Should I be taking notes?"

"No need for sarcasm, missy," Reba Mae chided. "Pinky told me always water from the bottom and make sure the water's room temperature. If it's too cold, it chills the plant's poor little roots and makes its leaves curl."

I opened and shut the drawer of an end table. A true-crime novel, a crossword puzzle book, and dog-eared copies of *TV Guide* were the only items.

Reba Mae trailed after me. "Pinky said avoid gettin' water on the leaves at all costs. It causes spottin'. And one last thing — never use soft water, because it changes the pH of the soil."

"The tutorial over?" I asked, heading for

the kitchen with Reba Mae on my heels.

The telltale odor of bleach still lingered. I peeked into the pantry cum laundry room. "Only thing missing is the empty bleach jug. The GBI guys must've taken it for prints."

Reba Mae examined the contents of the refrigerator. "Once the festival's over, we need to give this thing a good cleanin' out. No sense hangin' on to half-empty bottles of catsup and salad dressin'."

"McBride's going to need more than a broken fingernail to change his mind about the scene of the crime," I said, unable to keep the disappointment from my voice. "I don't know what I expected to find."

"The killer's name scrawled in blood?"

"Yeah, right," I muttered.

"Don't turn up your nose at the notion, missy. I saw that in a movie once — creeped me out. Problem was the cops couldn't figure out the victim's handwritin' and arrested the wrong guy. We done yet?"

"Almost." About ready to admit defeat, I opened the cabinet below the sink and found a two-gallon scrub bucket filled with cleaning supplies. Dish detergent, glass cleaner, all-purpose cleaner, furniture polish, and sponges were all jammed inside. Nothing out of the ordinary.

Or was there?

I stared at the items thoughtfully for a moment. I was about to close the cabinet when I was struck by a sudden realization. "Come here a sec, Reba Mae. Take a look and tell me if you see something odd."

Reba Mae scrunched down and stared long and hard at the inside of the cabinet. "Looks pretty much like stuff I keep under my sink except —"

"— there's no rubber gloves," I finished triumphantly.

"What are you gettin' at?"

"Doesn't it strike you as . . . peculiar . . . that a woman so fussy about her appearance, one who never left home without fresh lipstick or with chipped nail polish, doesn't own a pair of rubber gloves?"

"Well, yeah, I guess when you put it that way."

"What if — for the sake of argument — Becca *was* killed in her own kitchen?" My earlier suspicions seemed to crystallize. "What if her killer used bleach and gloves to remove the evidence?"

"Makes sense" — Reba Mae rubbed her arms — "in a scary sort of way. Now can we go?"

Reba Mae had no sooner driven off when my cell phone rang.

"Mom . . . ?" I heard Lindsey's voice. "Just wanted to tell you I won't be home for supper. Amber invited me over to look at bridal magazines. She has some amazing ideas for her and Dad's wedding."

Amber was my cross to bear. In a ploy to appear a "cool" stepmom, she'd asked Lindsey to be her maid of honor at a destination wedding. "Have the lovebirds decided on a location yet?"

"Right now it's between Costa Rica and the Dominican Republic. Turks and Caicos hasn't been ruled out either."

I envisioned somewhere else for the pair. A deserted island in the Pacific instantly sprang to mind. One with an active volcano. "Give the two my best," I said through gritted teeth. "Have a good time, but don't be late."

I hit the disconnect. During the short drive home, I mulled over what I should do about the absence of rubber gloves in Becca's house. McBride dismissed the importance of finding a broken fingernail. Being a dyed-in the-wool skeptic, he'd probably be even less impressed with missing rubber gloves.

When I turned down the street behind my shop, I spotted a police cruiser occupying my normal parking space. McBride slid out from behind the wheel. I slid out from behind mine, and we met somewhere in the middle. I felt a flutter in my stomach but blamed it on hunger. The sight of an alpha male had nothing whatsoever to do with my reaction. Tall, dark, and rugged wasn't my type.

I motioned at the soda cans, beer bottles, and food wrappers that accumulated in the empty lot like iron shavings to a magnet. "Passing out tickets for littering?"

"No, but if you're interested, I could deputize you for the job."

"I've often wondered how much money law enforcement actually collects from littering fines." I started down the weed-choked path leading to my back door.

He matched his stride to mine. "Not enough to buy a pack of gum."

"So if it's not busting miscreants, what brings you here?"

"I had an interesting conversation with one of our out-of-town guests. I'd like to hear your version of his story."

I shoved my key into the lock. "That sounds ominous."

"Ominous enough for me to skip dinner."

"Speaking of dinner, I haven't had mine either. Care to discuss this 'interesting conversation' over a chicken salad sandwich?"

He held open the door for me. "You dining alone tonight?"

"Lindsey had a better offer. She and Amber plan to look at pictures of bridesmaids' dresses."

"CJ and Amber. Does it bother you knowing they're planning a wedding?" he asked.

I shrugged. "I'm getting used to the notion. Most of the time, I think Pooh Bear and Sweetums deserve each other."

McBride followed me up the stairs. "I have to admit Amber does seem more his type."

Ouch! I swung around to face him and, being two steps above, found myself at eye level. My chin went up a notch. "Explain that remark, or I'll rescind my invite."

"You drive a hard bargain." His cool blue eyes warmed with humor. "The CJ that I remember always gravitated to taller . . . more sophisticated . . . girls. Not the petite and feisty sort. You're not who I pictured CJ would end up marrying."

"Oh." Unsure how to interpret his comment, I continued up the stairs, leaving McBride to follow.

Pleased at Casey's energetic welcome, McBride stooped to pet the wriggling mass of canine. I didn't have the heart to inform him that Casey greeted everyone with the same enthusiastic tail wagging.

"Make yourself comfortable while I fix the sandwiches," I told him. "I'd offer you a beer, but you're obviously on duty — besides, I don't have any. I'm more of a wine drinker myself."

"My guess would be Chardonnay."

I took chicken salad and lettuce from the fridge. "Actually, I prefer my wine sweeter, less dry. Riesling or pinot grigio. And when I'm feeling wild and crazy, I drink merlot."

While I worked, McBride wandered into the living room, where he stood looking out the window, his back turned. "You've got a bird's-eye view of the town square from here."

"Mmm," I murmured. I heaped chicken salad on multi-grain bread, topped it with lettuce, thin slices of tomato, and red onion, then added a handful of kettle chips and a kosher dill pickle to our plates. "Iced tea or soda?" I asked. "Or if you'd rather, I can make coffee."

He strolled back into the kitchen. "Soda's fine."

"It'll have to be diet," I warned as I set the sandwiches on the table.

"Diet's fine." He lowered himself onto a chair and stretched out his long legs.

Casey curled up under the table, transparent in his hope one of us would drop a morsel or two.

McBride popped a chip in his mouth. "This looks great. I wasn't able to eat much at the reception before the mayor called me away."

I watched him take a bite of his sandwich before I asked, "What did you want to talk to me about?"

"Ummm," he said, ignoring my question. "I've been living on pizza ever since that mutt of yours found a body. This is one helluva sandwich."

"I added a dash of curry powder," I replied, pleased at the compliment. "But you still haven't answered my question."

McBride washed down a mouthful with a swallow of Diet Coke. "Tex Mahoney stopped by my office a little while ago. Said he wanted a clear conscience."

"Tex . . . ?" I sat up straighter, all thought of food forgotten. "Did he confess to murder?"

"Nothing quite so dramatic." McBride munched chips. "Tex thought I should know about the confrontation he witnessed between Maybelle Humphries and the deceased. According to Mr. Mahoney, this 'confrontation' took place in your shop the same day Becca Dapkins was murdered."

Uh-oh. Another nail in Maybelle's coffin. "Exactly what did Tex say?"

"Mahoney stated the women had words. Threats were made. In his opinion, if you hadn't intervened their argument could have turned physical." McBride lasered me with his icy blues. "What I don't understand, Piper, is why didn't you tell me this?"

I broke off a small piece of bread and dropped it on the floor for Casey. "They were both upset. Maybelle's still hurting over Becca stealing Buzz Oliver. When they're angry, people tend to say things they don't mean."

His gaze fastened on mine, McBride took a long swallow of soda. "I had Maybelle come down to the station for questioning. She claims she was home alone the night Becca died."

"Do you believe her?"

"Do you?"

I raised my shoulder and let it fall. "Single women often spend a good share of evenings home alone."

Shoving his empty plate aside, he crumpled his paper napkin and got to his feet. "I have to admit that in light of the threats made, Maybelle tops my persons of interest list."

I picked up the dishes and placed them in the dishwasher. "Any trace of the murder weapon?"

"A brisket? You're kidding, right? Either the killer took it with him or some animal carted it off."

I debated whether to run the risk of being ridiculed and confide in McBride about the missing rubber gloves. In the end, I opted for full disclosure. "Reba Mae and I went over to Becca's after work tonight."

"You two on plant patrol?"

"African violets are high maintenance." I busied myself wiping down the countertop. "While we were there, we discovered Becca's rubber gloves are missing. A woman such as Becca, who never answered her door unless every hair was in place, wouldn't clean house or wash dishes without gloves."

"How many times must I remind you to stay out of the investigation? This isn't a game for amateurs."

"But what if I'm right? Isn't it possible Becca was killed at home? That the killer put on rubber gloves and used bleach to clean up any traces? What if Becca's body was moved to make it *appear* a random act of violence?"

McBride's expression grew even stonier

— if that was possible. "Whoever's responsible for Becca Dapkins's death is still at large. No telling what lengths he — or she — might go to if they find you sticking your cute little nose where it doesn't belong." He started for the stairs. "I've got enough problems without having to worry about your safety."

"Maybelle wasn't the only one to have words with Becca that day in my shop!" I called after him.

He paused on the stairs. "Who else?"

"None other than Miss Barbie Q. Seems she and Becca Dapkins had a history. Becca even accused Barbie of being a former stripper. Barbie's no pushover. She's able to hold her own quite nicely. You might want to check her alibi for the night in question."

Without another word, McBride headed down the stairs. Casey whined at the sharp sound of a slamming door. I wanted to do the same — whine, that is, not slam a door.

CHAPTER 18

The following afternoon, I'd just thanked the UPS driver when Doug burst through the door of my shop wearing a an ear-to-ear grin. Catching me around the waist, he whirled me in a circle.

Resting my hands lightly on his shoulders for balance, I laughed up at him, his good humor contagious. "Hey, what's the occasion? You win the lottery?"

"In a manner of speaking," he said, and planted a quick kiss before releasing me. "Your daughter came through for me."

"Lindsey? How's that?" I tilted my head to one side and studied him closer. Behind wire-rimmed glasses, his brown eyes sparkled with boyish enthusiasm. His prematurely gray hair was a bit disheveled, as though he'd run his hands through it countless times. Without further thought, I reached up to smooth it and found it surprisingly soft.

"Lindsey found two more members for my team," Doug said with a smile. "We're calling ourselves the Pit Crew."

"The Pit Crew, eh? It sounds hot and racy, like NASCAR." I walked over to the large package the UPS driver had deposited on the counter.

"Here, let me help." Doug followed and, before I could stop him, picked up a box cutter and slit open the box. Not even the thick plastic the peppers were encased in could smother their spicy aroma.

"Who are these new recruits?" I asked as I began to unpack the chilis — árbol and ancho, guajillo and chipotle, and the small but potent chili piquins.

"Clay Johnson, one of Reba Mae's boys, and Lindsey's friend Taylor."

"Clay's a hard worker. I'm not sure I can say the same for Taylor." I was pleased to learn Lindsey hadn't disappointed Doug. With summer school over, her social life had kicked into high gear. I'd noticed she had a tendency to forget casually made promises. Her intentions were good. Her follow-through not so much.

"Nothing like two pretty girls to pique the judge's interest in a lowly contestant." Doug picked up a large dark-purple ancho chili and set it aside.

"Good choice." I nodded toward the pepper. "Anchos are the backbone of most Mexican dishes."

He nudged a red-orange árbol pepper that resembled a slender but withered carrot toward the ancho. "My timing couldn't have been better. Looks like I get my pick of the peppers."

"Peter Piper picked a peck of peppers . . ." I sing songed.

Doug tossed an ancho into the air and caught it. ". . . a peck of peppers Peter Piper picked."

"If Peter Piper . . ." My voice trailed off and Doug turned to see what had captured my attention.

A white SUV pulled to the curb in front of Spice It Up!, and Barbie Quinlan emerged. In a concession to July-in-Georgia heat, she wore a sleeveless summer dress the color of lemon sorbet. Its fabric clung; the color flattered. Strappy sandals added a good four inches to her height. A side part allowed her platinum-blond hair to fall peekaboo style over one eye reminiscent of movie sirens of a bygone era.

Doug let out a low whistle. "Va-va-voom!"

I felt a spurt of jealousy at hearing Doug's remark but had to give credit where credit was due. Barbie tended to have a "va-va-voom" effect on men. With her knockout figure, she could have gotten the same re-action with a paper bag over her head. Without the paper bag, she was downright lethal. I felt frumpy . . . and short . . . in comparison. I smoothed my apron, aware I must smell like eau d'chili pepper.

Barbie glided into Spice It Up! as though she owned the place, flicked a glance at my shipment. "Looks like you're ready to turn up the heat. Chili piquins?" she asked, pointing a shellacked nail at a pile of small red shriveled peppers. "Hope you post a warning: USE WITH CAUTION."

"Hello, Barbie." I plastered on a smile. "What brings you here?"

Barbie aimed her considerable charm at Doug. Giving her long hair a toss, she extended her hand. "I don't believe I've had the pleasure," she purred. "Barbie Quinlan. Better known as Barbie Q."

I watched with irritation as Doug squared his shoulders and tightened his abs. I was surprised his glasses didn't fog. Judging from his reaction, you'd think he was back in junior high and the most popular girl in the class had just noticed him for the first time.

"D-Doug," he stammered at last.

"It's Doug Winters," I explained, taking

mercy on his befuddled state. "*Dr.* Doug Winters."

"Dr.?" Barbie drawled. "I'm impressed. You look the college professor type. Or maybe the cute high school science teacher all the girls have a mad crush on."

"I, um . . ." Doug struggled not to swallow his tongue.

What had come over the man? I wondered. It wasn't as though he'd never set eyes on Barbie before. She'd been McBride's date the night Doug and I *attempted* to have dinner at Antonio's — and settled for eggs at Chez Spice. But I suspected up close and personal the Barbie-Q Factor was an even more potent effect.

"Doug's a veterinarian." I went back to unpacking peppers. "He owns Pets 'R People, the animal clinic on Old County Road. He's also a contestant in the barbecue festival."

"First timer," Doug explained, adopting an aw-shucks tone. "Strictly amateur. Backyard division."

"Wholesome, earnest, good-looking." Barbie swept her gaze over him, making Doug blush to the roots of his silvery hair.

Hmph! The woman had some nerve slathering compliments all over a poor unsuspecting veterinarian. Even if they were true.

"You'll be quite photogenic should we decide to film you, but first you'd need to sign a waiver, which brings me to the reason for my visit," Barbie continued. Digging into a roomy tote bag, she extracted a printed form.

I eyed it warily. "What's that?"

She shoved it at me. "A standard release. I'll need your signature before Carter does the interior and exterior shoots. Don't bother to thank me for the unpaid advertisement."

Necessity makes salesmen of us all. I took the form from her and began to read the small print.

"That isn't necessary." She waved her hand impatiently. "Just sign on the dotted line."

"I never sign anything without reading it first. It's a poor business practice."

"Right, you were a lawyer's wife, weren't you?" she said, an underlying sneer in her voice. "I see CJ taught you a few tricks of the trade."

"Don't I wish," I muttered under my breath.

If I'd been more astute to "tricks of the trade," I wouldn't have listened to CJ poor-

217

mouth our finances. He'd gone on ad nauseam about pending medical school expenses for Chad, college tuition for Lindsey, the fluctuating stock market, the price of fuel in the Middle East, and the cost of tea in China. In the end, I'd agreed on a lump sum settlement in our divorce decree. I'd taken a gamble, rolled the dice, and invested the entire amount in a dream of mine. Owning my own business. Voilà! Spice It Up! became a reality.

My budget was tight, my profit margin minuscule, but I was squeaking by. While I "squeaked," however, CJ had transformed into the entire brass section of the Augusta Symphony, complete with French horns and tuba. He'd purchased a swank new home on a golf course, had his teeth whitened, hair dyed, peppered the interstate with billboards — and gotten engaged to a bimbo half his age. Such is life. I've gotten over feeling bitter. I'm reinventing myself and proud of the results.

"Later, I'd like to do an interview," Barbie said, interrupting my musing.

I glanced up from the release form. "Interview . . . ?"

Barbie's lips curved, but there was no warmth in the smile. "Only a few simple questions. For instance, what spices were your bestsellers before the festival? We might talk a bit about the heat units of various capsicums. 'Capsicums,' " she explained, turning to Doug, "is another name for chili peppers."

"Doug knows all about capsicums," I informed her. "He's a gourmet cook specializing in Indian cuisine."

"Indian, hmm . . ." Barbie's pale-aqua gaze focused on Doug with renewed interest. "Chicken Tandoori is one of my favorites. Too bad I'm not going to be in town longer, or I'd persuade you to make it for me."

Doug swallowed and managed a weak smile.

"More's the pity," I said brightly, and handed back the signed consent. "By the way, Barbie, I didn't see you at the reception after Becca's memorial service."

"That bitch?" Barbie jammed the waiver into her tote bag. Color rode high on her cheekbones. "I wouldn't give Becca Dapkins a drink of water if her heart was on fire. She was an evil, nasty woman. The world's better off without her."

Barbie turned and marched out.

"Well," Doug breathed, "that was interesting."

"It certainly was," I concurred.

■ ■ ■ ■

Doug left after reminding me to check out a video on shag dancing on YouTube. He also pointed out that the shag contest was only four days away. I promised again to meet him for the street dance and fireworks that would take place after the festival. He took along a bag of capsicums fresh out of the box. Unable to make up his mind, he'd decided to purchase some of each.

Soon after, Buzz Oliver arrived wearing a ball cap and blue work uniform that bore a smiling bug logo. Truth is, I'd nearly forgotten about calling an exterminator. I hadn't seen another scorpion, but didn't want one to appear and send Lindsey into a hissy fit.

"Hey, Buzz." I put the cardboard box from the chilies under the counter where I'd remember to take it to the recycle center later.

"Sorry if I kept you waiting, Piper." He set a large stainless-steel canister with a nozzle on the floor, took off his cap, and wiped perspiration from his brow. "Expected to get here sooner, but I had a follow-up at the Beaver Dam Motel. The owner wanted me to give the place another spray for bedbugs — just in case. Bedbugs are the bane of the hotel/motel industry, you know. In addition to mattresses, they like to hide in box springs, carpets, drapes, you name it."

"I can understand how that would be bad for business."

"Got that right." He replaced his cap over his crew cut. "Bedbugs are no better'n little baby vampires. They sneak out at night and suck your blood. That's where I come in. First sign of 'em, call a licensed technician like me to deal with the little buggers — pardon the pun."

"I'll keep that in mind." I shuddered at the thought of a possible bedbug infestation. "I found a scorpion yesterday. My daughter is deathly afraid of spiders, so —"

"Say no more." He grabbed his sprayer and pumped it a few times. "You probably saw what we in the trade know as a devil scorpion. It's one of two types found here in Georgia."

"You might want to pay extra attention to the storage room. Especially under the cupboards."

"Will do." Buzz took his canister and trudged toward the rear of the shop. "Scorpions get a bad rap if you ask me."

Had I asked him? No, didn't think so, but it didn't seem to matter.

"Scorpions aren't out looking for folks to sting. No sirree," Buzz continued his lecture. "Most of 'em only venture out in search of food or to mate."

Too much information? I hadn't enrolled for a tutorial in entomology, but at least it was free of charge. "Well," I said, "I wish they'd do their searching and mating elsewhere."

Buzz aimed his nozzle and spewed chemicals. "What many don't realize, scorpions are a natural form of pest control, preying on all kinds of pesky insects."

Humming to myself, I checked the shipment against the itemized invoice. I couldn't help wonder if Buzz's bug expertise somehow qualified him as a babe magnet. It certainly seemed to work with Maybelle, then Becca. Did he routinely regale the ladies with tales of bedbugs and scorpions?

I brought myself up short. *Shame on you, Piper.* The poor man had just lost his girlfriend. And here I was being totally insensitive. Talk of creepy crawlies probably was a form grief therapy.

"How are you doing, Buzz?" I said, looking up from the invoice. "You must miss Becca something fierce. What happened to her was shocking."

"Yes, ma'am, it sure was." He stopped

spraying, took off his cap, and scratched his head. "Rumor's flying around that it was Maybelle who beaned Becca on the head with a brisket. Shoot, I've known Maybelle for years. She won't step on an ant."

I placed a handful of guajillo peppers on the scale. "I don't believe Maybelle would harm Becca either."

Buzz resettled his cap, a worried look on his chubby face. "Ever since we broke up, I've taken to driving past Maybelle's place at night — just to make sure she's all right. Never get up enough nerve to stop. Don't think she'd want to see me anyways, but I feel better knowing she's safe. Funny thing is, she's never home Tuesday nights."

My ears perked up at hearing this. "Tuesdays? I think that's when she volunteers at the food bank with Gerilee." As soon as I said this I recalled Maybelle had canceled the night of Becca's murder. She'd said she didn't feel well. That she was home alone.

"Maybelle only works at the food bank on the second Tuesday of each month. I'm saying lately she's never home Tuesday nights."

Generally I subscribe to the philosophy that if you don't want an answer, don't ask the question. But I just couldn't help myself. "What about the night Becca was killed?"

"Nope." He shook his head. "No lights on in her house. No car in the carport."

"Are you sure about that?"

"Positive." Apparently well-versed in multi-tasking, Buzz went back to spraying. "After I finished at the Beaver Dam Motel, I did a drive-by, thinking for sure she'd be home since it was already late, but no sign of her."

This information certainly put a whole new spin on things. I felt stunned. Maybelle had lied not once, but twice, about her whereabouts the night Becca was murdered. And she'd lied to McBride as well. She hadn't been home alone. She hadn't even been home.

CHAPTER 19

The instant Buzz left, I reached for the phone. "Reba Mae? Pack some snacks. We're going on a road trip."

She was ready and waiting when I arrived in front of her house. "I love road trips," she announced, stowing a small insulated bag behind the front seat. She slid into the passenger side and buckled up. "I made a couple ham and Swiss on rye with Russian dressin' case we get hungry later on. Road trips — and stakeouts — always work up an appetite. Where we goin'?"

"You'll see." I put the Beetle in Drive, and we headed for Maybelle's. I parked halfway down the block in the shade of a sweet gum where I hoped we'd go unnoticed.

Reba Mae narrowed her eyes. "This your idea of a road trip? This close we coulda walked."

"Oh, ye of little faith," I scolded. "We need to do a little detective work. Find out what

Maybelle is up to on Tuesday nights."

"Why do we care what the woman does with her free time?"

" 'Cause she lied to us — again. She wasn't 'home alone' the night Becca was killed. She just plain wasn't home — alone or otherwise."

"You're kiddin', right?"

"Wish I were." I donned an oversized pair of sunglasses. "Buzz confessed he drives past her place every night to make sure she's all right. He said she's never home on Tuesdays. It was late when he finished fumigating the No-Tell Motel the night of the murder — and her car wasn't in the carport."

Reba Mae's eyes widened as she digested this. "You don't really believe Maybelle killed Becca, do you?"

"No, of course not, but why lie to us if she has nothing to hide? And lie to McBride as well? In order save Maybelle from herself, we need the truth — the whole truth and nothing but the truth."

Reba Mae reached into her purse and drew out a handful of Hershey's Kisses. "Here, take some," she said. "Chocolate always helps me think clearer."

"I thought you told me it helps relieve stress."

"That too." She unpeeled the foil and popped one in her mouth.

Three Kisses later, I saw Maybelle get in her Honda and back down the drive. "Get down," I hissed.

We slouched as far as we could, hoping we wouldn't be spotted. McBride had once warned me that kiwi-green VW Beetles weren't the best choice for covert operations. Cautiously, I peeked over the steering wheel. Maybelle headed in the opposite direction, so I took off in hot pursuit.

After driving two blocks, she signaled a left turn and took the highway leading south out of town. I followed keeping a respectable distance between us.

"How many car lengths are we supposed to stay behind?" Reba Mae asked, unwrapping another Hershey's Kiss.

"Beats me. I've never tailed anyone before," I replied, proud I knew the lingo. "Tailed" sounded, oh, so much better than "followed."

"Want me to call McBride and ask 'im?"

"No!" My head snapped around to glare at her. "Jeez Louise, I don't need another lecture on minding my own business." Let's check the situation out for ourselves before we decide what to do next."

We were heading in a southeasterly direction. I'd come this same way too many times to count on my way to the Augusta Mall. I slowed at an intersection to allow a logging truck loaded with loblolly pines access onto the highway. These trucks were a common sight in the Southeast. The logs weren't really logs but more of a pile of long, skinny trees stacked on top of one another like toothpicks.

"I hate gettin' behind these trucks. Always worry what would happen if one of those logs pokin' out the back end came loose. Could ruin a transmission. Take out the converter. Ruin a driveshaft."

Time for a change of subject. "How was your date with Wally last night?"

"Okay, I guess." Reba Mae flipped a candy wrapper into the trash. Might've gone better if the boys hadn't shown up when they did. I don't think they cared for him much."

I concentrated on staying a safe length behind the logging truck and still keeping Maybelle in view. "Why do you say that?"

Reba Mae pulled out a pack of gum and offered me a stick. "Could've been 'cause he's not a Braves fan."

"Yeah." I nodded sympathetically. "In this part of the world, that's a deal breaker."

When I refused her offer of gum, she dropped the pack in her purse. "Clay tried to strike up a conversation. Sports mostly, but Wally isn't big on sports. To put it in a nutshell, he went home early. Speakin' of kids, what's Lindsey up to these days? Seems like she's spendin' more time at your place."

"She has been ever since Amber moved in with CJ. Seems Sweetums and Pooh Bear need their alone time. Having a teenager underfoot cramps their style."

Lindsey's defection had been a sore spot of mine. Our daughter was the quintessential daddy's girl. She'd taken our breakup hard. CJ had won her over with fancy gifts — the kind that start with an *i,* as in "iPod," "iPad," and "iPhone." A sporty red Mustang didn't hurt his cause either. It wasn't until lately the tide had turned and she started spending more time at my place.

Leaning forward, Reba Mae peered through the windshield. "Where do you suppose Maybelle's goin'?

"We'll soon find out."

The logging truck eventually turned into a mill that would chew the towering loblollies into particleboard eventually used in the manufacture of furniture. I maintained a respectable distance of at least two car lengths between Maybelle's Honda and my Beetle. Traffic thickened the closer we came to Augusta.

At the junction of Interstate 20 — a major east–west thoroughfare spanning from Texas to South Carolina — Maybelle flicked on her turn signal and merged with eastbound traffic. I followed suit. Surveillance was simpler now. I had no problem staying hidden from view behind a beat-up truck and a Toyota.

"This is the route I take to the mall," Reba Mae commented. "S'pose we have time to duck into Dillard's? They're havin' a big shoe sale."

I blew out a breath. "Reba Mae, we're on a mission, not a shoe-shopping expedition."

"Seems a shame, is all, to waste a perfectly good opportunity. I saw their ad in the paper. All their summer stuff is marked down. This time of year you can find some real good buys."

"We don't know for sure that Maybelle *is* going to the mall."

No sooner had the words left my mouth when I saw Maybelle's turn signal blink. I followed her onto Interstate 520, known locally as the Bobby Jones Expressway. Bobby Jones, as I'd quickly learned upon moving to Dixie, was a legendary golfer and Georgia's fair-haired son. The most successful amateur golfer to ever compete, he retired from competition at the tender age of twenty-eight. He's credited with founding the Augusta National Golf Club, home to the prestigious Masters Tournament, which CJ and I were once fortunate to attend.

"I knew it." Reba Mae pumped her fist in the air when Maybelle turned onto Wrightsboro Road. "We're goin' shoppin'."

The Augusta Mall loomed ahead of us. Maybelle drove past Macy's and pulled into a parking spot near Dillard's. I continued down the row but didn't stop.

"What are you doin'?" Reba Mae cried. "We're gonna lose her."

"Watch and learn," I said. I continued along and found a parking spot the next row over where I had a clear view of her car. "We can either sit and wait — or follow on foot. What do you have in the way of a disguise?"

Reba Mae stared at me blankly for a second, then pawed through her purse like a gopher digging a hole. She produced sunglasses and a silk scarf in a bold geometric print, which she proceeded to wrap around her head and tie. "How's that?"

"You look like my Polish grandmother setting out to buy kielbasa back in Hamtramck,

Michigan."

"Nothin' wrong with kielbasa."

Twisting around in my seat, I rummaged through flotsam and jetsam on the floor behind me. "Ever try *golombki* or taste a pierogi?" I asked, suddenly nostalgic for Sunday dinner at my grandmother's house in what once had been a Polish enclave surrounded by the city of Detroit.

"More likely to feast on shrimp and grits."

"*Golombki* is stuffed cabbage." I managed to unearth a floppy-brimmed straw hat I used on occasion to lower the freckle factor and jammed it on. "Pierogies are these little crescent-shaped dumplings. My grandmother filled hers with potatoes and cheddar cheese. Then she'd fry them in butter and onions. People think Paula Deen loves butter, but they never met my *babci*."

"Get a move on, girl. We're losin' daylight," Reba Mae urged. "You can reminisce on our way home."

We scrambled out of the VW and, darting around parked cars, made our way toward the entrance. I caught my reflection in the rearview mirror of a Camry and giggled. "Think people will think it's strange we're wearing sunglasses indoors?"

Reba Mae opened the department store door and held it for me. "Sure they will,

232

sugar, but folks in the South are too polite to say anythin'."

"There she is," I said, pointing at our quarry. "Looks like Maybelle's making a beeline for the escalator."

We waited till she rose midway to the next floor before we stepped on board. I was careful to keep my head down but my eyes peeled. Reba Mae kept her head turned, studying the racks of summer clothing below. I knew she secretly longed to plunge through the sale items in search of a bargain.

Upon reaching the second floor, Maybelle briskly exited the store and headed in the direction of the food court. When she paused and gazed around expectantly, I grabbed Reba Mae's arm. The two of us pretended interest in a display in the window of a jewelry store.

As I continued to watch out of the corner of my eye, Maybelle walked to the Chic-fil-A kiosk, ordered a soft drink, and sat down at a table for two overlooking the lower level of the mall. A quick glance at her wristwatch told me she was waiting for someone. But who?

"What now?" Reba Mae whispered.

I grabbed a mall directory from a rack. In movies, private investigators always hid behind newspapers, but let's face it, in real life a girl's got to be flexible, learn how to improvise. Reba Mae, following my sterling example, grabbed a directory, too.

We sidled over to the food court and plunked ourselves down at a table partially hidden behind a pillar along the perimeter of the food court. I peered over the top of the directory, which I held in front of me like a shield. "Why do you suppose Maybelle is acting so weird?" I asked, my voice low. "She looks different, too."

"Yeah," Reba Mae concurred. Only the top of her bright scarf was visible above the directory. "I was just about to say the same thing."

"Think she's meeting someone?"

"Her accomplice . . . ?"

"Accomplice . . ." The directory slipped from my hands and flew underneath the table. I scrambled to pick it up without drawing undue attention. "Surely you don't think Maybelle had anything to do with Becca's murder?" I hissed once I'd righted myself.

Reba Mae shrugged. "Just sayin'."

We lapsed into silence. Watch and wait seemed key when it came to stakeouts. Lesson number one at the Piper Prescott School of Detectivology.

"Think we'll be here long?" Reba Mae

asked. "I'm thinking of getting one of those giant chocolate-chip cookies. Want one?"

"Sure," I said. "While you're at it, see if that Chinese place over there has a menu. We can use it as a screen in case people wonder why we're so engrossed in a mall map."

"Good idea."

When Reba Mae nonchalantly sauntered off in search of sustenance, I studied Maybelle. The woman did appear different in a subtle sort of way. Then it dawned on me. She was wearing makeup — lipstick and a little blush. She'd exchanged her plain blouse — usually white — for one of light blue. I saw her sneak peeks at her watch, her expression alternately hopeful and anxious.

"I think she's meeting a man," I told Reba Mae the instant she returned, cookies in one hand, egg rolls in the other. "She's actually wearing makeup."

"Well, I'll be." Reba Mae tipped down her shades for a better look. "Never expected to find Maybelle waitin' on a man."

I'd just popped the last bit of egg roll into my mouth when a middle-aged man in a striped golf shirt approached the food court. Hands in the pockets of pressed khakis, he took up a post near our table. His eyes narrowed, expression thoughtful, he scanned each of the tables in turn, his gaze resting on Maybelle. After a long hesitation, he turned and left.

"Did you see what I saw?" I asked in hushed tones. "I think Maybelle's just been stood up."

Reba Mae clucked her tongue. "Poor woman. She sure has rotten luck when it comes to men."

I took a bite of my chocolate-chip cookie, wanting to test Reba Mae's theory that chocolate helped one think more clearly. I didn't want to embarrass Maybelle by letting on we'd witnessed her rotten luck with the opposite sex from a ringside seat. Being stood up on what appeared to be a blind date was downright humiliating.

CHAPTER 20

"How long do you think she'll wait before she gives up and goes home?"

I let out a sigh. "Maybelle strikes me as the patient sort. We could be here for a spell."

"Why don't I round out our diet and get us a frozen yogurt?"

"How do you figure that's rounding out our diet?"

"Yogurt's dairy. The egg roll was protein."

"And the chocolate-chip cookie?"

"Dessert." She waggled a finger at me. "An often-neglected — but, nevertheless, essential — food group."

While Reba Mae trotted to the yogurt stand, I surreptitiously watched Maybelle. The woman's expression became increasingly glum as the minutes ticked away. I worried she might burst into tears any moment.

"I ordered the fat-free version. Had the

kid pile on extra berries," Reba Mae said when she returned carrying two waxed cups filled with yogurt topped with strawberries. "Experts recommend lots of fruits and vegetables."

"Since when are you the poster child for a well-balanced diet?" I asked, dipping my plastic spoon into the frozen concoction.

"A gal's gotta watch her figure if she wants a man to watch hers," Reba Mae retorted.

Maybelle maintained her vigil long after mine and Reba Mae's sundaes were demolished. Finally admitting defeat, Maybelle rose from the table, tossed her empty soda container in the trash, and started to exit the food court. Head down, preoccupied, she approached the area where we were seated.

"Showtime," I said. Reaching out, I lightly tapped Maybelle's arm as she was about to pass our table.

Before she could shriek, Reba Mae whisked off her scarf and dark glasses. "Don't scream, Maybelle."

"It's us." I removed my sun hat and glasses.

Maybelle's face registered shock at seeing us. "Piper, Reba Mae. What are you ladies doing here?"

Reba Mae gave her a feeble smile. "Would

you believe Dillard's summer clearance?"

Maybelle might not be a good judge of men, but she was no fool. Her eyes darted about searching for telltale shopping bags. "You're spying on me," she said, shock changing to anger.

I patted the empty chair next to me. "Sit down, Maybelle. We need to talk." She opened her mouth to protest, but I cut her off. "You need to be honest with us. No more lies."

The wind seemed to go out of her sails. She dropped down on the chair, her purse clutched to her meager bosom like a life vest in a storm. "I was supposed to meet someone," she admitted, her tone subdued.

"I know," I said.

Reba Mae nodded vigorously. "We saw what happened."

Maybelle's eyes pooled with tears. "Then you know my secret."

Oh, Lordy, were we about to be privy to a confession? Reba Mae and I exchanged nervous glances. "I . . . um . . ." I cleared my throat. "You'll feel better once you talk about it. Get it all out."

"How will I ever be able to look anyone in the eyes again once folks know the despicable thing I've done?" Maybelle wailed.

Despicable thing? As in murder . . . ?
Shouldn't Maybelle be at a nice cozy police station where a hunky police chief could read her rights?

Maybelle placed her purse on the table and put her head in her hands. "I'm so ashamed," she moaned. "I swear, I don't know what made me do it."

Was this the time to call CJ? I shifted uncomfortably in my chair. Reba Mae fiddled with an earring.

"Where did I go wrong?" Maybelle sniffed. She plucked a napkin off the table and dabbed her eyes. "I'm so embarrassed I liketa die. Thousands of women do it every day. I shouldn't have to feel ashamed for giving Internet dating a whirl."

"Maybelle, you have to —" I paused midsentence. "Did I just hear you mention Internet dating?"

Maybelle nodded, her head bowed. Reba Mae shoved another napkin at her, and she blew her nose. "Some women even find husbands on the Internet," she said, sniffling some more. "What's wrong with me? I can't even find a man who wants to meet for coffee Tuesday nights."

"Maybelle," I said, my tone sharper than usual, "are you saying what I think you're saying? That all the time you had us believing you were home alone, you were trying to hook up with men you meet on the Internet?"

"How mortifying!" She wiped her eyes. "A spinster has to resort to drastic measures to catch a man's attention. Unlike Becca, who was pretty and flirty, I blend into the woodwork."

I shook my head in disbelief. "Would you rather have people think you killed Becca?"

"No, of course not, but I don't want to become a laughingstock either. A woman has her pride, you know."

Reba Mae tucked her sunglasses into their case. "When McBride finds out you lied — and, trust me, the man's smart as a whip — it won't sit well."

I nodded agreement. "You're going to look guilty as sin."

"How did the two of you figure out I wasn't home alone?"

"Buzz let it slip when he came to exterminate for spiders," I explained.

"Buzz?" Maybelle frowned. "How would he know how I spend my nights?"

"He admitted that he drives by your place every night. Checks to make sure you're all right. He worries about you."

"Ask me, his conscience is botherin' him for jiltin' you," Reba Mae offered.

"It's that darn man's fault I'm in this predicament." Maybelle tore her wadded-up napkin into shreds. "If not for him, I wouldn't have to get all dolled up and meet strange men."

I nudged Reba Mae with the toe of my sandal, a signal to keep it zipped. If this was Maybelle's notion of being "dolled up," no wonder she had trouble attracting the opposite sex. She was expecting a payback of tsunami proportions from a little lipstick and blush.

"I signed up with a site called Mature Minglers." Maybelle tucked a salt-and-pepper strand behind her ear.

"How's it goin'?" Reba Mae folded her arms on the table and leaned forward. "I've seen their ads and thought about joinin' myself."

I looked at her in surprise. "That's news to me. You never mentioned this before."

Reba Mae shrugged. "What's to mention? My love life is nonexistent."

"Looks to me, it's picked up some with Wally Porter in town."

"Hmph!" she snorted. "Wally will be leavin' soon, and I'll be right back to spendin' Saturday nights watchin' the Lifetime Movie Network on TV."

Maybelle perked up at hearing this. Reaching across the table, she squeezed Reba Mae's hand. "Maybe we can get together some Saturday. Be nice to have company for a change."

"Sure thing." Reba Mae squeezed back. "I'll make us a nice big bowl of buttered popcorn."

It was nice to witness girl bonding in action, but the time had come to get down to brass tacks. "All right, Maybelle," I said, using my stern, no-nonsense tone, "since you weren't home alone the night Becca was killed, where were you?"

"Right here." She blinked back fresh tears. "And I was stood up that night, too."

"I don't suppose you know the man's name?" I asked.

"No." Maybelle shook her head sorrowfully. "He said his first name was Don. He never gave me a last name. Like a ninny, I waited around until the mall was ready to close hoping he'd show, but he never did. By that time, I was real upset and knew I wouldn't be able to sleep. Instead of heading straight home, I took in a late movie."

Ignoring my philosophy that if you don't want the answer don't ask the question, I forged ahead. "Can you prove it?"

Maybelle placed her hand on her purse.

"Course I can. The ticket stub's here in my wallet."

I breathed a sigh of relief. "Did you see anyone you know? Someone who can verify your whereabouts?"

"Not that I recall." Maybelle's frown returned; then she brightened. "I remember stopping for gas before leaving Augusta. Didn't want to drive all the way home on a half-empty tank. I put it on my credit card and kept the receipt."

"Well, that's that." Reba Mae jumped up and collected our trash. "Still time to check out shoes before the stores close."

"Hold your horses, Reba Mae," I said, then turned to Maybelle. "First thing tomorrow, Maybelle, you need to see Chief McBride. Admit you lied about your alibi. Show him the receipts so he can see for himself you weren't anywhere near Brandy-wine Creek at the time Becca was murdered."

"Whatever you think best, Piper," Maybelle promised.

"One thing I don't understand," I said, climbing to my feet. "Why didn't you tell the chief the truth at the outset? Why lie?"

"Foolish me." Maybelle gave a self-deprecating smile. "I thought if I waited Chief McBride would find the real killer and the fact that I'm a failure at Internet dating would never come to light."

The three of us started the trek toward Dillard's. "You positive you saved those receipts?" I asked Maybelle when Reba Mae paused to window-shop.

Maybelle patted her imitation leather purse. "All safe and sound."

Finding Becca's body had taken the shine off jogging. However, the next morning it was time for me to get back into the saddle — make that sneakers. The day was still in its infancy, with heat and humidity waiting in the wings. During summers in Georgia, the best time for strenuous exercise is early in the day. Before the mercury climbed and energy plummeted. Ideally, afternoons were spent lounging in the shade with a good book and a cool drink.

I donned gym shorts, sports bra, and a faded University of Georgia T-shirt with GO DAWGS scrawled across the front. If the barbecue festival brought in swarms of customers as I hoped, I had planned to reward my hard work with moisture-wicking running shorts and a snazzy racerback tank top. My dream shorts went by the wayside when I wrote a check to the exterminator. I still hadn't given up on the racerback top.

Casey, ready and waiting, thumped his tail on the floor, urging me to hurry.

"Okay, buddy, let's go," I said, clipping on his leash. "Cadaver dog or not, no more dead bodies. Deal?"

I started off at a brisk walk, breathing deeply and swinging my arms, to warm up my muscles. After five minutes of breathing and swinging, I picked up the pace. Casey trotted obediently alongside. Birds chorused from the thick foliage of trees and shrubs. I waved to a man on the porch of a brick colonial as he sipped coffee and read the morning paper. I called out a greeting to Wanda Needmore, CJ's paralegal, who was deadheading petunias, and narrowly avoided being sprayed by water spouting from her neighbor's irrigation system. The tangy, mouthwatering aroma of roasting meat wafted through the air. Dress rehearsal, I surmised, for the festival's rapidly approaching judgment day.

I elected a circuitous route, one that would bypass the town square with its reminder of Becca Dapkins planted among the azaleas. As I rounded the corner of the street behind my shop, I slowed to catch my breath.

"Ready for some kibble?" I asked Casey. I interpreted his *woof* to mean "yes."

Together we angled through the vacant lot toward my rear door. Judging from the amount of debris that had accumulated since the last cleanup, I realized it was time for litter patrol. Maybe I should ask McBride to deputize me so I could write citations. The coffers of Brandywine Creek would soon overflow. They might even dedicate a park in my honor. Better yet, the Piper Prescott Recycling Center.

Preoccupied with thoughts of discarded cans and bottles, I dug in the pocket of my gym shorts for my key. Then realized a key wouldn't be necessary. The back door of Spice It Up! stood ajar. Even an amateur sleuth such as myself could distinguish scratch marks on a lock.

When I gave the door a tentative shove, it swung open. To enter or not to enter? Or should I call the police and stay put? Undecided, I caught my lower lip between my teeth. I didn't want to be like the girl in a horror movie who, dumb as a box of rocks, went down creaking steps into a darkened basement while the audience screamed a warning. Instead, I fumbled for my cell phone and dialed 911.

Dorinda, the dispatcher, recognized my voice. "Don't tell me you found another dead body."

"Not this time." I managed a shaky laugh. "I think someone broke into my shop while I was jogging."

"Stay right where you are," Dorinda instructed. "An officer's on the way."

I gingerly lowered myself to the ground and rested my back against the warming brick. Casey hunkered down beside me. I dreaded another lecture from McBride. I could hear him already: *Get a stronger lock, don't play detective, leave police work to the police.* Yada yada yada.

To my immense relief — and equally immense disappointment — it wasn't McBride who responded to my call but Sergeant Beau Tucker, one of CJ's poker buddies.

"Hey there, Piper." Beau hitched his trousers higher on his paunchy stomach. "Dorinda said to hustle on over. That you had a break-in."

I rose and brushed dirt from the seat of my pants. "The back door was partially open. I debated whether to check things for myself, but decided to call you instead."

"Good thinkin'." Unsnapping his holster, he drew out his service weapon. "No tellin' if the perp is still on the premises."

I resisted the urge to pace while Beau entered my shop, his gun at the ready. Casey sat near the door, his little body tense, his dark eyes shiny as buttons. After what seemed an eternity, Beau returned, reholstered his pistol, and spoke into a radio clipped to his shoulder. "Place secure, Dorinda. Tell McBride no need for backup."

I felt foolish now that my nerves had settled. "Thanks for coming."

"No sense takin' chances. Like I tell my wife, follow your gut." He took a small black notebook and a pen from the pocket of his uniform shirt. "How much cash do you keep on hand?"

"Not much. Fifty dollars usually." I rubbed my arms to erase the sudden chill. "Why? Was I robbed?"

Beau jotted this down. "Your cash register's been pried open. Looks like the crook did a smash and grab. In and out. Speed and surprise. It's all over in a jiffy. I want you to go inside, take a good look around. See if anythin' missin' beside the cash."

I did as he directed, but other than an empty cash drawer, nothing seemed to be disturbed. I offered up a silent prayer of gratitude that Lindsey had spent the night at a girlfriend's. No telling what might have happened if Lindsey had woken up and confronted a robber. She could have been hurt or killed. If McBride's theory that

Becca had been the victim of a robbery gone awry proved true, Lindsey might have suffered the same fate. I broke out in a cold sweat. The very thought turned my knees to jelly.

"I'll send a man over to dust for prints." Beau tucked the notebook back in his pocket. "In the meantime, I'd splurge on a new lock."

As soon as he left, I reached for my cell and called Gray's Hardware. My trendy racerback jogging top would have to wait a bit longer.

CHAPTER 21

"Honeybun, you all right?" Reba Mae, accompanied by a dapper-looking Wally Porter, hurried into Spice It Up! "Jolene phoned, said you were robbed."

"Still a little shaken, but otherwise I'm fine."

News travels fast in small towns. Bad news even faster. In olden times, word traveled by tom-toms, Pony Express, telegraph, telephone. None of these would've been necessary if Jolene Tucker had been on the scene. Jolene's the wife of Beau Tucker, part-time poker player, full-time cop. She's Brandywine Creek's version of Gossip Girl. Dottie Hemmings and Ned Feeney were nothing to sneeze at either when it came to spreading the news but couldn't compete with Jolene.

"Sure you're okay?" Reba Mae's pretty brown eyes mirrored her concern. "Wally and I were shocked at the news."

Wally bobbed his shaved head. "Anything we can do?"

"No, but I appreciate the offer." I made an expansive gesture to encompass the tidy shelves stocked with spices from the four corners of the earth. "As you can see, nothing else was disturbed."

"I hope you aren't in the habit of keeping a lot of cash on hand," Wally said.

"No, I usually deposit the day's receipts after closing. I only keep fifty dollars in small bills to make change the next day."

"That's wise. Lots of people on drugs these days are looking to score fast bucks. That sort doesn't worry if someone gets hurt in the bargain."

"First thing I'm goin' to do when I get to the Klassy Kut is check the locks," Reba Mae declared. "No tellin' where the robber's gonna strike next."

"You ladies might think about investing in a good security system," Wally advised. "If you like, I can give you the names of some reputable companies."

Reba Mae squeezed his arm and beamed up at him. "Wally has connections."

"Thanks for the suggestion, but Ned Feeney is coming by later to install the finest lock Gray's Hardware carries. For the time being, it's the most I can afford."

"Locks are good but, in my estimation, not much of a deterrent for anyone serious about breaking and entering. A woman living alone can't be too careful."

Wally's words made me nervous. I ran my hands down the sides of my apron. "I'm not alone. Most times my daughter's here. And my guard dog is ready to go into attack mode the instant I give the signal."

Wally's muddy-gray gaze darted to the rear of the shop where Casey rested behind a baby gate. "Cute dog," he commented. "Border terrier?"

I glanced over my shoulder. Casey lazily opened one eye, then promptly went back to napping. "Mutt," I admitted. "From a long, distinguished line of mutts. He shows great potential, however."

Reba Mae hooked her arm through Wally's. "My first client of the day canceled — her mother-in-law fell and broke her hip. So I invited Wally over for breakfast this morning."

"Eggs Benedict." Wally patted his trim midriff. "I'd have to join a gym if I stayed in town much longer."

The man was built solid as a fire hydrant, and, to me, it looked more muscle than fat. "Reba Mae's a fantastic cook," I concurred.

Wally placed a manicured hand over Reba

Mae's. "I told her it's a damn shame she didn't enter the competition. She'd give the others a run for their money."

"Speaking of barbecue," Reba Mae said, trying hard not to look too pleased at the compliment, "our next stop is the Chamber of Commerce. Wally needs a final count on the number of entrants. Maybelle promised she'd have the information for him this morning."

"Have a good one." I waved them off with a smile.

No sooner had the door closed behind them when Tex Mahoney sauntered in looking larger than life in cowboy boots, Stetson, and faded jeans with a silver and turquoise belt buckle the size of a small platter.

"Mornin', ma'am." He tipped his hat. "Heard tell you had your share of excitement this early in the day. Sorry to hear about the break-in. Glad to see you're all right."

I went behind the counter and switched on the computer. "The thief got away with fifty dollars in petty cash. In return, I get a new lock for my door."

He tugged his ear. "Coulda been worse. Even so, it makes a body feel vulnerable."

"It certainly does." *Vulnerable.* Tex's comment nailed the sentiment I was experiencing. With an effort, I shook off the feeling and concentrated on business. "Is there something special I can help you with?"

"I'm on the prowl for somethin' that imparts a unique flavor to my sauce. Subtle but not overpowerin'. I thought I'd add a smidgen of anise and see what happens."

"Anise is an interesting choice." Tex followed me as I left the counter and headed for the Hoosier cabinet where I kept the majority of my baking spices. "Anise should impart a sweet, licorice-like taste, warm and fruity. Most of my customers use it when baking cookies or cake, but in the Mediterranean it's in demand to flavor aperitifs and liqueurs such as ouzo and anisette."

Tex grinned. "I'll keep that in mind should I get a hankerin' for one or the other."

I picked up a jar containing the small, oval seeds. "Would you like the anise whole or ground?"

"Ground if you would, ma'am."

I brought out the coffee mill I used exclusively for grinding spice. "While I'm doing this, take a look around. You might find other spices you'd like to experiment with as well."

He prowled the aisles, picking up and setting down, before finally settling on a half-ounce container of cardamom pods. "Not every day one can find spice this fresh," he commented. "I'll be sure to recommend this place to friends who might be travelin' through this part of the country."

"Please do." I smiled at the prospect as I placed his purchases in a bag and added one of my business cards for good measure. "I also accept mail-order requests."

"Service with a smile." He handed me his Visa. "You'd make a good Texan, little lady."

Little lady? It was impossible to take offense when the words slipped out so naturally. I ran his card through my machine and waited until it printed a receipt. "Did you know cumin and anise are in the same family? Caraway too."

"You don't say." He gave his earlobe another tug, then let out a long sigh. "I need to make a confession. My conscience's been botherin' me somethin' fierce. Wish I woulda kept my big mouth shut, but that's not my strong suit."

I'm no shrink — not a bartender or hairdresser either — but the man seemed to be in a quandary and needed to unburden himself. "If you want to talk about what's troubling you . . ."

He scuffed the floor with the toe of a well-worn boot. "Truth of the matter, I'm ashamed of myself for tattlin' to Chief McBride about a conversation I overheard between the woman who was killed and that nice Miss Maybelle. The lady doesn't strike me a cold-blooded killer. I know she's a friend of yours. S'pose she'd forgive me once I apologized?"

Tipping my head to one side, I eyed the man as I mulled over my response. Maybelle wasn't much for sharing recipes, and except for Becca Dapkins, I've never known her to harbor a grudge. "Only thing you can do is ask," I said slowly. "This time of day, Maybelle can usually be found at the Chamber."

"Maybe I'll mosey over, see for myself. Thanks for your help, Miss Piper." He touched fingertips to the brim of his Stetson. As I watched him stroll off, I couldn't help but think that perhaps Maybelle wasn't the failure with men she believed herself to be.

Since there were no customers at the moment, I released the latch on the baby gate and let Casey roam. I began to clean the spice grinder but dropped the cleaning cloth on the floor. Before I could retrieve it, Casey pounced on it. I ordered him to drop it, but apparently thinking it was a game, he ran off with the cloth clamped between his jaws. I got a clean cloth and went about my task. When I finished a short while later, I noticed Casey running around in circles chasing his tail.

"What are you doing, you crazy little dog?" I asked, both exasperated and amused by his antics.

Casey responded by lying on the heart pine floor and rolling around. I watched his bizarre behavior for several minutes. Then, like a lightbulb going off above the head of a cartoon character, the answer occurred to me. I recalled an article I'd read that said some dogs go crazy over anise seed like cats do over catnip. The effects would wear off shortly, but in the meantime Casey was in doggie heaven.

The morning passed quickly with people stopping by to ask questions about my stolen cash but leaving with a jar of this or that. I'd just finished a late lunch — the last of the chicken salad — when Amber Leigh Ames, dressed in a cherry-red tank top and a white twill skirt that showcased her long, tanned legs, breezed in,

"Hey there, Piper." Miss Peach Pit stood hands on hips and gazed around. "Pity your place isn't doin' much business. Guess folks don't care much for bare brick walls and old floorboards."

I tossed my paper plate and napkin in the trash. "Spice shopping?" I asked, ignoring her snide remark.

"Heavens no. The less time I spend in a kitchen, the better I like it." She flicked a disparaging glance at my sunny yellow apron. "Aprons remind me of my meemaw. I wouldn't be caught dead wearin' anythin' so tacky."

Since I was feeling my temper rise, it was time to cut to the chase. Sliding off the stool behind the counter, I folded my arms across my apron-clad bosom. "Out with it, Amber. You're not here to discuss the merits of ancho chili peppers versus árbol."

"Well," she drawled prettily, "CJ and I were talkin' the other night, and —"

I placed my hands over my ears. "If this was pillow talk, please, I don't want to hear it."

"No." Amber tossed her long brunette tresses. "Our conversation took place over dinner."

I slowly lowered my hands, my expression wary. "Exactly how do I fit into this 'conversation' of yours?"

"CJ and I think it would be a show of solidarity and goodwill if you paid half of Lindsey's expenses to our weddin' — room, airfare, incidentals, and such. Let her know we're one happy family."

"Room, airfare, *and* incidentals?" I sputtered. I needed a new lock on my back door, a high-tech security system, a cute little jogging outfit, not a trip to the Caribbean in peak season. "I'm afraid I can't afford to be so . . . extravagant," I said at last.

"I found this absolutely amazing five-star resort in Punta Cana with a spa," Amber prattled on. "The Christmas holidays are popular travel times to the Dominican Republic, but if we book early we can get a discount on airfare."

"If CJ wants Lindsey at his wedding, he's going to have to pick up the tab," I said with finality.

I was spared further discussion when Ned Feeney, local handyman and gofer, meandered in. "Hey, Miz Piper." He brandished the paper sack he held. "Mr. Gray sent me over to put a new lock on your back door. Hope I'm not interruptin'."

"Hey yourself, Ned. Your timing's perfect." I felt like giving the man a hug. "Miss Ames was just leaving."

Amber opened her mouth to speak, then snapped it shut. Turning on her heel, she stalked out.

Ned sniffed his armpit. "Hope it wasn't me."

"You're fine, Ned." Ned Feeney was a lanky, affable man somewhere between the ages of thirty and sixty. His loopy grin and prominent Adam's apple always put me in mind of the Gomer Pyle character on the old *Andy Griffith Show*.

Shoving back the bill of his ever-present University of Georgia ball cap, Ned asked, "Heard the news?"

"You mean news other than me being robbed of petty cash?" I asked as I started to straighten a shelf.

"Everyone's talkin' about how Brandywine Creek's undergoin' a crime spree, the likes of which never been seen before."

"Surely you're exaggerating." Ned relished gossip more than catfish and sweet tea.

"No sirree." Ned shook his head. "First off, Miz Dapkins gets bashed on the head and her purse stole. Next your place is robbed. And now Miz Humphries at the Chamber reported her wallet stole out of her purse while she was attendin' to folks."

Maybelle's wallet stolen?

Not only her wallet but her alibi also.

CHAPTER 22

"Ned, that's awful! Are you sure?"

He crossed his heart. "Sure as church on Sunday."

I was stunned to learn about Maybelle's wallet being stolen. My first instinct was to trot over to the Chamber. Hear the details firsthand. But I couldn't very well run off and leave Ned Feeney in charge of Spice It Up!

"Folks are havin' a conniption," Ned continued. "Mr. Gray said he's keepin' a .38 under the counter. Ever think about gettin' a gun, Miz Piper?"

"No. Not now, not ever." I resumed the task of straightening shelves. "Besides, I have a better weapon — a bona fide guard dog."

As though sensing he was the topic of conversation, Casey lifted his head off his paws and yawned.

"Right cute little dog you have, but he

didn't keep your store safe this mornin', now did he?"

"Casey wasn't here at the time," I replied, feeling compelled to defend my mutt.

"Lots of ladies have little pistols. Carry 'em in their pocketbooks. Miz Hemmings has a pink one. If you ask all nice, she'll probably show you. Might even tell you where she bought it."

"Shouldn't you get started on my lock?" I suggested. "No telling how long it might take."

"Yes, ma'am. I'm on it like white on rice." His stride ungainly, he headed toward the rear of the shop. " 'Preciate Mr. Gray at the hardware givin' me some odd jobs. Mr. Strickland over at the Eternal Rest hasn't had a single customer since Miz Dapkins passed last week. Not even any from the old folks home."

I fervently hoped the undertaker's business remained slow. I didn't care that funerals were classified as major social events. I'd had my fill.

Ned was still puttering with the lock when Lindsey returned from her friend Taylor's. "Someone said you were robbed!" Lindsey rushed over and pecked me on the cheek. "You okay, Mom?"

I ran my hand down her hair. "I'm fine,

sweetie. Thankfully, the thief only made off with the petty cash."

"I meant to get home earlier, but Taylor and I stayed up late watching a DVD and we overslept. Then with all this humidity, I couldn't do a thing with my hair. Lucky for me, I remembered Amber has a ceramic flatiron she said I could borrow, so I went over to Daddy's before coming here." Then, like quicksilver, her mood changed. "Is it true?" she asked, fisting her hands on her hips.

"Don't take that tone with me, young lady," I said sharply. "Is what true?"

Her blue-gray eyes stormy, Lindsey jutted her lower lip out much like she used to do as a toddler gearing up for a tantrum. "Amber said you refused to let me go to her and Daddy's wedding."

I slammed a jar of vanilla beans down on a shelf. "I merely told Amber that if they wanted you as maid of honor, Daddy's going to have to foot the bill."

"How much can a plane ticket cost?" she asked plaintively. "Amber said there's a discount for booking early."

Amber said. Amber said. I was sick and tired of "Amber said." "It wasn't only the cost of round-trip airfare," I said through clenched teeth, aware of Ned, still at the back, latching on to every syllable. "We're talking gown, shoes, room, *and* 'incidentals,' which I translated as spa treatments. We're talking at least a thousand dollars, maybe more. I can't afford that kind of money."

"Hmph," Lindsey sniffed, but I could tell she was doing the math. From the hours she'd spent working behind the counter she knew I struggled to make ends meet. "Maybe I can earn enough to pay for the airfare by babysitting. There's still time between now and December. I'll talk to Daddy, see if he'll pay the difference."

I nodded, grateful she understood and accepted the situation. "Say, I've got an idea. I can't pay more than minimum wage, but keep track of the hours you work. I'll write you a check the end of each month."

All traces of pique vanished, and she smiled. "Deal, but I'll work for free till you earn back what you lost this morning."

"You can start right now." Untying my apron, I handed it to her. "I want to run over to the Chamber. Have a chat with Maybelle."

"Okay." Lindsey donned an apron, careful not to muss her newly straightened locks. "Don't wait up for me tonight. I'll probably get in late. Doc wants the entire Pit Crew at his place to review plans for the festival.

He's even fixing us dinner."

I gave a lock of her hair a playful tug. "Let me guess. Ribs or brisket?"

"Neither." She laughed. "Doc said by the end of this week we'd have our fill of barbecue. He also told me to remind you to practice your steps for the shag contest."

I was nearly out the door when she called out to me, "Oh, I nearly forgot. Doc said you need to make an appointment to have Casey neutered!"

Neutered? I mentally cringed at the thought. Casey looked up at me, trust in his big brown eyes. My sweet little puppy had no idea what was in store for him. I beat a hasty exit.

I found Maybelle behind her desk at the Chamber of Commerce staring blankly at the computer screen. She glanced up as I entered, then promptly burst into tears at the sight of me.

"Y-you h-heard?" she sobbed.

"So it's true," I said, handing her a tissue from a box on the counter. "Ned told me the bad news."

"What am I going to do, Piper?" she wailed, dabbing her eyes. "I kept both the movie stub and the receipt for gas in my billfold. I wanted them to be safe until I showed them to Chief McBride."

"There, there." I clumsily rubbed her back. "I thought you were going to see the chief first thing this morning."

"I was," she sniffed. "I did."

Confused, I sank into a chair next to hers. "What happened?"

"Dorinda was on the desk. She said the chief was in an important meeting with the mayor and city council. Asked if I could come back later. I had to open the Chamber so told her I would."

I blew out a breath. This was a fine pickle. I was convinced of Maybelle's innocence, but McBride would be a hard sell without evidence to back up her claim.

"You've got to help me, Piper." Maybelle broke down in a fresh bout of weeping.

I promised to do what I could, but with all the crying going on I'm not sure whether she heard me or not.

"We need to look through Butch's old yearbooks. ASAP," I said the instant Reba Mae answered her phone.

"Sure, but what's the rush?"

"Maybelle's alibi is gone with the wind. Somebody — probably the same jerk who helped himself to my petty cash — made off with her wallet while she was busy helping a tourist."

"Oh no," Reba Mae groaned. "That's terrible. How she holdin' up?"

"Not well," I said. "That's why we need to look for possible suspects — other than Maybelle. Do you have plans for this evening?"

"Free as a breeze. Wally's doin' paperwork tonight, but he's invited both of us for dinner at Felicity's Friday night. He claims to be quite a cook and wants to show off."

"Count me in. Maybe we can persuade Felicity to give us a guided tour of her bed-and-breakfast. I've been dying to see what she's done with the place. Don't bother fixing dinner. I'll bring Chinese." I disconnected.

Half an hour later, I arrived on Reba Mae's doorstep toting a large paper sack from Ming Wah. "Hope you're hungry," I said, plunking the bag down on the kitchen table.

"Famished," she replied, taking wineglasses from the cupboard. While I unpacked a series of waxed containers, Reba Mae brought out a bottle of chilled pinot grigio and poured us each a glass. "Butch's yearbooks were in the attic exactly where I thought they were. Are we lookin' for anythin' specific or just want to make fun of the crazy hairdos?"

I divided the wonton soup into bowls while Reba Mate got out silverware. "Tempting as that may be," I said, "I have something different it mind — albeit a long shot."

"I'm all ears."

I heaped plates with sweet-and-sour pork, egg rolls, and rice, and we dug in. "Becca Dapkins never would have won the Miss Congeniality award if she was the only contestant."

"Sing it, sister." Reba Mae speared a chunk of sweet-and-sour. "Hell's bells, Becca wouldn't even be runner-up."

"Since we're assuming Maybelle's innocent, we need to look elsewhere for the perp. Think outside the box, so to speak. Ask ourselves who might've wanted Becca dead."

Reba Mae scooped up a forkful of rice. "Think how many folks she might've ticked off at her job with the water department alone. She could've added late charges to water and sewer bills. Late charges add up in a hurry. Or worse yet, she could've had someone's water shut off."

"Good point, but I thought we'd start with the obvious and work from there." I opened a packet of soy sauce and drizzled it over my rice. "Normally the number one suspect is the vic's husband or boyfriend. According to McBride, however, Buzz Oliver has an ironclad alibi. So the question is: Who else had it in for Becca?"

Reba Mae took a sip of wine. "You're assumin' Becca's murder wasn't a random act of violence. Not a robbery gone wrong. Who's to say Becca didn't resist when some creep tried robbin' her — and she died as a result?"

I tucked an errant curl behind my ear. "As hard as I try, Reba Mae, I can't shake the feeling that Becca was attacked in her own home."

Reba Mae scraped the last piece of pork from the carton. "Don't get your panties in a twist, hon. I'm just saying, is all."

I topped off my wine, needing time to think more than I needed the wine. "I keep remembering the broken fingernail we found in Becca's kitchen. Knowing how vain she was, I'm certain she'd never leave the house without repairing it. Then there were the missing rubber gloves and empty Clorox jug. How many TV shows have you seen where a killer cleans up a crime scene with bleach?"

"Yeah, I guess."

"And another thing's been bothering me." I sat straighter and leaned forward. "I didn't notice any sign of forced entry, did you? No busted locks, no broken windows. If my theory is right, it means Becca probably knew her killer and let him — or her — into her house."

Reba Mae shuddered dramatically. "That's downright scary. Are you gonna tell me where Butch's high school yearbooks fit into the picture? Or keep me guessin'?"

"Barbara Bunker Quinlan," I said slowly and succinctly. "Becca and Barbie hated each other. Too bad you missed the fireworks the day Barbie pulled into town. Becca called Barbie 'trailer trash' and asked if she'd worked as a stripper. For a minute or so, I thought there was going to be a catfight in the middle of my shop. Why, just yesterday Barbie declared Becca a bitch and said the world was better off without her."

"That still doesn't explain why you want to pore through musty ol' yearbooks."

I idly broke open a fortune cookie. "It's a long shot, I know, but I hope it will give me a little more . . . insight . . . into Barbie's character."

"Okay then, let's get to it. But first" — Reba Mae grinned — "I want to see what's inside my fortune cookie."

I raised a brow when she burst into laughter. "Care to share?"

" 'A new pair of shoes will do you a world of good.' How perfect is that?" she asked. "Now read yours."

" 'A conclusion is simply the place where you got tired of thinking.' Mine's even more perfect," I said with a grin. "Ready or not, yearbooks here we come."

We quickly cleared the table and loaded the dishwasher. Wineglasses in hand, we adjourned to the living room, where four yellowed and dusty yearbooks awaited our perusal on the coffee table.

"Way I figure, Barbie must've been in the same class as Butch. McBride and CJ were a couple years ahead of them."

I picked up the book on top. "Let's start with Butch's freshman year and work our way from there."

Reba Mae and I sat side by side on the sofa, flipping through the pages, exclaiming over the hairstyles and fashions. Her lips curved in a wistful smile at seeing photos of Butch in his football uniform, his helmet tucked in the crook of his arm, a big grin on his face.

"The boys remind me of their dad," I said.

There were other familiar faces, too. Wyatt McBride, member of both the varsity football squad and softball team, stared squarely into the camera's lens. CJ, president of his class, smiled confidently into the camera. But in the space Barbie's freshman photo should have occupied was the notation "Unavailable."

Reba Mae opened Butch's sophomore yearbook. "Here's to better luck this time."

More photos of Butch, McBride, and CJ. Senior year, McBride had been quarterback and captain of varsity football. CJ had again been elected class president and been voted homecoming king. I'd almost given up finding anything of value when I spotted the person I'd hoped to find.

"There she is!" I cried, pointing at a girl half-hidden in the second row of girls from the Future Homemakers club.

"You sure?" Reba Mae squinted for a better look. "She looks totally different."

"There's her name. It's her all right." I looked long and hard at the unsmiling teen with drab, stringy hair. She looked unhappy, awkward. Barbie bore little resemblance to the bombshell she was today. "Except for those spooky eyes of hers, I don't think I'd have recognized her."

"Look at the girl standing next to her." Reba Mae jabbed the page with her index finger. "The book gives her name as Claudia McBride. Must be Wyatt's sister."

I drew the book closer for a better look.

Claudia and her brother shared a strong family resemblance. Same dark hair, high cheekbones. I couldn't tell from the photo, but I'd bet she had the same electric-blue eyes.

"Does Wyatt ever mention her?"

"A time or two. From the little he's said, I gather she's living somewhere in California. I don't think they're close."

By her senior year, Barbie had undergone a metamorphosis. Though still unsmiling, she'd developed a knockout figure with full breasts, trim waist, and slender hips. And, according to a photo showing members of the National Honor Society, she was also smart.

While it was all very interesting, I still hadn't found anything that would explain the animosity between Becca and the much younger Barbie. Or anything that would connect the two women. I was about to snap the yearbook closed when my eyes fell upon a page with a banner titled STAFF AND FACULTY. There, staring back at me, was the answer to my questions. I'd found the missing link.

I was barely able to contain my excitement. "Reba Mae, do you see what I see?"

"Jeez Louise!" she breathed, peering over my shoulder.

" 'Arthur Dapkins, Assistant Principal,' "
I read. " 'Becca Ferguson, School Secretary.' "

We looked at each other, then down at the photos again. "Becca née Ferguson Dapkins," we said in perfect two-part harmony.

I sat back to digest this tidbit. The plot thickened. Becca, it seemed, had worked in the school office the whole time CJ, McBride, Butch, and Barbie were students. *Hmm . . .*

CHAPTER 23

After leaving Reba Mae's, I didn't feel like going home to an empty apartment. Instead, I procrastinated by looping around the square several times, then repeated the performance by driving around the block. I even drove past Maybelle's house to see if she was "home alone" and spotted her Honda in the carport. For a split second, I toyed with the notion of stopping, seeing if she was in the mood for company, but decided against it.

Next, I considered joining Doug and his Pit Crew at Pets 'R People for chatter and companionship. When I'd called earlier to schedule Casey's nip and tuck, Doug had mentioned he was making his team New York–style pizza — complete with New York–style pizza dough and homemade sauce. Yummo! Alas, I was too full to eat another bite, yet too weak not to give in to temptation. Rather than cruise around aimlessly — or consume extra calories — I elected to take a walk.

Upon hearing my key in the lock, Casey seconded the motion. His tail swished back and forth like a metronome when I reached for his leash. Together we strolled down Main Street; then on a whim I turned down a side street. We veered away from the business district into a residential area populated with well-maintained older homes, my ex-mother-in-law's among them.

The balmy night was a gentle caress against my skin. The temperature warm, but without the heat of the day. The high-pitched melody of cicadas was occasionally punctuated by the trumpet of tree frogs. A full moon hung suspended from a blue-black canopy pinpricked by thousands — maybe millions — of tiny stars. A perfect night for sitting on a porch swing. For holding hands and sharing secrets.

A night for lovers. Times like this I longed for porch swings, hand-holding . . . and intimacy. Casey, oblivious to my mood, lifted his leg and watered a crepe myrtle.

Though it was still relatively early, not yet ten o'clock, I was surprised to find lights still burning in Melly's windows. I was about to pass quietly, but Casey had other ideas. Straining on the leash and yapping his silly head off, he tugged me toward the walk leading to Melly's front porch.

"Hush, boy! Quiet!"

My admonition had little effect. Before I could silence him, Melly appeared in the doorway, her figure backlit by light from the foyer. Opening the door a crack, she peeked out.

"Piper, dear, is that you?" she called.

The porch light flashed on, its beam strong enough to illuminate half the neighborhood. No energy-saving bulbs for her, no sirree, Bob.

"See what you've done," I hissed at Casey, who seemed immune to my scolding. "Hey, Melly," I said, stepping closer.

"What brings you out wandering this time of night?"

"I'm just taking Casey out for a spin."

"Well, why don't the two of you come in? Sit a spell."

"I don't want to be a bother," I said, trying to find an excuse but failing abysmally.

"Nonsense," she pooh-poohed, holding open the door. "I was about to have a cup of herbal tea. I made a batch of gingersnaps today," she added, taking unfair advantage of my weakness.

"All right then, but we won't stay long."

Casey trotted up the walk ahead of me as

though he owned the place. Melly held up one hand, stopping me as I started to fasten his leash to a leg of a porch chair. "Don't bother, dear. He's welcome inside. Your little pet is always on his best behavior whenever Lindsey brings him to visit. Besides, he knows if he's a good boy I have treats for him. Make yourselves comfy while I get the refreshments."

"You little beggar," I scolded when Melly left for the kitchen. "No wonder you started barking and refused to budge."

Unabashed, Casey sat at my feet, a semblance of a smile on his furry little face.

It had been a while since I'd been inside Melly's home. Except for the presence of a flat-screen television that took up half a wall, nothing seemed to have changed. The large screen reminded me of the one at Becca's. Apparently the women shared a passion for watching television.

Melly returned carrying a tray set with a pretty rose-patterned tea set, hand-embroidered linen napkins, and a plate of cookies, which she set on the coffee table. She looked different, I mused; then it dawned on me. She was dressed more casually than usual in a flowered cotton top, pale-blue capris, and, of course, her pearls.

"It's nice to have company. Evenings can

be lonely." After handing Casey a doggie biscuit, she poured tea into porcelain cups.

"Yes, they can be," I agreed. Maybe I should suggest the formation of a lonely hearts club. Reba Mae could be the reigning president, Melly and Maybelle charter members. It could lead to all sorts of . . . interesting . . . exchanges. Thank goodness the presence of Doug Winters in my life saved me from such a membership. Once the BBQ festival was over, I planned to make sure we spent more time together. I helped myself to a gingersnap. "I hope we're not keeping you up past your bedtime."

"Good gracious, no. I've become somewhat of a night owl these past couple years." Always the epitome of well-bred Southern womanhood, she daintily spread a napkin across her lap.

We sipped and nibbled in companionable silence while Casey lounged contentedly on the floor at my feet. I had to admit Melly really did make the best gingersnaps ever. I liked to think they were even better since she started using Spice It Up! spices exclusively. Ginger, cinnamon, and cloves. I'd finally convinced her to toss out all her old tins and buy fresher spices in smaller quantities. She'd even begun to purchase whole nutmegs grown in Grenada and grate them herself for maximum flavor.

I happened to glance into the adjoining dining room. Instead of the Victorian soup tureen that had always occupied pride of place on the Queen Anne–style table, there was a sleek state-of-the-art laptop.

Melly followed the direction of my gaze. "Solitaire," she said. "I like to play solitaire." Jumping up so quickly her napkin fell to the carpet, she hurried to the computer and snapped it shut.

"Solitaire's fun," I said, puzzled by her strange behavior. Was Melly keeping secrets? If she'd started Internet dating like Maybelle Humphries, I wanted to be the last to know. "I read a recent magazine article that said games are a good way for seniors to keep the minds sharp. To stave off dementia."

"Mmm." Melly replaced her napkin on her lap and sipped her tea.

I wondered if the day had come for *me* to take preventative measures to ward off memory loss. I could start small, maybe buy a book of crossword puzzles or Sudoku. Lessen my odds by regularly watching American's favorite quiz show, *Jeopardy!* Keep track of the number of times I won the final round.

I drew one leg up under the other and

snuggled more comfortably into the corner of the sofa. "Melly, you've lived your entire life in Brandywine Creek. How well did you know Becca Dapkins?"

"Becca . . . ?" Melly's hand flew to her throat to fiddle with her pearls. "Why?"

I would've thought the interest obvious. After all, Casey, my trusty sidekick, and I were the ones who found Becca sprawled in the azaleas. "Curious is all," I said with a casual shrug. "Just trying to make sense out of what happened."

"I'm not one to speak ill of the dead, but . . ."

". . . but?"

"Becca Dapkins was a vile, mean-spirited woman is all."

So much for not speaking ill of the dead, I thought. I swirled the tea in my cup, careful not to spill a drop, knowing Melly would send me the cleaning bill. "I confess, I didn't know her all that well, but she just never struck me as being a happy person."

"Becca was never happy unless she got her own way. She was like that even as a girl."

"So you've known her a long time."

Melly picked a crumb from her napkin. "Becca Ferguson Dapkins came to live with her grandmother in Brandywine Creek when she was barely into her teens. Both the girl's parents had been killed tragically in an automobile accident somewhere up north. Philadelphia or maybe Baltimore. Her grandmother did her duty best she could, but she wasn't the affectionate sort."

I felt a pang of sympathy for a newly orphaned adolescent at the mercy of an indifferent relative. "It must have been a hard adjustment for a young girl."

"If it was, you'd never know to look at her. In no time flat, Becca seemed to take charge. She was the ringleader. Cheerleading captain. Homecoming princess. I don't think many girls were brave enough to stand up to her and risk being an outcast. Girls at that age can be vicious, underhanded."

"What about Maybelle? Weren't she and Becca classmates?"

"Maybelle always seemed content doing her own thing. She was the studious type and, to my knowledge, never seemed to mind not being part of the inner circle."

"What became of Becca after she graduated from high school?" I asked. "Did she go on to college?"

"Her grandmother didn't have that kind of money. Unfortunately, Becca's studies came in a poor third behind pretty and popular. Since she didn't qualify for a scholarship, she had to find a job."

I recalled her photo as school secretary. "She found a position with Brandywine Creek schools."

Melly raised a brow. "I'm surprised you know this. It was well before you married my son and came to live in Brandywine Creek."

Leaning over, I set my cup on the coffee table. I snatched another gingersnap in the process. "Reba Mae unearthed Butch's old high school yearbooks in the attic. Becca was school secretary during the time CJ and McBride were students." *And Barbara Bunker,* I almost added.

"That's correct. It wasn't long after that Becca got herself engaged to that nice young assistant principal, Arthur Dapkins."

I brushed crumbs from my capris, which Casey, now awake, lapped up with the alacrity of a Dyson vacuum cleaner. "Funny, but I was under the impression the newlyweds didn't stay in Brandywine Creek very long."

"Shortly after their wedding, Arthur received an offer to be a high school principal in another state. I'm afraid I lost track of the couple until their divorce several years ago, when Becca moved back to live in the house her grandmother left her."

"Any idea what led to their divorce?"

"Just one of those things." Melly spread her hands. "I suspect Becca wasn't an easy woman to live with and Arthur had had enough. Jolene Tucker said Art joined the Peace Corps after the divorce. Told folks he wanted to get as far away from Becca as possible. I believe he's in Thailand. Couples grow apart, as you well know."

I took that as my cue to exit. "Thanks for the tea and cookies," I said, getting to my feet. "I'll let you get back to your solitaire."

"That can wait till later." Melly reached for the remote control. "Now it's time for *Vanished,* my favorite show on the True Crime channel. It was Becca's favorite, too. Probably the only thing we had in common. Neither of us ever missed an episode. I DVR mine and often watch them over again."

"*Vanished . . . ?*" I paused, one hand on the doorknob. "Melly, you're always able to surprise me. I'd never take you for a fan of crime shows."

"You can't tell a book by its cover." She laughed.

"What's the show about?"

"It's about people who've simply vanished without a trace. Some nights it's about wives or husbands who wandered off for a quart of milk, never to be seen again. Other times it's about famous people who've disappeared."

"People like Amelia Earhart," I offered. "Or Jimmy Hoffa."

"Precisely." Melly aimed the remote at the television and clicked a button. "Care to stay and watch?"

"I'll take a rain check."

By the time the door shut behind me and Casey, Melly was already engrossed in her show. Flat-screen television. Fancy computer. DVR and crime shows. Guess you can't judge a book by its cover — at least not this particular cover encased in twin sets and pearls.

CHAPTER 24

A telltale squeak on the fourth stair from the bottom woke me up. "Lindsey . . . ?" I called out, more asleep than awake. I'd been determined to read for a while after returning from Melly's, but my eyelids wouldn't cooperate. I'd finally surrendered and switched off the light.

"It's me, Mom. Go back to sleep."

Hearing Lindsey's voice, Casey hopped off the bed and padded toward the door. "Deserter," I muttered, flipping over on my side.

The red numerals of the alarm clock informed me Lindsey was an hour past curfew. I was about to issue a reprimand when I remembered she'd been at Doug's preparing for the barbecue festival, which was only days away. I'd cut her some slack this time, but . . . Yawning, I drifted back to sleep.

The next time I woke, sun slanted through

the bedroom window. I peeked in on Lindsey, but she was sound asleep, with Casey snoring softly at the foot of her bed. Deciding to forego jogging in favor of baking — no sense overdoing a good thing — I took out the carton of blueberries I'd bought at the Piggly Wiggly. I toyed with the idea of pie, but muffins called my name.

I poured batter into muffin tins, then sprinkled on a topping rich in sugar and cinnamon with a hint of nutmeg. For a while now I'd been experimenting with various types of cinnamon. This morning I used a blend made from a variety of extrasweet cinnamon from China and cassia from northern Vietnam. Cassia and cinnamon are often used interchangeably, I'm aware, although, in the United States cassia is often preferred due to its more pronounced flavor and aroma.

While the muffins baked, I showered and dressed for the day in a white scooped-neck T-shirt and navy capris embroidered with tiny red ladybugs. Returning to the kitchen, I brewed a pot of Kona coffee that I'd been hording. Even in my sleep, my mind had replayed details surrounding Becca's death until it drove me bonkers. The unanswered questions were worse than the elusive seven-letter word in Sunday's crossword. I kept wondering if McBride was any closer to solving the case.

Or closer to reading Maybelle the Miranda rights.

When it came to motive, means, and opportunity, Maybelle scored high on two out of three counts. Would that be enough for an arrest warrant? If she couldn't convince McBride of her innocence, would she fare any better in front of a jury? The thought was troublesome, to say the least.

The scent of spicy muffins and freshly brewed coffee spread through the kitchen. I reached for a mug and was about to pour myself the first cup of the day, then hesitated. McBride loved coffee. Loved it even more than I did. And I owed him a cup after drinking his the other day.

Before I could talk myself out of it, I filled a thermos with robust Kona coffee and a wicker basket with muffins. I hoped McBride wouldn't think baked goods and coffee constituted a bribe. I viewed them more as incentives to tell me what he knew. I'd act as a sounding board. Or if he wanted, I'd listen while he ranted and raved. Vented his frustrations and uncertainties. Then I'd offer sage advice and leave knowing I'd performed my civic duty. I'd also leave better informed who topped his persons-of-interest hit parade. Maybe then I could quit worrying and wondering.

I scrawled a note for Lindsey, telling her to take Casey out "to do his thing," then hurried off with the basket in the crook of my arm. I was Little Red Riding Hood on her way to Grandma's house. I fervently hoped I'd meet up with the friendly woodsman in the guise of a handsome cop and not the big bad wolf.

As I hurried toward the police department, my gaze strayed to the opposite side of the street. I couldn't help but notice that yellow crime scene tape no longer festooned the azalea bushes in the square. Vendors were starting to set up colorful booths as if nothing bad had happened. Life went on. Business as usual.

I was happy to spot McBride's F-150 pickup parked in its designated space. I was also happy to note that there was no white Cadillac Escalade anywhere in sight. It would've been just my luck to have Miss Barbie-Q-Perfect arrive with a batch of homemade croissants.

As I pushed open the door of the police station, Precious Blessing glanced up from her computer and smiled. "Hey there, Piper."

"Hey yourself." I returned the smile.

"Didn't expect to find you on duty. I thought you worked afternoons."

"Dorinda asked me to switch hours with her. Company's comin' from Alabama to see the new baby, and she wanted to help Lorrinda get ready. With the little one wakin' every two hours for a feedin, Lorrinda's feelin' sleep deprived."

"Lorrinda's lucky to have her mother live close enough to help out."

"You can say that again, girlfriend. What you got in that there basket?" Reaching over the counter, Precious peeked under a corner of the cloth covering my basket. "Those blueberry muffins? Blueberries my favorite."

Taking the none-too-subtle hint, I presented her with a muffin. "I saw the chief's truck out front. Suppose he'd mind an interruption?"

"Not if the interruption comes bearin' gifts. Give him a minute or two before you bust in on him. He's finishin' a call with the GBI."

"So, Precious, how are things going?"

Precious beamed, her dark face glowing. "Goin' good, real good. The new man in my life likes a woman with a little meat on her bones. Says he doesn't go in for those anorexic types."

"Glad to hear it. Bring him around

sometime soon. I'd like to meet him."

"Might do just that," she said, taking a bite of muffin. "He's gonna be helpin' my brother Bubba with his barbecue. Bubba's callin' his outfit *Bub-Ba-Cue.* Catchy, ain't it? My brother Zeke will be at the festival, too."

"Does he cook?"

"Heck, no," she chortled. "Zeke can't fry taters without burnin' 'em. But there's hardly an instrument he can't master. He plays in a blues band. They're performin' downtown Friday night. You oughta stop by. You're in for a treat."

"I'll do that," I told her. "I promised Doug I'd meet him for the shag contest on Saturday. It'll be fun to see his moves on the dance floor."

"Since Jolene Tucker's still recoverin' from a broke ankle, others should have a chance at winnin' this year. Her and Butch used to party down in Myrtle Beach. They learned the shag from pros."

"Word's out this year's crowd will be bigger than ever."

"Damn straight." Precious nodded, causing the colorful beads woven into her braids to clack together. "Nothin' like a killin' to get folks' attention. Bubba's all fired up waitin' for the festival to start. He's braggin his ribs are so tasty it'll make your momma cry."

All this talk of food reminded me I hadn't eaten yet. "I hope your brother will be giving out samples."

Another nod, another clank of beads. "He's plannin' enough 'samples' to feed a battalion. Claims word of mouth is the best advertisement."

"Let him know I got in a fresh shipment of chili peppers."

"I'll be sure to tell 'im." Precious glanced at the switchboard and gave me a thumbs-up. "Chief's done with his call. Get outta here with those freakin' good muffins while there's still some left."

When I cracked the door and poked my head into his office, I found McBride poring over pages in a folder. I held out my basket of goodies. "Busy?"

He smiled, one of those rare genuine smiles that showed off his dimple. It might reflect poorly on my character, but I'm a sucker for dimples. "If this is a bribe, I have to warn you there might be consequences."

"I'll take my chances." Entering the office, I placed the basket on an uncluttered corner of his desk. I took out plates, napkins, coffee mugs, a thermos, and a larger plate of muffins. Not even Melly could fault my presentation.

"What's the occasion?" he asked, a bemused expression on his face.

"Rumor around the department has it you like your java good and strong. I thought you might enjoy Kona coffee along with some blueberry muffins."

"My instincts warn me to beware of pretty redheads bringing fancy coffee and baked goods to an overworked, underpaid civil servant."

I felt my face grow pink and my pulse quicken. I told myself his compliment didn't effect me in the least. *Liar, liar, pants on fire.* "One muffin or two?"

He flashed that darn dimple again. "One — for starters."

I centered a muffin on a small tangerine-colored Fiestaware plate. Next, I poured steaming Kona coffee into a mug the color of lemongrass. I repeated the process for myself, then sat down in the chair across from him. I raised my mug in a toast. "Cheers!"

"Cheers!" he toasted back. He let out a sigh of appreciation when he tasted the rich brew, another when he bit into a muffin. "So," he said at last. "What's the occasion?"

"Would you believe I'm here to make amends for drinking your coffee the day Casey found Becca's body?"

"It's a little late for 'amends.' What's the real reason you're here?"

I fluttered my lashes, vamping it up. "Can't put anything over on you, can I?"

"Not for lack of trying on your part." He helped himself to another muffin. "I suppose you'd like to ask if we found the culprit who helped himself to your petty cash."

"When you do, kindly inform him it cost me a new lock."

"I'll do just that." He washed down a bite of muffin with a swig of coffee.

"I heard there was a second burglary."

He stared at me over the rim of his coffee mug, his blue eyes cool, his expression unreadable, and waited for me to continue. I recognized his give-her-enough-rope-to-hang-herself tactics.

Clearing my throat, I elaborated, "Maybelle Humphries had her wallet stolen while at work when her back was turned. Ned Feeney told me all about it when he came to replace my lock."

"We're checking into it. Miss Humphries admitted she never kept more than twenty dollars in her purse. From the way she was carrying on, I suspect there was more to the story than she was telling. I don't suppose you know why she was so upset."

I studied the half-eaten muffin on my plate. Apparently Maybelle hadn't come clean, admitted to McBride she lied, and told him her alibi had disappeared along with her twenty bucks. What kind of friend would I be if I ratted her out? What kind of law-abiding citizen would I be if I didn't? A conundrum of the worst kind.

"Somehow I can't rid myself of the notion that you're on the receiving end of information I'm not privy to," McBride said, his voice calm and deliberate.

My gaze flew to his face. It had been a mistake thinking I could ferret information from a grand master of ferreting. The all-around champ of prying information from hapless miscreants. I started gathering the Fiestaware and loading it into the basket. "Hope you enjoyed breakfast, but I have to go. It's nearly time to open my shop."

He zapped me with a look from his laser blues. "I'm planning to question Miss Humphries later today. I also intend to speak with Buzz Oliver again. See if he can shed any light on the situation. Like I always say, memory's a funny thing."

I wedged the empty thermos into the basket. "I only came this morning out of curiosity. I keep wondering if you're any closer to finding Becca's killer," I said, trying for casual. "Are you?"

"This is an active investigation. I'm not at liberty to discuss details."

"What do I look like? A reporter from the *National Enquirer*?" His pat answer annoyed me. "If you recall, I happen to have a vested interest since I . . . er, my dog found the body."

"Thanks for the coffee and muffins." McBride picked up the file folder he'd been perusing before I entered.

Case dismissed.

CHAPTER 25

My impromptu meeting with Wyatt McBride had proven counterproductive. I returned home to find Lindsey behind the counter wearing a crisp apron and a sunny smile. Her long blond hair fell to her shoulders in loose curls befitting a shampoo commercial. Her makeup was prom perfect.

"Don't you look nice," I commented. "Beauty pageant material. Ready to be crowned Miss Spice It Up!?"

"Mo-om." She rolled her eyes.

I headed for the kitchenette at the rear to wash the Fiestaware. When designing Spice It Up!, I planned to host occasional cooking demonstrations. My first had been a disaster, pure and simple. I wasn't quite ready to climb back on the horse that threw me, but every now and then I'm tempted. I'm thinking of persuading Doug to demo his Chicken Tandoori, which incidentally calls for saffron. I stock top-grade Spanish coupé-quality saffron, the priciest of the priciest. "Why the outrageous cost?" people often ask. Saffron comes from the stigma of the crocus, which makes harvesting labor-intensive. It takes a plot of land the size of a football field to grow enough flowers to produce a single pound.

"Need help?" Lindsey joined me.

"Sure," I said, handing her a dish towel. "I'll wash; you dry."

She made a face but didn't mutiny. "Ms. Quinlan called while you were out."

I squirted liquid detergent into a small sink and turned on the tap. Although Lindsey was valiantly trying to rein in her excitement, I could see she was bursting at the seams to tell me her news. "Did Ms. Quinlan state what she wanted?"

"She wanted to ask you if it would be all right if she and Carter came by after lunch to shoot a segment for her show. How exciting is that!" Lindsey squealed. "Isn't that the most amazing thing ever?"

Amazing? My daughter and I differ when it comes to choosing adjectives. I rinsed a plate and handed it to her to dry. "Mm, sweetie, I'm not sure I'm ready for my TV debut."

She gaped at me. "How can you *not* be 'ready'? This is the most fabulous thing to have ever happened to Brandywine Creek. Just think, Mom, you'll be famous! Spice It Up! will be famous!"

Spice It Up! famous? I rinsed a coffee mug under the tap. "I don't know. . . ."

"Oh, come on, Mom. It'll be a blast!"

Lindsey looked so flushed and happy at the prospect that I set my reservations aside. "Fine," I said. "It would be foolish to turn down a chance for free publicity. After all, it's not as if I'm going to be talking in front of a huge audience. I'm perfectly capable of handling a one-on-one conversation."

"Awesome!" Beaming, Lindsey practically did a happy dance.

I rinsed out the thermos. "Does she expect me to call her back?"

"That isn't necessary." Lindsey draped the dish towel over a hook to dry. "I told her you'd be happy to do an interview."

"Pretty sure of yourself, weren't you?!" I drained the water from the sink.

"Turn around," Lindsey ordered. "Let me look at you."

I obeyed, both puzzled and amused.

Narrowing her eyes, she looked me over from top to bottom. "You might want to change clothes."

"Why?" I asked, glanced down at my ladybug capris. "What's wrong with what

300

I've got on?"

"Amber says the best way to stand out from the crowd is to wear a color that pops. Navy blue doesn't 'pop.' "

"Pop . . . ?" I laughed. "Are you saying I should aspire to look like a bowl of cereal?"

Lindsey gave me a blank stare. "Is that a joke of some sort?"

"Snap, crackle, pop! Remember the Rice Krispie Treats I used to make for you and Chad?" From Detroit, Battle Creek, Michigan, otherwise known as Cereal City, was a straight shot down I-94. Guess my Yankee roots were showing, but I'd birthed Southerners.

"You need to get busy, Mom. We don't have much time for a makeover."

"Makeover?" My voice rose. "Why do I need a makeover?"

"Amber said first impressions are important." Lindsey tilted her head to one side and studied me. "I bet if you ask Miz Johnson, all nice and polite, she'd squeeze you in. Do something with your hair."

My hand flew up to brush an unruly curl off my brow. "My hair? I like my hair. It's fine the way it is."

"It's just so . . . curly . . . and wild. It needs to be styled. And," Lindsey continued, unfazed by my outburst, "I bet

Miz Johnson would loan you earrings, dangly or sparkly ones. She has the coolest jewelry. One last thing, Mom. You need to apply more foundation to hide those freckles." She dug into her apron pocket and pulled out her iPhone. "I have to call Taylor. She'll freak when she hears Carter's filming us."

I stared after her as she went to the back of the storeroom where I couldn't overhear her conversation. Apparently, in my daughter's estimation, my appearance was sorely lacking. My clothes didn't "pop"; my hair was wild and unruly. I didn't hide my freckles and, what's more, I had a lame sense of humor. Truly her father's daughter. I was a wreck and hadn't even realized it. What's a mother to do?

Once I explained my dilemma, Reba Mae offered to come to my rescue. She said she'd make an exception in my case and make one of her rare house calls. She'd be there within the hour.

I'd barely hung up when Melly entered Spice It Up! toting a large cardboard box. I rushed over to take it from her. "Gracious, Melly. What do you have in here? Bricks?"

"A complete tea set." She brushed dust from her hands. "Must I remind you, dear, that I promised to bring teacups so you didn't have to serve your customers refreshments out of tacky Styrofoam."

"Must've slipped my mind." I set the box on the counter and peeked at the items wrapped in newspaper. "You really shouldn't have gone to all this trouble."

"No bother." She unwrapped a delicate china cup. "CJ's father and I received this set as a wedding present from his aunt Agatha but never used it. Agatha, bless her heart, had absolutely no taste. I swear the woman was color-blind."

I removed a second cup. Melly wasn't the only one questioning Agatha's taste. The bone china was decorated in a garish floral pattern awash in blues and purples. If that weren't enough, the wide gold band around the rim proclaimed these babies needed to be hand washed and dried.

"It's very generous of you, Melly, but I simply can't accept family heirlooms." Rewrapping and replacing the cup, I shoved the box in her direction.

Melly shoved it back in mine. "No, dear, I insist. I've held on to these much too long as it is."

Smiling thinly, I nudged the tea set toward her when inspiration struck. "Why, Melly, the tea set is an heirloom. I think you should give it to Amber and CJ when they get married."

"Hmm." Melly's hand rested on the box. "Perhaps you're right, dear. Agatha always did have a soft spot for CJ."

I heaved a sigh of relief. "Good, that settles it. As soon as Lindsey's off the phone, I'll have her carry the box out to your car."

"No sense holding on to things. I still have my mother-in-law's china as well as my mother's. At my age, a person can only use so many tea sets." She frowned and then brightened. "But never fear, I intend to make good on my promise. I'll raid my cupboards and find a few mismatched cups and saucers that ought to be good enough for your little store."

"Hey, Meemaw." Lindsey, her phone call concluded, greeted her grandmother with a hug. "Did Mom tell you she's going to be on TV?"

"No, dear," Melly said with a tight-lipped smile. "She's been holding out on me."

I shot Lindsey a see-what-you've-done-now look. "It's no big deal."

"I beg to differ," Melly corrected me. "It is a 'big deal.' It's not every day that a family member — make that 'former family member' — makes a television appearance."

"Barbie Quinlan is going to interview Mom for *Some Like It Hot.* Isn't that awesome?"

Melly turned her full attention on me. "Certainly you're not wearing what you have on, are you? And your hair," she continued, before I had a chance to answer, "well, perhaps Reba Mae can work a miracle."

"Sweetie, would you please carry this box out to your grandmother's car?"

Melly didn't take the hint that it was time to leave. "Piper, you'll need help while you're being interviewed. What time do you want me to return?"

"Really, Melly, that isn't necessary. I wouldn't dream of imposing."

"Nonsense." Melly dismissed my objection with a flick of her wrist. "I wouldn't dream of not being here when you're in dire need. After all, that's what families are for. Now I must run home and find something to wear. Something bright, something that pops. I think my blue silk blouse might be just the ticket. Folks always say it brings out the blue in my eyes. And I need to reapply my makeup — you too, dear. Bright camera lights cause one to appear washed-out and sickly." She was at the door when she turned and asked, "Do you suppose Reba Mae could fit me in? I want my hair to look especially nice when my friends watch the show."

"I'll ask," I replied, tempted to imitate Lindsey and roll my eyes. Unbelievable! Wardrobe, makeup, hair. Hollywood calling?

Lindsey was useless the remainder of the morning, alternating between peering at her reflection in a mirror and giggling on the phone. Shortly before noon, I sent her to the post office on an errand. When she offered to take Casey with her, I cheerfully shooed them both out the door.

I thought I'd fill the time before my makeover by sprucing up my shop. Grabbing a feather duster, I set to work. I might not "pop," but Spice It Up! would. High on adrenaline, I was making progress when Doug Winters wandered in. I felt my pulse kick at the sight of him. "Hey, Doug." I set my duster aside to greet him. "What brings you into town the middle of the day? Did you run out of helpless puppies and kittens to spay and neuter?"

That brought a smile. "My last owner got cold feet. She decided to breed her Corgi one last time before taking the plunge. I thought since Lindsey was working today, I'd invite you out for lunch. Afterward, I thought we might practice a few dance steps."

Uh-oh. Busted. "Dance steps?" I echoed. "Sorry, but I've been too preoccupied trying to prove Maybelle's innocence to give the shag contest much thought."

"No problem, pretty lady, you're about to get lesson number one." Doug took hold of my hand before I could object. "When doing the shag, keep in mind that eight words equal eight steps. One-and-two, three-and-four, five, six."

I watched in amazement as he proceeded to demonstrate the basics. His movements were slick as ice. The man possessed slippery feet and rubbery knees. Who knew Fred Astaire was reincarnated in the guise of a mild-mannered veterinarian?

Doug ended the demo by twirling me under his arm in a dance move that left me dizzy. I wondered if it was the shag or the man himself who made me feel that way.

I'd forgotten I had work to do until my gaze chanced to fall on the feather duster I'd carelessly tossed aside. I quickly reclaimed my hand from Doug's and hurried to retrieve the duster. "You've distracted me long enough. I have to finish cleaning."

Doug looked crestfallen at my abrupt

defection. "Can't you postpone your housekeeping chores till later? The longer you wait, the more dust that'll collect. That means you can collect twice the dust in half the amount of time. My way's more efficient."

"What . . . ?" I paused, feather duster in hand. "Did you just make that up?"

He grinned sheepishly. "Guilty as charged."

"Mind if I take a rain check?" I swept the duster over jars filled with vanilla beans and cinnamon sticks. "Barbie's coming to film me for a segment of *Some Like It Hot*. Between now and then I have to get this place shipshape, change clothes, tame my hair, hide my freckles, and find dangly earrings."

"Hey," he said, snatching my duster and kissing the tip of my nose, "no need for drastic measures. I, for one, happen to like your freckles."

I felt my cheeks warm at the compliment, but determined to finish my task, I grabbed the cleaning tool away from him. "I should lecture you on keeping the Pit Crew working till the wee hours," I said, referring to Lindsey coming home past her curfew.

"Sorry. I didn't realize ten o'clock was too late."

I dropped the feather duster. "Ten?"

He retrieved it and handed it to me. "Why? Anything wrong?"

"No, no. Nothing wrong," I managed. "Sorry about lunch. Another time?"

When I was alone, my mind shifted into overdrive. If Lindsey had finished at Doug's by ten, three hours were unaccounted for. I made a mental note to sit her down, find out what was going on. Though she hadn't specifically said she'd been at Doug's the entire time, she had certainly led me to believe that's where she'd been.

My maternal antenna twitched like crazy.

CHAPTER 26

My cleaning spree finished, I was besieged with a fresh set of worries. Maybe I should go all out and serve refreshments when Barbie and her shaggy-haired cohort came to film. *Tea and crumpets?* I wondered. Problem was I didn't know exactly what a crumpet was — and didn't have time to find out. I made a mental note to Google them later.

I'd just returned downstairs after putting away the dishes I'd used that morning to bribe — I meant feed — McBride when the front door of the shop swung open. Reba Mae, carrying a large duffel bag, barreled toward me. Dropping the duffel, she caught me in a bear hug. "Honeybun, you're gonna be ready for your close-up by the time I'm done with you."

I carefully extricated myself from her exuberant embrace. "Everyone's making this into a big deal. Barbie's going to ask a few questions; I'm going to give a few answers. Piece of cake, right?"

"Make mine a slice of Red Velvet loaded down with cream-cheese icing." Steering me over to the stool behind the counter, she gave me a gentle push. "Hush now, and let Aunt Reba work her magic."

I took the cowardly route and complied. "For all I know, this could end up on the cutting room floor." I had no idea of the accuracy of this statement, but I'd heard celebrities complain about this sort of thing on *The Tonight Show.*"

Reba Mae reached into her bag and pulled out an arsenal of styling tools. Some, like a curling iron and hair straightener, I recognized from watching Lindsey primp, but others looked like holdovers from the Inquistion. "Most folks would give their first-born to be in your shoes," Reba Mae said as she set an industrial-size can of hair spray next to a series of brushes.

"I'll gladly donate my favorite stilettos."

"Don't look a gift horse in the mouth," she scolded. "This will be great publicity for Spice It Up!" Head tipped to one side, she took a step back and studied me. "Looks like I've got my work cut out for me."

With a sigh, I surrendered. No sense charging headlong into a losing battle.

■ ■ ■ ■

Strike up the band. Bring on the piccolos, flutes, oboes, and bassoons. Barbie's arrival in her shiny white Cadillac had all the fanfare of a presidential motorcade or papal visit. More townspeople than usual, everyone dressed in their finest Sunday-go-to-meeting clothes in case they were caught on camera, leisurely strolled along Main Street. All pretense of window-shopping, however, vanished the instant Barbie Bunker Quinlan, aka Barbie Q, stepped foot on the pavement. They flocked around the platinum blonde and Carter Kincaid, aka the cute video guy, like flies to a summer picnic.

Barbie smiled graciously at her adoring public, then headed into my shop. The crowd parted in her wake with an alacrity that would have impressed Moses. *Sheesh!* I thought. *How would people react if it really was someone important? Like the president. Or the pope.*

Barbie stood on the threshold and whipped off her movie star–large sunglasses. She looked every bit the diva in a silky turquoise top and formfitting black jeans. Her blond hair fell loosely around her shoulders, her makeup flawless.

Melly sidled up behind me and nudged me in the ribs. "Don't just stand there like a ninny. Say something," she hissed.

Her admonition freed me from my momentary paralysis. I surreptitiously wiped sweaty palms on my apron. "Hello, Barbie," I said, my smile stiff.

"I don't believe I've met your sales staff," Barbie said, eyeing Melly and Lindsey, who hovered nearby.

"This is my daughter, Lindsey," I said, belatedly recalling my manners. "And this is Melly Prescott."

Barbie's eyes were hard and bright as aquamarines. "Melly Prescott? CJ's mother?"

Melly beamed with pleasure. "How nice that you remember my son."

"Even though we weren't in the same class, I remember him quite well," Barbie replied in a tone frosty enough to chill champagne.

It was clear to me, if not Melly, that Barbie's memories of CJ weren't fond ones. Fortunately, just then Carter Kincaid, weighted down with electrical cables and a huge video camera, shouldered his way through the door.

Giving her hair a toss, Barbie slipped on

an invisible cloak of professionalism. "While Carter's setting up I'll have Lindsey and Mrs. Prescott sign waivers. Standard procedure," she explained, taking forms from her leather tote bag. "These grant *Some Like It Hot* permission to use any and all footage not only when the segment is aired but for promos."

I smiled to myself at the sight of Melly and Lindsey scrambling to find pens and write their signatures. Celebrities for a day. Wish I shared their enthusiasm. Instead I felt as nervous as a cat in a room full of rocking chairs.

"Aha!" Carter exclaimed suddenly. I watched him plug a mile of thick black cable into an electrical outlet. "That ought to do it. Keep your fingers crossed, everyone. Not all old buildings can handle the demand for this much juice."

I felt obligated to defend my "old building." "Even though this place dates back to Prohibition, I had it rewired to meet code when I bought it."

He continued to look doubtful as he clipped a small microphone to the bib of my apron.

"Listen up, ladies," Barbie barked. "Let me tell you what I expect. When the camera pans the shop, I'd like you, Mrs. Prescott —

Melly Prescott — to remain in front of the counter. Act as though you're a customer. Do you think you can handle that?"

"My dear," Melly bristled, "I'll have you know I've been a 'customer' the better part of my life. That makes me eminently qualified for this little charade."

Ignoring the jibe, Barbie turned to Lindsey. "Lindsey, I want you to pretend you're making a sale. Be sure to smile."

Lindsey grinned as if to demonstrate. "Got it."

Now it was my turn to be on the receiving end of Barbie's transition to drill sergeant. "Piper, pay attention!" she snapped. "Carter is going to pan your shop while I do an intro. If I'm not happy with it, I'll do a voice-over later. Next, I'll ask you a few simple questions. Nothing to worry about, I'm sure you'll do fine."

"First off, I need to do sound and light checks," Carter announced. He fastened a mike like the one I wore to the neckline of Barbie's top. Taking a gizmo out of his cargo pants, he held it in front of her. Satisfied, he turned to me. "Speak into this in your normal tone of voice."

I did as directed and the gizmo's needle wobbled back and forth.

"Good," he said, seeming pleased I'd

passed the talk-into-a-mike test with flying colors. "Now hold still while I check you with the light meter."

I did my rendition of a bug under a microscope while he scrutinized me from various angles from behind a handheld device. "Sorry, ma'am," he said. "You're much too pale. You need more makeup. Try adding blush."

While I dabbed on another layer of blush and foundation, Barbie and Carter conferred in hushed tones. At last Barbie beckoned me over.

Curtain time. Like Reba Mae said, a piece of cake. I knew spices like the back of my hand, inside and out, backward and forward. I could speak for hours about their countries of origin, harvesting, and their different uses. I practically had a Ph.D. in spiceology. A simple interview. Nothing to get my panties into a twist about.

Carter donned a headset, then hoisted the camera to his shoulder. "Camera, sound, action!" he shouted.

My gaze flew wide. For the first time, I noticed that a crowd had gathered on the sidewalk outside my front window. Dottie Hemmings and Ned Feeney were in the front row, their noses pressed against the glass. Ned gave me his lopsided grin; Dottie signaled thumbs-up.

"Hey, y'all," Barbie drawled for the benefit of the camera, her voice sweet as a Georgia peach. She went into a brief but concise account of what was about to take place during the barbecue festival, then turned to me. "Let me introduce Piper Prescott, the charming proprietor of Spice It Up!, a quaint little spice shop I happened to stumble upon. Her shop is located on Main Street in Brandywine Creek, Georgia, right across from a picturesque town square where a body was recently discovered."

Body? I didn't know bodies were going to be discussed.

"Piper, would you explain to our viewers why you believed a tiny specialty store would prosper in a town with only two stoplights. I bet many of its citizens thought you were crazy when they heard your plan."

"I . . . ah . . ." I ran the tip of my tongue over my lips, which were suddenly dry. "I'm certain some thought I'd lost my marbles, but I'm happy to report most changed their minds once they realized the amazing difference fresh spices bring to their family's favorites."

"Still, Piper, you must admit it was a gutsy move for a recently divorced woman who'd never worked a day in her life."

"N-never worked . . . ," I stammered. Who the heck did she think she was talking to? Did she labor under the delusion that I spent most of my life watching soap operas and eating bonbons? I made a mental note to add "bonbons" to my Google search along with "crumpets." Taking a calming breath, I regained a degree of equanimity. "Do you have children?" I asked, keeping my tone pleasant with effort.

"No, I don't."

"Didn't think so." I smiled into the camera. "Raising children is the most important — and the most difficult — task a woman can ever undertake. I'm certain your women viewers will agree."

"I didn't mean to imply otherwise." A telltale pink seeped through the layers of Barbie's pancake makeup. "Allow me to rephrase. What I meant was that before starting your own business, you never held down a steady job."

"I'm afraid you were misinformed, Barbie," I said sweetly. "In the early days of my marriage, I worked two jobs to support my husband through law school. I worked as a hotel maid during the day and waited tables at night."

Unable to hold her tongue an instant longer, Melly marched over. "I don't want folks to get the wrong impression," she said, leaning into the microphone pinned to my apron. "For those of you who don't know me, I'm Melly Prescott, Piper's mother-in-law."

"Ex-mother-in-law," Barbie and I chorused.

Melly continued, undaunted, "As soon as my son CJ graduated law school — with honors, I might add — he insisted Piper quit work. He treated her like a queen. They even belonged to the country club. Unfortunately, Piper never did develop a decent backhand and boasted the highest handicap in the women's golf league."

"Cut!" Barbie made a slashing motion across her throat, a signal for Carter to cease filming. "Mrs. Prescott, if you don't mind, I'd like to restrict this interview to just Piper and myself."

Lindsey, her face crimson with embarrassment, scooted over, took her grandmother by the arm, and dragged her off into neutral territory.

"Let's get back to the subject at hand, shall we?" Barbie smiled brightly as filming resumed. "As the barbecue festival gets ready to fire up, could you tell us, Piper, which spices the contestants are clamoring for?"

Familiar territory at last. I inwardly heaved a sigh of relief. "Well, Barbie, as you know, all pitmasters are searching for the perfect degree of heat. Chili peppers, either ground or crushed, are by far my most popular items. They range from the mild chipotle to the fiery habanero."

"Speaking of heat, I hear Brandywine Creek is experiencing plenty of heat these days but of a different sort. Sources tell me this picture-perfect little town is undergoing a serious crime spree."

We'd gone off script — again. Unsure how I should respond, I let my gaze roam. In addition to the crush on the sidewalk, people filled the opened doorway. Reba Mae, Wally Porter at her side, gave me a finger wave and nod of encouragement. Bob Sawyer, reporter for *The Statesman,* was there, too, his Nikon at the ready for a photo op.

I cleared my throat. "I hardly consider having petty cash stolen a 'crime spree,' " I answered, deliberately misinterpreting her.

"I referred to a crime of a more serious nature," Barbie continued, shifting into investigative reporter mode. "Kindly tell the audience what it's like to find the body of a woman who's been bludgeoned by — of all things — a brisket. How fitting" — she winked at the camera — "practically on the eve of Brandywine Creek's biggest tourist event of the year?"

"Quite frankly, my dear, it sucks." I made the same throat-slashing motion I'd seen Barbie make earlier. "Interview's over."

Filming came to an abrupt halt to a smattering of applause from the audience. Barbie didn't linger to have her picture taken or to sign autographs. If this interview had been a "piece of cake," I'd have to describe the flavor as Devil's Food.

CHAPTER 27

The black snakes of cable had been coiled and stowed. The camera laid to rest in its foam carrying case. Barbie and Carter drove off muttering such things as "splicing" and "editing." The show over, the crowd drifted away. Lindsey, Melly, and I had polished off the last of the gingersnaps Melly had supplied.

"Mom, I promised Amber I'd tell her all about the taping. She invited me to spend the night — if it's okay with you." Lindsey brushed crumbs from the shorts she'd changed into after the "cute video guy" left. "She's scared to spend the night alone in that big house of Daddy's with a murderer on the loose."

I guess Lindsey didn't stop to consider her defection would leave her poor mother alone and unprotected "with a murderer on the loose." Bending down, I picked up Casey, who had whisked the floor clean of errant cookie crumbs. "Don't worry about me being alone, sweetie," I said, making no effort to hide the sarcasm. "I'll be just fine with my trusty guard dog at my side."

"Maybe I should get a dog," Melly mused. "A big one with a loud bark."

Lindsey and I stared at Melly in amazement. Was she serious? I'd never thought of my former mother-in-law as a pet owner. She smiled at seeing our expressions. "Why the looks?" she asked. "I always wanted a dog, but CJ and his father always claimed they were allergic. It's never too late. . . ."

Lindsey brightened. "I'll let Doc know you're in the market for a pet. He said lots of times a client's dog has an unplanned litter. Big ones, small ones. All kinds of breeds to chose from."

Melly reached over and patted Casey on the head. "I was thinking more along the line of the Humane Society. A rescue dog like your mother's."

I couldn't help but smile at Melly's remark. I may not have a decent backhand and I can't hit a golf ball to save my soul, but when it came to pets I'm an ace. "Lindsey," I said, "you never mentioned your father being out of town."

"Daddy's at a seminar on criminal law in Atlanta."

"Criminal law?" I asked. "What happened to him suing folks for finding a dog hair in the Puppy Chow?"

"Daddy said he needed to expand his horizons. To follow the money trail." Lindsey's phone played a tune telling her she'd just gotten a text. "So is it okay if I spend the night with Amber?"

"Fine." I set Casey on the floor. "Aren't you scheduled to work at the animal clinic tomorrow?"

"Not until afternoon," Lindsey replied absently, reading the message on her iPhone. "Doc's having a butt-rubbin' party tomorrow night."

"Mercy!" Melly exclaimed. "A butt-rubbin' party? What's this world coming to?"

"Not that kind of butt rub, Meemaw." Lindsey laughed and gave her grandmother a hug. "The butt — in this case — is the pork shoulder."

"I knew that," Melly sniffed. "A butt-rubbin' party just doesn't sound very lady-like, is all."

"Doug's specialty is pork butt," I explained. "He's positive his pulled pork will be a winner."

"Tomorrow night, we're not only mixing the rub, but we're rubbing it in. That chunk of meat will be so well massaged, it'll think it's at a day spa." Lindsey tapped out a quick response to her texting buddy. "Meantime, I gotta throw some stuff into my backpack and get over to Daddy's."

"Not so fast, young lady. Doug mentioned you left his place around ten. Please explain how you managed to come in after curfew."

"Sorry, Mom." Lindsey slid her phone into her shorts pocket. "I gave a friend a ride home. We got to talking, and I lost track of the time."

"Well," I said, deciding to cut her some slack, "don't let it happen again."

"Well, that's that," Melly said a short time later as Lindsey raced off, slamming the door behind her.

"What did you think of the taping?" I asked, curious to hear Melly's unvarnished reaction.

"I must confess, dear, I found the entire process . . . fascinating." She fiddled with her pearls, her expression thoughtful. "But I have to be honest, I don't care for Miss Barbie Too-Big-for-Her-Britches. Mark my words, her show's never going to be a success unless she learns how to focus on barbecue, not gossip."

"Amen." I pulled my apron over my head, not caring if it messed Reba Mae's artistry.

"I'd hoped being interviewed for *Some Like It Hot* would be good for Spice It Up! That folks visiting Brandywine Creek for the barbecue festival or a play at the opera house might drop in. Instead everyone will think we're murder central."

Melly tucked the container that had held the gingersnaps into her carryall. "If you want my opinion, Barbie Quinlan, née Bunker, has an axe to grind. That's the only reason she returned to Brandywine Creek. For goodness' sake, even Yankees have barbecue festivals. Ask yourself why did she choose this particular one?"

"Barbie grew up here. It's not unusual for people to get nostalgic for their hometown." I couldn't believe my ears. Here I was actually defending the woman.

"Do you ever get nostalgic for Detroit?" Melly fired back.

"Detroit isn't such a bad place. It's home to the Red Wings and Tigers. Furthermore, how many big cities are there where you can look across the river and see Canada?" There I was doing it again, champion of the underdog. At this rate, I'd be telling folks Jack the Ripper was just a poor misunderstood serial killer.

"Needless to say, a visit to Detroit isn't on my bucket list." Melly smoothed the collar of the silk blouse that brought out the blue of her eyes. "Barbara Bunker grew up on the wrong side of the tracks. A lazy no-'count father, a barfly for a mother. The girl's clothes were the thrift store variety. To make matters worse, she was bookish and sorely in need of braces. Kids picked on her mercilessly. You know how cruel children can be."

I paused in the act of folding my apron. "Are you saying Barbie was a victim of school bullying?"

"More than a victim, I'd say. The girl practically had a bull's-eye painted on her back. Then she hit puberty, and suddenly things changed. Boys overlooked the fact her teeth needed straightening and her clothes weren't stylish. They were more interested in other . . . attributes."

I stashed my apron, then rested a hip against the counter. "No wonder Barbie doesn't have many fond memories of home. What else do you remember about her?"

Fine lines formed between Melly's brows as she concentrated. "I remember once during bridge, the women were gossiping about a certain faculty member who took her under his wing. Tried to guide her, offer counseling. He was investigating possible scholarships. Like I said, the girl was bright."

"I didn't see Barbie's graduation picture in Butch's yearbook."

"That's because she dropped out of school senior year."

Curiouser and curiouser. "Do you know the reason why?"

Melly clucked her tongue. "Pity she didn't finish, but I believe the rumors were just too much for her."

"Rumors . . . ?"

"Vicious ones," Melly said on a sigh. "Promiscuity. Possible pregnancy. The type intended to ruin a girl's reputation."

I winced. Even though Barbie and I weren't destined to become BFFs, I felt sorry for anyone subjected to that sort of cruelty. "Do you have any idea who was responsible for the rumors?"

Melly shrugged, her expression troubled. "I can't say for certain — and I hate to speak ill of the dead — but I'd be willing to bet my entire Social Security check that Becca Dapkins was behind them."

"Becca?" I asked, astonished at the notion. "Why would Becca do such a thing?"

"Back in the day, Becca worked in the school office. Remember the faculty member I just mentioned? The one who took Barbie under his wing?"

"Yes," I replied. I had a sick feeling in the pit of my stomach where this conversation was leading.

"His name was Arthur Dapkins. Arthur was the assistant principal at the time."

"Becca's ex?"

"One and the same." Melly retrieved her pocketbook from a drawer where she'd stashed it. "Becca had her sights set on Art and, in my opinion, felt threatened by his attention to Barbara. She waged an all-out campaign to win him over. It was pathetic really, the lengths she went to. New hairdo, lots of makeup, short skirts. The whole kit and caboodle. The woman couldn't have been more obvious if she'd tried. The two married a year later, then Art took a position elsewhere, and the couple moved on."

Long after Melly left, I sat thinking over everything she'd just told me. I'd finally connected the dots between Becca and Barbie. Becca must have seethed watching the good-looking assistant principal, a man with a promising future, one she had designs on, show interest in a stunning younger woman. If Becca had generated the rumors and innuendos as Melly suspected, then I could understand why Barbie hated her. The sixty-four-thousand-dollar question was: Did Barbie hate Becca enough to kill her? There was only one way to get to the bottom of this: go directly to the source.

Six o'clock had come and gone. It was way past my normal closing time when I flipped the sign in the window from OPEN to CLOSED. I opted to take Casey along for my little outing. He must have like the idea, too, since he hopped in the car the instant I opened the door. I rehearsed in my mind what I wanted to say to Barbie as I headed toward the historic district. I needed to use finesse rather than come right out and ask, *Did you bean Becca over the head?*

The Turner-Driscoll House was a pristine two-story square structure. Heavy white columns supported a broad porch. Multiple chimneys covered in English ivy flanked the sides. Built by a businessman prior to the War Between the States — or the late unpleasantness, as I'd heard it called — the house had been in Felicity's husband's family for generations. Though it had languished from neglect under various tenants, since Felicity had taken over the reins it had been restored to its former glory. I parked my VW behind Barbie's Escalade in a side drive under an oak probably almost as old as the house itself.

Leaving the car window open a crack, I

instructed Casey to behave himself in my absence, then marched up the front walk and rang the bell.

Felicity greeted her unexpected guest — *moi* — with a gracious smile. "Piper! What a lovely surprise."

"Hey, Felicity," I said. "I know that the dinner Wally invited me to isn't until tomorrow night, but I'd like to have a word or two with Barbie if she's available."

"Of course." Felicity held the door wider. "Is she expecting you?"

"No." I peeked over her shoulder into the spacious rooms that opened off a wide entrance hall. Gleaming mahogany antique furniture, rich brocade draperies, Aubusson carpets. The rooms were every bit as elegant as I'd heard. "I have a couple questions I'd like to ask Barbie. It shouldn't take long."

"You'll find her in the front parlor." She stepped aside to allow me to enter. "Barbie mentioned reviewing her notes."

I followed Felicity across a broad marble foyer in a black and white checkerboard design. To my right, a curving staircase wound its way to the second floor. A console table held a stunning arrangement of deep-blue hydrangeas. I caught a glimpse of myself in an ornate gilded mirror. I scarcely recognized the woman with the soft, orderly curls and flattering makeup staring back at me. *Darn!* I looked good if I did say so myself. Maybe I should let "Aunt" Reba Mae get her hands on me more often.

My footsteps echoed on the marble tile. Felicity's, on the other hand, were noiseless in her sensible rubber-soled Keds. She knocked softly on the doorframe.

"Barbie, you have a visitor."

Barbie, wearing tortoiseshell reading glasses, sat on a crushed-velvet settee, a clipboard in one hand. She looked up and frowned when she saw me. "If you're here to talk about the taping, you need to reread the fine print on the waiver you signed. It's legally binding."

"No," I said, taking offense at her defense. "There's another matter I'd like to discuss."

Felicity's head swung back and forth, as she sensed the tension between me and Barbie. "Um" — she cleared her throat — "can I get you refreshments before I go? Sweet tea or lemonade?"

"No thank you," I said. "I don't expect to stay long."

"Well then, I'll leave you girls to talk." She drew a pocket door closed as she left, giving us privacy.

Barbie regarded me wordlessly. Since she made no move to make room for me on the settee, I perched on a Queen Anne–style chair opposite her. It was every bit as uncomfortable as it looked.

Silence stretched between us like a rubber band ready to snap. I was beginning to have second thoughts about coming here. But my questions needed answers.

Barbie huffed out a breath. "Say what you came to say, and let me get back to work."

My tongue felt glued to the roof of my mouth. I regretted having refused Felicity's offer of a cold drink. In for a penny, in for a pound. Clasping my hands in my lap, I blurted, "Did you murder Becca Dapkins?"

CHAPTER 28

Barbie tossed her clipboard aside. "Are you out of your cotton-pickin' mind?"

I wasn't quite sure how to respond. Was that a rhetorical question? Even if I were out of my mind, I'd come too far to back down. "It's a simple question, Barbie. Did you kill Becca or didn't you?"

Bright splotches of pink dotted Barbie's cheekbones in clown-like fashion. "You have some nerve, barging in, questioning me."

I might've lost my mind, but I hadn't lost my nerve. "There are dozens of barbecue festivals — hundreds maybe — all over the country. Big ones, fancy ones, in places like Charlotte, Nashville, and even New York City. Why Brandywine Creek?"

She flung both hands in the air. "Why not? I grew up here. Who's to say I wasn't overcome by a sudden urge to visit my hometown?"

"From all accounts, you weren't happy here."

"Where did that come from?" she snapped. "You've been asking questions about me, haven't you? Snooping around behind my back."

My cheeks grew warm. Considering the conversation I'd just had with Melly, I could hardly dispute the truth of Barbie's accusations. So instead of disputing, I did the next best thing. I ignored them. "Is it true you were subjected to school bullying?"

"I don't see where that's any concern of yours." Barbie shoved her reading glasses to the top of her head.

"Kids can be cruel."

"Yes, they can be, but I doubt you'd know about that." She gave her hair an angry toss. "You were probably one of the popular girls. Not someone on the outside looking in because of you didn't have nice clothes, or lived in a trailer park, or your daddy drank himself stupid most every night."

I sensed she didn't want my pity, but that's what I felt for the picture she painted. "In spite of your hardships, Barbie, you emerged a stronger person. You're a attractive, successful — a woman of means."

"Don't try flattery. It won't work." Barbie sat back, crossed her legs, folded her arms over her chest. "If you want more details about my high school days, ask your ex."

"What does CJ have to do with any of this? You two weren't even in the same class." Fact of the matter, other than his glory days on the softball team, CJ rarely talked about his teen years.

She smirked at my stunned reaction. "I take it CJ doesn't boast about his high school prowess. Did you know he was elected president of his class senior year? Voted most likely to succeed? Crowned prom king?"

I shrugged, tried to act nonchalant and pay no-nevermind to the vitriol. "High school days are a long way behind him. These days, CJ's more an in-the-present look-to-the-future kind of guy. Tell me about Art Dapkins," I said, deliberately shifting the focus from CJ and back to the matter at hand — Becca.

Barbie's expression underwent a subtle change at the mention of his name, softened, became less hard-edged. "Mr. Dapkins was a nice man. As good as they come. He was the only one to give a damn about me. He kept encouraging me to apply for scholarships."

"Why did you drop out of school without graduating?"

She stared into the near distance, her pale-aquamarine eyes cold as glass. For a moment I didn't think she was going to reply. "I stayed as long as I could," she said softly.

What the heck did that mean? "I'm not good at riddles."

"Rumors started circulating." Pursing her lips, she framed her words carefully. "Not only was my reputation at stake, but that of Mr. Dapkins as well. I thought the best thing to do was get out of town. I went to live with my grandmother in Tennessee."

"Rumors? What kind of rumors?" Pretending ignorance, I shook my head as if that would magically snap all the puzzles pieces into place. It's not unheard of, I knew, for a teacher to develop "feelings" for a student. "Were there any . . . extracurricular activities going on between you and Art Dapkins?"

"No," she spat. "Mr. Dapkins wasn't that kind of person. A certain party, however, started a tale that I was the aggressor in a student–teacher relationship. The same 'party' who, though I can't prove it, also started lies about my promiscuity and hinted at a possible pregnancy. Finally, I'd had enough. I couldn't take any more. So, I packed my bags and bid this town good riddance."

"Until now . . ."

"Yes, until now."

"What made you come back after all these years?"

"My shrink." Barbie lowered her reading glasses and reached for the clipboard. "He advised me that, if I wanted to get on with my life, it was time to put high school behind me. The debut of *Some Like It Hot* coincided nicely with Brandywine Creek's annual barbecue festival. I decided to show the town for what it's really like beneath its postcard-pretty surface. All its backstabbing, gossipy, narrow-minded ways. I view Becca Dapkins's murder as icing on the cake, an unexpected bonus."

"You suspect Becca was responsible for the vicious rumors?"

"Damn right I do." Beautiful, hard, and cold, Barbie's face could have doubled as a porcelain mask. "The bitch was so worried I'd steal the man she'd set her sights on that she'd go to any lengths to make my life a living hell. I hated the woman then; I'm not sorry she's dead now."

I rose from the uncomfortable chair I'd been sitting on. Our discussion had come full circle. "Did you kill her?"

Barbie pointed an index finger shellacked bloodred at the door. "Out! Now!"

I started to leave, but halfway across the room I hesitated and turned. "Do you have an alibi for the night Becca was murdered?"

From the way Barbie's eyes narrowed in anger I thought for a second she was going to fling her clipboard at me. "If you're not out of here by the time I count to ten, I'm calling the police."

I didn't need to be hit over the head with a brisket to know when I wasn't wanted. "I'll see myself out."

I left the Turner-Driscoll House trying to figure out my next move. Barbie certainly had motive to want Becca dead. Matter of fact, Barbie had it in spades. As for the weapon, how hard was it to get one's hands on a chunk of meat days before a barbecue festival? All that was missing from the unholy triad of motive, means, and opportunity was the o word — opportunity. Barbie had tossed me out on my ear without revealing where she'd been the night Becca was murdered.

"All right, Casey. Let me run this past you," I said aloud to my little pup, who raised his shaggy head, one ear cocked, and assumed a listening pose.

"Becca Dapkins, née Ferguson, a school secretary, had designs on a certain good-looking assistant principal. This nice man had taken an interest in a particular student — a late bloomer, a target of bullying, and very smart. As a result, Becca felt threatened by his attention to this vulnerable . . . and voluptuous . . . young girl."

Casey thumped his tail against the car's seat to indicate he was following the gist of my lopsided conversation.

"Becca saw her dream of marrying Mr. Assistant Principal going down the toilet," I continued. "Rather than risk losing him, she conjured a series of mean and nasty rumors about the girl's morals. In so doing, she forced the girl into dropping out of school and leaving town, thus effectively removing all roadblocks to her romance with a good-looking young man with a promising future.

"Now," I said, addressing Casey, who commendably hung on my every word, "this is where it gets interesting. The young girl grows into a beautiful, successful career woman. Years later she returns to her hometown with a score to settle. One of the first people she runs into when she gets there is none other than the woman who wronged her. They meet; they clash; only one survives. So far, how does my theory hold up?"

Casey let out a *yip* and thumped his tail again.

That was the only affirmation I needed.

I turned right and cruised toward the Brandywine Creek Police Department. Since it wasn't busy this time of day, I pulled into one of the vacant slots designated for visitors. Sand was trickling through Maybelle Humphries's hourglass. McBride needed to find the real killer. And sooner rather than later.

"Be patient a little longer," I advised Casey, giving him a scratch behind the ears. He looked back at me, a reproachful expression on his doggie face. *Promises, promises, promises,* he seemed to be saying.

Before I could talk myself out of it, I scooted from the car, hurried down the walk, and shoved open the doors of the police station.

"Hey, Piper." Precious Blessing stopped filing her nails. "Find another body?"

"Ha-ha," I replied. "Not funny."

"Oops." She grinned, not the least bit repentant. "My bad."

I found myself grinning back. It was hard not to when confronted with Precious's good-natured sass. "The chief in?"

"You just missed him, girlfriend." She pointed her nail file at the door. "Last I heard of him, he was mutterin' somethin' about a cold beer and a burger."

"Drat!" I drummed my fingers on the counter separating the public area from the restricted one. "I need to run something past him."

"Bet you can find 'im home 'bout now. Be a shame for him to miss out on how pretty you look with your hair and makeup all done up proper." She gave me a wink. "Do you want directions or can you find the way?"

I felt a telltale blush creep into my cheeks. "I think I can manage, but thanks."

Precious chuckled at my reaction but, thankfully, didn't pursue the reason why I didn't need a road map to find McBride's place. "You gonna take time to have some fun come Saturday? You know what they say about all work and no play."

"Put your mind to rest," I said. "I plan to be at the dance and fireworks. Dr. Doug's fairly confident he's going to be one of the winners. My daughter, Lindsey, is part of his team. You should've seen the look on her grandmother's face when she said that she was going to a butt-rubbin' party."

Amusement shimmered in Precious's dark eyes. "Lordy! I bet Miss Melly was fit to be tied, hearin' that comin' from the mouth of her sweet grandbaby."

As I headed out the door I couldn't help but think "fit to be tied" might also describe McBride's reaction when I told him my suspicions about his old friend the comely and voluptuous Barbie Q.

CHAPTER 29

Following an impulse — another of my bad habits — I headed down Route 78, a narrow two-lane county road. I'd been to McBride's once before after Lindsey and her friends engaged in a bout of underage drinking on prom night. At the time, he'd been renting a fixer-upper with an option to buy. According to the local grapevine, which boasted a 95 percent accuracy rate, he'd since made an offer and was now the proud owner of a handyman special.

A spanking-new mailbox with MCBRIDE neatly stenciled along one side marked the drive. As the gravel crunched under my tires, I began to doubt the wisdom of my decision. Kona coffee and fresh-baked blueberry muffins aside, it wasn't as if McBride and I were buddies. Our relationship was strictly professional — except when it wasn't.

Like now.

I spotted him casually reclining on the porch steps, beer bottle in hand. He'd exchanged his starched navy blues for cutoff jeans and . . . nothing else. My mouth went dry at the sight of his bronzed torso and well-defined abs. A hint of five o'clock shadow along his square jaw only added to the sexy image. My libido kicked into overdrive. No need to get my estrogen level checked. Heck, my ob-gyn could avoid billing for expensive blood work by parading him through her office from time to time. The man was a living, breathing hormone barometer.

His icy-blue gaze unwavering, McBride watched me brake to a stop at the foot of his drive. He took a long pull from his beer as I approached with Casey romping at my heels. "What's the occasion?" McBride asked

"Would you believe I'm just being neighborly?"

A corner of his mouth twitched. "I was referring to the hair and makeup 'occasion.' "

"Oh . . ." I ran my hand over less curly curls thanks to Reba Mae's wizardry with a flatiron. "Today marked my TV debut. Barbie and her video guy came by and filmed a segment for her show."

"I thought you and the vet might have a hot date — or maybe you were trying to seduce me."

My eyes widened. "McBride, shame on you. And to think, all this time you've been keeping it a secret."

He frowned. "Keeping what a secret?"

"Your sense of humor."

"Every now and then." He grinned, and my favorite dimple popped into view. "As my daddy used to say, even a blind squirrel finds an acorn sometime."

I sat on a lower step. Casey sprawled at my feet. I looked out across a yard bordered by sweet gum, loblolly pines, and oak. The last of daylight slanted through the boughs, forming a filigree of sunlight and shadow. Crickets chirped in the thick grass. "It's a nice night," I said for want of clever repartee.

"Can't argue with that." He took another swig of beer. "Haven't had much company, so excuse me if my manners are a tad rusty. Care for a beer? It's the best I can offer in the way of adult beverages."

I shook my head. "No thanks. Never been much of a beer drinker, not even in college."

"Didn't think so. Had you pegged for a white wine sort of gal from the get-go."

"Don't sprain your arm patting yourself

on the back. I like red wine, too."

"I'll keep that in mind," he drawled, letting a hint of Georgia creep into his voice. "How about a Dr Pepper?"

"I'd love a Dr Pepper."

He nodded his approval. "Now we're dancing to the same tune. Stay put; I'll be right back."

I rested my arms on my knees and stayed put. I felt oddly content. Peaceful. I wished I didn't have to spoil it all by bringing up Larry, Moe, and Curly, otherwise known as Becca, Maybelle, and Barbie. Wished it were simply an evening spent in the company of an interesting and attractive man. After my divorce from CJ, I'd sworn off men for good. Time heals all wounds, as the saying goes. Guess it's true in my case, too.

"Here you go." McBride handed me a cold can of soda. I noticed he'd taken time to pull on a T-shirt and ruin the awesome view of his bare chest. "Say," he said, settling back on the top step. "What happened to all those cute freckles?"

Cute freckles? Never in a million years would I have "pegged" McBride as a sucker for freckles. "Blame their disappearance on Carter Kincaid, the videographer. He complained I looked pale and washed-out. The extra foundation and blush were his idea, not mine." I popped the tab on my Dr Pepper and took a sip. I felt a pang of guilt. As though I were being disloyal to Doug for enjoying McBride's company.

He gestured toward the can of soda. "I'd offer you a glass with ice, but I keep forgetting to refill the damn ice cube trays."

"No problem," I assured him. "It's nice and cold."

"One of these days, I'm planning to replace the relic that came with the house. I looked at Lowe's, but came away even more confused. Guess I never realized there are so many choices when it comes to a fridge. Freezer on top. Freezer on the bottom. Side by side. White, black, or stainless steel. Only thing I'm sure of is I want a built-in ice maker. No more fooling around with ice cube trays."

"Built-in ice makers are great features." I swept a glance over the exterior of the house. "Doesn't look like you've done much since the last time I was here."

He grimaced. "Truth of the matter, I'm afraid I bit off more than I can chew. Got carried away by the low price — and the fact the property sits on five wooded acres with a stream running through it. Realtor kept stressing it was a steal. A do-it-yourselfer's dream. When I questioned her, she said the price reflected the need for redecorating. Now that the house is mine, I don't know where to start."

For a tough cop he seemed flummoxed at being a homeowner. I was torn between laughter and sympathy. "Somehow I never pictured you as a do-it-yourself kind of guy."

"I own a hammer. I can read directions." He shrugged. "How hard can it be?"

"I could be wrong, but owning a hammer isn't the equivalent of being a licensed contractor."

"Before you drove up, I was about to fix myself a burger," he said, stretching his long legs. "Care to join me?"

"Sure," I said, surprised by the offer. "As long as you let me help."

Getting to his feet, he held out a hand. "Nothing fancy. Burger and chips. If you're in the mood for dessert, I've can dig out a bag of Oreos."

"Oreos . . . ?" I laughed. "I'll definitely be in the mood for dessert."

He held open the screen door and Casey scooted through before I could stop him. "Don't worry," McBride said. "I like dogs. Might even get me one someday."

I stepped inside and got my first up close and personal of the handyman special. A small entryway led into a living room. A leather recliner was the sole item of furniture. At the far end, a large flat-screen television backed up to a corner cabinet made of knotty pine. Next to the living room was a small dining room with a card table and a couple folding chairs.

"Bedrooms and bath are on either side. Kitchen's to your right. Like I told you, the place needs work."

"Let's see the kitchen."

He led the way. I felt I'd entered a time warp. Cracked red and black linoleum, worn thin in spots, chipped gray Formica countertops, and antiques for appliances. A drop-leaf table, layered with yellowing paint, and two chairs that looked like garage sale cast-offs completed the vintage look.

"I know it's not much. . . ."

"Not yet," I agreed. "But think of the potential. All it needs is —"

"A ton of cash." He dragged a hand through his hair.

"With a little imagination and the right budget, you'll get a big return on your initial investment."

"Tell me you're not serious. You're beginning to sound like my Realtor." Crossing to the fridge, he took out a package of ground beef.

"Let me make the patties while you start

the grill."

"My 'grill' consists of the plug-in George Foreman variety. A gas grill is another item on my list." He handed me the meat and rummaged through a cupboard for the George Foreman. "I lived in a furnished apartment in Miami. If I wanted a steak, I'd use the grill out back by the pool."

I shaped the burgers while he set the table with inexpensive plastic dinnerware. "What do you have in the way of seasoning?" I asked.

"Will good old salt and pepper do?"

"They'll work just fine." When the burgers began to sizzle, I sliced a couple tomatoes I found cowering behind a stack of mail.

"Precious brought in a whole sack of them. She said her brother has so many he can't give them away."

"Nothing better than homegrown tomatoes," I replied, arranging them on a plate.

McBride opened a bag of potato chips and set bag and all on the table. Brought out mustard and catsup. I still hadn't broached the subject I'd come to discuss. And felt oddly reluctant to do so. When our conversation shifted to the impending barbecue festival I leaped at the chance.

"Melly and I had a rather interesting

conversation after Barbie finished filming."
I slid the burgers onto buns, put one on
each plate, and sat down at the table.

Taking the chair opposite me, he squirted
catsup on his burger and added a dollop of
mustard and a slice of tomato. He nudged
the bag of chips closer to me, a signal for
me to help myself.

The man knew how to turn silence into a
weapon, I thought grumpily, putting a
handful of chips on my plate. "Melly said
Barbie wasn't happy while growing up in
Brandywine Creek. Said the kids teased her,
made fun of her. That Barbie was the target
of bullying."

He raised a dark brow but waited for me
to continue.

I broke off a small piece of my burger and
fed it to Casey curled beneath my chair.
"Melly remembered a certain vice principal
took a special interest in the girl. Then, all
sorts of vicious gossip started. Melly believes
that the bullying and subsequent rumors
were the reasons Barbie dropped out of
school and left town."

Finishing his burger, he folded his arms
across his chest and leaned back. The legs
of the chair creaked in protest. "And your
point is . . . ?"

He wasn't making things any easier, I realized with mounting frustration. "The vice principal was Arthur Dapkins. During this period, Becca Dapkins, née Ferguson, worked as the school secretary. According to Melly, Becca had set her cap for Art. She wanted him for herself and wasn't about to let some buxom high school student steal him away. We — Melly and I — think Becca started those rumors and Barbie knew it. I witnessed firsthand the animosity between the two women the day Barbie arrived in town."

"And your point is . . . ?"

"Stop repeating yourself," I snapped. I gave Casey what was left of my burger, which I realized wasn't very much. I didn't even remember eating most of it. "My point is, Barbie had a motive for killing Becca."

"Just because two women dislike each other doesn't necessarily equate with murder."

I hated it when I came to him all fired up and he doused my conclusions with ice water. Now it was my turn to fold my arms. "Will you at least ask Barbie if she has an alibi for the night Becca was murdered? I tried," I admitted, "but she threatened to call the police if I didn't leave."

He got up from the table and, rummaging through a drawer, produced a half-eaten bag of Oreos. "Dessert?" he said, offering me some.

I took one. Reba Mae claimed chocolate helped her think. This was as good a time as any to test the theory. "You're the one enrolled in the motive, means, and opportunity school of police work. Becca Dapkins's reprehensible behavior destroyed the reputation of a young girl. Why not ask Barbie where she was the night Becca died?"

"Because I know where she was."

I blinked. "You do? Where?"

"Barbie was in exactly the same spot you're sitting right now."

"Here . . . ?" I asked when I found my voice again. "In this chair?"

McBride stood, leaned against the chipped Formica counter, arms braced behind him, and looked me square in the eye. "Barbie dropped by when she first got into town. Stayed for a few beers. We sat around and reminisced."

"I didn't realize you were that close." *Why should the fact he and Barbie-Q-Perfect were "close" bother me?* I wondered. I channeled Scarlett O'Hara and told myself I'd worry about it tomorrow.

"Barbie and my sister, Claudia, were inseparable when they were growing up. I stepped in a time or two when kids picked on Barbie, and she remembered. She and my sister still keep in touch."

"I see," I said slowly. It wasn't a stretch to picture McBride as the protective older brother, coming to the aid of his sister's little friend. Even then he was living under the credo "to protect and serve." My earlier irritation faded. "Thanks for dinner," I said. "I don't want to overstay my welcome."

"I'll walk you out."

We paused in the drive while Casey watered the shrubbery. "Since you've blown my theory all to smithereens that must mean Maybelle still tops your list of suspects. You don't know the woman like I do, McBride. She's a gentle, caring soul, who'd give you the shirt off her back. She woulnd't hurt a fly."

Darkness had fallen, making it hard to read his expression. Reaching out, he skimmed his thumb over the bridge of my nose and rubbed lightly. For a split second I thought he was going to kiss me. Did I want him to? Or didn't I? My reaction to Tall, Dark, and Lethal made me feel like I was cheating on sweet, dependable Dr. Doug.

"There," McBride said, his voice humming with satisfaction. "The freckles are back just the way I like them."

I stepped back, panicked and flustered.

"If you're seriously thinking about renovating, I have a lot of ideas," I said in a rush to regain my emotional moorings. "You might want to consider adding shutters and possibly flower boxes to the front of the house. Your hydrangeas need pruning, and you might want to do some replanting. Gardenias and holly are always nice."

"Anything else?"

I hurried to the car, and Casey hopped inside. "Well, as for the interior, I'd knock down the wall separating the dining room from the kitchen and living room and go with an open concept."

"No sweat. I'll get right on it with the aid of my trusty hammer."

Still on a roll, I slid into the driver's side. "While you're at it, tear out that corner cabinet. It would be a great spot for a gas-log fireplace. You might also want to knock out the windows along the back wall and put in French doors. They'd look great leading out on to a deck with its new grill."

"That's all?"

"For now." I gave a friendly wave as I backed down the drive. The beam of my headlights showed him looking even more flummoxed than he had earlier. For some reason, which I didn't stop to examine, that gave me a distinct feeling of satisfaction.

CHAPTER 30

Not many cars out at this hour. As I drove toward town, I tuned into a country-western station playing oldies. A female singer was lamenting that certain men cause good girls to go wrong. Wyatt McBride instantly came to mind. The man had a way of getting to me. With a look he made my tummy flutter. A touch made my toes curl. Tummy flutters and curling toes, as most women know, are unreliable predictors of compatibility. McBride spelled danger with a capital *D*.

And a capital *D* stood for "Doug." Doug Winters was safe, sweet, and — another *d* word — dependable. Those were qualities I admired in a man. Not bare chests, weight-lifter abs, and cute dimples. I liked a man who knew his way around a kitchen. One who owned a grill that you didn't have to plug in. Who owned more tools than just a hammer.

I switched to one of Lindsey's favorite stations. I wished I could change my train of thoughts just as easily. Wyatt McBride obstinately stayed at the forefront. Specifically Wyatt and Barbie. I had to own up to the fact I felt a twinge of jealousy. They were consenting adults. Considering their history, it was understandable they'd spend time together. Perfectly natural they'd spend a night reminiscing. What a lucky happenstance for Barbie that none other than the chief of police himself could supply an alibi for the night her nemesis was bludgeoned to death.

Reaching over, I idly scratched Casey behind the ears. The pup opened one eye, then let it drift shut. I felt restless — a mood that struck me with increasing frequency these days. With Lindsey spending the night babysitting Amber, I wasn't in a hurry to return to an empty apartment. I cruised past the town square where a handful of people milled about in front of partially erected booths.

Though it was late by Brandywine Creek standards, it wasn't late in other parts of the world — or maybe even the next county over. Now was as good a time as any to check on Becca's beloved African violets. While I was at it, I'd box up a few to take with me. I'd keep the plants next to the register along with a sign: FREE TO GOOD HOME. Down deep, I hoped to find something — anything — that might lead to Becca's killer. I couldn't ignore the steadily increasing sense of urgency that time was running out

"Stay here, Casey. I'll be back in five," I told him upon reaching the little bungalow.

I debated asking Reba Mae to meet me but remembered she and Wally were on a "date." Over the past couple days, she must have reminded me a dozen times that we were to be Wally's guests at the Turner-Driscoll House for a gourmet meal on Friday. Using Reba Mae's key, which I'd forgotten to return, I let myself in the front door. Fumbling in the dark, I found a wall switch and turned on a table lamp. The dim light from an energy-efficient bulb showed nothing had changed since my last visit. If anything, the dust was thicker, the musty odor stronger. The drawn drapes added to the gloom. A client had told Reba Mae that the appraiser Becca's children had hired was expected next week. The remainder of Becca's personal belongings would be shipped off to Goodwill or the Salvation Army. After that, the house would go on the market. All traces of her existence here in

Brandywine Creek would be erased. How sad.

Heaving a sigh, I reminded myself of my late-night mission. I confiscated a plastic laundry basket from the top of the clothes dryer and filled it with the finicky but pretty blooms. Becca's fondness for pink was evident in her choice of plants. The flowers ranged from dainty baby-girl pink to the more vibrant bubble-gum hue.

My task completed, I sank down on the overstuffed chair opposite Becca's flat-screen television and was nearly swallowed in its cushy softness. I absently ran my hand along the piping of a throw pillow embroidered with the saying THE TRUTH WILL SET YOU FREE. Poor Becca. What an untimely end to an otherwise unhappy life.

Who hated her enough to want her dead? Certainly not Maybelle. Didn't the fact Maybelle was dipping her toe into the Internet dating pool prove she'd moved on with her life? Barbie had sufficient motive but a rock-solid alibi. Or was I overcomplicating matters? Becca's death could have been a random act of violence. A simple crime of opportunity. A mugging gone awry. Whatever the case, she deserved justice.

I shifted my weight slightly and heard paper rustle. Glancing downward, I discovered a crumpled sheet of newspaper wedged between the cushions. Pulling it free, I recognized the TV section from the newspaper. Becca had circled several programs with a black marker. I got goose bumps when I realized the date coincided with the night of her death.

Keeping Up with the Kardashians was one of the shows circled. No big surprise there. The other was *Vanished* — saints and sinners who vanished into thin air — which also happened to be Melly's guilty pleasure.

A sound, soft and subtle, caught my attention. It seemed to emanate from the rear of the house. I sat up straighter, listening, my senses heightened. The creak of a hinge? A footstep? A tickle of fear raced down my spine.

"Who's there?" I called, pushing free from the chair's cloying embrace.

No answer.

The ensuing silence was even creepier. Had the slight sound been a trick of my imagination? Why had I left my trusty little guard dog snoozing in the car? Worse yet, why had I left my purse under the seat with my cell phone in it? Careless of me. I edged toward the door while keeping my eyes trained on the darkened dining room and the even darker kitchen beyond. In my imagination, the living room suddenly took on the dimensions of a football field.

"Hello!" I called a second time, hoping I sounded braver than I felt.

Silence. Again.

The little hairs at the nape of my neck stood on end. I half-turned on the balls of my feet, ready to sprint, when a banging on the front door nearly made me jump out of my skin.

"Yoo-hoo!"

I went weak in the knees at recognizing Gerilee Barker's voice. Racing to the door, I yanked it open. I barely refrained from throwing myself into the woman's arms.

Gerilee stood on the front porch, straining to keep a short leash on a large dog. The dog — a black Lab if I had to make a guess — growled deep in his throat. "Bruno, stop it!" Gerilee scolded, then turned to me. "I was taking Bruno for his nightly walk when I noticed your car out front and saw a light on. Thought I'd stop, make sure everything was okay."

I let out a shaky sigh. "Everything's fine."

Bruno kept up his low, throaty growl. "I can't imagine what's gotten into him tonight. He's usually very even tempered and well behaved."

"Gerilee, can you wait a sec while I lock up?"

Before she had a chance to refuse I darted back to collect the laundry basket of plants from the living room floor. I almost dropped it on the worn carpet at what sounded like the crack of a gun.

Bruno barked and lunged on the leash.

"Bruno, hush! Bad dog," Gerilee tried to quiet her pet. "Mercy, what was that?"

"Bring Bruno along, and we'll check it out."

"Has this old house gotten you spooked?" Gerilee laughed — rather nervously, I thought — as she and her pet stepped inside Becca's poorly lit home.

"Of course not," I said. A lie, a lie, a bald-faced lie.

I headed toward the kitchen feeling much braver having reinforcements. I stumbled to a halt in the doorway. A door that opened on to a small concrete back porch stood open.

Gerilee noticed it, too. "The Realtor or appraiser must not have closed it all the way when they left. A gust of wind probably caught the door and slammed it against the wall."

Hurrying over, I shut the door and twisted the dead bolt. "Let's go."

Pausing only long enough to pick up the basket of houseplants, I forced myself to walk when I wanted to run. Do not pass go! Do not collect two hundred dollars! I couldn't get out of the place fast enough.

Once I was safe and sound in my apartment, my heart rate gradually returned to normal. I still felt a bit on edge. I blamed it on the Dr Pepper I drank at McBride's. Probably heavy on caffeine and loaded with sugar. I wandered to the window overlooking the square. The statue of the Confederate soldier was clearly visible through the maze of tents and booths. If only statues could talk . . .

I hugged my arms around myself. I couldn't stop thinking about my visit to Becca's. As I sat in an empty house, thinking of a dead woman, my imagination slipped into overdrive? Still . . . I could have sworn that someone besides me was in the house. True, the Realtor or appraiser could have left the door unlatched and a sudden breeze could have sent it crashing open.

Yet how would that explain what sounded like a muffled footstep?

I paced the length of my living room. Becca's house had belonged to her grandmother. Old houses and old buildings, such as mine, often creaked or groaned. The previous occupants of Spice It Up! — a tanning salon/movie rental business — insisted the building was haunted by the ghost of a bootlegger killed when his still exploded, setting fire to half the town. Personally, I believed the tanning salon/movie rental owner smoked dope. Or indulged in too many magic mushrooms.

But the question remained: Who, and why, would anyone sneak into Becca's place that time of night unless they were up to no good? Question followed question. If Barbie was truly innocent of the evil deed, who else hated Becca enough to kill her? A disgruntled water department customer? Possibly but, in my opinion, highly unlikely. Then who? Had Becca grievously offended someone in town connected to the barbecue festival? Or was the culprit someone who resided right here in Brandywine Creek all along?

Finally, I gave up trying to find the answer.

After changing into pj's, I washed off my makeup, brushed my teeth, then climbed into bed and hit the remote. A guest on a late-night program was belting out her latest and greatest. The refrain caught my attention. Words to the effect that it was easy for a good girl to go bad. The sentiment was similar to one I'd heard earlier after leaving McBride's. Guess some messages bear repeating. I clicked off the television and turned off the light. Tomorrow was a new day.

CHAPTER 31

Before things got too wild and crazy, I decided an early-morning jog was in order. Jamming a ball cap over my stubby wannabe ponytail, I was out the door with Casey in no time flat. In the square across the street, tents colorful enough to inhabit a box of Crayolas seemed to have popped up overnight — a kaleidoscope of green, red, yellow, and blue. The clang of metal against metal assaulted my ears as men worked to erect still more booths. I plugged the earbuds of my MP3 player into my ears to drown out the noise, then started off to the upbeat music of Sugarland.

Although the actual judging wouldn't take place until tomorrow afternoon, the atmosphere in town already felt supercharged. The streets surrounding the square were blocked off with bright-orange barrels to allow contestants easy access. In spite of the hour, vendors were already beginning to congregate. Ladies from the Methodist church chattered and called out to one another as they toted plastic bins filled with arts and crafts back and forth for their two-day bazaar. Later tonight, a free blues concert would take place on a stage erected in the parking lot of Cloune Motors. It always drew a crowd. In addition to the regular bunch of tourists, news of Becca's murder had generated a great deal of media atttention. Mayor Hemmings must be dancing a jig at the turnout.

After a five-minute brisk walk, I picked up speed and settled into a slow, steady jog with Casey keeping pace. I traded the bustling commercial district for a quieter residential one. Squirrels chased each other up trees. Cardinals — or redbirds as they're called in the South — flitted in and out of the holly bushes in Pinky Alexander's yard. It was a lovely morning, perfect really, sunny with a clear blue sky. I wished I could capture its essence in a spray bottle. I'd use it like expensive perfume on gloomy days.

I was singing along with Jennifer Nettles when I was hit by a blast of cold water so powerful it nearly knocked me off my feet. Then, just as suddenly, the blast ceased. I was drenched. I stood in the middle of the sidewalk and shook myself until my earbuds fell out. My poor pup. He looked like a drowned rat from his unexpected bath.

"Oh boy. Man, oh man, I'm so sorry. My apologies." Thompson Gray, owner of Gray's Hardware, rushed across his yard, all red in the face. Tall and lanky with thinning brown hair, Thompson lived with his widowed mother. The hardware store had been in the family for three generations. "Sorry, Piper. I'm testing a new rotor for my irrigation system. Must've had the nozzle set to spray in the wrong direction."

Beads of water dripped from the bill of my cap. Casey shuddered, sending water droplets flying every which way. I jogged in place, holding my T-shirt away from my wet skin while Jennifer warbled about something — or someone–being stuck like glue. "If you don't make an adjustment, your walk's going to turn into a wading pool."

"Right, right," Thompson said, clearly distressed. "Anything I can get you? A towel maybe."

Pushing the earbuds back into place, I waved his offer aside. "Thanks, Thompson, but I think I'll head on home."

Due to the unforeseen circumstances, I looped around the block and detoured through the square. I ignored people who gawked curiously as I jogged past and pretended I wasn't soaking wet. I had Spice It Up! in the crosshairs when McBride stepped out of the bushes near where I'd found Becca's corpse.

I let out a startled yelp and skidded to a halt. "McBride, you scared the daylights out of me!"

He gave me the eye, a smile tugging at the corners of his mouth. "Thinking about trying out for a wet T-shirt contest down at High Cotton?"

I squinted up at him. "Hi what?"

He plucked the earbuds from my ears. "I asked if you were auditioning for a wet T-shirt contest."

I glanced downward. My shirt clung to me like tissue paper. My cheeks burned with embarrassment. Mortified, I crossed my arms to cover my chest the best I could while maintaining a grip on Casey's leash. "Thompson Gray had a rotor of his irrigation system aimed wrong," I said. "Must have had it on a timer."

"Well, as they say," McBride drawled. "Timing's everything."

I tried to dart around him, but he moved slightly and blocked my path. "I wanted to go over the crime scene one more time," he explained. "Make sure nothing was overlooked. Couldn't help but notice again

370

how you have a clear view of the exact spot where the body was found."

I shivered, but the chill had nothing to do with my damp clothes and everything to do with Becca. Casey hunkered down at my feet, content to track the flight of a hummingbird.

"Cold?"

Absently I rubbed my arms to warm them. "I'm not sure I mentioned it earlier, but I had trouble sleeping the night Becca was murdered. For a long time, I stood staring out that window thinking how peaceful everything looked. The whole time Becca was laying half-hidden under the azaleas."

McBride's gaze sharpened. Only now it wasn't my wet shirt he was looking at but my face. "No," he said slowly, "you never mentioned this. Did you recall anything unusual? Something out of the ordinary?"

"Of course not," I replied indignantly. "I would have told you if I had. Are you still working under the assumption Becca's death was a random act of violence?"

"And you're still convinced Becca was murdered elsewhere," he countered, more statement than question. "Off the record, let me say we're checking out all possibilities."

"You can't seriously think Maybelle

Humphries killed Becca in a fit of jealousy over Buzz Oliver?"

"The woman's got motive, means, and opportunity. That puts her at the top of my list."

"She has an alibi," I blurted. "Or she did."

"Ms. Humphries told me she was home alone, but couldn't prove it."

"She wasn't home — alone or otherwise. She was in Augusta." Maybelle would be furious with me for telling her secret, but I'd cross that bridge when I came to it. "Maybelle's been trying her hand at Internet dating. She got stood up that night. Rather than go home, she went to a movie. She has — had — the ticket stub and a receipt for the gasoline she bought on the way home."

He raised a brow. "Had . . . ?"

"They were in her wallet when it was stolen."

"Did you actually see this ticket stub and receipt?"

I huffed out a breath. "Well, no, but —"

"Never been a believer in coincidence. First Ms. Humphries deliberately lies to an officer of the law about her whereabouts. Now her so-called alibi disappears. Sounds fishy, if you want my opinion."

"Maybelle was positive you'd find the

killer and no one would ever need know her secret. She has too much pride to let everyone in town think she's desperate for a man. Are you going to arrest her?"

McBride's cop mask had slipped firmly into place. His grim-lipped silence told me all I needed to know. Maybelle was toast.

"Wait!" I cried as he started to walk away. Suddenly an idea had struck me with enough force to knock the wind out of my sails. For the life of me I don't know why it didn't occur to me sooner, but I'd kick myself later. "Don't places like movie theaters and gas stations have surveillance cameras? Wouldn't they prove Maybelle was miles away when Becca was murdered?"

"Without the receipts to back up her claim, how do I know the woman isn't lying? She doesn't exactly have a sterling track record when it comes to telling the truth. I've got too much on my plate right now to spend hours poring through video footage for what, in all likelihood, will turn out to be a colossal waste of time."

As I watched him stroll away, I wanted to stomp my foot in frustration. I should have insisted Maybelle go directly to McBride the night I'd first heard about her proof. Better yet, I should've gone *with* her. What kind of friend was I? I'd let Maybelle down.

Well, I vowed, busy or not, I wouldn't let McBride off the hook without checking into this more thoroughly.

I stood behind the counter, but my mind was elsewhere. If Maybelle didn't kill Becca, who did? Too bad the No-Tell Motel could verify that Buzz Oliver had been on bug patrol the night Becca died. With Buzz out of contention, my odds-on favorite would have been Barbie Quinlan. Who would've guessed Wyatt McBride himself could vouch for her whereabouts? With both Buzz and Barbie out of the equation, I needed to search elsewhere for Becca's killer. I decided to take a closer look at everyone Becca had contact with on the day and the days prior to her death, and that included barbecue aficionado Tex Mahoney and esteemed judge Wally Porter. In addition, I'd trace Becca's actions backward from the time of her death in the hope of finding a clue to her murderer.

"Mom . . . ?" Lindsey's plaintive voice broke into my musings. "You haven't heard a single word I've said."

I snapped to attention. "Sorry, sweetie. Tell me again."

Lindsey rolled her eyes. "I was talking about how amazing Carter and Barbie are.

You wouldn't believe how they piece together a story about a boring little town like Brandywine Creek and make it sound interesting."

"Mmm-hmm." I tried — but not very hard–to work up a shred of enthusiasm. Lindsey had been rambling on and on about the dynamic duo ever since she returned from her overnight at Amber's.

"Barbie is *really* nice. And talented, too. You ought to make more of an effort to get to know her, Mom. And Carter says Barbie has great instincts about what works and what doesn't."

"That's nice, sweetie." I reminded myself the festival would soon be over and Barbie would ride out of town on her broomstick.

Lindsey ran a feather duster over a shelf holding various forms of ginger — crystallized, sliced, powdered, and cracked. "According to Carter, Barbie's very creative. Her husband was quite a bit older. He left her a boatload of money when he died, so she doesn't really have to work like you do."

Now I was the one to roll my eyes. In my dreams, I too was drop-dead gorgeous, independently wealthy, talented, creative, "really" nice — and drove a white Cadillac Escalade.

"She had this amazing idea for *Some Like*

It Hot. She pitched it to an executive on the Cooking Network, and he signed it up like that." Lindsey snapped her fingers to demonstrate. "The rest, as they say, is history."

Or the world according to Carter Kincaid.

"Carter's showing me how to frame a subject through a viewfinder. He's a gifted videographer. Even Barbie thinks so."

If I heard Lindsey mention Barbie's and Carter's names one more time, I'd scream. "Carter Kincaid is much too old for you," I pointed out. I picked up a handful of credit card receipts and proceeded to sort them. "How is it you've been spending so much time around him?"

Lindsey flipped her ponytail over her shoulder. "Carter filmed Doc's team for possible inclusion. He wanted to document what goes on behind the scene."

The door swung open, and Clay Johnson squeezed through holding a kettle grill. Lindsey ran to help. Clay, young and fit from working construction, looked strong enough to manage without Lindsey's assistance, but I didn't quibble.

"Mama said you wanted this old thing for a display of some sort," he said.

"Hey, Clay," I said. "You can set it in that space I cleared near the front window."

"Got more stuff in the truck." He left and returned with a cardboard box filled with grilling tools, oven mitts, and an assortment of cookbooks. "Mama thought you might could use these, too."

"Thank her for me, will you, Clay." I added a chef's hat and red-checkered tablecloth to the collection of props I planned to transform into an eye-catching window display.

Clay turned his attention on Lindsey. "Hey, squirt."

"Hey yourself."

Clay dusted off his hands. "My brother's busier than a one-armed paperhanger down at the garage these days," he said to Lindsey. "Caleb told me he probably won't have the brakes changed on your Mustang until tomorrow. Seein' as how we're both on Doc's team, he wondered if I would give you a lift to the butt-rubbin' party."

Lindsey shrugged and smiled prettily. "Sure."

"Guess that settles it then. I'll be by around six to pick you up. See you, Miz Prescott."

I'd watched the byplay between my daughter and Reba Mae's son with interest. Her twins were twenty, the same age as my Chad. The three boys had been inseparable until Chad went off to college and enrolled in pre-med. Clay always did have a soft spot for his friend's baby sister, whether it was punching the kid who stole her doll in grade school or offering a ride to a butt-rubbin' party.

I went back to sorting credit card receipts when I noticed a piece of paper protruding from a drawer. When I opened the drawer, I discovered the crumpled TV section I'd found wedged into Becca's overstuffed chair. I must've stashed it there after returning home with a basket full of African violets.

Lindsey peered over my shoulder. "What's that you're reading?"

"Nothing." I stuffed the paper into the pocket of my beige crop pants. "Sweetie, I need you to keep an eye on the shop while I run a few errands."

"Whatever." She sighed the sigh of a martyr. "Taylor's going to do my nails before the party and I'm going to do hers, so don't be too long."

"Promise." I stripped off my apron and hurried out the door.

Becca had circled the show *Vanished* with a bold black marker. She'd had every intention of staying home and watching television the night she was killed, not going gallivanting across town brisket in hand. *Vanished* also happened to be my ex-mother-in-law's favorite. Melly mentioned she was in the habit of DVRing episodes. I needed to find out if she'd recorded the episode from the night in question.

This could turn out to be a wild-goose chase, but I had nothing to lose. Who knew, finding a crumpled TV section might be a genuine clue or even Divine intervention. McBride claimed he didn't believe in "coincidence." I decided to keep my options open. From down the street I could hear the high school band practicing for tomorrow's awards ceremony. The clash of cymbals and the thud of a bass drum reverberlated in my ears as I hurried toward Melly's, which only added to my growing unease that time was running out.

CHAPTER 32

Melly greeted me with a warm smile. "Piper, dear, this a nice surprise, but shouldn't you be working? Taking a morning off is no way to run a business."

I gritted my teeth. "Mind if I come in? I need a favor, though you might think it's strange once you hear it."

She stepped aside for me to enter. "All you have to do is ask."

"I remembered a comment you made the other night. Something about how you and Becca shared a fondness for a certain TV show — *Vanished.*"

"Of course I remember," she said peevishly. "Just because I'm getting up in years doesn't mean my memory isn't as sharp as ever. And yes, I never miss an episode."

We were still in the foyer, but from the corner of my eye I could see the large flat screen in the living room. Next to it was a small black box, the type a cable company provided. "Did you happen to record the show the night Becca was killed?"

"I programmed my DVR to automatically record every new episode." Melly walked over to the set, picked up the remote control, and pressed a series of buttons. "Have a seat, dear. I'll demonstrate."

I complied, sinking down on the sofa. "That particular episode would have aired a week ago."

Melly navigated the remote with the ease of a seasoned gamer. I should be taking notes, but then maybe not. A pricey cable service wasn't in my budget.

A number of screens appeared and disappeared until Melly found the one she searched for. Aiming the remote, she clicked a drop-down menu and scrolled through a lengthy list. Whoever said you couldn't teach old dogs new tricks obviously had never met Melly Prescott.

"Melly!" I exclaimed. "Where did you learn how to do all this?"

A pleased smile lit Melly's lined face. "It's not all that difficult, dear. I've discovered I have a natural aptitude for computers, TVs, and such. I'm considering purchasing one of those newfangled smartphones. One where I can download apps."

Duly impressed, I smiled, too. Underneath the pearls beat the heart of a geek. In no time at all, she'd be texting with her thumbs. Clearing my throat, I reminded myself of the purpose for my visit. "It's a long shot, I know, but I wondered if *Vanished* was in any way related to Becca's death."

"I don't see how." Melly sat down in a wingback chair that converted into a recliner.

"Like I said, it's a long shot. I'm grasping at straws. Becca had every intention of watching her favorite TV show the night she died. It struck me as odd that shortly afterward she was killed in the town square." *Or possibly in her own kitchen,* I thought, but kept the suspicion to myself.

"I hope you don't fancy yourself a detective like Miss Jane Marple in an Agatha Christie novel. Need I warn you, dear, that you're playing with fire? Last time you meddled, it nearly got you killed." Melly made tsking sounds, then added, "I trust you'll be more careful."

I'd learned my lesson well at the hands of a narcissistic sociopath. "I will, Melly. Don't worry."

Placated, Melly asked, "Can I get you something to drink? Coffee or tea?"

"No, thank you." As the credits began to

roll, I settled back to watch. I already felt foolish for making a big deal out of what in all likelihood would turn out to be nothing.

The program Becca had circled focused on the Witness Protection Program operated by the U.S. Marshals Service and administered by the Department of Justice. Their spokeswoman — a PR dynamo dressed for success in a tailored suit — related that more than eighty-five hundred witnesses and nearly ten thousand family members had participated since the program's inception. To its credit none of the participants who followed the program's stringent guidelines had been harmed while under its active protection.

I sat straighter and paid closer attention when the interviewer asked if anyone had ever opted out of the program. The PR lady gave a rueful laugh and explained that though rare, it has happened. She cited an occasion when a witness complained that his new identity and new location were "boring as hell."

A photo of a tough-looking guy with a wiry build, bushy hair, and port-wine stain marring one cheek flashed across the screen. "After living high on the hog," the narrator explained, "life in the sticks was pretty dull for mobster Louie Coccetti. Nicknamed

Vino due to the port-wine stain on his face, Coccetti was used to wearing Armani and driving a Porsche. The best WitSec could offer was a modest subsistence and medical care."

"Fascinating, isn't it?" Melly commented as she fast-forwarded through a series of commercials.

"Um-hum," I agreed. "What happens to those who leave?"

"Be patient, dear, and watch the show."

No sooner had the program resumed when the interviewer asked the very same question I'd wondered about. "Some fade into the woodwork," the narrator stated, "never to be seen again. Others can't resist their old life of crime. Unfortunately, most who sign themselves out don't fare very well." The PR gal stared directly into the camera. "The Mob has a long memory and an even longer reach."

The program over, Melly clicked off the television. "Did that satisfy your curiosity?"

I got up to leave. "Like I said earlier, grasping at straws."

Poor Maybelle. Some help I turned out to be. I wasn't any closer to finding Becca's killer than I had been the day I'd found her body. I wondered if Miss Jane Marple ever felt this discouraged.

■ ■ ■ ■

When I returned to Spice It Up!, my conscience gave me a swift kick at seeing the harassed expression on Lindsey's pretty face. She gave me a look as if to say, *How could you go off and desert me?* I'd seen the same look countless times on Casey's furry face. Wordlessly I donned an apron and set to work.

Business was brisk. Grill masters, amateur and pro alike, came in to purchase last-minute ingredients. My supply of chili peppers was nearly depleted. The grinder I used for spices overheated from all the use. I forgot to eat lunch. It was mid-afternoon before the shop experienced a lull. Tired, famished, and frazzled aside, I felt elated that Spice It Up! was thriving.

"Is it okay if I go take a look around?" Lindsey asked hopefully. "I don't think I've ever seen Brandywine Creek this busy."

"Take the rest of the day off," I told her. "Go!"

Lindsey didn't need further encouragement. She tugged off her apron and stuffed it under the counter. "I'll take Casey with me."

I felt a twinge of envy as I watched the

two head toward the square. All day long, we'd watched rigs pull into town and set up operations. These rigs ran the gamut from customized RVs — some bigger than my living room — to the hook-behind-a-pickup variety. Most were creatively christened with names such as *Pig 'n a Pit, Skin and Bones,* and *Smoke This.* The grills, I'd observed, were just as diverse, ranging from stainless-steel monstrosities large enough to roast an elephant to battered oil drums. I drew in a deep breath and smelled woodsmoke. Hickory, or maybe oak or pecan, most pitmasters agreed woods were where barbecue got its flavor.

Lindsey had no sooner left than a weary-looking Maybelle appeared clutching a large manila envelope. "Just saw Lindsey with that cute little pup of yours. It was hard to tell who was taking whom for a walk."

I took the apron Lindsey had carelessly stashed and smoothed the wrinkles. "Have you ever considered owning a pet, May-belle?"

"It's on my bucket list."

I stared at her, curious. "You have a bucket list?"

Maybelle gave me a feeble smile. "Once this is over — provided I'm not behind bars — I've decided to make some changes in my life."

"What sort of changes?" I refolded the apron and put it away.

Maybelle shrugged her narrow shoulders. "Becca's death hit me hard — harder than I ever would've imagined. You might say that it sent me into a tailspin."

"Reba Mae and I were worried about you."

"I know you were, and don't think I don't appreciate your friendship," Maybelle said. "Hearing Becca was dead started me thinking. My life's a shambles. No husband, no children. A dead-end job. I don't want to look back and know I've spent my lifetime handing out brochures to tourists. I want to travel, see something of the world. I want to see if the Grand Canyon is really grand. Watch the ball drop on New Year's Eve in Times Square. Go to Disney World. Visit Niagara Falls. Pretty pathetic, isn't it?"

"No, not at all. You deserve some happiness."

"Folks I've known since childhood are starting to give me funny looks. I keep expecting Chief McBride to barge into the Chamber of Commerce and lead me out in handcuffs," Maybelle confessed.

"McBride will get to the bottom of this, Maybelle," I said, patting her shoulder.

From the expression on her face, my words seemed to have little effect on her doom and gloom. "Nice of you to say, Piper, but things don't look good. It's public knowledge Becca and I had it in for each other. To make matters worse, it doesn't help that I don't have an alibi for the night she died."

"Try not to worry," I counseled, knowing full well how empty those words were when your freedom — your life — was at stake.

"Thanks, Piper," she said, summoning a smile. "This year crowd's even bigger than expected. I had to turn away a couple of last-minute entrants. They said they'd heard about Brandywine Creek and Becca's killing on TV. Thought they'd stop and try their luck here before heading up to Gatlinburg."

"Too bad it takes a murder to catch some folks' attention."

"Gracious! I nearly forgot what brought me here." She produced a wad of coupons from the envelope she carried and handed them to me.

"What're these?"

"Each coupon entitles the bearer to sample barbecue from any of the participating vendors. It also entitles them to cast a vote for their favorite."

"Great idea." I set the coupons next to

the cash register where I wouldn't forget to hand them out. "I don't recall doing this in the past."

"It's something new." Maybelle's face brightened. "Tex Mahoney's been dropping by the Chamber from time to time. The coupons were his idea. Tex said this has worked well in some of the other contests he's been in. He said it encourages visitors to patronize local businesses during the course of the festival. I had to get the town council's approval, of course, but Mayor Hemmings finally agreed to give Tex's suggestion a try."

"One to a customer it is."

"Tex is a bona fide barbecue expert. A purist." Maybelle hugged the envelope to her bosom like a schoolgirl. "He told me he gets furious when contestants try to cheat. He went on and on about the stunts folks try to pull. Tex said competition is something fierce, but rules are rules. Meat can't be marinated, injected, precooked, or pretreated. Those are grounds for disqualification according to the sanctioning organization."

Long after Maybelle left to deliver coupons to the rest of the merchants, I mulled over what she'd just said. I recalled the drawer full of flavor injectors in various shapes and sizes that Reba Mae and I found in Becca's kitchen. A woman who used cream of mushroom soup as liberally as others did catsup had little use for a flavor injector. To the best of my knowledge, the recipe for green bean casserole didn't call for one.

Becca had bragged about bringing home a trophy. She wanted to show everyone once and for all she was an award-worthy cook. How far would she go to prove her point? Knowing Becca, she intended to win — even if it meant cheating to do so. What if Tex had discovered her plan? Maybelle had mentioned cheating made him furious.

But furious enough to kill?

I was restocking shelves, my mind on autopilot, when Doug entered wearing his bright-orange Pit Crew T-shirt and jeans. "How's my favorite spice girl?" he asked.

I stopped what I was doing long enough to return his smile. "I've been dancing to the tune of a busy cash register most of the day. What brings you into town?"

"Wally Porter called a mandatory meeting for team captains. He wants to go over rules and regulations a final time. Answer any questions. Make sure there are no misunderstandings."

"I heard the rules are quite strict."

"Yeah, they are." Doug took off his wire-rimmed glasses and polished them with a handkerchief. "Five pages' worth of strict. Everything from no controlled substances to no pineapple rings on the pork. Off with their heads to anyone caught deviating."

Off with their heads . . . ? I cringed inwardly. The phrase brought to mind Becca's bloody skull.

"Sorry I haven't been very attentive recently," Doug continued. "Been too caught up trying to find the perfect rub, the perfect sauce, but I'll make it up to you once the festival's over. Dinner, maybe take in a movie. I heard about a terrific new restaurant in Augusta I'd like to try."

"Sure," I said, noting it was time to order more cardamom. "Dinner and a movie would be great."

He studied me, a worried look on his face. "I don't detect much enthusiasm on your part."

"Sorry," I apologized, taking his hand and squeezing it. "Guess I'm distracted by all the goings-on."

"Apology accepted," he said, then brightened. "Say, better yet, why don't I take you dancing? I heard about a club not far from here that has a live band every Saturday night."

"Sounds like fun."

"That's more like it." He drew me in for a kiss, and for blissful seconds my mind emptied of everything else.

"Guess I'll see you tomorrow night then for the street dance," Doug said when we broke apart. He started for the door, then turned and grinned at me over his shoulder. "Hopefully, you'll be able to spot me behind the big trophy I'll be carrying."

"Good luck!" I called after him.

As I slowly walked back toward the storeroom, I was unable to escape the niggling feeling that the window of opportunity for finding Becca's killer was about to slam shut. The barbecue festival would soon be over. Would the chance to find the murderer be over as well?

CHAPTER 33

It wasn't every day I was invited to dine at a home dating back to the 1820s. I was looking forward to the occasion. It would be the perfect opportunity to learn more about Tex and Wally, too. I dressed with care in a black and white floral jacquard skirt, sleeveless black top, and peep-toe patent-leather pumps. The Turner-Driscoll House had been the talk of the town as the once-neglected grande dame had flourished from tired into fabulous.

I alighted from my carriage — er, make that my VW Beetle — beneath the boughs of a stately magnolia and sashayed up the front steps to the portico. I had no sooner rung the bell when the door was opened by a young black girl.

"Mrs. Driscoll is expecting you, Mrs. Prescott," the girl informed me. "She said you were to join the others in the parlor. If you'll follow me . . ."

The girl looked vaguely familiar, yet I couldn't quite place her. She was slender and quite pretty, with skin the warm brown of an acorn. I guessed her to be in her late teens. "Excuse me, but have we met?"

"I graduated from high school with your son, Chad." She flashed a smile over her shoulder. "I'm Lakeisha Blessing."

"Then you must be related to Precious."

"Yes, ma'am," Lakeisha acknowledged. "Precious is my auntie."

"Ahh, yes," I said. "Chad, I recall, was quite upset when you beat him out for class valedictorian."

Lakeisha simply smiled and, upon reaching the parlor, excused herself.

"Piper!" Felicity rose from the settee and hurried over to greet me. Her other guests had already assembled and were enjoying cocktails in stemmed glasses. Tex and Wally, gentlemen that they were, rose when they spotted me. Reba Mae waggled her fingers and grinned.

Linking her arm through mine, Felicity drew me into the room where I'd been only the day before. "Wally is making martinis. Care to join us, or would you prefer a nice Chardonnay?"

"I'll have a martini," I heard myself reply. I resisted the urge to go all James Bond on her and add *shaken, not stirred.* Luckily I caught myself in time. I have to confess I've never tasted a martini. The drink — or maybe it was the fancy glasses — always seemed glamorous and sophisticated, so I put any misgivings aside.

"Excellent choice." Wally nodded his approval. "One olive or two?"

What was with the quiz? Was there a right or wrong answer? What if I didn't like olives? With these questions zipping through my brain, I contemplated my options. Reba Mae cleared her throat. I darted a glance in her direction and, much to my relief, saw her hold up her index and middle fingers.

"Two," I replied. "I prefer martinis with two olives."

While Wally measured gin and vermouth into a silver shaker, Tex indicated a chair across from Reba Mae. "Have a seat, little lady."

I cautiously lowered myself onto a chair that looked to be museum quality. The kind usually seen behind a velvet rope and inaccessible to humble tourists. Felicity offered me hors d'oeuvres prettily arranged on a silver tray.

"Try 'em, Piper," Reba Mae urged. "They're to die for."

"Those little triangles are a variation of

cheese straws," Felicity explained, looking pleased at Reba Mae's ringing endorsement.

"Cheese straws and deviled eggs are part of every Southern cook's repertoire," Reba added, helping herself to another golden triangle.

"You're absolutely right, Reba Mae." Felicity passed the tray to Tex. "As you can see, Piper, I used both the black and white sesame seeds I purchased in your shop."

Wally handed me a martini. "Here you go."

"I'm afraid I'm not familiar with black sesame seeds," Tex confessed.

"Americans are more familiar with white sesame seeds," I explained. "The black variety is used more commonly in Chinese and Japanese cooking."

"Hmm, interesting." Wally eyed me over the rim of his martini glass. "In my experience, black sesame seeds tend to be bitter."

"True, but not if the dry roasting is done lightly."

"I bow to your expertise."

Wally's smile didn't reach his eyes. I got the impression he wasn't pleased I'd contradicted his opinion. I took a tiny sip of my martini and tried not to make a face when I discovered the drink stronger than anticipated.

When thirty minutes later Lakeisha Blessing announced dinner was ready, I was amazed to find my glass empty. I felt grateful for Tex's steadying arm as he escorted me into the dining room. Martinis, it seemed, packed a punch. I made a mental note to steer clear of them in the future.

Seated at an antique dining room table, I experienced once again the sensation of stepping back in time. Felicity had pulled out all the stops to make dinner a memorable occasion. Bone china, crystal, and silver sparkled against the white damask tablecloth. I doubted the room looked much different than it had when news arrived that General Sherman and his troops were marching across Georgia. The only things absent were hoop skirts and frock coats.

Felicity sat enthroned at the head of the table and requested that Tex and Wally sit on either side of her. I was seated beside Tex while Reba Mae sat across from me next to Wally. At a signal from Felicity, Lakeisha served a salad of field greens, toasted pecans, and mandarin oranges drizzled with raspberry vinaigrette.

Wally, assuming the role of sommelier, circled the table and poured wine. "I selected a full-bodied cabernet sauvignon to pair with the beef bourguignon. My specialty is really Italian, but tonight I decided to serve French instead."

"Wally's spinach and eggplant lasagna with sun-dried tomatoes was superb," Felicity said.

Leaning over, Tex whispered, "Me, on the other hand, a burger, a brew, and I'm happy."

Felicity passed a basket of flaky dinner rolls. "I consider myself fortunate at having Lakeisha help when I entertain. I'll miss her when she returns to Georgia Southern in Statesboro. Her father, Bubba Blessing, is an entrant in the amateur division."

Tex stopped slathering butter on his roll. "What's your father's specialty, Lakeisha?"

"Ribs, sir," she said, pride in her voice. "Daddy's are the best. They melt in your mouth."

"You're not trying to influence one of the judges, are you, Lakeisha?" Wally asked, quick to remind us of his esteemed position lest we had lapsed into dementia.

Lakeisha's dark eyes rounded. "No, sir. I didn't mean . . ."

Felicity clucked her tongue. "I'm certain Mr. Porter was merely teasing, dear."

Wally gave the girl a stern look. "Now would be a good time, Lakeisha, to plate the entrée. Remember to do it exactly as I instructed."

"Yes, sir." Lakeisha hurried out.

"Speaking of specialties," Felicity continued, "I don't think I've ever tasted better brisket than the one Tex made for us."

Brisket . . . ? I paused in the act of reaching for my wine. *As in bludgeoned with a brisket?*

From across the table, Reba Mae shot me a look. "I heard Pete Barker at Meat on Main had a run on brisket," she said, picking up the conversational thread. "Could hardly keep up with orders."

"Dottie Hemmings told me Becca Dapkins bought his entire stock," I said, improvising like mad.

"You know what they say about timing." Tex raised his wineglass and winked. "Lucky for me Pete found one lonely brisket, froze hard as a brick, hiding in the back of his meat locker."

"Don't suppose you're of a mind to share your recipe?" Reba Mae all but batted her eyelashes.

"Sorry, ma'am, but wild horses couldn't drag it out of me. It's been in the family for years. Family secrets are hard to part with—even to a lady as pretty as yourself."

Reba Mae speared a slice of mandarin orange. "Can't blame a girl for tryin'."

"I tried to persuade Reba Mae to divulge her secrets for Hungarian goulash, but with no success," Wally grumbled. "I even tried bribing her with an excellent Bordeaux."

Lakeisha returned to clear the salad plates. I would've liked to find out more about Tex and his magic way with a brisket that was "hard as a brick," but talk drifted to other topics. I promised myself I'd corner Felicity later in an effort to learn more.

The beef bourguignon lived up to the hype. Wally's chest swelled like a pufferfish in the Georgia Aquarium at all the praise. He celebrated his resounding culinary success by opening a second bottle of red wine. He failed to notice I'd barely touched the first glass he'd poured me.

My chance to speak privately to Felicity came when she announced it was time for dessert. "I'll help," I said, hopping up from my chair before she could refuse. I raced after her as rapidly as my high heels and pencil-slim skirt allowed.

I caught up with her as she was about to enter a kitchen that seemed surprisingly modern in a house nearly two hundred years old. "That's very thoughtful of you to offer help but unnecessary," she said.

"Lakeisha and I can manage quite nicely."

"I wanted to ask you a question," I told her, glancing down the hall to make sure no one was within earshot. "I wondered if you recalled exactly when Tex cooked his brisket."

"Well now, let me think." Felicity's brow furrowed; then her expression cleared. "Oh yes, I remember. It was shortly after he arrived in Brandywine Creek. Matter of fact, it was the very day Becca's body was discovered. I remember thinking how considerate of him to distract us from the terrible tragedy that had just transpired."

"Oh . . ." *Coincidence? Or just plain creepy?*

Felicity studied me worriedly. "You look a bit pale, dear. Are you feeling all right?"

"I just need a breath of fresh air is all."

"I should have warned you that Wally's martinis are potent. Not to mention all the wine." She patted my arm. "Why don't you sit a spell while I check on the peach cobbler?"

My head was reeling — and it had nothing to do with alcohol. Tex Mahoney had just zoomed to the top spot on my persons-of-interest list. By his own admission, he hated cheaters. And judging from the drawer of flavor injectors, Becca had intended to cheat her way to success. Had Tex discovered her plan? Did a mean temper lurk under the lazy drawl and good ol' boy charisma? Was the out-of-this-world brisket he'd prepared the day I'd found her body a clever attempt to destroy the murder weapon?

For Felicity's benefit, I fabricated a tipsy smile and wobbled unsteadily down the hall. Pausing outside the dining room, I waved my arms to flag down Reba Mae's attention. She glanced up, about to speak, but I held my finger to my lips and beckoned her.

Muttering an excuse about needing to visit the little girls' room, she joined me in the hallway. I caught her arm and pulled her toward the curving stairway that led to the upper level. "I need to search Tex's room."

She regarded me suspiciously. "Girl, how many martinis did you drink?"

"I think Tex murdered Becca."

"Let me smell your breath," Reba Mae ordered. "You never could tolerate hard liquor."

"I don't have time to explain," I whispered. "All I'm asking is that you keep everyone occupied downstairs while I look for clues."

Reba Mae stared at me as if I'd taken

leave of my senses. "Honeybun, you're crazy as a loon."

"We can debate that later, but right now I need you to watch my back."

"Well," she said at last, "if you're gonna sneak around you'd better do it barefoot. High heels make one heck of a racket on these hardwood floors."

If I had time, I would have hugged her. Instead, I slipped off my shoes and hid them behind a plant stand with a trailing Boston fern. Giving my BFF a thumbs-up, I hiked up my skirt and darted up the stairs.

I found myself in a wide center hallway, its heart pine floor cushioned with a runner in subdued colors. Doors with bronze nameplates bearing names of various military leaders opened off either side. Names such as those of Brigadier Generals William T. Wofford, George T. Anderson, and Henry Benning. If I had to venture a guess, these officers served in the Confederate army.

From below I could hear the soft murmur of voices and I knew I didn't have much time. My heart hammered in my ears as I pushed open the door on my right. Women's clothing was strewn across a chaise lounge. The antique dresser was cluttered with jewelry, cosmetics, and expensive perfume bottles, telling me the room belonged to the barbecue princess.

I left quietly and moved on. I struck pay dirt when I entered a room labeled: BRIGADIER GENERAL MATHEW D. ECTOR. Unlike Barbie's, it was neat as a pin. Distinctly masculine. Who was the neatnik? I wondered. Wally or Tex?

I ventured farther inside, cautiously shutting the door behind me. There were no closets to sift through, since homes of that period favored bulky armoires rather than spacious walk-ins. My question as to the room's occupant was answered when I eased the armoire open and found it crammed with Tex's Western-style shirts and jeans.

Any lingering doubt vanished at spying a silver belt buckle inlaid with turquoise on the dressing table. I eased open a drawer of the nightstand, but the only thing it contained was a Gideon Bible. I was about to close it when something caught my eye. Several scraps of paper protruded between the pages. Had someone used them to mark a favorite passage? My curiosity piqued, I picked the Bible up for a better look, and two small pieces of paper floated to the floor. Even before I scooped them up, I sensed I'd just found Maybelle's missing alibi.

I stared down at them. What to do? What to do? I gnawed my lower lip and pondered my options. I needed to show McBride my find. I'd worry later about explaining how I found proof of Maybelle's innocence. I knew from past experience he'd be a hard sell. There were dozens, maybe even hundreds, of movie tickets sold any given night. Everyone has gas station receipts. This particular station was located at a busy intersection. Tex could have filled his tank there as easily as Maybelle. But what about fingerprints? What if Maybelle's — and now mine — were on the credit card receipt? Wouldn't that be significant? I slipped both of them into my skirt pocket.

Nervously I glanced over my shoulder. I'd dawdled long enough. It was time to skedaddle. I replaced the Bible and hurried out of the bedroom. I was congratulating myself on a clean getaway when Tex met me halfway down the stairs.

"These yours, little lady?" he asked, holding up my peep-toe stilettos.

Forcing a smile, I reached for my shoes, but he held them just out of reach.

"Any reason why you're parading around upstairs in your bare feet while the rest of us are corralled below?"

I thought I detected an underlying hardness in the soft drawl. "I wasn't feeling well," I fibbed. "I thought Felicity might have some aspirin in her medicine cabinet."

Snatching my shoes out of his hands, I squeezed past him on the staircase. I felt his eyes bore into my back as I fled.

CHAPTER 34

I drummed my fingers on the steering wheel. The *click, click* sound made by my nails seemed the equivalent of Chinese water torture on my frayed nerves. The two receipts I'd retrieved, confiscated, appropriated — or blatantly robbed — from Tex Mahoney's room were burning a hole in my pocket. To my way of thinking, they were tantamount to proof positive that Tex murdered Becca and had tried to frame Maybelle. Problem number one was how to convince McBride. Problem number two was how to explain why I was in possession of two incriminating pieces of evidence. I wasn't a fashion maven, but neither was I fond of orange jumpsuits.

Put on your big-girl panties and stop being a wuss. Problem number three was to locate the lawman. Would I find him behind his desk at the police department? Or had he already left for the day? Deciding to swing by the station, I shifted into Drive. If I didn't see his truck in its usual parking spot, I'd drive by his house. I'd smile nicely while asking him to check the receipts for fingerprints. Next, I'd suggest he haul Tex down to the station and grill him like a rack of ribs.

I cruised down Lincoln Street, bypassing the stage set up for Zeke Blessing and his blues band and slowing when I reached the Brandywine Creek Police Department. There was no sign of McBride's vehicle in the adjacent lot, so I continued on my merry way. I was contemplating confronting McBride on his home turf when I recognized his big black Ford F-150 parked down the block from North of the Border. Who was I to argue with fate?

Lights blazed in the windows of the Mexican restaurant. Cars lined both sides of the street. People waiting for tables congregated in the doorway. Tomorrow barbecue would reign supreme, but tonight was meant for mariachi music and margaritas. As if from a stroke of a magic wand, a SUV pulled out of a parking space, and I pulled in. I still hadn't devised a tactful way of confessing I'd committed a felony, or at least a misdemeanor, but I refused to let that deter me. I hurried from my car and pushed my way through the crowd.

Waiters bustled back and forth with trays of burritos and fajitas. Nacho greeted me with a harried smile. "Señora, we have no empty tables, but if you'd care to wait . . ."

"That's quite all right, Nacho," I said. "I'm here to meet Chief McBride."

"Ah . . ." Worry clouded Nacho's round face. "The chief is here, señora, but he's with a lady friend."

Lady friend . . . ? That bit of information stopped me dead in my tracks. Barbie Q? Of course, why hadn't the possibility occurred to me sooner? That explained the woman's absence at Felicity's dinner party. And who better to have a date with than a macho police chief? Not that I cared.

I craned my neck, hoping to spot the couple. "Just point me in McBride's direction, Nacho."

"He's in a booth, señora, at the back. Would you like —"

I didn't wait to hear the rest of the sentence. Weaving my way through a maze of waiters and patrons, I zeroed in on my prey. I instantly recognized the back of Barbie's bleached-blond head. I dodged a portly gentleman with a bad comb-over just as McBride looked up. True to his calling, his face mirrored suspicion at seeing me.

Barbie, observing the change in her date's expression, glanced over her shoulder. I didn't have to be clairvoyant to know what she was thinking. Her displeasure was written all over her face. "What do you want now?" she demanded the instant I arrived tableside.

I ignored her — or at I least tried to. "McBride, we need to talk," I said, not bothering with a *sorry to interrupt.*

"Can't it wait?" he asked.

"We just ordered dinner," Barbie snapped. "Go away!"

"It's a matter of life or death."

"Really, Piper," she said plaintively. "Stop being such a drama queen. Isn't it obvious Wyatt's off duty?"

It was obvious all right. The jeans and T-shirt were a dead giveaway. At the word "dead," a sense of urgency washed over me. Impatient, I shifted my weight from one foot to the other. Soon I'd be reduced to hand-wringing. "It's important," I said.

Leaning back, McBride eyed me with his electric blues. "So speak, then."

"In private." I wanted desperately to take McBride's arm and bodily haul him to his feet. "It'll only take a minute."

Tossing his napkin aside, he eased himself

410

from the booth. "This better be good. Let's go."

He started toward the front entrance, but I jerked his sleeve. "No," I said. "There's too many people milling around. Better if we use the rear entrance."

He scowled but followed my lead out the back door and into a narrow alley. "What's with the cloak-and-dagger? Ever think of applying for a position in the CIA?"

Now that I had McBride all to myself I didn't know where to begin. Would he see my actions as breaking and entering? I'd confess to the entering, but since I hadn't broken anything had I really committed a crime?

"The clock's ticking," he said, then waited for me to continue. Say as little as possible while allowing the other person to babble like the village idiot. Must've been a technique he'd mastered over the years.

"I . . . er," I stalled, digging the receipts out of my pocket and shoving them into his hands. "Here."

He glanced at them, then back at me. "And these are . . . ?"

"Maybelle's alibi. They prove she was at a movie and stopped for gas during the time Becca was killed, therefore she's innocent."

"I'm not going to like the answer, but how

do these happen to be in your possession?"

"I found them." And that was the truth, the gospel truth, and nothing but the truth.

"I see," he muttered. "Exactly where did you find them?"

"Where?" I repeated. *Dang!* I'd hoped he wouldn't ask.

"You heard me. Don't pretend you've suddenly gone deaf."

I looked down at the ground and nudged a pebble with my patent-leather peep-toe. "Perhaps 'found' isn't the correct word," I conceded grudgingly.

He blew out a breath. "Kindly clue me in to the correct word."

"They fell out of a book — a Bible — if you must know. They fell and I found."

That was a hair closer to the truth. The two scraps of paper had succumbed to the law of gravity and fallen to the floor, where I'd picked them up. Surely that constituted finding.

"I see," he murmured. Should I remind him that he was repeating himself? I wondered. A peek at his face, however, warned me to hold my tongue.

"I'm curious, Piper," he continued. "Care to tell me where this Bible was when you happened to pick it up and Maybelle's alibi just happened to fall to the floor?"

"Mmm." Nervously I started to look at my wristwatch for the time, then realized I'd forgotten to wear it. "Ah . . . the Bible was at the Turner-Driscoll House. You know how those Gideons are about putting a Bible in every room."

McBride's patience was wearing thin. "Let's narrow it down a bit, shall we? Which room was it in? And what were you doing there — conducting a prayer service?"

"If you must know, I was looking for the ladies' room when I happened into Tex Mahoney's room by mistake," I lied, keeping my fingers crossed. "That's where I found the receipts. I think Tex murdered Becca," I blurted. There, I'd gone and done it — stopped being a wuss.

McBride studied the ticket stub and gas receipt. "Who's to say Tex Mahoney didn't go to a movie and stop for gas on the way from Augusta to Brandywine Creek?"

The thought hadn't occurred to me. "I suppose it's possible," I said slowly.

"These, in and of themselves, don't prove Maybelle's not guilty of murder. Dozens of movie tickets are sold every evening. As for the gasoline receipt, the station's popular. I've stopped there a time or two myself."

"But don't you think it's strange that Maybelle told Reba Mae and me about having an alibi and shortly afterward her wallet was stolen? Isn't it odd Maybelle and Tex would go to the *same* movie and stop at the *same* gas station on the *same* night Becca was murdered? I didn't think you were a great believer in coincidence. Besides, Maybelle's credit card info should be on the gas receipt along with the time of purchase."

"Do you realize the danger you've put yourself into if Mahoney discovers you took the receipts and gave them to the police? If he killed once, he could do it again."

I gulped noisily at the mental image. I'd met Tex coming up the stairs at the Turner-Driscoll House. Did he suspect I'd searched his room and found Maybelle's missing alibi in his nightstand?

"What do you expect me to do with these?" McBride asked.

"Sheesh!" I threw up my hands. "I 'expect' you to make like *CSI* and have them checked for prints. If Maybelle's telling the truth, her fingerprints will be all over them along with those of the person who stole them from her. Or," I added, making no attempt to hide my sarcasm, "you might find time in your *busy* schedule to requisition the surveillance tapes from the movie theater and gas station."

"Fair enough, but on one condition." He carefully tucked the receipts into a plastic protector inside his wallet. "Swear to me that you'll put an end to your nosing around. No telling what trouble you'll land in."

Before I could swear to anything, the rear door of the restaurant swung open and Barbie's head poked out. "Your 'minute' could go on record as the longest one in history. Dinner's getting cold."

"Sorry," McBride told her. "Be right there."

But Barbie didn't budge. Instead, she flicked a disdainful glance in my direction. "The woman's so transparent it's ridiculous. I'm surprised, Wyatt, you haven't caught on to her ways. She's using any ploy available to attract your attention."

I felt my cheeks burn. How dare she accuse me of the very thing she was guilty of? Baby sister's best friend turned TV celeb, Barbie Quinlan had made a play for McBride from the moment she drove into town. She'd used all her ammunition — designer clothes, flawless makeup, flowing blond locks, and drop-dead figure. Give me a break. Did she seriously view little ol' me as competition?

McBride gave me a curt nod. "I'll check into it."

Barbie shot me a spiteful look as they both disappeared inside. I was left standing alone in a deserted alley worrying if curiosity would kill the cat — the feline in this particular case being none other than me.

Giving up on late-night television, I tossed and turned until my sheets were a tangled mess. As mothers of teens the world over can attest, you never sleep easy until your chicks are safely back in the nest. I pried open one eye and peered at the bedside clock. It was 12:45 A.M. And my chick still hadn't come home to roost.

I was about to climb out of bed and start pacing when Casey's head popped up. Ears cocked, he made a throaty growl. The slamming of a car door sent him galloping from my bedroom to assume a stance at the kitchen door, where he commenced a spate of barking and vigorous tail wagging.

Between barks, I heard a key twist in a lock downstairs followed by footsteps of the tiptoeing variety. "Linds!" I called. "That you?"

"Shh," Lindsey said, trying to hush Casey's enthusiam as she opened the door of the apartment. "Yes, Mom, it's me. Go back to sleep."

Going back to sleep wasn't an option, so I flung aside the covers and flicked on a light. "Do you have any idea what time it is, young lady?"

Lindsey stooped to pet Casey, who wriggled with delight. "Sorry. I was hanging out with Taylor and the gang and I lost track of time. I tried to be quiet coming in."

I just bet you did. I leaned against the doorjamb, arms crossed over my sleep shirt, my bare foot tapping the hardwood floor. Did my daughter think I was born yesterday? Did she think I'd never tried to sneak in after curfew without disturbing my parents? Did she really think I wasn't on to her tricks? Jeez Louise, I could give the girl pointers. But that could wait until she turned forty.

"Doc's pulled pork is going to be fabulous," Lindsey said, stifling a theatrical yawn. "I had no idea all the work involved when I volunteered. I'd better get to bed. Busy day tomorrow."

"Make that today," I corrected, stopping her in her tracks as she headed toward her room. "Once the festival's over, no more excuses for coming home late. Understood?"

"Fine." Lindsey heaved a put-upon sigh

that would have made Meryl Streep weep with envy.

"And Lindsey, next week I want you to help Meemaw sort through her tea sets. Everything needs to be hand washed and either returned to her cupboard or boxed up and delivered to Yesteryear Antiques."

Lindsey's pretty blue-gray eyes widened in alarm. "Mo-om . . . ," she wailed. "Do you know how long that will take? Meemaw has a china cabinet filled with cups, saucers, and teapots. It'll take forever."

Question asked and answered, I thought with a nod. "Forever is just what it felt like waiting for you to come home safe and sound — and late."

Lindsey trudged off with Casey trotting behind. I switched off the light and crawled back into bed. I drifted off to sleep blissfully unaware of what the day held in store.

CHAPTER 35

"I'm off. Wish us luck." Lindsey flew out the door, bagel in hand, a blur of blond ponytail and bright-orange T-shirt.

"Good luck." I called, but doubt that in her haste she heard me.

Casey watched her departure with censure in his doggie-brown eyes. I'd become adept at reading the expressions on the cute furry face. Lindsey had left without giving him a pat on the head or a scratch behind the ears, and he wasn't pleased at the oversight. The pup looked even more unhappy, if that was possible, when I banished him behind the baby gate fastened across the foot of the stairs.

Customers began filtering in the instant I turned the sign on my front door from CLOSED to OPEN. The tang of woodsmoke drifted in along with the tantalizing aroma of roasting meat. Mouthwaterin' and finger-lickin' good, as Reba Mae would say.

Melly, prim and proper in a starched shirtwaist and her signature pearls, hurried in and took her place beside me at the counter. "Sorry I'm late, dear, but I ran into Gerilee Barker at the pancake breakfast. You know how Gerilee loves to talk."

The mention of pancakes served up by members of the Brandywine Creek Fire Department at their annual fund-raiser made my stomach rumble. I took another swig of coffee and hoped that would appease the hunger gods. If business was as brisk as I hoped, I might not get a break until dinnertime.

"The American Legion is sponsoring a yard sale." Melly donned an apron, careful not to muss her perfectly coiffed hair. "Gerilee said Pinky Alexander finally sold the solar-powered birdbath she received from her daughter-in-law last Christmas."

"I'm happy for her," I replied. "She tried getting rid of it at the Humane Society's silent auction, but no such luck. It was ugly as sin."

"I remember." Melly wagged her head. "Not a single bid. She practically begged folks to take it off her hands."

A barrel-chested man wearing bib overalls entered and made a beeline in our direction. "Some darn crook made off with my cumin. I need more for my sauce."

"Let me show you," Melly said as she led him away. "Would you like whole or ground? My ex-daughter-in-law carries both."

A tall, gangly youth, a worried expression on his pimply face, approached next. "My uncle sent me here for coriander. Said don't come back without it. I don't even know what the heck it is."

"Coriander is one of the few plants that can lay claim to being both an herb and a spice." I plucked a jar from a shelf and handed it to him. The boy's tension seemed to ease. "Did you know coriander and cilantro are related?" I asked as I made change from the five-dollar bill he'd given me.

"No, ma'am," he admitted. "I'm new to cooking. My mom sent me here from Macon to spend the summer with my aunt and uncle. Said the fresh air and outdoors would keep me away from computer games while she was at work."

"Well, if you're into trivia, cilantro, which is used extensively in Mexican cooking, is the leaf of the coriander plant. The seeds, such as your uncle requested, add flavor to foods that cook for a longer period of time."

"Thanks," he said, the jar clutched to his

bony chest. "I'll use that info to impress my uncle."

I'd no sooner rearranged a window display when Dottie Hemmings sailed in. She beamed me a smile. "I just popped in to say hello."

"Hello, Dottie." Dottie was generous with hellos. Not so much with actual purchases. She adhered to the policy that spices retain their potency for a lifetime. I tried to convince her otherwise, but so far my advice fell on deaf ears.

"Looks like business is booming." She glanced around at the customers who were filling little wicker baskets with a variety of spices. "My husband the mayor says this is the biggest crowd Brandywine Creek has ever seen. Pity it took poor Becca dying to bring 'em to our town," she said mournfully, but her expression quickly brightened. "Nothing's so bad it's not good for something, I always say."

I removed extra bags from beneath the counter and placed the stack next to the cash register where they'd be handy. "Maybe your husband could arrange for a murder every year," I said tongue-in-cheek. "That way every festival would be assured success."

Dottie's penciled brows crept high on her

forehead. Her round face mirrored shock. "Piper . . . !"

"I'm joking, Dottie," I said, never thinking for a second she'd would take me literally.

"Of course. I knew you were only pulling my leg." She patted her sprayed and teased helmet of Clairol's natural blond. "Folks are excited Barbie Quinlan is in town filming the goings-on. Maybe it's just me, but it seems everyone took pains to look extra nice in case they wind up in front of the camera. No one wants to look frumpy with the whole world watching."

I seriously doubted the "whole world" would be tuned into Barbie-Q-Perfect's show but refrained from saying so. Let Dottie have her illusions.

"Dorinda, over at the police department," Dottie continued, "said the EMS set up a booth to treat medical emergencies. My husband the mayor says they're just trying to look good so the city council will approve funds for new equipment."

"That seems a worthwhile cause," I said absently as I rang up a sale.

"Dorinda said the EMS already treated a couple entrants for burns," Dottie prattled on, refusing to take the hint when customers demanded my attention. "If the weather prediction is right about today, they might see a bunch of heatstrokes. Wish I could visit longer, but I want to stop by the Chamber and see if I can help out. Maybelle, bless her heart, is worn to a frazzle worrying about the festival and if she's going to be arrested any minute. Toodleloo." With a waved of her plump fingers, she marched out the door.

Melly joined me behind the counter. "I swear that woman never tires of spreading doom and gloom. For heaven sakes, would it kill her to refer to her husband the mayor by his Christian name? Everyone knows it's Harvey."

I looked at my former mother-in-law in amusement. "Getting a little testy, are we?"

"If you want my honest opinion, her husband the mayor also happens to be a pompous windbag."

"No argument there." I glanced at the regulator clock on the wall, surprised to see it was nearly two o'clock. "I think we deserve some lunch."

While Melly minded the shop, I ran across the street. Scores of people in shorts, T-shirts, and flip-flops jammed the square. If noise alone was any indicator, the Brandywine Creek Barbecue Festival was a resounding success. The steel guitars of a country-western band performing down the block were nearly drowned out by the laughter and chatter. Heat from dozens of cookers added to the day's already-blistering temperature. I felt a bead of sweat trickle between my shoulder blades as I made my way down a long row of vendors. Ribs, brisket, and hash. Everything looked and smelled delicious. Guided by the sweet and savory aroma of barbecue sauce, I finally settled on a booth where trophies from previous competitions were prominently displayed. I stood in line behind a couple debating the merits of pulled pork versus baby back ribs. When they finally moved on, I purchased a sample platter for Melly and myself. As I started back, I narrowly avoided colliding with a small boy intent on licking a cone that dripped homemade peach ice cream.

Upon my return to the relative peace and quiet of Spice It Up!, I poured Melly sweet tea and popped the tab on a Diet Coke for myself. We feasted like royalty on pulled pork, barbecue chicken, hash, baked beans, and coleslaw.

"Glad to see you're wearing sensible footwear," Melly commented, eyeing my running shoes. "Are you going to the dance tonight?"

"Doug — Dr. Winters — invited me." I tried the hash but found it too bland for my taste. I'd like it better with more black pepper, more thyme, maybe a dash of chili powder. "What about you, Melly? Are you going to the dance?"

"Believe it or not, I cut a fine figure in my day. Alas," she sighed, "that day has come and gone. I'm planning to spend the evening watching reruns on TV."

"Reruns such as *Vanished*?"

"As you know, it's one of my favorite programs," she said primly. "Do you think Becca saw the episode about the Witness Protection Program? She would have enjoyed it."

I sampled the pulled pork. It had been basted with a tangy yellow mustard-based barbecue sauce popular in South Carolina. Pulled pork, as many foodies know, is the South's contribution to American cuisine. Who was I to disagree?

"That might have been the last one she saw, since she was killed soon after," I said, licking sauce from my fingers.

"Oh, dear. . . ." Melly looked stricken at the thought. "How horrible."

I was instantly sorry for what I'd just said. I opened my mouth to apologize but was interrupted by drumroll and a roar of applause coming from the square.

Melly discarded her empty paper plate in the trash. "Winners in the various categories must have been announced."

As if in response to her comment, Doug bounded in, wielding a trophy in the shape of a pig. "Second place. Backyard division," he said, his face wreathed in triumph.

I hurried over to admire his prize. "That's wonderful, Doug."

"Who took first place?" Melly inquired innocently.

"Bubba Blessing and his *Bub-Ba-Cue* team," Doug replied, too happy at the outcome to be upset. "Best of all, we're both invited to compete next year in the professional division."

"Doug, that's terrific!" I said, hugging him.

Hugs, especially in this part of the country, are spontaneous and plentiful. Even so, I could feel the zing of Melly's disapproval. I know for a fact she didn't condone CJ's trading me in for a twenty-four-year-old with prefabricated boobs and glow-in-the-dark teeth. It never crossed my mind, however, that Melly might resent me moving forward with my life. It had taken me a while, but I'd finally made peace with being a divorcée and forsaken my vow of celibacy.

I was ready to dip my toe into the relationship pool and test the water.

"A grillmaster from North Carolina and his team, Hogs Gone Wild, won the professional division," Doug said, readjusting his grip on his trophy. "I asked for the recipe for his mop sauce, but he refused to give it up. He said he's been perfecting it for the past fifteen years."

Melly wrinkled her nose. "Most mop sauces are too vinegary."

"Bet you'd like this one," Doug told her. "I think it might've had coffee in it. The guy kept swabbing it on the brisket the whole time it cooked. The meat was so moist and tender it fell right off the bone."

"What about the taster's choice division?" I asked.

"Canceled," Doug said. "Mayor Hemmings told the entrants it was being withheld out of respect for Becca Dapkins. That was the division she was determined to win. In a way, Becca did win, but posthumously."

How had Tex taken the news that taster's choice had been canceled? I wondered. The man was a fierce competitor. After seeing the expression on his face when he nearly caught me snooping the previous night, I suspected a temper lurked behind the good ol' boy façade.

Business slowed to a trickle after Doug left, so I sent Melly home. She'd been a trooper, tirelessly ringing up sales and waiting on customers. I don't know how I would've managed without her. Now that peace and quiet returned to Spice It Up!, I used the time to enter data into my point-of-sale software. As I did so, I had to admit the changes Melly made, though minor, were time-savers. I wondered if she'd ever followed up on my suggestion to submit her ideas to the company that marketed it.

I glanced up when the shop door opened. Lindsey, her cheeks flushed, rushed in. "We did it, Mom," she said, catching me up for a hug. "Our team placed second, but Doug said not to worry. Next year, we're going to finish first; just wait and see."

"Now that's what I call a positive attitude," I told her, stepping back. "Now about curfew . . ."

"Mo-om!" she cried. "Isn't it bad enough I have to wash all of Meemaw's tea sets? Can't your lecture wait till tomorrow? Right now I need a shower. My clothes reek of smoke and barbecue."

"Fine," I conceded. "Just make sure you're home on time tonight."

"Promise," she agreed. "Barbie and Carter filmed the entire trophy presentation.

Wait till Amber hears I'm going to be on TV."

"Oh, happy day," I muttered under my breath as she danced away with Casey happily prancing after her.

A shower and a change of clothes were on my agenda as well. Fueled by the knowledge Spice It Up! showed a healthy profit, I was ready to celebrate. After my shower, I dressed in a swingy skirt and sleeveless top and put on my dancing shoes, which in this case happened to be ballet flats. Doug had advised leather soles were a must when it came to dancing the shag. He said to pretend my shoes were magnets and the floor was made out of metal. I added a collection of thin bangle bracelets to my wrist and I was ready.

It was an easy walk on a balmy summer night. The dance was being held in what had once been a pre-owned car lot belonging to Cloune Motors. The stock of vehicles had recently been liquidated, and the business was up for sale. In the meantime, Caleb Johnson, Reba Mae's boy, continued to operate the automotive-repair end of the business.

I heard the music from a block away — beach music. The kind that made you want to kick up your heels and swing your hips. *But,* I reminded myself, *no bouncing allowed in the shag.* I needed to "glide," not bounce. I stood on the fringe and scanned the crowd for a familiar face. I'd told Doug that I'd meet him here, but he was hard to spot with all the people.

I thought I saw Reba Mae's head bobbing on the dance floor. I was about to wave and get her attention when Clay Johnson approached.

"Hey, Miz Prescott, lookin' for someone?"

"Hey yourself, Clay," I said. "I'm supposed to meet Doug — Doc Winters — but I underestimated the turnout for the dance."

"The shag contest is the draw. I saw Doc over at the bandstand talkin' to Mama." Clay stuffed his hands into the pockets of his cargo shorts.

"Thanks," I said.

I started off in the general direction of the dance floor when he stopped me. "Wait up, Miz Prescott."

I paused. "Something bothering you, Clay? You know you can always come to me."

"Yeah, you're cool. You didn't even lose your temper when I was a kid and my base hit flew through your kitchen window."

"Having girl trouble?"

"Not exactly." Rocking back on his heels, he studied the ground.

"Then what is it?" I prompted. The poor kid looked so upset, I wanted to put him out of his misery.

"I'm worried your daughter's headin' for trouble."

"Lindsey?" My voice rose loud enough to turn the heads of a couple standing nearby. "What do you mean, 'headin' for trouble'?"

His expression said he wanted to be anywhere else but where he was. "I hate to be a snitch, but . . ."

"But . . . ?"

"Lindsey's been spendin' a lot of time around Carter Kincaid."

"The videographer?" I asked in disbelief. "Why, Carter must be seven years older than Lindsey."

Clay stared off into the near distance. "I'm not sure he knows her actual age. Once she sets her mind to it, Lindsey can easily pass for older than sixteen."

I squared my shoulders. "Don't suppose you know where I might find them?"

"Yes, ma'am." Clay nodded. "Saw them a few minutes ago over at the beer tent."

CHAPTER 36

I stormed off in search of a certain young couple. And found them right where last spotted — outside the beer tent. Carter held a frosty bottle of Yuengling, a popular beer, in one hand. Lindsey, praise the Lord, was drinking a soda.

She looked none too happy to see me. "Hi, Mom," she muttered.

My scowl wiped the smile from Carter Kincaid's face. Typhoid Mary would have received a warmer welcome. "Mrs. Prescott —"

"Carter's been teaching me about photography and videotaping," Lindsey said in a valiant attempt to head off the storm she saw brewing. "I'm thinking of majoring in communications."

"I see," I drawled, attuned to her tactics. "What happened to becoming a veterinarian?"

"Carter's opened a whole new career path

for me. Isn't that awesome?"

" 'Awesome' hardly begins to describe the way I feel right now."

"A degree in communications can lead to a variety of job opportunities," Carter began an erstwhile pitch for his chosen profession.

"College is still a year away," I snapped. "Lindsey has plenty of time to decide what she wants to do when she grows up. Carter . . ." I paused for effect. "Do you realize my daughter is only sixteen?"

He blanched. "Sixteen?"

I simply nodded. Smart lad. He'd latched on to the key word. I felt inordinately pleased to see him squirm under my steely-eyed glare.

He turned toward Lindsey so abruptly he nearly spilled his brew. "You told me you were almost nineteen."

Lindsey had the grace to look embarrassed by her deception. "Sixteen, nineteen. They're just three years apart."

"Sixteen," I said, my voice flat but my eyes shooting sparks. "Jailbait."

Carter heaved his unfinished beer into a nearby trash barrel. "Gotta run. Barbie wants me on the road at first light tomorrow."

"How humiliating!" Lindsey stomped her foot as she watched him disappear into the throng. "You're treating me like a child."

"Then stop acting like one," I hissed. "That's what you deserve after pretending to be 'almost nineteen' and hanging out with men seven years older than yourself."

"Six," Lindsey corrected. "Carter's twenty-two."

"In the future, limit your dating to boys your own age. And for good measure, I'll make sure your daddy knows — and abides — by the rules."

Lindsey's lower lip jutted mutinously. "Why is it okay for Daddy to have a fiancée half his age? What make it all right for Amber to marry a man so much older than herself?"

Because Amber wants a father figure; Daddy wants a trophy wife, I wanted to say, but took a calming breath instead. "That's a conversation you need to have with your father — and Amber."

Every time I thought Lindsey had come to terms with mine and CJ's divorce, something new bubbled to the surface. Rather than confronting the issue head-on, she acted out with inappropriate behavior. I had to remember that while she looked grown-up on the outside, she was still a child in many ways. We — the three of us, CJ, and Lindsey, I — needed to sit down and air any grievances that still festered.

"Whatever," Lindsey retorted, but the word had lost its usual sting. "Now that you chased Carter off is it all right if I find Taylor and hang out with friends my 'own age'?"

"Fine," I said. "As long as you're home by curfew."

"Fine." She turned on her heel and marched off.

Hoping I'd taken the right approach with my daughter, I turned in the opposite direction and plowed into McBride. "Trouble with your teen?"

What McBride omitted saying was trouble *again.* He'd already witnessed the problems a single mom faced raising a sweet but sometimes rebellious daughter. "The fire's under control — for the moment."

"Good," he said. Taking my elbow, he steered me away from the crowd.

"What's up?" I noticed that though he was out of uniform, there was a discreet bulge under his navy-blue polo shirt. I guessed Smith & Wesson hugged his waist.

McBride pulled me into the darkened doorway of Dale's Swap and Shop. "I got a surprise hit on the movie stub and gasoline receipt that just happened to fall out of a Bible in Tex Mahoney's room on your way to the ladies' room."

I gaped at him. "Whose?"

"Call it the granddaddy of surprises," he said. "The GBI lifted a set of prints belonging to a former Chicago mobster. AFIS ran them and came up with a guy who ratted out his former associates in order to avoid prison. His testimony led to more than two dozen convictions."

"Wow!" I breathed. "Do you suppose that person is Tex Mahoney?"

"It's a possibility. Either that or someone deliberately planted them in Mahoney's room to throw suspicion elsewhere. The information I received said this guy opted out of the U.S. Marshals Witness Protection Program. The bulletin went on to state that it's believed he changed his name and moved to an undisclosed location."

My jaw dropped at hearing this. Unanswered questions buzzed in my brain like bees in a honeycomb. Before I could voice one of the many, McBride's cell phone trilled. "I have to take it," he said, glancing at the display. "Join the dancers till I get back. I want you in plain sight until I can sort this mess out."

I nodded and moved toward the people crowding the makeshift dance floor. Beach music continued to blare over loudspeakers.

The Witness Protection Program, or WitSec as McBride called it, had been featured on *Vanished* the night Becca was murdered. Karma or happenstance?

The DJ, mike in hand, called out instructions. "One and two. Three and four. Five, six!" Couples gyrated in what appeared to me a modified version of swing dancing. Craning my neck for a better look, I zeroed in on Doug with Reba Mae as his partner. I felt a stab of guilt for letting him down, quickly followed by admiration. The guy knew how to move.

He and Reba Mae shag-danced together as naturally as breathing. Their fancy footwork was greeted by cheers from the bystanders. Twisting, turning, and twirling, they took center stage. It was plain to see by their smiles that they were having fun.

"They make a nice couple," Wally Porter said.

I looked over and found Wally standing next to me. His shaved head was turned to study the dancers, which allowed me a clear view of his profile. Something about him nagged my memory. Then it dawned on me. Barely yet distinctly visible under what appeared to be a thin layer of make up was a birthmark. A purplish birthmark — a port-wine stain I'd wager — marred one cheek.

Was the man next to me the Chicago mobster featured on *Vanished*?

Impossible. It couldn't be.

Or could it? Was the mystery mobster really Wally Porter, not Tex Mahoney?

Had Becca, after watching her favorite TV show, put two and two together and come up with four? Had she threatened to expose the man? Extort or blackmail a vicious gangster? Had Wally Porter, aka Louis Coccetti, aka Vino, aka master barbecue Judge, and not Tex Mahoney, murdered Becca Dapkins?

Wally must have felt me staring at him. "Anything wrong?" he asked, his tone mild.

"N-no, nothing."

"Good, good," he muttered, and turned his attention back to the dancers. "I heard shag dancing described as the jitterbug on phenobarb. Did you know it originated during the Big Band Era back in the nineteen-thirties and forties?"

"Er, no," I said, my mind still trying to reconcile the smooth-talking snappy dresser with a Chicago criminal. Pretending to concentrate on Doug and Reba Mae's gliding and pivoting, I observed Wally out of the corner of my eye. The photo I'd seen of Louie Coccetti showed a man with a wiry build and bushy hair. If Wally and Louie were one and the same, he'd packed on the pounds, bulked up over the years, shaved his head. And attempted to conceal the port-wine stain. Not all that difficult as transformations go. Maybe I was way off base. Maybe Wally Porter was the person he purported to be. I decided to test my theory.

"How about those Sox?" I said, referring to the Chicago White Sox.

"I'm a Cubs fan," he replied, his gaze on the dance floor.

So far so good, I thought. "Chicago's a great town. When it comes to pizza, nothing beats Chicago-style deep-dish."

Wally jerked his head around. "Why all the talk about Chicago? You planning a trip?"

I took a half step back, stunned by the barely controlled fury I'd unleashed. "I-I thought Reba Mae mentioned you were from the Midwest."

"What business is it of yours?"

I shrugged. "Just making small talk."

He stared down at me, his eyes hard as agates. Before I could guess his intent, he caught my elbow. "Let's go," he whispered. "Someplace quiet where we won't be disturbed."

"If we leave now, we'll miss the fireworks."

"Screw the fireworks," he hissed. "Get a

move on."

I opened my mouth to scream but felt something hard jab between the ribs. A gun? I gulped down a surge of fear.

"Don't try anything stupid unless you want something bad to happen to that daughter of yours. I'd hate to see that pretty face of hers scarred."

Wally's threat caused the blood to drain from my head. It was one thing to threaten me, another to threaten my child. Frantic, I looked around for McBride. His advice about being safe in plain sight just plain sucked. Just then the crowd surged forward in an attempt to see the winners of the shag contest crowned. No one paid the least bit of attention to a bald barbecue judge and his frightened red-haired companion — *moi*.

I tried to wrench my arm free from a grasp as strong as a bear trap. Tightening his grip, Wally dragged me away from the noise, the lights, and safety. As I struggled to break free, one of my bangle bracelets slipped off my wrist. He propelled me around a corner down a side street. When he was sure no one was around, he pulled me between two buildings and slammed me against the brick wall.

"What's your game, spice girl?" he snarled. "If it's the same as your friend's, you might want to rethink it. We both know how that ended."

"You killed Becca." Even to my own ears, my voice sounded flat, lifeless. In the dim glow of a distant streetlamp, I saw a toy-size pistol in his hand. How much damage could such a little gun inflict? I knew the answer without being told. Lots.

Wally moved so close our bodies were only a hair's breadth apart. "Damn right I killed that stupid broad. Did she think she'd get away blackmailing Vino Coccetti? The crazy woman demanded a small fortune to keep her trap shut."

"Becca recognized you from the television show."

"That ridiculous show picked the worst possible time to rehash the past. Just couldn't let sleeping dogs lie. I've spent years creating a new identity after leaving WitSec. Went as far as having laser surgery to remove that damn port-wine stain on my face. Trouble is they tend to reappear."

"I don't want your money." I squeezed the words past vocal cords that felt paralyzed.

"Good." He chuckled. "I wasn't planning on giving you any."

"Then let me go." Like a bolt of lightning, the actor's name I'd been trying to remember dawned on me. It wasn't Yul Brynner whom Wally reminded me of but Michael Chiklis, the star of a defunct TV show, *The Shield.* Chiklis could instill fear with a single glance. So could Wally.

" 'Fraid I can't do that, doll. Can't take a chance you might blab that Vino Coccetti is alive and well. My former associates have long memories. I'd be an easy target for some punk looking to make his bones. Word hits the street, I'd be dead within a week."

I attempted to swallow, but my mouth was too dry. "What do you intend to do?"

"In case you haven't noticed, that's my Lincoln parked at the curb. As soon as the fireworks start you're going to take a little nap — a permanent one — in the trunk of my car. With all the racket, I won't even need to use a silencer."

Round and round I nervously twisted the bracelets on my wrist. Another one slipped off and wobbled down the sidewalk like a drunken sailor on shore leave. Wally didn't seem to notice, didn't seem to care.

"Tomorrow, after breakfast," he continued, "I'll dump your body on the way out of town. Disposing of the bodies used to be one of my specialties when I worked for the Mob."

I nearly jumped out of my skin when a

loud bang signaled the beginning of the fireworks display. The night sky exploded with brilliant colors. Red, blue, and green stars shot into the heavens, then slowly drifted back to earth. Wally casually reached into his pants pocket and, using a fob, popped the trunk of a Lincoln parked at the curb. He stepped away and motioned with the barrel of his gun for me to move toward the car.

For an instant I thought I saw a shadow creep along the building's brick wall. I dismissed the notion as a trick played by a desperate mind. It was foolish to hope a white knight would ride to my rescue. But hope springs. "Tell me," I said, stalling for time. "Did you kill Becca in her home, then try to make it look like a mugging?"

"Get in the trunk," he ordered. "I'd shoot you first, but I'd rather not get blood all over my clothes."

I hesitated, trying to delay the inevitable, wanting to find an escape. I could run only to be shot in the back. I could scream, but no one would hear it over the noise of the fireworks. That depleted my short list of options. A whistling and hissing sound directly overhead was followed by a cascade of yellow pinpricks. In the afterglow I glimpsed a figure flattened against a doorframe. My white knight, in the guise of Wyatt McBride, had arrived on the scene.

Emboldened by his presence, I said, "I'm not budging an inch until you answer my question, Vino. Once and for all, did you, or did you not, murder Becca in her own kitchen?"

Vino blew out a breath. "Guess there's no harm granting a dying woman one last wish. The Dapkins bitch phoned, insisted I come over, claiming it was urgent. I didn't go to her house intending to kill her. I wasn't even packing that night. Don't ask me how, but she recognized me after watching that stupid program on TV. She demanded money to keep quiet. I couldn't let that happen. I used the only means at hand — a frozen beef brisket on the kitchen counter — to silence the broad. Call it a crime of opportunity if you will." He shrugged. "Necessity is the mother of invention, or so they say."

I moistened dry lips with the tip of my tongue. "How did you get Becca to the square without being seen?"

"I waited till the middle of the night, when I was sure everyone was sound asleep. Then I used a suitcase I found stashed in the attic to move the body. Let me tell you, I got quite a start when I glanced up and saw a figure in the upstairs window of your shop."

"Hormones," I muttered. "I have trouble sleeping some nights."

"I was tempted to pop you the night I went back to check the Dapkins woman's house and found you there instead. Hadn't been for that neighbor showing up with her dog . . ."

"Why did you go back?" I ventured. What the heck was taking McBride so long? Wasn't it time for him to make his move? If he didn't do something, and do it soon, it would be time for my "nap."

"It's been years since I retired from the family. I wanted to double-check. Make sure I didn't leave behind anything incriminating."

"Drop the gun, Coccetti," McBride's voice cut through the darkness.

Wally spun toward the sound, his gun leveled at McBride's chest. "How about you drop yours, McBride?" he said. "You won't be the first lawman I iced. Your disappearance will coincide nicely with Ms. Busybody here. Guaranteed to set tongues wagging until I've cleared the state."

My gaze darted from one man to another. I felt like I was witnessing a standoff in an old-time Western. Neither man looked willing to back down. Overhead, a rocket zoomed skyward and rained down a shower of yellow and green. In that instant I glimpsed Wally Porter's expression as his finger tightened on the trigger.

More by instinct than design, I lashed out. My foot connected solidly with Porter's kneecap. His gun fired as he crumpled to the ground clutching his leg and yowling in pain.

Rushing over, McBride kicked the pistol out of reach while keeping his weapon trained on the writhing man. "Piper," McBride said quietly. "I need a favor. Would you dig my cell phone out of my jeans and dial nine-one-one?"

It was then I noticed he was bleeding.

CHAPTER 37

Humming to myself the next morning, I peeked into the oven and was pleased to find my quiche browning nicely. A chilled pitcher of Bloody Marys waited in the fridge. Reba Mae had called earlier to tell me she'd be late. Even though she never worked on Sundays, she was making a rare exception for this particular client.

"Come in!" I called when I heard footsteps on the stairs. I assumed they belonged to my BFF, so I didn't turn around. "You must've finished sooner than you thought. Brunch won't be ready for another twenty minutes."

A familiar-looking stranger with flaming red hair burst into my kitchen. "Hey, Piper. It's me, Maybelle."

"Maybelle Humphries." I laughed. "Why, I almost didn't recognize you. You look amazing!" I stared in disbelief at the slender figure dressed in dark denim jeans and a

Western-style shirt. A pair of Reba Mae's chandelier earrings dangled nearly to her shoulders.

"I feel like a new woman." She pivoted so I could get a better look at the total package. Carefully applied makeup made her skin glow and her eyes sparkle.

Reba Mae, beaming ear-to-ear, stuck her head in the door. "What do you think of our Miss Maybelle now? Isn't she a knockout?"

I nodded in agreement. "The transformation is remarkable. From church mouse to va-va-voom."

Maybelle fiddled with a pearl button on her shirt. "I've given the matter a lot of thought, Piper. I'm tired of the old me. I decided if the day ever came and I was no longer a murder suspect, I was going to make some changes."

"Wait till you hear the rest," Reba Mae said, nearly busting with excitement.

"I quit my job at the Chamber," Maybelle said in a rush.

"And . . . ," Reba Mae prompted.

"And" — Maybelle blushed — "Tex asked me to come with him on the barbecue circuit. He thinks we'd make a good team, seeing how we're both good cooks. He swears we'll win more trophies than we know what to do with."

My jaw dropped at hearing this. "Maybelle, are you sure this is what you want to do? Have you thought this through? It's a big change."

"Change is what I'm looking for, honey." She reached over and squeezed my arm. "Today is all we got, Piper. The past is dead and gone. There's no guarantee about tomorrow. I'm grabbing today with both hands and making the most of it."

Reba Mae and I exchanged glances, then smiled.

"I owe it all to you, Piper," Maybelle confessed. "I'm ever so grateful for all your help. You risked your life trying to save mine. If I live to be a hundred, I'll never be able to thank you enough."

I blinked moisture from my eyes. I saw Reba Mae do the same. "Just be happy."

The three of us looked up when a horn beeped.

"That's Tex," Maybelle said. "He's waitin' on me downstairs."

After promising to stay in touch, Maybelle gave each of us a bone-breaking hug and disappeared.

"Well, well, well," Reba Mae sighed. "Who would've thunk it?"

"Who would've thunk it?" I echoed.

Over spinach quiche and Bloody Marys, Reba Mae grilled me for all the gory details of what happened the previous night. By the time we'd finished, the King Ranch chicken casserole that I'd made earlier was ready to come out of the oven and the lasagna ready to pop in.

"How's McBride doin', by the way?"

"It took a dozen stitches to close the wound in his arm. The ER doc said the bullet tore through muscle, so it'll take time to heal. Last I saw of him, McBride was grumbling because he had to wear a sling."

"Scared it'll ruin his macho image?"

I shrugged. "He claims things would've been worse if I hadn't kicked Wally in the knee."

"It would've been worse, honeybun, if McBride hadn't of shown up when he did." She gave a dramatic shiver. "How *did* he find you anyway?"

I held up my wrist and pointed to the bangle bracelets. "He came looking for me. When I was nowhere to be found, he spotted my bracelet where it had fallen and followed the trail."

"Who needs bread crumbs when a girl's got jewelry?"

I poured the rest of the Bloody Marys into Reba Mae's glass. No more for me, because

I had a little road trip planned for later on. "When it comes to injuries, Wally got the worst of it," I said. "He's going to need surgery to repair his ACL."

"ACL?" Reba Mae stirred her drink with a celery stalk. "Sugar, stop speakin' Greek to a l'il ol' country gal."

"Anterior cruciate ligament," I elaborated. "It connects the femur to the shinbone."

"Okay," she replied good-naturedly, "so I didn't ace anatomy class. Then what happened?"

Now it was my turn to grin. "McBride suggested I take up kickboxing. Said I'd be a natural."

"I meant what happened after my dream guy, Wally, was carted off? I can't believe what I ever saw in the guy."

"Where Wally Porter was concerned, Maybelle Humphries was the perfect fall guy. Especially since she couldn't prove her alibi."

Reba Mae glanced down, shamefaced. "It's my fault her alibi got stolen. I let it slip to Wally that Maybelle had proof she was miles away the night in question."

"Don't beat yourself up. It all worked out in the end." I put the plates we'd used in the dishwasher. "McBride says Wally Porter, aka Louie Vino Coccetti, has a record a mile long. And that's only for the crimes where he was caught red-handed. Who knows how many people he whacked?"

Reba Mae ran a finger down the side of her glass, making a path in the condensate. "Sure as shootin' Becca picked the wrong guy to blackmail. What was she thinkin'?"

"She saw dollar signs dance in her head," I said, wiping down the counter. "Becca was never satisfied living in Brandywine Creek and working a job she hated just to make ends meet. She wanted bigger, better. More."

"And look where she ended up." Reba Mae crunched down on a celery stick. "Planted facedown in an azalea bush."

Trying for a distraction, I looked into the oven at the lasagna that was just starting to bubble. I didn't need a reminder I'd nearly disappeared without a trace. I didn't doubt for a minute that Vino Coccetti could dispose of a body where it would never be found. "Let's change the subject, shall we," I said.

"Fine by me." Reba Mae leaned back contentedly and sipped her drink. "Clay mentioned Lindsey's been seein' a lot of Barbie Q's video guy. Isn't he a lot older than she is?"

My kitchen spick-and-span, I draped the

dishcloth over the faucet and sat down again. "I caught the two of them together last night — in the beer tent of all places."

"Lindsey . . . ? Drinkin' . . . ?"

"Nothing more than a soda, but I let Mr. Carter Kincaid know in no uncertain terms that my daughter was only sixteen. He labored under the assumption that she was about to celebrate her nineteenth birthday."

"More like sixteen goin' on twenty-five," Reba Mae said. "Glad I had boys. If you ask me, boys are much easier to raise than girls."

"Lindsey and I had a come-to-Jesus meeting when I got home last night. I found *her* waiting up for *me*. Imagine!" I shook my head at the memory of the indignation on her face. "She didn't like having the shoe on the other foot. When I explained what had happened, she told me I was the one in need of a curfew. She went as far as to accuse me of always being the one in trouble."

"You gotta admit the girl has a point."

"Next thing I knew, Lindsey jumped up and hugged me so tight she almost broke a rib. She refused to go to bed until I promised I'd take a self-defense class."

"If you sign up, I will, too."

I absently tucked a stray curl behind my ear. "Lindsey admitted Carter was too old for her. She realized that when she mentioned a rock group and he admitted he'd never heard of it. However, because of his influence, she's now talking about going to film school. She has her sights set on being an editor or producer."

"I thought she wanted to be a vet like Doug."

I sighed. "That was last month."

"By the way, Dr. Doug's one terrific dancer. Who knew? That man's got moves. Did I show you the trophy we won for shag dancing?"

"If you mean the trophy that's prominently displayed on my kitchen counter, then, yes, you did. I think Doug's even prouder — if possible — of winning a dance contest than having placed with his barbecue. From the little I was able to watch, I was duly impressed with his fancy footwork."

Restless, I jumped up and opened the cupboard over the sink. "Do you suppose bringing McBride chocolate-chip cookies along with the casseroles would be overkill?"

"Nah." Reba Mae wagged her head. "Man can't live by casseroles alone."

It was late afternoon when I traveled down the winding gravel drive leading to

McBride's small house. The first thing I noticed was the white Escalade parked beside his Ford F-150. Through the screened door I could make out McBride's tall figure.

And he had a handful.

Barbie Quinlan was wound around him tighter than a kudzu vine. Clinging, climbing, coiling, and noxious. My first impulse was to get the heck out of Dodge, but it was too late thanks to Casey's excited yipping. The couple broke apart as I got out of my car. McBride held the door open, and the two of them stepped out onto the porch. Even wearing a sling, he looked better than an invalid ought to.

Casey scampered out, eager for a tummy rub from his favorite lawman. I followed more sedately, lugging a wicker hamper.

"Look, Wyatt. Isn't that sweet," Barbie cooed. "Looks like Little Miss Homemaker is bringing you a basket of goodies to make you all better."

"Hello, Barbie." I tried not to let my irritation show.

Barbie, I noticed, didn't bother to entice a man with baked goods. She opted for the more direct approach with formfitting white jeans and semi-sheer aquamarine blouse opened to reveal the lacey cups of her bra.

Under Barbie's watch, Victoria's secret had just gone viral.

McBride took the basket from me. "That looks heavy. Let me take it inside."

"Hope I didn't interrupt anything important," I said, not the least bit apologetic.

"You didn't." Barbie gave her platinum hair a toss. "Wyatt and I were just saying good-bye. I'm taking off for Memphis. Their festival should make for a great episode. It's ten times the size of Brandywine Creek's."

"Well, good luck." *And good riddance,* I wanted to add, but didn't. I was a better person than that.

Barbie started down the porch steps, then turned back. "Sorry if I came across as . . . abrasive. I'm never at my best around other women — especially those who pose a threat of any sort."

Not knowing what to say in response to Barbie's admission, I mustered a smile. "Drive safe."

McBride returned just then and we stood side by side on the porch while Barbie climbed into her SUV, executed a perfect three-point turn, and disappeared from sight.

"Barbie's had a tough time." McBride slipped the hand of his uninjured arm into the pocket of his jeans. "Makes me feel good to see the success she's making of her life."

Mimicking his actions, I stuck my hands into the pockets of my denim skirt. "I don't think she likes me very much."

"Barbie . . . ?" He lifted a brow. "It's not you she dislikes; it's CJ."

"CJ?"

McBride rocked back on his heels, his expression pensive. I noted his jaw was covered with bearded stubble, but his lack of a shave only added to his rugged appeal. "CJ played a mean trick on Barbie back in high school," he said. "The kind a girl — especially one who has a mad crush on a guy — doesn't forget. Or forgive. She's still harboring a grudge and it might've rubbed off on you."

I stared at him, perplexed,. "On me, why?"

"Call it guilt by association. As a prank, your ex asked Barbie to the prom, then stood her up. Made her a laughingstock. According to my sister, Barbie used every penny she'd saved from babysitting to have her hair done and buy a dress. Seems like half the school was in on the joke."

I was shocked by CJ's callous behavior. Granted, he'd been young at the time, but old enough to know the difference between right and wrong. "That's more than just plain mean; that's downright cruel."

"Yes," McBride agreed, "but not as cruel as the rumor someone started about a possible pregnancy."

"Becca Dapkins." The name seemed to float on the breeze rifling the leaves of the sweet gums.

McBride nodded. "Barbie suspected Becca but couldn't prove it."

"Melly informed me Becca wanted Arthur Dapkins for herself. She wasn't about to let a certain well-endowed student railroad her plans. Because of Becca, Barbie packed up and left Brandywine Creek for good."

"Small wonder you thought Barbie clobbered her old nemesis with a brisket."

I watched Casey chase a squirrel up a tree. "It seemed a logical conclusion at the time. What I still don't understand is how Maybelle's alibi happened to show up in Tex's room."

"Porter's kicking himself for not destroying those receipts when he had the chance. He admitted putting them in Mahoney's room so, if they were ever found, it would point suspicion at Tex. By then, he planned to have disappeared without a trace. Unfortunately for Wally, his plan backfired."

"What about the break-in at Spice It Up!?"

"Wally wanted it to appear Brandywine Creek was experiencing a rash of burglaries. He thought everyone would assume the person who broke into your shop was the same one who stole Maybelle's wallet, which happened to be his real target."

I let out a sigh. "So that's how a criminal mind works."

"Say." McBride smiled suddenly, showing off that cute dimple of his. "Why don't you come inside and tell me what I'm supposed to do with all the food you brought?"

"Deal," I said.

McBride held the door open, then followed me inside and looked on while I unpacked the casseroles along with an assortment of small glass jars.

"What's all that?" he asked, frowning.

"Since you favor the basics when it comes to seasonings, I brought you salt and pepper." I held up a jar for his inspection, set it down, and picked up another. "A blend of black Tellicherry and white Sarawak peppercorns. And salt. Sea salt, kosher salt, garlic salt, and onion salt."

He pointed to a bottle filled with a reddish-orange substance. "That doesn't look like salt or pepper."

"Chili powder," I explained. "In case you ever decide to try your hand at cooking, chili is a good place to start."

He flashed a wicked grin. "Never know when I might want to spice things up."

Spice things up? I nearly dropped the pan of lasagna at hearing that. Surely by spicing things up he referred to cooking with items I sold in my shop. Things like cumin, cinnamon, and paprika.

Or did he? Oh, dear . . .

GUIDE TO PEPPERS

Hot, hotter, hottest. Not only are chili peppers hot, but many of them also are similar in appearance. One thing they do have in common, however, is that they all contain capsicum, the compound responsible for the sensation of heat on the tongue. Wilbur Scoville was the first to quantitate the amount of heat in chili peppers in the early 1900s, and his method is still used today. His scale starts at 0 for green peppers (no heat) and goes to the high end of 250,000 units for chilies like the habanero.

PIPER'S HOT TEN

Ancho: Deep red-brown, wrinkled, fruity, and sweet, the ancho is a dried poblano. It is Mexico's most popular pepper and is used in many of their favorite dishes.

Arbol: Bright red even when dried, the árbol is slender, curved and pointed and packs a punch in the heat department when added to barbecue sauce or chili.

Cayenne: The cayenne remains green on the plant but once picked may turn red. In its powdered form, it is known as "red pepper." They are used for heat rather than flavor.

Chipotle: Tan to coffee-colored, wrinkled, and leathery, chipotles have a sweet, smoky flavor with a chocolaty smell. Chipotles are often used to flavor soups and stews.

Guajillo: Maroonish-brown, long, and slender, this pepper possesses a smooth, tough skin. It is perfect for chili and chili-based dishes.

Habanero: The brilliant orange color is nature's way of saying, *Handle with care.* Rubber gloves are recommended when handling this hottie. Remember the adage "less is more" and use only the outer flesh and not the seeds or membranes.

Jalapeno: These bright-green torpedo-shaped peppers have a light flavor and are medium hot. Fresh, canned, or pickled, they are a widely used table condiment.

Piquin: These little red peppers are petite but potent. They are used in Mexican moles and sauces, stewed meats, and barbecue sauce.

Poblano: Poblanos ripen to a dark green and are triangular in shape. Their rich flavor pairs well with corn and tomatoes.

Tabasco: Tabasco chilies ripen from yellow to red and have a sharp, biting taste with a hint of celery. They are used to make Tabasco sauce.

DR. DOUG'S BUTT RUB

1/2 cup paprika
1/2 cup fresh ground pepper
1/4 cup kosher salt
1/4 cup turbinado sugar
2 tablespoons chili powder
2 tablespoons garlic powder
2 tablespoons onion powder
2 teaspoons cayenne
1 teaspoon dry mustard

Mix spices thoroughly before rubbing on meat. Can be stored covered in a cool, dark pantry.

BUBBA BLESSING'S
BBQ SAUCE

2 cups ketchup
1/2 cup brown sugar
1 bottle of beer (use your favorite)
2 tablespoons red wine vinegar
2 tablespoons steak sauce (such as A1)
1 tablespoon Worcestershire sauce
1 tablespoon Dijon mustard
1/2 teaspoon black pepper
1/2 teaspoon hot sauce (I use Tabasco)
1/2 teaspoon cayenne
1 clove of garlic, minced
1 cup chili sauce

In saucepan, whisk together all the ingredients and bring to a boil while stirring frequently. Reduce heat and simmer for 30 minutes, stirring occasionally.

BECCA DAPKINS'S CHICKEN TETRAZZINI

1 (7 oz.) package linguine
1 (8 oz.) package of fresh mushrooms, sliced
2 tablespoons butter
3 cup cooked chicken, chopped
1 cup shredded Parmesan cheese
1 (10 3/4 oz.) can cream of mushroom soup
1 jar of Alfredo sauce (can substitute a container of refrigerated)
1/2 cup chicken broth
1/4 cup Marsala wine
1/4 teaspoon fresh ground pepper
1/2 cup slivered almond

1. Preheat oven to 350°F. Prepare pasta according to package directions.
2. Melt 2 tablespoons butter in skillet over medium-high heat; add mushrooms and sauté for 4 to 5 minutes.
3. Stir together mushrooms, chicken, 1/2 cup of the Parmesan cheese, and next six ingredients. Stir in pasta. Spoon mixture

into a lightly greased 11 × 7-inch baking pan. Sprinkle with almonds and remaining 1/2 cup of the Parmesan cheese.
4. Bake at 350° F. for 40 minutes or until bubbly.

Note: The dish can be made earlier in the day and reheated. It also freezes well.

ABOUT THE AUTHOR

The author of the Bunco Babes mystery series, **Gail Oust** is often accused of flunking retirement. Hearing the words "maybe it's a dead body" while golfing fired her imagination for writing a cozy. Ever since then, she has spent more time on a computer than at a golf course. *Kill 'Em with Cayenne* is the second novel in her Spice Shop mystery series. She lives with her husband in McCormick, South Carolina.